MW01125243

ARSEN

a broken love story

MIA ASHER

Dear Danielle,
Love is infinite
Mia Asher

Published by Mia Asher

Editor: Jennifer Roberts-Hall
Cover Designer: Regina Wamba, Mae I Design
Interior Design: Angela McLaurin, Fictional Formats

Chapter images © CanStock

dedication

For my beautiful family, you illuminate the darkness within me.

"As I watched you walk away, I watched every dream I had never dreamed, I saw every wish that was yet to come true, I felt every ounce of love in my heart, I knew it all when I saw you walk away...but I know you knew it too, because you took all of me with you."

~Unknown

prologue
broken

I'm lost.

I'm drifting away…

Drowning in a sea of sorrow and pain as waves of regret keep pulling me down where an undertow of resentment won't let me break free.

Maybe I should just give up?

As I stare blankly into Dr. Pajaree's beautiful dark eyes, listening to her prognosis in her pragmatic, yet friendly voice, I can't help wondering where the magic has gone? Is real life contaminating our fairy tale romance with all its ugliness?

Yes.

Maybe.

"It's better known as habitual abortion…recurrent pregnancy loss… RPL…three or more pregnancies that end in misca…"

With my arms tightly wrapped around my stomach, I rock back and forth as I try to listen to what she's saying, her words drifting in and out of my consciousness.

I know I should be paying more attention because she's explaining to me why I'm not woman enough, why I can't keep a baby in my body long enough to be able to hold it in my arms, but all I want to do is shake off the cold blanket of numbness that enfolds me.

It's not working. I'm still so very cold, so very dead inside. Feeling Ben's strong arm wrap around my shoulders stops the manic rocking, but even his warm embrace can't help me get rid of this helplessness threatening to take over.

I wonder why doctors wear white coats. It's such an ugly color.

Sterile.

Ben gives my shoulder a supportive squeeze, waking me from my drunken-like stupor.

"Tell us what to do, where to go, who to see…it doesn't matter. We will do it, Dr. Pajaree. No matter what the cost is," Ben says, not letting go of me. Focusing my gaze on Dr. Pajaree's face once more, I listen to her next words.

"Yes, Ben." Dr. Pajaree looks at Ben with understanding in her eyes for a moment, then turns in my direction. "Cathy, since this is your third miscarriage I think it's time we ran some tests on both of you. I'm talking about parental chromosome testing, blood tests for thrombophilia, thyroid function, ovarian function…if we can identify the cause for RPL, then we can look at treatment options."

"E-Excuse me. I need to use the ladies' room. Sorry."

The chair makes a horrible screeching sound as I forcefully push it backwards and leave the room, but I don't care. Running to the bathroom, I lock myself inside and stand in front of the sink. I notice a sheen of sweat covering my forehead and my entire body seems to be shaking slightly.

Swallowing hard, I close my eyes as I try to compose myself.

I can't have another panic attack.

I can't.

"Cathy! Open the door, Cathy! Please, let me in," Ben pleads as he bangs on the door.

"Please, Cathy. Open the door." There's a hint of desperation in his voice.

Not wanting to draw more attention to us, I open the door and let Ben in. As soon as he walks through, he enfolds me in an air robbing, soul crushing hug and buries his face in the curve of my neck.

"Babe, please…don't give up. It will be okay. I promise you, I'll leave no stone unturned. There's no place in the world where I won't take you, there's nothing I won't do until we have a child to call our own. I promise you, Cathy." Tightening his grip around me and pulling me closer to him, he roughly whispers, "For you I will do anything. Anything."

As I return his embrace, I believe the earnest prayer he's chanting in my ear, and I believe his words with my whole heart, but even Ben can't stop the numbness settling around me, settling around my heart.

I can feel myself withdrawing from him.

From his love.

From my marriage.

And there's nothing I can do to stop it.

Nothing.

1

present

"Babe, can you pick up the dry cleaning today? I may be running late. Amy needs me to go to the airport and pick up the new guy."

My husband lifts his brown eyes from the newspaper he's holding, and smiles the same smile that robbed me of my breath the first time I met him eleven years ago.

It doesn't rob me of my breath anymore.

Sometimes it feels as if I am living with a man who I don't know. A man whose face seems familiar but remains a stranger.

Sometimes I feel like the normalcy of our lives will drive me insane.

"Sure, no big deal. Just remind me who this new guy is?" He puts the newspaper down on the table and runs his hand through his short black hair. Looking at my husband now as his lips touch the rim of the coffee mug, I realize how handsome he really is. The realization that I seem to have forgotten what he looks like, truly looks like, hits me like a running bull in Pamplona.

Am I so desensitized to him that I have forgotten how his maple-brown eyes shine like the brightest gemstone when he looks at you straight on? How his gaze is as penetrating as the tip of the needle when it pierces your skin? I seem to have forgotten that when he smiles a little dimple appears on his left cheek. That dimple is taunting me, begging me to kiss it, but I don't. I really don't have time to be sitting here, admiring my husband. I have to get to work.

"Cathy? Are you listening to me?" He's waving his large hand in front of my eyes, trying to get my attention back. I snap out of my reverie, refocusing on his face and his mouth. He's speaking to me, but all I hear is the annoying electric buzzing of the landscaper working outside in our garden.

Buzz - Buzz - Buzz - Buzz

Trying to clear my thoughts, I shake my head. "Sorry, babe. The landscaper is distracting me. What were you saying?"

Tenderly smiling at me, Ben says, "Your boss, Cathy. You said Amy wants you to go to the airport and pick someone up tonight?"

"Oh, yes. I'm not sure who the guy is, but apparently he's coming with his son and wife. I think he's going to take over the company. I don't know. Anyway, I've got to run."

Standing up, I make my way to my husband and bend down to kiss him on the cheek. As I'm straightening, Ben grabs the back of my neck and guides my face back to kiss him on the lips. Startled, I don't immediately kiss him back until I feel his tongue trying to make its way inside my mouth. I open my lips to welcome him in, and we begin to kiss earnestly. His tongue tangles with mine as I feel his hand sneaking up under my skirt, making its way to my core. When his thumb hooks under the edge of my panties and moves them aside, his middle finger enters me and I break the kiss.

I straighten my body completely and look down at Ben who just grins widely at me. His lips look moist from our kiss, and I can't help laughing out loud when he smiles at me like that. I think he has two speeds—horny or tired.

"Seriously, Ben? I have to get to work." I turn around, but Ben's hands grab my waist from behind and pull me back to sit on his lap.

Oh, my...

He laughs in my ear as he nudges my ass with his huge erection, "Can't help myself around you, Cathy. You're just so damn sexy in the morning. Come on, it will be a quickie." His tongue is inside my ear, tracing its contours while his hand goes back to work under my skirt.

"Ben, stop it. I have to get to work. I'm already late...as...it...is..."

"Yes, baby?" he huskily whispers in my ear.

Oh, those fingers of his...

Recognizing what is going on, and what I don't want to happen, I push his hands off my body, and stand up. As I look down the length of my body trying to smooth my skirt free of wrinkles, and pacify the rapid beating of my heart, I notice that my hands are shaking. After taking a few calming breaths, I look up to see him watching me with a raw and naked hunger as he brings the finger that was just inside me to his mouth and sucks it.

Hard.

Ben pulls his finger out and his tongue follows behind, tracing the lingering flavor of my body on his lips. I feel a powerful shot of heat surge straight where his hand was not too long ago.

When Ben realizes that I'm not moving, he chuckles then grabs me by the hand, pulling me forward and lifting me until I'm straddling his hips.

"Babe, I've missed you," he says roughly.

As he leans down to nuzzle my neck, I sense some sort of desperation growing within me. I do want him. I want him to take the lead, make everything go away. His hands close around my wrists, moving them to wrap around his neck, then he grabs my ass, pushing me against his erection.

"I need you, babe. So fucking much," he says before he lets go of me and begins to slowly unbutton my silk shirt, pulling down my bra and exposing my breasts to him. Without breaking the kiss, I let go of his neck and unbuckle his belt, unzip his dress pants and pull down his boxer briefs. I take his hard erection in my hand and begin stroking him, feeling the strength of his dick in my fingers.

"Enough," he says roughly as he puts a hand over mine, stopping me. "Let me."

I nod, allowing him to do whatever he wants to me. We become frantic, our need for each other vibrating through our bodies, and we barely have time to lift my skirt and slide my panties to the side until he pushes forward.

"Fuck, you're wet." We both look down to where our bodies are connected and watch as he begins to pull out of me. There's nothing more sensual than watching your lover's arousal as it leaves your warmth covered with your body's reaction to his touch. Covered in want.

Connected as we are, I'm overcome by this feeling of wanting to be owned by Ben. To drive him mad with desire.

"No more talking, Ben." I pull his head down towards mine and kiss him once more, letting the rhythm of his thrusts set the pace of our lovemaking.

After I reach my release, Ben allows himself to do the same. "Jesus Christ," he mutters.

Breathing heavily, with our arms still around each other, my legs wrapped around his waist, and our bodies cooling off, we look at each other and smile. Whatever desperation I sensed in me before has dissipated.

For now.

"Damn, wife, if that's what you call breakfast," he grips my hips, "I think I may never skip it again." He smirks.

"Better than coffee?" I ask, blushing.

Ben throws his head back and laughs. He cups my cheeks, and makes me stare at him until I lose my way in his brown eyes.

"Yes, so much better than coffee," he caresses my lower lip with his thumb. "I love your smile, wife. Even after all these years it can go straight to my…" he nudges me gently, still inside me, "and my heart." He leans down and plants a soft kiss on my smiling lips. "I love you, babe."

"I love you, too. I guess we need to take another shower before work." I untangle my legs from his waist, our bodies disconnecting, and get off his lap. Wrapping my shirt around my bare chest, I make my way to our bedroom with Ben following close behind.

When my hands land on my empty stomach, I shut down the voice inside my head, reminding me of the overwhelming emptiness spreading inside me like a black hole, sucking all the happiness around me.

The voice telling me that everything remains the same.

Or not.

2

past

I didn't fall in love.

I walked smack into it and then fell flat on my ass.

I hate rain.

Okay, that's a lie. I like it just fine when, say, I have an extra set of dry clothes on hand and an umbrella. So you could say, I'm pretty pissed off at Mother Nature right now.

As I stand outside Lerner Hall and watch the rain pouring angrily down from the sky, I contemplate whether I should take a cab or walk to the nearest subway station. Either way, I'll be soaked to the bone as soon as I step away from the student center. I swear sometimes I feel like the song *Ironic* by Alanis Morissette should be my personal soundtrack.

Sighing, I get ready to step into the rain when I hear my phone ring. As I'm about to answer, a group of gorgeous and intimidating sorority girls walk past me throwing condoms my way, shouting as they go, "No Glove, No Love!"

Embarrassed, and blushing like some silly heroine from a regency novel, I pick up the condoms off the ground and shove them quickly in my bag before anyone notices them surrounding me. Great. I don't even have a boyfriend, and now people are going to think I'm a sex addict.

Now I really need to get out of here.

The moment I start to walk, my phone begins to ring again. I struggle with the zipper on my bag to get my phone while dodging a student with a huge-ass umbrella. As I avoid a big puddle coming up, I completely miss the guy who is walking straight at me.

When our bodies collide, I fall on my ass in the very puddle I was trying to avoid in the first place, smashing my bags on the ground.

What the hell just happened?

More surprised than anything else, I stare at the pair of wet leather loafers in front of me.

Stupid puddle. I want to cry. Shit, my ass is wet. Now, I'm getting very angry.

Okay, Cathy. Breathe. Get your act together and give this guy a piece of your mind.

With all these thoughts running through my head, I don't even notice what the guy who'll soon be getting some major shit from me even looks like. So when he kneels down in front of me, trying to shield my face from the falling rain with his own hands, I am frozen. Paralyzed. Gone are the thoughts of my wet ass.

Are those lips for real?

Shit, I feel my face lighting up like the Macy's Fourth of July fireworks. I need to say something, and quick, but all I can think as I stare into his maple brown eyes is that I want pancakes with syrup...lots of maple syrup.

Snap out of it, Cathy!

I open my mouth to say something to the gorgeous guy with the yummy lips and laughing eyes kneeling in front of me, when he awkwardly says, "Um, I think you better stand. Your things…um, your things are getting wet. Here," he says, offering me his hand.

As he helps me up, I notice that everything has fallen out of my bag, of course.

What else could go wrong?

Scanning the mess, I quickly realize why he wanted me to get my stuff. Next to my wallet, between the books scattered all over the wet pavement, are about ten, guilty looking, condom packages.

Mother. Fucker. Shit.

Now I really want to die.

I mean, carrying protection is great, but these aren't my condoms!

Quickly, I kneel down, keeping my eyes to the ground. Feeling so embarrassed by the whole thing, I don't notice that Mr. Loafers has done the same until we end up knocking heads as we both try reaching for the condoms at the same time.

"Ouch!"

Rubbing my head, I look up at him and watch him mirroring my movements as he tries really hard not to smile. It's impossible, really. The whole situation is hilarious, so when our eyes meet, my stomach doing Olympic-level pirouettes, we burst out laughing.

When we stop, we stare at each other for a minute too long. Oblivious to the rain falling down on us, I let myself get lost in the moment and in the color of his laughing eyes. It's almost as if gravity is suspended and we're floating in slow motion.

I'm thinking of ways to break this electric silence between us when he clears his throat about to speak, and that's when it happens.

One moment I'm staring into his eyes and feeling butterflies in my stomach, and in the next we find ourselves drenched in dirty water from the streets of the Bronx.

Yes.

Slimy, smelly, yucky water is on my hair, my face, my clothes, and all over him as well.

"What the fuck, man!" The beautiful boy shouts after the car that just drove past us splashing us with water. He turns to look at me and lets his eyes stare at my wet t-shirt a little too long before we make eye contact again. Instead of blushing or stammering an apology for so blatantly staring, he grins. "Guess we better move. With our luck, if we linger here any longer we might get struck by lightning."

I'm slow at reacting as he speaks to me because, for one, I am truly stunned by his low baritone voice, and two, the way the light is hitting his wet hair makes the black curls shine like an expensive mink.

I nod in agreement since it seems I have not only lost my ability to think but also speak. Together, we collect all my belongings and put them away.

Yep, even those stupid condom packages.

Once we are ready to get up, he sticks his hand out, saying, "Let me help you up."

By the time we're standing, my hand still in his, we look at each other without moving, one willing the other to say or do something, but nothing happens. The rain continues to fall all around us, more heavily now than before, but it doesn't seem to faze us. It's like we're in our own little time capsule, where everything seems to have stopped. I can barely see his face without constantly wiping the raindrops from my eyes as his very tall figure looms above me.

Slowly, his face moves towards mine. Halfway, he stops and looks at me as if asking for my permission to do what I think he's about to do. My mind is chanting the words, "Kiss me…Kiss me…" as if they are a holy communion. Throwing all logic and caution to the wind, I close my eyes, stand on my tiptoes, and let the moment take over.

When we finally kiss, our lips touch so softly, so intensely, so magically, but I don't feel like lightning has struck me, or that the world has stopped moving. No, the feeling is unique. Special. Like I am being cleansed from the inside out, the rain washing away all my past mistakes, my sorrows, my hurt. And in their place, taking root, is hope.

Magic.

As the kiss comes to an end, my body feels like it's floating on air and my mind is slightly aware of four facts:

My feet are not touching the ground.

He has his arms wrapped around my waist. Tight.

I just kissed a total stranger in the middle of a busy street.

And last but not least…

It felt amazing!

When he lowers me to the ground, his wavy black hair falls over his eyes, covering his expression. He takes a deep breath as he pulls his hair behind his ears and looks at me. Once again, butterflies are attacking my stomach as if they are bullets shot from within my soul.

I need to say something, ask him for his name and maybe his phone number.

Yes, I definitely need his number.

But all I can do is stare at him, afraid he might disappear. I watch as he lifts his hand and softly cups my cheek. His hand feels like it was meant to be there all along—so natural. Closing my eyes, I feel a warm shiver run down my spine, raising goosebumps on my skin. With my eyes shut, I don't see that his mouth is close to my ear until I feel his breath tickling it and hear him whisper words that make my knees go weak. His words take me by surprise.

When I open my eyes to ask him what he meant, he gives me a cocky smile, and then turns around and walks away, leaving me all alone on a busy street. I feel shocked, breathless, and stunned.

Did I imagine what just happened?

No, I don't think so.

It was real.

He was real.

I can still taste the tangy flavor of the apple he must have eaten on my lips. I can still feel the warm imprint of his hand on my cheek.

I shake my head and turn around quickly to see if I can make out his retreating figure amongst the sea of people. I want to catch up to him and ask him for his name. I need to know his name. But I'm too late.

He's already gone.

Suddenly, I feel so alone.

He is gone.

Feeling dazed, and knowing that I must look like a drowned rat, I try to look for a cab. I thought this kind of thing only happened in movies or books, not in real life. At least not in mine.

A cab finally stops in front of me, and I'm about to get in when I feel a tap on my shoulder. Turning around, I come face to face with the last guy I ever expected to see again. Standing in front of me is the stranger I just kissed.

"Hey," Mr. Cocky Smile says.

The way he's smiling at me opens a floodgate of shivers as powerful as a storm surging inside me, shivers that inundate my senses, running up and down my body.

I'm glued to the ground, and I think my mouth might be hanging open.

It's not until the cab driver yells at me that I snap out of my rude ogling trance.

I cannot believe it's him.

Again.

"Miss, are you getting in or not?"

My attention on the driver first, I turn to look at the handsome stranger, wondering what to say to him, but he speaks first.

"I was halfway to class when I realized I hadn't asked your name," he says, watching me closely.

I don't know what to do or say, so I voice the first words my brilliant mind can come up with, "Um…"

This guy is making my face burn like a bonfire.

"Nope. You definitely don't look like an Um. More like a Wow." He smiles, making the same delicious dimple deep on his left cheek appear once more.

How can a guy be this perfect?

If my face felt hot before, now it feels like it's burning. Forest fire burning. What do you say to that? It's all kinds of sweet and funny. Come on, Cathy! Say something.

"Ha. You're funny. You know that, right?"

"No, I wasn't trying to be funny. I was just stating a simple fact."

Still blushing, I notice that he's watching me closely once more. Thinking that there must be something wrong with my appearance, my hands go straight to my hair as he steps closer to me. "I-I…Is there something wrong?" The closeness of his body sends my mind spiraling into an abyss where coherent speech seems to be nonexistent.

Without answering my question, his hand moves towards my face. When his thumb strokes the crest of my cheek, I can feel the softness of his finger against my skin. It has been so long since I felt a guy touch me so tenderly.

I notice his face is much closer to mine than before, his hot breath hitting my lips. He's watching me with eyes that roam my face as if memorizing every single feature of mine…my nose, my cheeks, and lastly, my mouth.

When he looks up, our eyes connect for a brief instant, and he takes a deep breath. "Um, may I have your phone number?"

"Is she getting in or what?" The cabdriver yells once more.

Without breaking eye contact with me, he addresses the cabdriver, "Give us five, man."

"B-but why?" I ask stupidly. I know what I want but could he possibly want the same?

"Isn't it obvious?"

I shake my head because it's not.

"You really don't know, huh?" he says huskily.

"Um…"

"Listen, how about this, I'll let you get in that cab under two conditions. You must give me your number, and you must agree to go on a date with me three days from now."

Can this really be happening to me?

"But that's Friday."

Shouldn't this beautiful man already have a date for Friday? Only dateless losers stay home on a Friday night. Example. Me.

"So what?"

"It's a Friday. Shouldn't you be busy? With a date, or something?"

"I'm trying to get myself a date, but the stubborn girl won't give me a chance." Smiling, he looks at me. Like, really looking at me.

"Oh. You want to go out with me?" Holy shit. He *does.*

"I want to do more than that. But for now, I would be more than happy if you would give me your Friday night."

"Why?" I blurt the question before I realize that I kind of don't want to know his answer.

"Why, what? Why do I want to take you out?"

I nod my head yes.

"Besides the obvious." He pushes himself closer to me and whispers in my ear, "Because I can't fucking wait to kiss you again."

Oh.

"Why don't you do it now?" Shit. Where the hell is this Slutty Cathy coming from?

"Simple," he says. I can feel the heat radiating from his body onto mine as his eyes roam my face once more. "Because I want to pick you up at your doorstep. I want to bring you flowers. I want to tell you how beautiful you look. I want to see you blush when I compliment you. I want to see you fuss over the flowers while you offer me a glass of water. And if you live with your parents, I want to shake your dad's hand and tell him that I will take care of his daughter and that I won't bring her home too late. Then, I will compliment your mother with how beautiful she is. Because only a beautiful woman could have given birth to someone as pretty as you."

He caresses my cheek tenderly. "Then, you will blush and take my hand in yours to get me out of the house as fast as possible so I don't embarrass you anymore. When we're outside, I will take your hand in mine and walk you to my car. I'll open the door for you, let you in, and then once the door is closed, I'll make my way to the driver's seat. But before I start the engine, I want to turn to look at you, sitting there, blushing. I want to grab you by the neck," his words reflect his actions as he grabs the back of my neck tenderly and brings our faces closer together, "bring your perfect lips close to mine. And then…"

"Yes?" I swallow hard.

"And then finally kiss you," he whispers huskily, his eyes boring into mine.

Oh my God.

"So, do we have a date?" he says, smiling smugly.

"Yes," I say breathlessly as my pulse begins to race.

"You won't regret it, Wow," he says, smiling.

"My name is Cathy," I smile in return.

"I like that. You look like a Cathy. Sweet, innocent, and perfect."

"Oh."

I seriously want to pinch myself to make sure I'm not dreaming.

"My name is Ben, by the way."

"Nice meeting you, Ben," I murmur softly.

Putting my hand out for a handshake, Ben totally rocks my world when he takes it and brings it to his lips, planting a kiss I feel all the way to my bones. Dumbstruck, I let go of his hand and watch Ben step to the side, opening the door wider for me to get in.

Is this guy for real? I don't know whether to swoon, or burst out laughing. I kind of want to swoon, though.

"Okay. Thank you. I, um, I guess I'll wait to hear from you?"

"Sure." He smiles.

After we exchange numbers and say a quick goodbye, I get in the cab and give the driver my address. I feel in a daze as if I'm standing still while the world moves around me at a fast speed.

I feel my phone vibrating. Well, I guess it didn't die after all. I take my cell out and notice I have a text from an unknown number.

1(347) 886-8688: Hey, Cathy. I meant what I said on the street.

I smile as I remember what he whispered in my ear.

"Too late. Lighting has already struck."

I burst out laughing, then look out the window. As I gaze at my reflection, I decide that maybe I don't hate the rain after all.

Ben.

Oh, yes.

Most definitely.

3

present

Ben: On my way home. Picked up the dry cleaning and some dinner from Past-Tina's. Wasn't sure if you're going to have dinner with Amy and the new guy, but figured you might be hungry when you get home if you didn't. Good luck, babe.

That is Ben for you, always thoughtful. Looking down at my screen, my fingers hover over the digital keypad on my phone. I really should reply to his text and thank him for thinking about me, but I don't. Not sure why. Maybe it's because I don't feel like starting a text message conversation with him, maybe it's because I am running late, as always, and I need to get to the airport pronto. Or maybe it's because I just don't feel like typing.

Shoving my phone in my Burberry bag, I decide to give Ben a call on my way to the airport. I'll be leaving as soon as Amy gives me the information on Mr. Radcliff's flight, anyway. Yippee…can't wait to meet another Hotel Magnate jerk who thinks the sun rises and sets on his ass.

Bruno Radcliff just acquired the hotel where Amy and I work. The chain was known as Dreams Hotels, but now we are part of the bigger and more exclusive Radcliff Conglomerate. So yes, Mr. Radcliff is a big deal in the hotel world.

Amy, my boss, is the director of sales and marketing. She manages all the top accounts and key clients. I'm a sales coordinator, and my job is to support whatever Amy needs help with. I look after clients who want to book their hotels, VIP celebrities, corporate clients, and handle complaints.

Feeling a little nervous. I make my way to the bathroom to touch up my makeup and hair. As I'm running my fingers through my shoulder length blonde hair in front of the mirror, I hear my phone ringing.

"Cathy Stanwood."

"Hi, babe." Hearing Ben's deep voice makes me smile at my reflection. After eleven years together, not a day goes by when he doesn't call or text me just to say hello and ask how my day is going. Sometimes I wonder if he will ever grow bored with me, with married life, kissing and having sex with just one woman, the same woman, for the rest of his life.

Does he ever imagine he's fucking someone else when he's inside of me?

I don't have fantasies of other men, but I am bored…so bored. I often wonder when the ticking time bomb of our relationship will explode. If Ben will wake up one day and ask himself what he's doing with me, and where his life has gone. If he'll wonder what would have happened if he hadn't met me, if we hadn't bumped into each other on that rainy day, if we hadn't met and fallen in love…

I know I do.

"Hi." Holding the phone between my shoulder and ear, I take the pocket size perfume I always carry with me and spray it on my body. Rubbing the perfume on my wrists, I'm enveloped by the fruity and citrusy notes of my favorite smell.

"What are you doing?" I say in the flirty voice that he enjoys so much. I rarely use it anymore. When we were young and deeply in love with each other, that voice came out only when I wanted two things: forgiveness or sex.

"Just got home. And I'm petting your pussy," his deep voice rumbles in the phone.

"What?"

"Get your mind out of the gutter, babe. I would like to, don't get me wrong, but you aren't here at the moment, so instead I'm cheating on you with Mimi." I hear him chuckling as I picture what he's doing at the moment.

Ben is probably sitting on the leather chair in his office, running a hand through his hair as our cat, Mimi, tries to crawl under his white Brooks Brothers dress shirt. His suit jacket will be thrown carelessly over the old worn out leather sofa that he refuses to get rid of because it reminds him of our first years as a married couple. He even named it.

Having just finished a vigorous round of sex, I laid on the couch with only his unbuttoned shirt on me, revealing my body. With one of my legs hanging off the couch, and the other tucked under my ass, I was exposed for Ben. I felt so sensual and beautiful after each time he made love to me. I didn't care that I wasn't perfect like him, or that my hips were nonexistent, or my breasts too small. He made me feel beautiful.

He came back from the kitchen wearing nothing but an I-just-fucked-you-silly kind of grin; it made me smile and my insides felt like they were performing somersaults. Watching him walk towards me in all his naked glory, I admired his tanned chest, and the way the sweat made his large muscles shine. He had a glass in his hand with only ice in it. His hair was a complete mess from me pulling it…I could only imagine what mine looked like. Sex hair was the best thing in the world; it kind of made you want to give it another go.

A smiling Ben kneeled next to me on the couch as his fingers slowly opened the shirt wider, baring me to him. With my front completely naked to his eyes, he took an ice cube out of the cup. "I think we should name this couch."

I laughed and closed my eyes as I felt the ice cube in his fingers hit my warm skin. "Yes? What…are you…um…thinking about?"

I was wondering why it was taking him so long to answer my question, when I felt the heat of his tongue tracing the path of goosebumps the ice was leaving behind. He traced the ice cube around the tip of my nipple, making it pebble. The numbing sensation of the ice made my nipple hurt, but it felt delicious.

Just as I was about to protest, his mouth closed around it, sucking it deep inside. I moaned long and hard. The cold of the ice and the warmth of his mouth were the perfect recipe for disaster; even a nun would have a hard time keeping her legs closed. When I felt the ice cube caress my clit, then move lower, entering me, I opened my eyes.

Wow.

I didn't know whether I should be shocked or turned on. Smiling, Ben spread my legs open for him as he positioned himself between them. The ice was melting inside of me, making me shiver. I watched Ben's head lower as his tongue licked his lips whilst withdrawing the ice cube from inside of me and popping it in his mouth.

My limbs trembling, I whispered, "Again?"

"Yes. Again, and again, and again, until you can't remember your name. And it should be the love couch…" he replied huskily.

My laughter got lost in a moan when I felt his cool tongue inside of me again, licking the mixture of ice water and me.

Yes, those were the days.

Those were the days when the sight of one another would make us so horny and desperate that we would end up making love. Sometimes it was rough; all you could hear were the slapping sounds of our bodies, moans, groans, a lot of curse words too. Other times it was tender and sweet; Ben would hold my hand, our fingers intertwined the entire time he was inside of me, moving, filling me, never looking away.

Ben would whisper in my ear how hard I made him…how much he wanted me…how the world meant nothing to him without me in it. But no matter whether we made love or screwed each other's brains out, two things remained the same—the couch and our thirst for each other.

However, nowadays our sex life is a complete and totally different story.

Is there even a sex life to speak of?

What happened this morning in the kitchen is sadly not the rule anymore, but the exception to how much sex we have. We're lucky if we both make it to bed at the same time. Early in our relationship, we lived and breathed for the sole reason of being with each other; spending pretty much every second we were together naked and having sex everywhere we could think of, trying to break our own record of how many times we made each other come with our mouths and our bodies. These days, though, I feel adventurous if I wear one of his tees without any underwear on. And, most times, if Ben doesn't initiate sex, I avoid it.

What is the point?

It hurts to think that we are just wasting our time. I miss the closeness and intimacy sex brought us, but the hoping and waiting that comes after every time we are physically together only chips another piece of me away, of our relationship away, until there will be nothing to put back together. It makes it seem like work.

And it hurts to know that it's only the two of us, our cat, and my empty womb.

"Cathy, are you there?" Coming out of my reverie, I realize that I had completely tuned Ben out of my thoughts…again. Am I a terrible person because I can't even pay attention to my husband? God, I really do need therapy.

"Sorry, babe. What were you saying?"

"Daydreaming again, love?"

"You could say that." Looking down at my watch, I realize how late I am. "Ben, I've got to go. I'm running late again. I'll see you tonight. Not sure about dinner, I guess I'll have to play it by ear, so if you don't hear from me assume that I went out with Mr. Radcliff and his family. I'll text you to let you know what's going on when I get a chance. Alright. I've got to go. Love ya."

I almost hang up before letting Ben say something back to me.

Almost.

I don't know why, but sometimes his familiar deep voice pisses me off.

I know women find him very attractive, and almost every intern at his law firm has a crush on him, but sometimes I can't bear to see his face.

"Babe, is something bothering you?" Ben asks, curiosity in his voice.

Can't I hide anything from him? Must he always be able to read me like a flipping open book? I want my privacy back. And yes, I sometimes want Ben to stay the hell out of my life and mind his own damn business. Sometimes his niceness drives me fucking insane.

"No…I really have to go. Bye, babe. Love you."

I hang up before I give him a chance to answer me back, or say goodbye.

Shoving the phone back in my bag, I straighten to leave, looking at myself in the mirror one more time. As I'm about to turn around and head for the door, something catches my attention. Walking back, I look closely at my reflection. Lifting my left hand to touch my lips, I notice my bare ring finger. When I took my rings off this morning to put lotion on my body, I must've forgotten to put them back on.

In the six years we have been married, not once has that ever happened.

Until today.

Buildings, people crossing the streets, walking, laughing, living; cars speeding or slowing down as the traffic lights direct them. Shapes blending with one another, creating a blur of color flashing through my eyes. It is beautiful and alive.

It is New York City.

After the limousine leaves the Midtown Tunnel behind, escaping into the freedom of the night, we speed through the Long Island Expressway heading to JFK. The Radcliff's estimated arrival is roughly 8:00 P.M. At first, I thought they'd be flying commercial, but I should've known better. They're traveling on his personal jet. Really, after so many years working in the hotel business, I shouldn't be surprised by how much money some of these people make.

Ben's family has a lot of money, too. The kind of money that would afford us to live without working and let us travel the world, but Ben hates the idea of just living off his family's wealth. He loves his job as a lawyer, and he works because he wants to.

Pulling into the private landing strip, I don't see a jet anywhere near. I take my cell phone out and dial Amy to give her a heads up. She'll be happy to know that I got here before them.

After one ring, Amy answers the phone in that breathy voice of hers, "Are you with him?"

I chuckle because she doesn't bother saying hello. "Nope. They haven't landed. You owe me big time, you know? I should be having dinner with—"

"Yes, I know. You don't have to shove the fact that you have sex-on-legs waiting for you at home. I get it. If I were married to that divine husband of yours, I would probably be giving you shit as well, but I need you tonight."

"Which reminds me, I was about to call you because there has been a slight change of plans. Bruno's assistant phoned me about five minutes ago, letting me know that only his son and wife will be arriving tonight. Apparently there was an issue with one of his top clients that only he could take care of." She pauses, and I hear some shuffling on the other end, "Back, sorry. What else…Yes! You need to take the wife and son to dinner."

Okay, this is so not what I wanted to be doing on my Friday night.

"Ugh, Amy! You're killing me here! I don't want to sit with a Stepford wife and an entitled rich child and make small talk when I could be spending it with Ben. You know better than anyone that we haven't been in the best place lately…"

And we haven't. Not at all. I mean, sometimes Ben and I are like friendly strangers living under the same roof; we say hello and ask each other about how our days went, but the intimacy ends there. If it wasn't for the sex, like today's rare occurrence, we would probably be more like roommates than a married couple. There's an emotional disconnect growing between us, and on bad days it seems like it'll be impossible to bridge.

"I know, Cathy. And I am sorry. If I had known this before you left, I would have sent Ryan, but hey, when you get home Ben may want a second round."

"Seriously, Amy? I shouldn't have told you why I was late this morning. And it's not going to happen again. I don't want it to happen—"

"Cathy, shut up and listen to the HBIC. Go have dinner with these people, get drunk, eat shrimp or something that's supposedly an aphrodisiac, then go home and fuck your hubby. All your issues are because you are not getting enough at home. If Ben were my husband, I seriously would be hitting that as often as he felt like it which is apparently pretty often. By the way, I didn't mean to pry into your business, but when you arrived late this morning you looked so flushed that I thought you had a fever. I only asked because I was concerned for my top employee."

Okay, that was funny.

"That's because I'm your favorite sales coordinator. And what in the world does HBIC mean?"

"Head Bitch In Charge, luvah…"

We both laugh at that. Amy, the red headed minx, is a spitfire of a woman with no shame. She is thirty-eight years old, twice divorced, and a force of nature. She has the balls that a lot of men lack, curses like a sailor, loves sex, younger men, and she uses her drop-dead gorgeous looks to her advantage…always. Seriously, that woman has perfected that swaying-your-hips-as-you-walk kind of thing.

"Alright, HBIC, should I take them to the Ritz for dinner?" I ask, smiling into the phone.

"Yes, darling. When you get there, let them know that you are Bruno's party. They should take you right to the best table available. And please, Cathy, play nice and use those green eyes of yours with the wife. She's probably the kind of woman who whines if her foie gras isn't cooked properly."

"Amy, I've got this. Why do you think you pay me the big bucks except to do my job, and do it right. I'm sorry I complained before. Too much going on."

"I know, but this is a big deal, honey. Bruno just bought the chain, and I need you to be more than your usual perfectionist self. This could mean we both get promotions. And you know how I feel about your marriage. If you would just tell Ben how you feel, a lot of pain could be saved," she says, sighing deeply.

"Yeah, yeah. It's easier said than done, but don't worry. I will take care of Mrs. Stepford Wife and their child as if they were my own in-laws."

"Well, in that case we're all good," Amy answers, laughing.

Hearing the loud noise of engines, I turn to look at the dark sky when I see the jet coming into view, "Amy, I've got to go. The jet is about to land. Wish me luck. Hopefully I won't disappoint you."

"You would never disappoint me, girl. Go get them, hot stuff."

Ending the call, I laugh at myself. I don't know why Amy insists on calling me hot stuff when I'm pretty average looking; straight blonde hair, green eyes, slightly too thick lips, and a skinny body. Petite to the tee.

Robert, the driver, gets out of the limousine and comes to stand next to me. Yelling over the noise, he says, "Well, Mrs. Stanwood, let's hope this new boss of ours is a good guy."

I look at Robert and smile. "I hope so, Robert. We don't want to work more than we already do, right?"

As the jet approaches us, I think back to what Amy said about not having enough sex with Ben being the root of our issues.

I wish it were that simple.

Sex is not a problem. Love isn't either. I love Ben as much as the first time we said those three beautiful words to each other, but as each baby was taken away from my body by fate, by life, a part of me died and was buried with them in the cold-hard ground. The first miscarriage ripped a painful hole inside of me, the second one widened it, and the third just about broke me.

Time has fed that hole with inevitable boredom, monotony, and resentment towards life, Ben, and myself for not being woman enough. Enter doubt, and what you thought was an already rocky ride becomes a turbulence-ridden journey with no relief in sight except for the end.

The very end.

Doubts. They seep into your bloodstream, they plague every unused crevice inside your brain with revolving questions and no real answers. Is love a strong enough glue to put me back together again? Is the love between Ben and I strong enough to keep us together and our marriage afloat?

With this huge gaping hole inside me, and my taunting doubts as constant companions, I'm left hollow, angry, and afraid of intimacy with my own husband. Physical intimacy won't close that gap.

After a perfect landing, the jet finally comes to a halt. I address Robert, "Well, it's show time." I wink at him and begin tapping my left high-heeled foot on the ground.

I hope this guy doesn't change the dynamics of the office too much.

When the door to the jet finally opens, a beautifully dressed blonde woman appears. She is statuesque, and her body clothed in all shades of cream looks like it belongs on the runway of a Chanel Paris fashion show. Her ashy blonde hair is tightly coiled in a French bun, showcasing a lack of wrinkles all over her face. If that is Mrs. Stepford Wife, I already hate her. Behind her, comes a…

Wait, is that supposed to be the kid? I expected a puberty ridden teenager.

Oh, my.

No. There is no boy in that body. He is all man. If that is, in fact, Mr. Radcliff's son, he doesn't look anything like I'd imagined. For one, this blond stud doesn't look like a teenager, at all. And two, there are no pimples on his perfect face. And well, he is at least ten inches taller than what I expected.

The man walking behind Mrs. Stepford Wife Perfect Skin No Wrinkles is wearing faded distressed jeans that hang so low on his hips you can see the waist-band of his Armani underwear as he walks, and a light pink oxford shirt with the first three buttons opened, exposing his tanned and very muscular chest.

This guy exudes confidence and sex. I bet that if I got near him, trying to catch a whiff of his scent, I would be able to breathe in what pure sex smells like. Even his leisurely walk is sexy as hell. My God.

When my eyes land on his face, I notice he is watching me with a lazy smile playing around his lips. He is beautiful. His chiseled face is the kind of perfect that belongs in an

Abercrombie & Fitch ad to which thousands of girls daydream about kissing someday. But there is a deceptive sweetness in his features too; when you look at those eyes of his, you know you are in trouble.

Big trouble.

William Shakespeare said that the eyes are the windows to your soul. When our eyes connect, I see danger, and maybe something exciting. Something forbidden. Some basic instinct in me instantly recognizes that this man doesn't make love to a woman.

He fucks her.

As I'm locked in his gaze, I am suddenly gripped by this feeling threatening to choke the air out of my lungs. A premonition or an omen, this feeling is shouting in my head, telling me to run and hide, to never turn back. I can't move. I can't breathe. I just blink. My hand goes to my chest as I start to rub the area surrounding my heart.

He is danger.

My head is shouting to get away, and my heart is yelling danger, but my body isn't letting me move. All I can do is watch as he makes his way down the stairs of the jet towards me. His grin has grown from lazy and crooked to a full-blown kilowatt-powerful smile.

His smile is electrifying.

His smile frightens me.

His smile hypnotizes me.

Shaking my head, I break my gaze from his hypnotic one. Get a grip, girl. Stop thinking about silly omens and wicked eyes. You need to listen to Amy and get laid. Like, as soon as you walk into your house, you better jump Ben.

Putting my best smile on, I clear my throat as I step forward. "Hi, my name is Cathy Stanwood. Nice to meet you."

4

On our drive back to the city, my cheeks are still tingling from where his lips touched my skin. I was definitely not expecting him to ignore my handshake and plant two of the most electrifying kisses I'd ever received on each side of my face. I felt my cheeks flush as I clumsily took two steps back, extending my hand for a now useless handshake. He must have seen how affected I was by the close contact, because out came that stupid lazy smile of his that seemed to be doing stuff to my lady parts, my very married lady parts, as he took my hand in his own very large one.

Shaking hands, I noticed the unique and exotic color of his eyes. They were a pure aqua blue. Beautiful. I also noticed how they slowly perused my body, sending a shiver so strong running through my spine it made me tremble. He seemed to like what he saw because as his eyes covered more areas of my body, his smile grew wider. When his eyes finally landed on mine, and he realized that I had been watching him the entire time, he winked at me.

He smiled again. "Nice meeting you, Cathy."

That smile should be illegal.

"I'm Arsen," he said, still shaking hands.

"Arson?" I repeated. "Like, Fire-raising Arson?"

"No, Arsen with an E instead of an O, but very close," he said, his eyes shining bright.

It's funny that his name reminded me of fire because he certainly looked like someone who could burn you to the ground. With just one look, he made me feel as if my body was burning scarlet. The clearing of a throat breaks me away from my trance. "Miss Stanwood…Cathy…"

Shit, I hope I haven't missed much of the conversation. Turning towards his voice, I see Arsen sitting on the leather seat with his legs spread apart. As he sips his water, his gaze lingers on my mouth for a moment longer than necessary.

"Cathy, my mother was wondering whether you happen to know if Amy has seen to the buying of that property in Purchase or not?"

"Yes, we closed two weeks ago. I've met and interviewed a couple of interior designers who—"

I'm cut off by Victoria Radcliff. Yes, Mrs. Stepford wife has a name.

"Oh, There's no need for an interior designer. I only use Charles." When she turns to look at her son, I am struck by how much they look alike. All American blonde perfection.

My phone rings, breaking my perusal of perfection.

"I'm sorry. I should probably take this phone call. It must be Amy making sure you arrived safely."

Victoria shrugs her shoulders and continues talking to her son as if I don't exist. Turning my body to the side so that I can give them and myself some privacy, I take the call.

"Cathy Stanwood."

"Babe, it's me. I know you're working, but I just got called into the office…emergency meeting. I'll probably be working all night long, so I don't think I'll be back until you're in bed and already asleep."

I can feel eyes on me. Suspecting Victoria is watching me because I'm interrupting her conversation with her son, I lower my voice.

"Okay…"

Ben must sense that I shouldn't be on the phone because he chuckles. "I'm probably getting you in trouble with this call. Tell them to go to hell. I'm talking to my woman."

"Ben…"

"Alright, babe. I just wanted to wish you a good night. And to let you know not to wait up for me. I love you."

He waits on the line for a second longer, probably expecting me to tell him that I love him back, but I can't. I don't know why. Sighing into the speaker I only say, "Night."

Wait. That's not fair.

I'm about to say something more meaningful to Ben when I hear him release a deep breath and end the call.

Shit. Fuck. Damn it. Why do I always behave like such a bitch to him when he's just trying to be sweet?

Frustrated with myself, I put my phone away and lift my eyes, expecting Victoria to be shooting daggers at me. She's not, though. She's looking out the window. Instead, my eyes connect with aqua ones.

It has been Arsen watching me all this time.

Arsen is making me very uncomfortable. He keeps watching my every move, and it's unnerving. I don't know why. He is much younger than I am, and I usually don't cower in front of men, not even when they are as drop dead gorgeous as the man sitting next to me.

I'm used to some of them watching me and flirting with me, but I'm never made uneasy by just a simple stare.

Not like this.

Not ever.

And, I never squirm in my seat, not even when Ben is trying to be funny and kinky at the same time. But this guy is seriously getting to me. The intensity in his gaze feels as if it's burning a hole through me.

I break our staring contest and reach for my glass of Pinot Noir. For a moment, I get lost in the taste of the wine, tasting its fruity flavors mixed in with warm spice and earthy undertones. Letting the delicious wine roll around in my mouth, seeping into the taste buds of my tongue, I avoid looking at the man sitting to my left and the woman sitting right across the table from me. Instead, I let my eyes wander around the restaurant that Arsen picked instead of going to the Ritz. Homme. It's the "it" restaurant in New York City at the moment. Zagat, the New York Times, and The New Yorker all swear by it. I'm surprised they let us in without a reservation because I've heard that the wait list is currently one month in advance.

I guess I shouldn't be though. Arsen seems to know a lot of the people here tonight, and so does Mrs. Radcliff. Looking around, I take in the very upscale and expensive décor. It's all white and glass. The light fixtures are a mix between classic designs of sparkly clear crystal and large modern Swedish-looking orbs of white, opaque bulbs. Aesthetically it is beautiful and very zen. On the other hand, the music is loud and very Ibiza. The juxtaposition of the techno blasting in your ears while you're trying to eat a hundred-dollar duck is pretty funny if you think about it.

But it works.

Smiling at the very cute waiter when he comes over to fill my almost empty glass, I don't see Arsen move closer to me until I feel the whisper of his hot breath against my ear.

"Why don't you smile like that at me?"

I feel his pinky finger touching the outside of my thigh as his hand supports his reclining body on the edge of my chair. His nearness is crowding me. The insignificant contact of our bodies makes me want to fidget in my seat, and his words make me want to get up and flee away from him and what they just made me feel.

Excitement.

I don't know what to do or say, so I turn to look at Mrs. Radcliff to see if she's watching us. But she's not. With her head lowered, I can see that she's texting someone. I try to move away from Arsen and his mouth when his hand is suddenly on my knee. His large hand manages to cover my entire knee and then some. "Why are you afraid of me? I don't bite unless you want me to. And if you do…"

I clear my throat and gently but firmly remove his hand from my knee. I don't know this guy, and he should not be touching me like this at all.

Meanwhile, ignoring the part of me, of my body, that enjoyed his touch.

Trying to think of Ben, I look at Arsen, about to say something cutting to put him in his place, but I stop short. Instead, I watch as he brings the pinky finger that was touching my leg not a minute ago to his mouth and slowly lets his tongue trace it. Somehow, I get the impression that he can taste me. My throat dry, I can't deny how erotic I find it.

Arsen watches me flush and squirm in my seat and cockily smiles at me. Then he reclines back in his seat, grabbing his glass of wine and draining the contents in one big gulp. I know I need to say something, but I can't. So many warring thoughts are running through my head; fear, dislike, shock, but the voice that is the loudest is lust.

His cockiness is doing things to my body. The way he is watching me, the way he is smiling at me, and the little touch of his finger is making me wet. I am shocked to discover that I want my tongue to be the one tracing his finger. I want to open my legs, take his head, and guide his tongue inside of me so he can drink me, swallow me just as if I were that glass of wine. I want his tongue to taste me.

Alarmed with the direction of my thoughts, I find my voice to shut him and my own imagination down.

"I…Excuse me—"

I don't finish my sentence because Arsen lifts his index finger to his mouth signaling me not to say anything more.

Is he kidding me? I can't.

Putting my napkin down, I push my chair back and excuse myself, saying that I need to use the ladies room. I don't bother looking at him or at Victoria.

I need to get away.

Walking out of the bathroom, calm but still lost in thought, I don't see Arsen approaching me until he's standing in front of me.

"Hey." There's a teasing tone in his voice.

"Hi," I say dryly. I need to get back to the table and get this night over with; he's making me very uncomfortable. Actually, the thoughts he's invoking in me are making me uncomfortable.

"Did I say something to bother you back at the table?"

"Um…No. Not at all…" I stutter nervously.

"Really?" He steps closer to me and lifts a hand, letting his fingers touch my shoulder and caress it slowly. I want to take a step back, but I can't move. I'm frozen under his spell. "Because when I did this, it looked like it bothered you a lot."

"Please stop doing that…" I shake my shoulder off.

"Why? How about we ditch my mom and have some fun?" he asks, reclining his shoulder against the wall and taking in my body.

"No. I can't." I feel myself blush under his scrutiny.

"Why not? I'm known to be a good fucking time."

"B-because…because I'm—"

Doesn't he know I'm married?

"I like you. There's something about the stiffness in your demeanor that makes me want to see if you have a wild side."

He's telling me all these things while he stands there looking cool and composed. Confident. Cocky.

"No. You didn't let me finish before. I can't. I'm married and not interested. Now can you please move to the side so I can get back to your mother?"

He seems shocked when I tell him that I'm married. Good. Whatever this is between us needs to be nipped in the bud.

"You're married? You're not wearing a wedding band," he says, pointing at my finger.

"Well, I forgot to put them on," I say, rubbing my hands together.

"I can still show you a good time, you know. Even better since it can be a one-time thing." He moves away from the wall, and leans down to whisper in my ear. "It can be our little secret."

I push him away. "What's with you? I don't even know you. Do you always insinuate yourself to women like this and it works?"

"Yes. Always."

"Well, it won't work with me. I'm married and not interested. End of story. Now please, let me go back."

Angry and offended, I turn around and walk away from him. I can't believe that man. I just met him, but he's saying these disgusting things to me.

Making my way to the table, I sit down next to Victoria and proceed to pretend that what just happened outside the bathroom between her son and me didn't actually occur. That those words were never exchanged.

Even if for a small fraction of a moment, maybe I did consider them.

I pretend that I wasn't tempted at all.

By the time Arsen comes back, he doesn't ignore me like I thought he would. He continues to be flirtatious, but now that kilowatt smile doesn't reach his eyes. Instead, they look cold and empty.

When I get home, I feel dirty and guilty. I don't know why. I shouldn't feel any of those things. It's not like I asked Arsen to follow me to the bathroom or to say all those things to me. It's not like I actually flirted with him.

I didn't. At all.

But the guilt is there.

The conflicting emotions stampeding through me are leaving such chaotic confusion in its wake that I feel as if my conscience is the resulting aftermath.

And maybe some small part of me wanted to say yes.

5

past

"What's with you?" My dad asks me as we sit down to have dinner.

"What do you mean?" I reach for my glass of water and notice that my hand is slightly shaking.

"Cathy, since you got back from school you haven't been able to stop smiling." He studies my face. "Did you meet someone?"

"Maybe..." I say before taking a mouthful of penne.

"I thought so. You have one of the biggest grins I've seen in a very long time. You should smile more, my darling. It makes me very happy."

I rarely smile. Not since my mom left. We haven't heard from her in over eight years, and I doubt we ever will, so smiles are scarce in my life. Only good grades, my dad, and a good book will bring them out.

"Don't worry, Daddy. And yes, I met someone today. I...I think it was the most amazing experience ever."

"Cathy..."

"No, nothing has happened yet, so don't panic. We just met in the rain."

"What do you mean in the rain?"

"Daddy, forget about it. Just know that I met one of the most beautiful guys I've ever seen in my life."

"Darling, I think you say that about every good looking guy you see."

"Yes, maybe…but he truly is, Daddy."

He's quiet for a minute while we stare at each other.

"Just be careful. I've never seen you this excited over a boy. Not even when you dated those two assholes."

"Dad…"

"I'll drop it, but if he wants to take you out, he better be ready to meet me."

"Dad!" I exclaim. Sometimes my dad can get quite carried away, but he's right. I have to be cautious. The last time I gave my heart away, it was broken badly.

My two ex-boyfriends, the only two boys I've ever loved and slept with, are long gone, but I still think about them. Jack had medium brown hair, wore glasses, and was lanky. He wasn't unattractive, yet he wasn't handsome. He was just like me—passable. My second boyfriend, Matt, was really good looking, so much so that I always wondered why he was with me. Our relationship was conventional, his love for me ordinary. I, on the other hand, loved him so much, wanted him so much. When he broke up with me because I wasn't doing it for him anymore, it broke me. He broke me. I haven't really seen anyone since high school ended and college began. I need to maintain my GPA and not jeopardize my scholarship.

When dinner is over, I run upstairs to get some work done before my dad can question me further. I quietly close my bedroom door behind me, then stand in front of my Ikea floor length mirror.

I notice what my dad is talking about. My cheeks look so rosy, and the smile on my face is so big that you can see how deep my dimples go. The girl staring back at me looks as if she has swallowed a big fat happy pill and is high on happiness

Covering my mouth, I silently scream into my hands, breaking into a little dance that might include some Mr. Roboto dance moves. Cheesy, I know, but I mean, come on! I'm so giddy and full of butterflies that I'm surprised my body is still here and not flying away along with them. I feel so light and alive.

The wait for Friday to come isn't nail biting after all. Ben calls me every time he says he will; his texts are the first ones to greet my eyes when I wake up, and his voice is the last sound I hear before going to bed.

The evening before our Friday night date, we talk on the phone for two hours. I'm falling asleep, and so is he, so I tell him we should hang up. He laughs. "I don't want to hang up. How about we just fall asleep listening to each other's voice? It could be kind of hot if you wanted to…"

I laugh at his silly joke while I imagine him wiggling his eyebrows in a cute but perverted way. "No freaking way. Nu uh, not happening, buddy. Get your mind out of the gutter. I am not having phone sex with you. I barely know you…"

Hearing a full-blown laugh, I smile into the receiver. When Ben speaks next, his voice has grown deeper, but I somehow know he's still smiling.

"Well, casual phone sex has been known to help attain a better night sleep…deeper if you know what I mean…" He teases me.

I laugh. "Really?"

"Yes. Best-Method-Ever. I am even offering myself as a test dummy." Laughing, I wish him a good night and end the call. If I know myself well, and I think I do, I'm pretty sure I'm already falling for someone I barely know.

But it is so easy.

I'm so nervous. I haven't eaten anything all day.

Tonight is a perfect early September evening. Warm, but with a cool breeze whispering on your skin. Not knowing where Ben is taking me, I pick a cute, light pink, short, baby-doll dress with lace applications on the sleeves and neckline. It's girly and pretty, but a bit sexy, too, paired with tanned wedges that make my legs appear longer. Really, dressing like this is way out of my comfort zone, but I want to look as pretty as possible for Ben. I really want him to think I look good tonight.

When I stare at myself in the mirror, I'm happy to notice that I look my best. The champagne eye shadow brings out the color of my eyes, and the little bronzer I applied to my face lends a sun kissed glow to my features. And, yes, my hair decided to help me out tonight because it doesn't look frizzy. Smiling at my reflection, I apply some light pink gloss on my lips and decide this is as good as it is going to get.

I'm looking for a pair of earrings when I hear a knock on the front door. Shit.

My dad is going to get the door.

Oh, my. This should be interesting.

Not bothering to put the earrings on, I throw them in my bag and run towards the stairs. I need to get down there before my dad starts embarrassing me. When I get to the foot of the stairs, I freeze on the spot. I can't believe what I'm seeing.

Ben is standing inside my house holding the largest bouquet of…

Wait…are those cupcakes? Yes, I think so.

Ben approaches me, leaving my dad standing there with a "Who the hell does this guy think he is?" expression written all over his face.

The sweetest smile touches the lips of the most handsome guy I have ever seen in my whole life, and it's for me—ME!

I thought I remembered what he looked like, but I'm so wrong. His maple brown eyes shine so radiantly that they appear to be crystalized syrup, and there's a hint of a blush blooming on his strong cheekbones.

Even with my wedges on, he still towers over me, and the way he's looking at me with such tenderness in his expression makes me want to faint. My knees feel all wobbly.

Ben just stands there, staring at me for a second…or forever. Who's keeping track of the time, anyway? When he finally speaks, his words are softly said and take my breath away.

"I wanted to say something witty and funny when I finally saw you again, but my brain seems to be fried." He closes his eyes and groans. "So, you look beautiful."

Blushing all kinds of red, I hear my dad clearing his throat, trying to remind us that he's still in the room. After he hands me the very heavy bouquet of cupcakes, I ask him why he brought me so many of them. There is no way I could eat them all.

Ben blushes again. "The other night when we were talking about favorite foods, you said you could have a cupcake every day of the week. I figured that if I brought enough to last you a week, you'd want to see me again next week when you ran out. If anything, just so I could bring you more."

Oh, my God. Now the two of us are blushing.

"Um, thank you." Is this guy for real?

Leaving my dad with Ben in the foyer, I excuse myself and head to the kitchen to deposit the cupcakes on the counter. When I come back, Ben and my dad are facing each other. Dad has his arms crossed over his chest with an angry look on his face, and Ben's hands are in his front pockets as he rocks on his feet. He looks uncomfortable. I want to laugh because Ben is probably four inches taller than my dad and a lot bigger too, but he actually seems nervous. It's quite cute to watch.

"She's only eighteen, so you better not take her to a bar. I remember when I was your age. I know where you guys hang out and what you like to do with pretty girls like mine, so you better watch it, son. If she comes home smelling like alcohol, or if her clothes are out of place, I won't be a happy camper."

Just kill me now. Seriously, Dad? I half expect Ben to jet and bail on me.

"No, sir. I won't let her hands touch anything with alcohol."

"How old are you, son?" my dad asks, studying him.

Flushing, but never breaking eye contact with my dad, Ben answers, "I'm twenty-two. I'm also in my first year at Columbia Law, Sir."

"Humph. A future lawyer. What kind of law are you interested in pursuing?"

Okay, this is bordering on harassment. I need to step in before my dad scares Ben out of the house, leaving me dateless…and sex-less. *You want to get to at least third base tonight with that hot stud!* Slutty Cathy reminds me.

I clear my throat, breaking my dad's interrogation. "Hi. Sorry. I'm ready, Ben. Are you all set?"

Ben looks at my dad, then at me, smiling. "Yep. Ready whenever you are."

Grinning, I give my dad a kiss and tell him not to worry about tonight. Ben helps me put on my denim jacket, but when I think he's going to follow me to the door, he steps away from my side and walks back towards my dad. He stretches his hand for a handshake. "Don't worry, sir. I'll take very good care of your daughter. Thank you for trusting me with her."

Wow. Hearing Ben speak to my dad like this is causing my insides to turn into mush.

My dad smiles for the first time tonight. Shaking hands with Ben, he wishes us a good night. I'm about to open the door, when Ben stops me.

"No, let me get the door for you. That was the deal, remember?" he says softly.

"Oh, yes."

Smiling, he takes my hand, intertwining our fingers tightly together. It's the first time we do. Holding hands is a big deal. The last time I held hands with a guy was with my ex two years ago.

Does this mean that Ben likes me? *Duh, girl.* Why do you think the guy brought you cupcakes to your house? To watch you eat them? Of course he likes you. It shows he put some thought into tonight. Count your blessings and open your legs.

Slutty Cathy always shows up at the most inopportune moments.

I barely register leaving the house and making our way to his car. I'm now sitting on the cool leather seat and thinking about holding hands and slutty voices, when I sense Ben's eyes on me. The way he's staring at me…

Suddenly the car feels hot, too hot. I watch Ben following the movement of my legs as I rub them together.

"Screw it. I can't wait any longer," Ben says.

He grabs the back of my neck forcefully as he pulls me on top of him. I knew he was strong by looking at the muscles on his body, but not like this. As I straddle him, our lips touch for the second time and it's like the air is being sucked out of me slowly, deliciously, tenderly. His lips, soft and sweet, kiss me as if mine are made out of glass. He's gentle at first, but when our tongues touch fire explodes inside of me, inside of him, inside of both of us.

His kiss isn't sweet anymore. It isn't tender. It turns into an aggressive, rough, hungry, hard, teeth clashing, tongue against tongue kind of kiss.

And, I love it. Oh, how I love it.

When our lips part, we're left panting and trying to catch our breath. As we look at each other in the little space we have allowed to come between our bodies, I notice the way our hands are tangled in each other's hair, fisting handfuls of it, pulling our faces closer, clutching as if we are the other's life support.

I can't believe it. I can't. This just doesn't happen in real life.

"Fuck, Cathy…just like that you make me lose control, huh?"

Gulping, and trying to untangle the thoughts coming from two different directions in my body, inside my head and inside my panties, all I can manage to do is shake my head and grin.

Ben laughs, plants a quick kiss on my lips and moves me off his lap. Once I'm back in my seat, he rests his hand on my knee. "I'm sorry about that kiss. I was planning to take my time tonight…go slow, you know…but when you came down wearing that sexy dress, showing those killer legs, and looking so fucking sexy and beautiful…I kind of wanted to jump you right then and there, even with your dad watching us, but I figured he wouldn't let me take his daughter out again. And after that kiss," pausing, he grabs my chin so I'm facing him, "Look at me, Cathy…I want to see your eyes." Applying slight pressure to my chin, "I need to see you again."

Blushing, I'm so glad that the car is dark.

"But the date hasn't really begun…how do you know you will want to see me again if we haven't even started the first one?" My voice is small. I'm afraid because I so want his words to be true. I like him. I like him a lot.

Letting go of my knee, he grabs my hand and brings it to his mouth, planting a kiss inside my palm. "I just do. I'm sure of a few things in life…that no matter what you do, death will always catch up to you. You've got to work hard to pay for life, party harder to enjoy life, and love hardest to live life, and now, you."

"Oh."

DING-DING-DING.

Have I just won the lotto?

When we are in Serendipity, a group of drop dead gorgeous girls approach our table to ask him if he is Benjamin Stanwood, the ex-quarterback for the University of Florida. Blushing a little, Ben says he was, making the girls squeal and ask him for his autograph. As the girls flirt with him, he reaches for my hand. They all look at me as if they're wondering how the hell a plain Jane has ended up with a hunk.

I've been wondering the same thing the entire night.

Ben clears his throat, "Sorry, girls. Here are your autographs. Thank you for coming over and saying hello. It's really cool of you, but I'm trying to impress my girl…and so far it isn't working."

The girls turn to look at me, anger and disbelief written all over their faces. I have never been the kind of girl to gloat over others when something right goes my way, but in this moment some hidden attitude-ridden part of me wants to stand up, give them my best Queens bad girl fuck you look, snapping my fingers in their plastic faces and say, "Suck it, Bitches."

But I don't.

Instead, I grip Ben's hand harder. His eyes meet mine and what I see in them elates me.

The rest of the date passes in a blur. I don't remember much except for the softness in his eyes when he looked at me, his sweet but flirtatious smile every time his hands "accidentally" grazed my butt or boobs, the very pleased and smug expression on his face after every kiss we shared left me dazed and unfocused. But the thing that I remember the most is the way Ben never let go of my hand, almost as if he owns it or like it belongs there.

After he drops me off and kisses the hell out of me, I make my way to my bedroom, walking like a living zombie. The crazy beating of my heart has to be proof that I am still alive, right?

Lying in bed, I can't remember getting out of my clothes and into my pajamas or removing the little make up I had left from the hot and heavy make out session we'd just had outside my house in his car. My lips feel numb, yet tingly like they are on fire. They are so hot to the touch; it's like I'm burning from the inside out.

My breasts are sore from his hands, my nipples still hard, and I'm swollen and raw in between my legs from his fingers, but it feels good.

So very good.

My body is humming with excitement because it's alive again. It has been so long.

Staring and looking at the shadows playing on my ceiling, I try to will my eyes to close, but I can't. The images of him touching me, whispering what he wants to do to me, what he is trying hard to refrain himself from doing…the feel of his erection in my hand…

I'm still in a daze when I hear my phone ringing. Answering without looking at the caller I.D., I smile when I hear his voice.

"Hi, Cathy."

"Hi."

"I miss you already," he says huskily.

"I…I am…me too."

"You're what?"

"Hmm…not sure I should say it." I whisper.

"Damn, Cathy. I'm still in a fucking daze. I have been since we kissed back in my car when I first picked you up. Haven't been able to shake it off. And I don't want to."

I hear him sucking in his breath, then releasing it. "I can't close my eyes because when I do all I see is you. When I breathe, all I smell is you. And I would much rather have the real deal next to me than a dream. When can I see you again? I promise not to jump you like a starved man…but man, Cathy, do you have any idea of the things you do to me? Of the things I want to do to you? What I almost did to you in my car?"

"Yes."

"You do? Well, shit."

"Shhh…let me talk. I know how you're feeling because I feel the same way. I'm feeling every single thing you just mentioned…just more," I say.

"Really?"

"Yes, really."

"I'll be damned."

Silence.

"Cathy?" Ben asks.

"Yes?"

"I like you. I really like you."

"I like you, too."

"Fuck, I want to…no, scratch that, I need to see you again."

"Me, too."

"Tomorrow?"

"Yes."

"And the day after tomorrow, and the day after that?"

"Yes, and yes."

"Cathy…"

"Ben…"

"Night, beautiful girl. And thank you for going out with me."

"Night, Ben. And thank you for asking me."

"Do we really have to hang up?"

"Yes! Night," I say, giggling.

Closing my eyes, I grab my pillow and scream into it as I let myself believe that this magic night wasn't a dream.

I can still remember being able to feel the smile on my swollen lips as I begin to fall into a deep sleep.

6

present

"Oh my God."

I stare at the stick with the plus sign once more. Can this be happening again? Can this be true?

"Oh my God."

My vision starts to blur as I keep staring at the pregnancy test in my trembling hands. Hope and fear wrestle against each other to be the strongest and loudest emotion growing inside my chest. Hope wins.

It always does.

After carefully putting the pregnancy test on the sink, my hands, shaking now, automatically go to my flat stomach. There is life growing inside of me once more. I don't want to feel hope; I don't want my mind to inevitably wander to our attic where there are pink and blue things still wrapped in gift boxes, unopened. I don't want to start wishing for things that may never happen. Gosh, but it is so easy to.

Feeling the tears rolling down my cheeks, I stick my tongue out to taste them, savor each and every single one of them. They are happy tears for once, and they taste so sweet on my tongue. Moving away from the porcelain tub, I run out of the bathroom in search of Ben.

As I make my way to Ben's office, I notice how bright the corridors look this morning. The rays of sun hit the windowpanes at just the right angle that as I'm walking by, rainbows of color are reflected on my skin. Funny, it has been a long time since I've noticed how pretty our home is. There are so many pictures of Ben and me, eleven years' worth of a life together to be exact, scattered throughout the walls. Hard to believe time has flown by this fast.

Sometimes, when passing by, I notice how young and happy we looked, so in love. Our smiles remind me of how promising we thought our life together would be. The look in the eyes of that young girl reminds me of a time when looking at Ben made me believe that the answers to life's secrets could be found within him. That he was my answer to everything. Sadly, I've come to discover that such a notion is not only false but impossible. No one has all the answers to solve the big puzzle that life is, and it is even less likely that another person can offer them to you.

The girl in those pictures doesn't look like she is plagued by uncertainty, though. If anything, the woman and the man posing in the pictures look like they believe everything is possible and within reach. I haven't seen those feelings when I look at my reflection in the mirror for a very long time.

Nearing his office, closing in the physical distance between us, a thought is planting its thick roots in my head and heart, spreading hope within me. Call it wishful thinking, but I hope that the small life inside of me is able to bridge the emotional space growing between us. An emotional gap so wide, that lately it feels almost insurmountable to close.

It is the source of our growing distance after all.

Well, mine mostly.

I find a frowning Ben when I walk in his office. One of the stems of his glasses is in his mouth while he looks down at the newspaper sitting on his desk in front of him. His dark, wavy hair looks messy, probably from pulling at it while lost in thought. Wearing an old gray t-shirt with the word Columbia written across his chest and faded jeans, he looks just as big and handsome as the day I met him. The years haven't done anything to alter his starting quarterback body; if anything, he looks more masculine and seasoned with age.

I hope our baby has his dark looks and not my boring blonde ones.

When he hears me enter his office, the frown disappears immediately and

a gorgeous smile appears, showing his perfect white teeth. He reminds me of a pirate sometimes when he smiles at me that way, with his tanned skin, dark hair, and glimmer in his eyes.

As soon as he notices the tears on my face, he drops his glasses on the desk, stands up from his leather chair and makes his way towards me. His hands go to my shoulders.

"Cathy, baby, what's the matter? Why are you crying?"

Looking up, the tears that were slowly flowing before begin to blur my vision as they fall in a torrent so fast and so strong that I can't do anything but feel them inundate my face as they overflow my eyes. I can't do anything but move between his arms and wrap him in a hug, tight and fierce. Yes. There is hope for us, after all. Our love is enough.

It is enough.

Ben wraps his arms around me, returning my embrace just as strongly and intensely, lowers his face close to mine and whispers, "Babe, talk to me. You're scaring me. What's the matter? Tell me so I can fix it. Shit, Babe…please."

I let go of his body, lifting my hands to cradle his face in between them. He truly looks concerned. Fear is written in the way he seems to be clenching his teeth, emphasizing how strong his jaw is. The frown that had disappeared when he heard me coming in is back, and he looks as if he is scowling. The half angry and half worried expression on his face makes a stupid watery giggle escape my mouth. The situation is growing more comical by the minute.

"Baby…no." Reaching out to smooth the temples of his lovely face with my fingers, I erase the scowl away. "No, baby. Nothing is the matter. Actually, everything is…oh my God. Ben, baby, I'm pregnant again."

Ben's body becomes statue-still. The arms that are wrapped so tightly around my waist go slack. He is looking at me as if I am a ghost, not blinking and barely breathing, he seems to be in a state of shock. I'm about to shake him, to make him react, when I see the first glimmer of tears flood his dark eyes.

He lets go of my waist and lowers his large body to kneel in front of me. Looking down at his dark head, I watch him as he lifts my light cashmere sweater, exposing my flat stomach to him, and gently and carefully leans over to softly place a tender kiss on the same spot where three babies have grown and died.

This poignant moment, so full of love and hope, feels like a new beginning.

A second chance for us.

Clearing his throat, Ben comes out of his shock. "Are you sure, Cathy?"

Nodding because that is all I can do, I hear Ben say, "Oh, babe. Really?" Nodding again as he looks up at me, he mumbles, "Shit…'Kay. We need to call Dr. Pajaree first thing tomorrow. Get you an appointment with her as early as possible. I don't care if she is treating the President of the United States, she will make time to fit you in. You need to call Amy, too. She will understand if you can't make it to work…fuck. Babe, shh. Don't cry anymore. We will do whatever it takes to make it work."

"I'm so afraid, Ben. I want this baby so bad…"

I'm crying so hard that I can barely make out Ben's features as I feel his mouth whispering kisses all over my body. Moving away from his embrace, I kneel in front of him, and we stare at each other. As Ben watches me intensely his eyes sparkling with unshed tears, I see all the love he feels for me written in his face. I hope he can see the love I feel for him reflected in my eyes as well.

I love him so very much that it hurts.

Thickly, Ben whispers, "Come here. It will be okay, babe. We will be okay whatever happens…"

Out of nowhere, as he is bringing our bodies in an all-encompassing embrace, an image of blue eyes crosses my mind, but I immediately bury it in the deepest confines of my guilty conscience. For the very brief moment that Arsen sabotages my mind, I am shocked to realize that not a day has gone by since I met him two weeks ago where I haven't thought of him. But like I've done every time the thought of him enters my mind, I pretend that Arsen and what happened between us never occurred. I go back to pretending that he didn't make me feel things I haven't felt in a long time; that he didn't make my body hum with something as temptingly delicious as it was forbidden, bringing it to life. No. He has no right to intrude in my thoughts right now.

As I feel Ben's arms tighten around me, I make myself believe that Arsen and his words are meaningless and that the only reason why I haven't been able to get him out my mind is because he will always remain an unknown. And I hate unknowns.

Returning Ben's hug, I believe my words, even if for a moment they sound like empty excuses to my own ears.

I feel Ben's breath on my mouth as he mutters that I make him so happy and that I am and will always be his Cathy just before he kisses me.

We are going to be okay. Yes.

The life growing inside of me will be able to seal all the empty holes I've carried with me for so long that not even Ben's deep love has been able to fill since the first time it happened.

God, I want this baby so bad.

When the kiss ends, a flushed looking Ben pulls slightly away to look me in the eye, our bodies still glued to each other. The smile I observe on his face is so big that I can see his dimples peeking at me, taunting me to kiss them. Planting a quick kiss on my nose, Ben gives me with that naughty look of his, the one that means he wants to get lucky.

"Hey, want to give the love couch a celebratory ride?"

I laugh out loud as I swat his shoulder. "Seriously, Ben?"

A smiling Ben lowers his nose to touch mine as he teases me, "Can't blame a man for trying. By the way, did I tell you how fucking happy you make me? I love you, Cathy."

7

"Cathy…Cathy…Earth calling Cathy. Oh, hi. Hello. Yes, I am still here."

I laugh as I turn to look at Amy who is sitting across the table from me. Her long red hair is blown out to perfection in soft curls that seem like natural waves flowing down her back and over her shoulders. Dressed in a black suit and crisp white shirt, she is so gorgeous.

It's not fair.

"Yes? By the way, I hate you. Only you could manage to look so freaking gorgeous in a plain black suit," I say, smirking.

She waves a piece of bread in front of my face before replying, "Please. Have you looked at yourself in the mirror lately, blondie? Even I, a 100% penis lover, would totally do you. Pregnancy suits you, you know? Anyway, what are you thinking about? You seem lost in thought and haven't touched your plate. I mean, shouldn't you be eating for two and enjoying the perks of being preggers, instead of sitting there watching me stuff my face while daydreaming about baby socks or whatever it is you pregnant women like to think about?"

"What makes you think I'm daydreaming about babies and baby gear?" I smile at Amy. Her light teasing about my pregnancy makes me feel better, almost as if it wasn't such a big deal when in reality it truly is.

I know it's insane to put so much on this pregnancy, but I feel like my marriage and my own sanity are hanging by a very thin thread, and only this baby can save us, save me. Amy's jokes help to alleviate the ever-present fear that lays dormant like a sleeping volcano at the back of my mind and in my heart. A constant fear that slowly and painfully gnaws my insides raw, yet, all I seem to be able to do is wish and pray.

Getting my hopes up when I know I shouldn't.

"Due to your medical history of pregnancy losses, Cathy, I must be completely honest with you. You are considered a high-risk pregnancy. According to the date when you had your last period, you are now five weeks pregnant. We need to be very cautious this early in your pregnancy. Until your first trimester is over we are on shaky ground, so I want to see you every two weeks to monitor the growth of the fetus; you must avoid risky substances…" Dr. Pajaree's words are still so fresh in my mind; I can hear her sweet voice telling me not to start thinking about baby names. So, yes, I need funny now. I need a lot of jokes.

"Look, I have been stuffing my face with empty but delicious complex carbohydrates that according to my dentist will not only make my ass bigger but give me cavities, so the least you could do is tell me what's going on in that pretty head of yours? Wait. Is my teasing bothering you? Because I'll stop. You know I just do it to try and make you feel better." The concerned and chastised expression on her face makes my smile grow wider.

"Woman, I love your face. No, don't worry about it. I was just thinking that Ben's birthday is coming up and what that means."

"What do you mean?"

"I thought you knew. Ben and I got *serious* sometime around his birthday. It depends who's telling the story, really."

"No, you hadn't told me that. How many years now? I know you've been married for six years, right?"

"Right. Six years married, but eleven together."

"That's a long time to be with one person. In the past eleven years, I've been married twice and who knows how many men I've slept with in between and after. But if I were married to your hunk of a husband, I would probably still be married. I mean, I remember how amazing he looked in swim trunks when we went to Turks and Caicos to celebrate your birthday. Cathy, no joke. He was built better than my gym instructor and my instructor was rocking a pretty lickable six-pack, just saying."

I can't help laughing. If I didn't know Amy so well, I would totally think she had the hots for Ben. I couldn't blame her if she did, though. Beautiful women, young or old, are always hitting on him, even when he's with me.

"Well, don't waste your time. He only has eyes for me, or so he tells me every time some young intern hits on him." I lean back in my chair and watch as Amy grins at me, acknowledging my comment.

"You're a very lucky woman. That man never, ever looks at another woman when you're in the same room. It's quite depressing actually. I mean, the way he looks at you even after all the years you've been together is as if you are the only person with a pair of breasts in the room. Hot and sweet."

"Mine are very small sadly," I say, laughing.

"I want what you have, though. Every woman wants that, a man who looks at her as if she were the only woman in the room. You're so lucky to still have that."

As Amy tells me how fortunate I am, all I can do is smile because I am lucky. A week ago, I thought Ben and I were going through a very rough patch in our marriage, and then I took the pregnancy test that changed everything. The results brought hope into my life again, hope that we will be okay after all, hope that we can grow closer again, bridging the space between us, and hope that we will finally get a chance to have that family.

Smiling, I realize that our future doesn't look bleak. Yes, I may be scared shitless of the what ifs, but as I glance around the restaurant full of people, my hands go to my stomach. My body is not empty anymore. There is magic growing inside of me. There is life.

However, I'm afraid that such hope won't last forever. Cruel reality has a way of always catching up to you, no matter how fast or how far you run; reality has a way to destroy one's hopes and dreams. Reality doesn't caress your cheek, letting you know what's to come. No, reality slaps you across the face harshly, reminding you that a dream is just that…a dream.

The naïve part of me wants to believe that those feelings are gone, gone since I found out we are expecting again, and that the love we feel for each other is enough. But the logical voice inside my head, the cynical one, tells me to stop fooling myself. It tells me that just because I'm pregnant, those issues, our issues, my issues, aren't going anywhere. They're still there, will always be there until I address them. They just happen to be concealed by a blanket made of happy feelings at the moment. A blanket that allows me to ignore the nagging sentiment that not everything is as it should be.

After lunch, I drop Amy off at the office and drive to SoHo to pick up Charles Parker. He's one of the most exclusive and expensive interior designers in the world. His clientele includes many people with famous last names, Hollywood A-listers, and members of the European Jet-Set. Charles has also been featured in every magazine geared for high-end homeowners and the very, very wealthy.

Curious as to what kind of man he really is, I'm excited to finally meet him in person and take him to the future Radcliff residence. Based on the estimates he gave me for his services, I hope he's amazing because I almost fell out of my chair when the numbers came out of his assistant's mouth.

"Yes, how may I help you today?" A very chic receptionist asks upon seeing me approach her desk.

"Hi. My name is Cathy Stanwood. I believe Mr. Parker is expecting me," I tell the drop-dead gorgeous brunette girl with the bluest eyes I've ever seen. She looks to be no older than twenty.

"Mrs. Stanwood. What a pleasure to finally meet you. I'm Natalie, we've spoken on the phone before." I notice that Sexy Natalie speaks with a slight Russian accent that only makes her more attractive in my opinion.

I smile. "Hi, Natalie. It's great to finally meet you."

Her red lips smile back. "Yes. Would you like to have a seat for a moment while I let him know that you are here? Charles has been waiting for you."

"Of course." I make my way to sit on a posh white leather couch that reminds me of one I saw not too long ago in Architectural Digest. As my hands caress the smooth texture of the leather, my eyes spot a newspaper on the coffee table in front of me. I open it and go straight to Page six, the gossip column.

I feel like the wind has been knocked out of my lungs. I stare at the headline of the article and the profligate beauty of the man whose face is plastered on the front of the page. A defiant Arsen is looking directly at the camera as a sexy smirk plays around the corners of his lips.

He's so beautiful.

The picture shows Arsen, drunk and exiting an exclusive nightclub with a famous model wrapped around each arm, and a third one on his back, piggyback riding him. He looks like a kid in a candy store. The hand of one of the girls is inside his pants, wrapped around his huge erection no doubt, and a thong is wrapped around his neck. I know how his *night ended.* Disgusted by his behavior, and with myself for not being able to look away, I read the banner of the article.

Arsen=Arson? Manhattan's new favorite bad boy.

That's an understatement.

Curiosity gets the best of me, so I read the article about him. According to the columnist, the photographers asked Arsen his secret to staying in such good shape.

"I fuck a lot."

When they asked him if it was true he banged the newest Hollywood "it" girl, he answered, "No comment. I'm a gentleman. I don't fuck and tell…unless they want me to."

"Handsome devil, isn't he?"

Lifting my eyes, I see a very attractive man in his mid-forties smiling at me. I blush because I've been caught reading trash about his clients, and my boss' son. I close the newspaper and place it on the table as quickly as possible and stand up to extend my hand.

"Hi, Mr. Parker. It's a pleasure to finally meet you. I'm Cathy Stanwood, your chauffeur for the day."

He takes my hand and shakes it. "Hi, Cathy. What a lovely surprise. Let's just say that I've never been so glad to be driven around as I am today."

"Thank you for the compliment, Mr. Parker."

"You're as beautiful as your voice is over the phone. And please, call me Charles." We've stopped shaking hands, but he hasn't let go of mine yet. "I love when pretty women like you call me by my name."

I can't help smiling into his grey eyes as he flirts with me. "Sure." Taking in his appearance, I note that he's wearing dark denim fitted jeans with a light blue button down shirt and a cream-colored sports jacket. His longish brown hair is parted to the side, lending his handsome face a very preppy and boyish look.

"You flatter me, but I feel obligated to let you know that I'm not that good of a driver. Anyway, should we go? Driving to Westchester is quite a hike at this time of the day."

"Of course. Please lead the way." He moves to the side to let me pass and walk in front of him.

"Well, what a gentleman," I tease as I grab my bag and move past him.

"Always, Darling. Always," he teases back.

Somehow he beats me to the door, opening it for me. "After you."

Laughing, the two of us get in my car. I turn to look at him as I start the engine. "About before…the newspaper isn't mine. It was just sitting there and…"

Charles shrugs as his gray eyes land on mine. "I was just teasing you. I've known that kid for a very long time. I'm what you could call a longtime family friend. Arsen definitely likes to have his fun in his own wild ways, but don't believe everything you read. They make a living on selling lies. But there is no denying he's guilty of at least half of those stories. If I have ever met a kid who knows how to use his pretty face and money, it's got to be him. He never hurts the women, though. He's always very forward and up front with what he's looking for and what he expects before getting involved with someone."

As I fight the Manhattan traffic, I say, "Yes, there is no denying he knows how to have fun and that women love him."

"Yes, the kid is so good looking that women throw themselves at him. I still remember Victoria complaining back when he was a boy how kids would tease him saying that he looked like a girl because he was so pretty."

"Well, he definitely doesn't look like a girl anymore. I don't think people tease him either," I say, smirking.

"No. I don't think so." We both laugh at the joke.

"I'm curious though…is his life always reported and scrutinized like that by gossip columnists? I can't imagine living under the microscope like that," I ask.

"He can go quite unnoticed by them when he's out and about and they leave him alone for the most part. It's only when he dates someone famous that he can't escape the rumors or paparazzi."

Dropping the subject of Arsen, we continue the car ride to the suburbs talking about everything else that strangers who like each other talk about upon meeting.

As we approach the impressive Radcliff residence, I decide that Charles Parker is a great catch. He is likeable, wealthy, and would be perfect for Amy. They both ooze sex from the pores of their perfect skin and would probably screw like bunnies. My mind goes back to Arsen, and for a brief second I wonder if I will ever see him again.

I want to.

Yes, even after what happened, or *didn't happen*, between us.

After the elderly housekeeper lets us in, Charles and I make our way to the kitchen. Charles has been to the house with Victoria plenty of times before, so he knows his way around the massive mansion just fine. When we walk into the kitchen, I'm surprised by how extensive the area is. Everything is made out of maple wood and black marble. It boggles my mind that Victoria would like to change the décor of the kitchen because the room is already breathtaking.

I follow Charles to the expansive black marble top island. Upon reaching him, I notice he has all sorts of designs, fabrics, and floor plans spread across the top. Charles studies the organized mess in front of him as if he's solving an algebra problem.

"This is a beautiful home. I hope it's finished soon so Victoria and Bruno can move in."

"I agree, but living at the Plaza is *not* a shabby thing either."

We laugh.

"Hey, Charles, would you mind if I step away? I need to make some phone calls to the office," I ask, wanting to give him some space to do his work.

Looking up from his study of the floor plans, he smiles at me. "Take your time. I'm going over some last minute changes that need to be addressed."

As I walk around the palatial mansion admiring its beauty, I realize for the first time that the Radcliff's and I will kind of be neighbors since Ben and I live in Greenwich, not even fifteen minutes away from here.

When I think about our home, I decide to give Ben a call. I haven't spoken to him since this morning and I miss him. Lately, I've made a conscious effort to seek him out, to reach out to him and it seems to be working. A couple of weeks ago I could go a whole day without speaking to him, but now I'm rediscovering how much fun it is to talk to him. Yes, his voice is making me feel things again.

About to press send, I hear extremely loud metal music coming from somewhere. My interest piqued, I forget about the phone call and decide to find the source of the music.

I follow the noise and make my way down the hall to where the song sounds loudest. I stand outside of a room left with its door ajar and watch the paintings on the wall shake in time to the bass. I wonder who could be listening to such an atrocity.

Thinking that I should do something, I walk through the threshold of the room as the answer to my earlier question is staring me right in the eye like a bulls eye target.

Well, Cathy. You wanted to know…

Stopping dead in my tracks, I see a naked Arsen going down on a dark haired woman on top of what I assume is his dad's oak desk. His muscular back and the woman's long tanned legs wrapped around his neck are all I can see from where I am standing. However, there's a large mirror sitting on the mantelpiece above the fireplace behind the desk that reflects everything.

As the loud thumping of the music surrounds me, drowning my own thoughts in the aggressive melody, I can see the reflection of Arsen's blond head in between her legs. The woman lying on the table is holding her ankles, spreading her legs open and offering herself to Arsen. Shocked, I want to move…I want to get out of this room as fast as my legs will allow, but I can't. Metal music continues to blast in my ears as I watch Arsen lick his lips and stand up, his hungry eyes landing on the woman's face. I can see him smiling as he fists his dick in his hand, pumping it up and down. Letting go of himself, he reaches for his jeans and takes a condom out of the back pocket. I watch as he rips the foil package open with his teeth. After rolling it over his length, he grabs the woman's ass in his large hands and pulls her closer to him. Remaining in her split position, the woman lifts her head to look at him. Her back is facing the mirror, so I can't see the expression on her face, but I see Arsen's half cocky smile…the barest lift of his lips…as he places the tip of his dick against her entrance. The woman throws her head back, exposing her long and elegant neck just as Arsen pushes all the way in, fully penetrating her. She appears to say something that pleases Arsen because, shaking his head, a short lived smile appears and disappears on his lips, a smile that is replaced with lust and want.

Looking down at his dick inside her sex, he begins to slowly slide out, then slam right back in her, each thrust harder and faster than the last, every slam of his hips pushing her body further across the top of the desk. I can hear her screams breaking now through the music, begging him for more.

Arsen lifts his eyes and notices me.

He notices the transfixed blonde woman standing on the threshold of the office watching their every move. Not stopping, Arsen keeps slamming his body into hers as I see his reflection smile into mine. He watches me as he lowers his smiling lips to kiss the dark haired woman. As their tongues connect with one another, he continues to watch me as he fucks her with his mouth.

It's his shameful smile that I feel slowly brandishing itself in my memory that finally brings me back to reality. I shouldn't be here. I shouldn't be watching him, watching them.

Appalled at myself, I turn around, leaving the study as fast as my stiletto clad feet will allow. I trip on my feet not once, but twice in my lame attempt at running.

Damn it! Stupid Louboutins and their lack of traction.

Feeling like I'm burning from the inside out, I make my way to an empty room. It looks like a sunroom with all its windows and the sunlight streaming in. With no furniture in sight, I lean my body against a wall. As I try to catch my breath and calm my beating heart, I close my eyes and attempt to expunge the image of Arsen and that woman out of my mind.

It isn't working.

The scene I just walked in on keeps playing over and over in my head. I can still see the way Arsen smiled at me as he had sex with her on the desk as if daring me to stop him…or join him. I can still see his blond head in between her legs. I can still hear her screams through the music, asking him for more.

Calmer, I open my eyes and realize I didn't feel anything when I saw him other than shock. Not one thing. I want to scream with happiness.

My infatuation, if you could even call it that, is over!

I obviously find him attractive, but who wouldn't. He's sex on legs. But I know that thoughts of him sabotaging my mind when I least expect it are gone. And funny enough, seeing him with her has helped to exorcise him from my mind.

Completely.

My hands go to my stomach as I feel a smile tugging at my lips. This time, brown eyes pop into my head and not aqua.

I am free.

Free.

8

My body feels light as a feather, and my conscience guilt free for the first time in a very long time as I leave the room in search of Charles. I need to get out of here, and fast, before I run into Arsen and Miss Spread Eagle again.

When I step into the kitchen, I find Charles talking to a bare chested Arsen. What the hell? How did he get here?

Arsen is the first one to notice me as I walk towards the granite island where floor plans and magazines remain scattered all over the countertop. His eyes scrutinizing me as he smiles.

I avoid making eye contact with him. It's a big mistake because my gaze lands on his very perfect and sweaty chest where his six-pack glistens with the moisture of sex.

Feeling an embarrassed blush cover my face, I turn to address Charles. "There you are. Are you ready to head back into the city?" I look down at my watch, noticing that it's already close to 4:00 p.m. "If we leave now, we could beat the rush hour traffic, but even then I can't guarantee that we won't be stuck in it. Shall we leave now?"

Someone clears his throat, making me lift my eyes.

Arsen.

Why is it always him?

His hair shines like gold in the sunlight, and there is a blush on his cheeks that wasn't there before. We stare at each other for a moment before he turns to face and address Charles.

"Charles, Catherine…Why don't you join my friend Amanda and me for drinks and dinner? I've made a reservation for 6:30 p.m. at Le Provencal in Greenwich."

Really? Just friends?

I take advantage of the fact that he's looking at Charles and not at me to steal a quick glance, admiring all of him again. It's not like I can shut his beauty out of my mind; he is gorgeous and there is no denying that. He'll always be a pleasure to look at, but what has changed is that he doesn't make me feel curiosity, temptation, or yearning anymore. Those feelings are gone.

Besides his wasteful beauty, I notice that there's a very girly pink butterfly tattooed on his skin, right where his heart is. I want to laugh because really the tattoo defies everything that Arsen stands for.

I shake my head and decide to step in because I most certainly don't want to spend my evening with him again. I can't wait to get back to Ben.

I smile at the thought of Ben.

Charles must notice it because he asks, "What is it? Ah, you've seen The Tattoo? Yes. It's quite comical, the story be—"

Oh, no. I don't want them to assume that I was checking Arsen out, which I was but not really.

"No, that's not it at all. Sorry. Your talk of dinner plans reminded me of something my husband said." I don't look at Arsen when I mention Ben. I stare down at my rings, which I made sure to put back on this time, when I say, "Would you mind very much taking a rain check, Arsen?" I lift my eyes to finally meet his and I'm taken aback by the look in his face.

He seems to be pissed.

Ignoring him, I address Charles, "Unless you would like to stay…" Charles seems to get the hint because he turns to Arsen. "Sorry, buddy. Seems that the beautiful lady already has dinner plans. How about—"

"No. Actually, never mind. I just remembered that there's something I have to do in the city. Would you mind very much if we rode back with you?" Arsen asks me. The way he's looking at me makes me think he's daring me to say no to him.

Whatever, two can play this game.

"Sure. I don't mind at all. But how about your friend?" Arsen crosses his arms on his chest, and an impish smile appears on his face.

"Oh, she won't mind. We're done here." He looks to Charles, "I've shown Amanda every room in the house. She loves it." Glancing in my direction, his teasing eyes land on my face again. "In fact, she begged me to come…back again."

"I'm sure she did. It looked like she was enjoying herself as she tested the sturdiness of your father's desk."

Take that, asshat.

But instead of pissing Arsen off, he bursts out laughing. "It was sturdy alright. Perfect for—"

"There you are! I've been…oh, hi."

Amanda is wearing Arsen's missing shirt and nothing else. Not even blushing or trying to button the shirt closed, she makes her way to him. As she stands on her tiptoes to kiss him, the shirt tugs up, showing her perfect, cellulite-free ass.

Seriously, that is not possible.

"I've been looking for you. You said you were going to get some water, so when you didn't come back, I decided to come and find you."

She pouts, her fingers lightly touching his chest. Arsen wraps one hand around her tiny waist and pulls her closer to him. Leaning down, he kisses her behind the ear while Charles and I watch. I don't know if Charles is as uncomfortable by the situation as I am, but I try to avoid watching him kiss her. Instead, my eyes land on his free hand as it sneaks up her thigh and disappears under the white shirt.

I smile to the girl and don't bother to look at Arsen as I greet her. "Hi. Nice meeting you, Amanda. My name is Cathy, and this is Charles. He's decorating the house for Arsen's mother. Anyway, it seems that we have detained him long enough. I'm sure he is ready to get back t—"

"Amanda, get yourself ready. We're leaving with them in a few," Arsen says, blatantly interrupting me.

The girl's confusion is written all over her face. "But…I thought we were meeting Alec and Sali for dinner and drinks?"

He lets go of her waist and speaks dismissively to her, "Forget that. Change of plans. Don't fuss, Amanda. I hate that shit. Now, go get ready."

Amanda leaves the kitchen, hopping away on her perfect legs. Soon it's just Charles, Arsen and myself again. Though, I have to admit that I forgot all about Charles for a moment there.

My companion seems to sense a weird kind of tension in the room. "My boy, that is no way to treat such a lovely lady. Are you sure you want to ride back with us? It seemed like you were having an awfully good time with her. I would hate to end your tour." Charles voice is dripping with sarcasm.

"Yeah. I'm done here," Arsen snaps back, then turns to look at me, a scowl on his face. "If I say that I want to ride with you, I mean it. I don't appreciate it when people butt into my damn business."

Oh. Seriously, I'm, what, five or six years older than this guy, yet he is talking to me like that? No way.

"Listen, kid…you can do whatever you want, but remember it's my car."

Arsen and I stare at each other for a moment. The energy this time around is so different from the restaurant, a silent challenge to see who will back down first.

It sure as shit won't be me.

Arsen must know I won't be intimidated because he backs off, the scowl gone off his face, replaced by his boyish grin. He turns to look at Charles. "She's a feisty one, dear uncle, but I guess I deserved that."

"Yes, my boy. I think you did. Now, go get ready. I'm not looking forward to sitting in traffic," he replies, laughing.

"Yes, sir." Turning to look at me before he leaves, Arsen says, "Sorry about that, Dimples. I didn't mean to upset you." I know he's apologizing for his rudeness, but somehow I also know that he is apologizing for everything.

I smile. "Whatever."

When we get to the city, I drop Charles first, then make my way to Prince Street where Arsen's loft is. After Charles got out, Arsen made his way to the front, sitting next to me as I drive through the crowded streets of Manhattan. Arsen and I don't speak to each other. He just stares straight ahead as I drive.

I'm relieved that I don't have to carry any sort of conversation with him.

And if I didn't know any better, I'd think Arsen is avoiding making eye contact with me, which is crazy talk. This is the same man who basically invited me to cheat on my husband with him.

Amanda hasn't stopped talking, though. Looking at the rearview mirror, I see her twirling her black hair around her index finger, the bright yellow color of her nail polish peeking through the strands of hair. She's talking about an audition she had for a Broadway show. Apparently Miss Spread Eagle is some sort of singer and dancer.

So not my thing.

For one, I cannot act, and if you have ever heard me sing, you would know that I belong in the back alley with a bunch of stray cats screeching at the top of my lungs.

As Amanda keeps going on and on, I can't help but wonder if she knows what silence means. You know? Just you and your thoughts. She should give it a try sometime. She may like it.

When I park in front of his building, Arsen turns to look at Amanda in the back seat, telling her to go ahead without him, and that he'll meet her in a few. After a quick, nice meeting you, I hope to see you again…not, a chirpy Amanda, with her very long legs and perfect cellulite-free ass, gets out of the car, making her way to the entrance.

As she walks into the building, I notice the way male heads turn in her direction, following the every move of her Sports Illustrated body. I can only imagine the amount of saliva being wiped off chins after all the drooling that just happened.

And this is the kind of girl Arsen is used to dating.

A disinterested Arsen watches her retreating figure until she disappears inside the revolving glass doors of his building. Once she's out of sight, he turns his aqua eyes over my way, connecting with mine for the first time since we left Westchester. An indescribable awareness passes between us by that one glance, thickening the air in the car with an almost tangible tension.

The stampeding images of his naked body having sex run through my mind like a herd of animals with no clear direction or purpose, just trying to cause havoc within me. Clearing my throat to try and break the tension filling the car and hide how uncomfortable being alone with him suddenly makes me, I turn to look out the window.

"Hey, listen." He rubs his hands on his face. "Sorry about the restaurant."

Surprised at his apology, I stare at my hands and begin to twist my fingers. "Oh, okay. There is no need to apologize."

"Are you kidding me? I was a fucking asshole to you." He takes a deep breath. "I was drunk and wasn't thinking. All I knew was that I wanted you. A lot. And you weren't interested. And that, Catherine, never happens. So, you pissed me off by ignoring me because I'm not used to that shit. You piqued my interest and then when you didn't return it, I wanted it more, but I was mean to you. And I'm not mean. Not unless that's the way you like it, baby," he says, smiling at me.

"No. I don't like it at all. And please don't call me baby. I mean, do you even know what boundaries are?" I say, shaking my head.

"I'm only teasing you. And, no. I hate any kind of shit that tells what I can and can't do. But, honestly. I'm sorry. It won't ever happen again. I know when no means no." Staring at me, he extends his hand out. "Friends?"

"Why?" I ask, crossing my arms. I'm not buying his act just yet.

Arsen smiles ruefully. "You're not going to let me live the restaurant incident down, are you?"

I purse my lips, trying not to smile because he's right.

Chuckling, he lowers his hand and stares out the windshield. "I like you. I like that you don't put up with my shit. Not many women are able to do that. And you'll be seeing a lot of me at the office. Apparently, my father wants to teach me work ethics. If I don't get my shit together, he has threatened to take my trust fund away. So I'm gonna be suckin' it up to the old man for a while. We'll be sort of co-workers, and for once I'd like to know someone who doesn't let me walk all over her, and who won't suck my dick if I tell her to…"

He grins when he sees the disbelief on my face. The ego!

"I am sure other interns and workers wouldn't mind getting to know you."

"Nah. They always want to fuck because they're attracted to me, or because they want the bragging rights. Don't get me wrong, I fucking love it, but for once I'd like to be just Arsen. I don't feel like being harassed for my cock or my money or last name while I'm trying to get in father's good graces. Kinda would backfire if daddy dear walked in on me fucking his executive assistant. However, I know you can't stand me and hate my guts. Plus, you're married. I promise I'll be on my best behavior. I'll be a good boy."

"How do I know you won't try to pull another one of your theatrics?"

"I told you…I'm sorry. It won't happen again. This…" he touches himself, "only goes where he's welcomed, and it's obvious that we aren't welcomed by you. I have moved on. Trust me."

"Okay." I want to smack him, really, but he is kind of funny when he's not hitting on me. I can't fault him for being honest. I like straight-shooters.

I extend my hand, saying, "Okay. Peace offering accepted."

Arsen accepts my handshake as we smile at each other. I feel a little like I'm making a pact with the devil.

I still don't fully trust him.

9

past

Ben: It cannot be healthy, the way I constantly dream of you.

18 dates.
63 phone calls.
1000+ texts.
4 weeks' worth of Ben.
The best four weeks of my life.

Falling in love with the wrong person is easy. Falling in love with the right person is easier. But falling in love with your soul mate is easiest.

It's meant to be.

I don't think falling is the right word when referring to my feelings for Ben, though. How about soaring? Every time I'm with him I feel like I can fly. I feel weightless.

I feel free.

It's not like I haven't felt the butterflies in my stomach before; the loss of sleep because you can't stop thinking about someone, the crazy high of making out; I've felt them all. But with Ben, butterflies don't just flutter inside me. They ricochet like flying bullets. Falling asleep under a pink and purple sky after a night spent with him is my new normal.

When he whispers between kisses how beautiful I am, how much he loves the way I smell, and how much he wants me, I feel high. And when I feel the scratch of his rough hands touch my body intimately, gently, roughly, but always with need, I am delirious.

Sitting on the steps of my front porch, I watch the falling rain wetting the asphalt. My skin pebbles with goosebumps when the cool autumn air sneaks in between my clothes, touching my body. The chilly air helps to cool down my hot cheeks, a physical reaction that appears every time I think about Ben and what this weekend could mean in our relationship.

Slutty Cathy screams in the back of my mind: It better mean some freaking sex, like, hello! Penis, meet my vagina.

"What's so funny?" my dad asks, scratching his head when I laugh out loud. He's sitting next to me while I wait for Ben to arrive.

I shouldn't be laughing when my worried father is so close to changing his mind about this weekend. Honestly, I was even surprised that my dad allowed it since this will be the first time in my entire life that I'm traveling with a sort of boyfriend, sort of seeing, guy. A guy he knows I'll probably be having sex with if I haven't already, on said vacation.

I turn to look at my dad, trying to control my laughter as he watches me with those wise green eyes of his. They are so knowing; they seem to hold the key to the secrets of life.

"Nothing, Daddy. Just something funny that happened during class."

"I don't believe you one bit, Missy, but I'm letting it go."

Sitting so close to him, his familiar scent wafting through my nose, I can see the years' worth of laugh lines around his eyes and the corners of his mouth. It reminds me how hard he's worked to make my life a happy one.

"Daddy, it's nothing," I say as I stare at him. "Do you remember when I was eight years old and I cried for an entire week because my best friend, Lisa, was going to Disney and I couldn't go with her?"

He chuckles. "Of course, how could I not? I tried to reason with you that we couldn't afford a Disney vacation, but how much logic can you instill in an eight year old?"

I can't help giggling. "I was quite stubborn…"

"No, you were my angel, and it was my fault." He takes my hand in his. "I couldn't take off work and be able to pay for it. But I remember seeing how heartbroken you were.'

"So, you bought me a princess dress instead and pretended to be a dragon," I state as I watch the man who I love the most in my life. My daddy.

His eyes crinkle as he smiles, remembering that time. "Yes, I took you to the nearest toy store and bought you a princess dress, then took you to Juniper Park where I chased you across the park."

"Hey! It was an enchanted garden!" I exclaim.

"Those were the days. Now my little girl is making someone else chase after her."

"Daddy!"

We look at each other and laugh.

My dad is perfect and means the world to me. Maybe one day I'll get lucky and meet a man like him and marry him.

My mind automatically goes to a pair of brown eyes, but I shut the image out. Really, Cathy?

Watching as the concern written on his face grows, I feel a pang of guilt for not telling him what has been going on between Ben and I, but seriously? How could I? Where would I even begin? Should I tell him that I'm falling so hard for Ben that just the thought of hearing his voice makes my body go hot and cold, sending shivers down my spine? That we can talk on the phone for hours about everything and nothing at all, and most importantly that he makes me giggle like a thirteen year old?

Should I tell him that I've waited this long to have sex with Ben because I'm not completely sure he's over his ex? And that if he were to get back together with her, ending whatever we have going on right now, it would cause some serious damage within me. The kind that makes it hard to breathe.

Should I also tell him that well, even though we "technically" haven't had sex, we've done pretty much everything you can do with two sets of very willing hands and mouths? And that each time we've been together, we push the physical boundaries further and further?

As understanding as I think my father is, if he knew exactly what was going on in my mind, I think he'd completely lose it. However, he knows I'm not a virgin anymore. He almost killed Jack, and his father when he found the condom wrapper under my bed.

Talk about awkward.

I reach for my dad and one arm hug him. Pushing my body closer to his, I nuzzle the edge of his sweater clad shoulder, breathing in the smell of rain, musty cotton and his ever familiar cologne. "The boy who happens to be chasing after me is a good guy." I try to reassure him. But I don't think he believes me by the look on his face. He knows I'm not telling him the whole story.

Fuck-Fuckity-fuck.

I so don't want to be having this conversation with my dad right before I leave.

He clears his throat, "Catherine, I know it's a bit late to be having this conversation."

And there you have it. Looks like we are having the discussion after all.

"I raised you well, and I know that you respect yourself and your body, but are you sure you're ready to be traveling with some boy who you've been seeing for less than a month?" My dad wraps his left arm around my shoulder, giving me a reassuring squeeze. Like that's going to help.

I recline my head on his shoulder. "Well. I think I'm ready, Daddy. Please don't ask for details. It's freaking me out having this conversation with you, but if you must know. I don't think you have to worry. We know what we are doing."

Staring at each other, my dad raises an eyebrow as if calling my bullshit. "Anyway, it won't be just the two of us. As you already know because I'm pretty sure we've gone over this before plenty of times, a bunch of his friends will be there. It's a house party, Dad."

"This is why I hate being a single father. I'm not sure what to do or say and I feel as if I'm throwing my little girl to the wolves," my dad mutters.

"Dad! I know you're far from being okay with this, but Ben is so nice and he treats me like a princess. Trust me."

It looks like he wants to say something else but Ben decides to finally show up. Thank goodness.

As I make a move to stand up, my dad stops me. "Just promise me that you'll be careful, Cathy. I don't want to see you hurt again," my father says, gently reminding me of the mess Matt made a year ago.

"Yes, Daddy, but somehow I have a feeling that Ben would never hurt me like that."

And as the words leave my mouth, I know they are true.

After an awkward and uncomfortable goodbye, we make our way to Ben's black Land Rover. When Ben opens the passenger door for me, he leans down and cups my cheeks in both of his large hands, lowering his face to plant a gentle peck on my lips. Even though the kiss is tender and sweet, it makes the tips of my toes curl inside my leather boots. I immediately want to deepen the kiss, but Ben pulls away before I get a chance to push my body closer to his.

"Damn, girl. Do you want your dad to shoot me? For a moment there, I thought he was going to go back inside the house to fetch his gun." Smiling, he looks like he wants to kiss me again, but he doesn't. "I seriously hope he doesn't own one."

Once I'm inside the car, I turn around to look at the front porch one last time. How I knew that my dad would still be standing there watching me getting ready to leave isn't really a mystery. He's always there for me. I wave goodbye with one hand and blow him a kiss with the other. He pretends to catch it, then tucks it inside his jeans pocket. It seems cheesy now, but when I was a little girl it rocked my world, so we never stopped doing it.

As Ben pulls away from the curb, he reaches for my hand, intertwining our fingers together. My starved body feeds itself on his warmth. "Hi, babe. I missed you."

I turn to look at him, feeling a smile tug at the corner of my lips. "Me too. Twenty-four hours is suuuch a long time. I don't know how I made it through," I joke, trying to play it cool. Teasing Ben is lots of fun because most of the time, he teases back…naughtily.

Ben's sexy little smirk grows into a full smile as he brings our connecting hands to his lips, kissing my hand. All of a sudden, the car feels very hot. Turning away from him, I fan myself with my free hand. I hate that Ben does this to me.

No, that's a lie.

I love it.

Ben drives for maybe five blocks when he pulls to the curb of a random house in my neighborhood. Not exactly sure why he's stopping when we just left my house. I'm about to ask what's wrong, but I never get a word out because his lips are suddenly on mine, devouring me like he's a starved man and I'm the first piece of food he's had in weeks. Tangling his hands in my hair, he pulls me closer to him, deepening the kiss. The moment our tongues touch, I hear him groan, but he continues to torture me with his mouth. When we end the kiss, I feel light-headed, but so darn horny.

Who needs oxygen? Oxygen is so overrated.

With his fingers still tangled in my hair, I cup his face in my hands, and we gaze at each other without saying anything at all. I see a blush covering the crests of his cheeks as his lips, swollen from my kisses, smile at me. I smile back.

"Well, that was nice," I say, trying to nip at his finger closest to my mouth.

"You better believe it. Now stop being so damn cute or we're never going to make it in time to Newport." Letting go of my hair, he brings the thumb of his free had to rub gently over my puffy lip. The rough texture of his finger over my mouth reminds me of where those fingers have been before, and it seems that Ben remembers too because he groans again and lets me go completely. "Damn, girl. You're driving me fucking crazy."

While Slutty Cathy is doing a 'Hell, Yeah!' dance inside my head, I try to hide the huge smirk starting to break through the surface of my face. "You're not the only one hot and bothered here, you know? What would you like me to do?"

Ben shakes his head while his gaze remains on me; his soft maple brown eyes look almost black with intense desire

Oh, boy.

"Hmm…well, smartypants, since I don't want us to get into a car accident, how about you stay in your seat and ignore me."

"Seriously?" I laugh, "What are you twelve?"

Smirking, he looks down at his pants then looks back up to me, wiggling his eyebrows. "Around you? Yes."

My eyes travel to his pants and…

Hello!

"Really, Ben?" I shake my head, but I can't stop the laugh that is fighting so hard to escape again.

With a beautiful smile on his face, Ben looks down at himself, then back at me. "Only for you, Cathy. I mean it." As the words leave his mouth, I know what he is trying to tell me. He is trying to reassure me that he wants me, only me. And at this moment, I believe him.

I truly believe him.

The trip to Newport, Rhode Island is a blur, but a few things stick in my mind: the comfortable silence, the stolen glances, Ben accidentally copping a feel here and there, and the warmth of his hand in mine.

When we arrive to Newport, I'm totally blown away. I knew Newport was where some "old money" people vacationed in their big houses, but you really have no idea what wealth of that magnitude is until you see one of these mansions up close. The one I'm currently staring at keeps getting bigger and bigger as we drive through the never ending gravel driveway.

The ocean front estate is gigantic. Holy shit! Did I just die and wake up in a scene from the Great Gatsby?

As Ben parks his car in front of the illuminated main entrance, I'm in a state of shock, awe, and to be honest, kind of freaking out. I knew Ben came from money and that most of his friends were wealthy as well, but I hadn't imagined we were talking about this kind of money. Rubbing my sweaty palms over my jeans, I observe the commotion that's taking place inside the house at the moment. Loud techno music is blaring through the open windows into the night, and I can see the outlines of some couples making out and dancing close together.

Overwhelmed with the realization of how far out of my comfort zone I am, I turn to look at Ben as my stomach begins to twist with the bad kind of nerves, "Umm…I…I…"

I know I shouldn't feel intimidated by a big house and the idea of spending a whole weekend with rich people. My dad raised me to know my own worth and to always be proud of what we have, who we are, but…

Shit, who am I kidding? Your ideas of self-worth kind of go flying out the window when you're standing in front of a mansion that accommodates a garage bigger than your own house.

Ben turns the car off, then reaches for my hand once more, giving it a supportive squeeze. "Cathy, it's going to be fine. Julian is the shit and his twin sister, Morgan, is pretty awesome as well. We're going to have a lot of fun this weekend." He leans over the console, plants a kiss on my forehead and nudges his nose against mine. "Trust me. You're here with me. No one will bother you."

I turn in his direction and hug him hard. I feel the strong muscles of his body wrapped within my arms, smell his masculine scent mixed with expensive cologne, and I make a decision about us.

Tonight will be the night.

I can't continue living my life in fear, worried that Ben will leave me one day. I can't. I must take a chance on him, trust my heart and let him take me to that place that only he can show me. After kissing his neck, I whisper, "Don't worry about me. I'll be okay. I was just shocked, but I'll get over it. Remember, I'm a tough Queens' girl. Just promise me one thing."

Ben leans back far enough to see my face. As I stare into a warm pool of deep brown, my hand caresses his cheek. Ben closes his eyes for a moment, but when he opens them, I see my answer gazing right back at me.

It will be fine.

"Just promise me that we'll have tonight to ourselves."

"Of course. We're staying in the same room."

"Um, yeah…I knew that. What I meant, uh…what I mean is that…well…I'm ready. You know, ready." Blushing, I hope that Ben gets my meaning because I don't think I could be any more direct without telling him to sleep with me.

Ben is quiet for what seems an eternity.

Oh my God. What if I read the signals all wrong? No.

He wants me. I know it.

He likes me. I know it.

But his silence is freaking me out. When I'm about to tell him to forget it, he finally speaks.

"No, Cathy. I can't do that."

"What? Come again?" That is so not what I was expecting. Where is Horny Ben when I want him?

Abruptly he lets go of me, shakes his head and looks away, speaking to the windshield. "No. Let's try this again. You know damn well that I want you. So damn much, but I didn't bring you here to get you to have sex with me. I'm better than that." Turning around, he immobilizes me with his stare. "You're better than that. Hell, I'm not that kind of an asshole, Cathy. You should know better."

Is he kidding me? "Ben, no. I want to…I'm ready." You would think that when you tell the guy you've been seeing that you're finally ready to have sex with him, he would say, "Hell yeah! Where's the bed?" Instead, I'm stuck with a righteous asshole.

"No, Cathy. Please, drop it."

I can feel shame beginning to burn my face, and the humiliation sinking deep within. Ben's eyes soften as he takes my hand in his. "Look, babe, let's talk about it tonight when we're alone. Not when we're parked outside Julian's house and—"

Confused and hurt by his rejection, I push his hand away. "I'm not dropping it. We've been seeing each other for a month now, and we've done pretty much everything but have sex."

Ben opens his mouth to say something, but I don't let him get a word out.

"I thought we waited this long for me to be ready. Well, I am now, so why the hell not? And I'm sorry, but I don't buy your excuse of," lifting my fingers in quotations marks, I throw his words back in his face, "I didn't bring you here to have sex with me."

I know I'm being illogical. It was me who asked him to take it slow just to make sure he was over his ex before sleeping together.

What if he's not over her?

But he wants me. He just said so.

A feeling of dread settles in my stomach. "Let me ask you something, Ben. How long did you wait to sleep with Ashley, huh? Did you tell her no when she offered herself to you? Because that's basically what I just did. Or are you making stupid excuses because you're not over her?"

I hear Ben groan as he puts his face in his hands. Waves of frustration radiate from his body, blasting me with their force. "What the fuck, Cathy? That's low, even for you. Why do you have to bring up the past?"

"I'm confused, that's why. I-I thought you liked me. That you wanted me and now, you don't…is it because of her?"

Silence.

Nothing.

Ben doesn't say anything.

He just looks at me.

His silence hurts.

His silence is majorly pissing me off.

"Well, I wanted to know, didn't I? I guess I have my answer."

Frustration is written in the frowning lines of Ben's face, his set jaw and the way he's tugging his hair. When he's about to speak, someone opens my door and interrupts our first fight.

And maybe our last.

Cool air hits me in the face, filling the warm interior of the car with a cold breeze. Ben and I turn to look at the person who rudely interrupted us mid argument. My eyes meet a pair of blue eyes on the face of a gorgeous guy. He has shaggy brown hair and some freckles on the crest of his nose, full lips, and a cleft on his chin.

He smiles as he seems to take in the scene. "Yo, Ben. I thought you were never going to get here, Man." He turns to look at me, a bigger smile on his lips now. "You must be Cathy. Nice meeting you. We've been dying to meet the girl that has Big Ben acting like a chick. Morgan is going to love you."

"Um, hi. And you are?"

"Sorry. Pretty girls make me act stupid. I'm Julian," he smirks arrogantly.

"Hi. Nice meeting you, Julian." I don't blush, but I can feel a reluctant smile tug at the corners my lips as I watch his contagious smile. Julian is a flirt, and he knows it works for him. I glance back at Ben and see him studying us both.

He doesn't look happy.

At all.

Good. I'm glad. Maybe Julian won't have a problem sleeping with me.

Ben's frown has been replaced by a mean scowl. "Back off, dude. You need those pretty hands of yours to play that pansy shit you call a sport."

Julian stares at us both as a playful grin replaces his flirtatious smile. "I play golf. And don't listen to him. I can take his juice-head body any day, any time."

If I weren't so upset with Ben, I would find this seriously funny. But I'm angry and hurt, so I decide to piss him off a little bit more. Remembering the way Lisa flirts with guys, I try to imitate her. Please, God, don't let me look like an ass. After slowly licking my lips and tilting my chin at just the right angle, I give Julian my best smile. "I'm sure you can. You have a beautiful home, by the way. I'd love a personal tour if you're available."

Julian's eyes dart from Ben to me, pausing on my face as understanding dawns. An approving look appears on his face as his smile grows wider. "I'd love to, and I happen to be available right now. Ben, you've seen the house before, I'm sure you don't need to come along, right? Anyway, it's fucking cold out here. Let's head inside before we freeze."

He reaches out for my hand and wraps his long fingers around mine. "Here, let me help you," Turning to look at Ben, Julian adds, "Dude, you know the way. Arthur will take care of the luggage, so head to the bar. Morgan is there with the usual crowd. You may want to skip the main living room, though, it's a fuckfest."

I don't dare to look at Ben when I get out of the car with Julian's help as we make our way to the entrance. I am halfway up the stairs when I realize how shitty I am being to Ben. Whatever his reasons are, he was trying to do the right thing by me. I stop dead in my tracks and face Julian with an apologetic smile.

"Could you give me a minute? I forgot to tell Ben something."

Spinning around after Julian nods his approval, I make my way back to the car. Ben is unloading the luggage, even though Julian said that someone was going to take care of them.

Gosh, he really is perfect.

When I reach him, he lifts his eyes and what I see in their depths scares me. The laugh is gone. He looks very angry. And hurt.

"Um, sorry about that. I didn't mean to run off with your friend like that. And I'm sorry for bringing up Ashley. It wasn't nice of me." I tuck my hair behind my ear with a sweaty hand. My skin feels clammy with nerves.

Ben closes his eyes and takes a deep breath. After a moment, he opens them again and the look he gives me lets me know in how much trouble I am.

"Whatever, Cathy. Go ahead. Julian is a shit load of fun. Hope you guys enjoy each other," he spits out.

He walks past me, picks up our suitcases in his hands and makes his way to the house, passing Julian without even acknowledging him.

What have I done?

My eyes follow Ben until he disappears inside the house. With a heavy heart, I turn to look at Julian who's watching me carefully. The anger I felt before has been replaced by guilt. Why did I have to let my craziness get the best of me?

When I reach the spot where I left Julian, I'm aware that I should say something to break the tension filling the air, but I'm at a loss for words. As I search my mind for an icebreaker, I hear Julian ask, "Why is Ben so pissed? Did I interrupt a fight or something?" Putting his hands in the back pockets of his jeans, he waits for my answer.

Tucking a stray piece of hair behind my ear, I decide to be somewhat honest with him. I don't know the guy, but if he's Ben's best friend, he must be trustworthy. Besides, I like him.

"Well…yes. It started as nothing, but then he said some stuff that really bothered me." Nerves make me rock on my heels. "And, uh, I might've let my bitchiness get the best of me which sucks because I took an already shitty situation and made it worse. And my running off with you didn't help at all. I mean, we've just met, so yes, I can see why Ben is so pissed off at me. And I'm sorry about before…you know, my lame attempt at flirting. I was trying to get to Ben."

"Don't give it a second thought. I could tell something was up. And, you don't suck at flirting. You were very cute." He grins as he stares at my mouth for a second too long. "As for Ben, I think he was pretty close to beating the shit out of me, but I don't give a fuck about that." He tilts his head and smirks naughtily, "In prep school Ben and I always solved everything with a good fistfight. *Always.*" He smirks, "However, that jealousy is new. Ben doesn't do jealousy, it's always the other way around. Not even when he was with Ashley."

When the name of Ben's ex crosses his mouth, an expression of disgust crosses his face, almost as if he'd swallowed a bitter pill, but it's quickly replaced with a grin. "And I gotta say, Cathy, that I like it. It means that he's getting over that bitch."

Pondering his words for a moment, and letting them sink in, I smile as I look down at the steps. "Do you really think so?"

I look up and meet his sincere eyes as he nods at me "Hell, yes. That bitch did a number on him. And trust me, the Ben I just saw didn't look depressed like the last time we hung out. This time he looked fucking mad because I was hitting on his girl."

"I hope you're right. I really do. You see…"

Then I remember the reason for our fight and his silence when I confronted him about Ashley, and I'm not sure how correct Julian is anymore.

"I don't see, so why don't you tell me? I like you. I can tell we're going to be good friends, so tell me. Maybe I could help?"

"Fine, but remember you asked. Just don't yawn if I bore you."

"You would never bore me. Now, go on. But, wait. I have an idea. I can tell it's going to be one of those long Morgan kind of stories where it's always the guy's fault and never the girl's."

I whack him on the shoulder, making him raise his hands out of his pockets in a surrendering gesture. "Hey! I was just being honest! But seriously, sometimes if you girls just spoke to us instead of acting all cryptic and shit, we would know what the fuck is going on. Anyway, I'm freezing my ass off, and you must be too. Why don't we go to my mom's greenhouse? We can talk there and avoid the orgy currently taking place inside my parent's home."

"B-but what about Ben? What if he gets the wrong idea when we don't come find him right away?"

"I don't give a fuck. He was rude to you just now, let him sweat it."

"Um, okay. But, wait. Before we go, I need to…um, make sure of one thing."

"Yes?"

"Well, since I just met you, I hope that "going to your mother's greenhouse" isn't code for hooking up because I'm not interested. I'm with Ben. And, well…yeah. I'm with Ben." Blushing, I can't believe what I said. I just told a very dreamy guy to not get any funny ideas with me. Me!

As if, Cathy. As If.

"Shit, Cathy. Really? One, I would never take you to my mother's greenhouse to hook up. I'd take you to my room. I have the best fucking bed in this place. Two, I don't poach, ever. Not even when the girl is as pretty as you are. Three, Ben is my best friend. And four, and I mean this, I want to help. I can already tell that Ben likes you, and Ben liking someone is a very good thing."

"Oh my God, I'm sorry. I just wanted to make sure. I didn't want to give you the wrong idea."

"Nah. I like that. You're cool. Now let's go. I am seriously freezing my ass off."

"Okay."

The greenhouse is beautiful. Glass and plants and trees are everywhere surrounding us. There are roses and orchids and so many other foreign plants whose names I don't know but have seen in bouquets on the covers of bridal magazines. As we walk deeper into the room, breathing the aromatic air, I can almost imagine myself in the middle of a jungle with all its exotic and abundant flowers and greenery towering over me. The moon, the only source of light inside the glass structure, allows me to see and follow Julian's tall form without tripping over flowerpots and stands.

Julian sits down on a bench next to what looks to be a funky tree with its spiky leaves, and pats the spot next to him. When I join him, Julian leans back, turning his body so that I can see his face clearly, an easy smile appearing on his lips. "So, here we are. Now you can tell me what's going on. Let's see if I can work my magic, unless you would like to have a sexcapade in here after all?"

"Ha Ha Ha. Very funny. And have my ass poked by one of those weird spiky plants? No, thank you."

"I had to try, ya know?" Julian says, laughter in his eyes.

I smile and look down at my lap, watching my hands twist. "Okay. So basically, I'm not sure what's going on between Ben and me. I mean, I know what's going on. I'm not stupid. It's just that, well, I'm not sure whether we're serious or just having fun. We haven't discussed labels or anything. It's not like I can say, hey Ben, do you want to be my boyfriend? I'm not that big of a loser, yet. I don't know if we're in a relationship or just dating. I don't even know if he wants to be exclusive. I know I do."

I lift my gaze and stare at the shadows of the plants playing on the wall. "The thing is I-I think I'm falling for him, Julian. Like in love. And we haven't even had sex."

"Wait, what? You guys haven't fucked? No fucking way. Man…his pissy mood is making a lot more sense. Shit." Julian's shocked expression reminds me of an old school cartoon where the eyes pop out of its eye sockets.

Nodding as I laugh at Julian, I continue, "Before you feel bad for Ben, don't. I'm not going into details, but trust me, he's doing just fine. But yes. We haven't gone all the way. I told him I wanted to wait to make sure he's over his ex. And he's been super sweet and understanding. On my way here today, I decided that I wasn't going to worry about her anymore, so I told him…okay, I kind of implied that tonight was going to be the night, and he freaked out. He went all righteous asshole on me, saying he hadn't brought me here for sex. So, yes, that's when I let my anger get the best of me and brought Ashley up and—"

I hear Julian groan and curse under his breath, causing me to look at him for the first time since I started talking. "What did he say?"

"Well, that's when things took a turn for the worse because he didn't answer me at all. I asked him how long he waited to have sex with her, and then I asked him if he was over her, and he didn't say anything. Just remained silent. And that's when you decided to introduce yourself. So now I really have no clue what's going on between us. If there's even an us to worry about."

Julian sits forward, resting his elbows on his knees. "So, let me get this straight. You guys haven't fucked. You're not sure what you guys are, and you're afraid that he hasn't gotten over that bitch. And now he's pissed off because he thinks you're thinking he brought you here to get him some ass. And you mentioned the ex, which probably pissed him off the most. Because now he thinks you don't trust him enough and let's face it, it was totally uncalled for."

"Yes, that's everything in a nutshell." Guilt covers my whole body in a tent of shame.

"What a pussy."

"Hey!"

"Sorry, but he is being a baby. He needs a lesson, and I think after I'm done tonight, you will definitely know what's going on between the two of you."

"What about Ashley?"

"I'm telling you. He's over her. You should've seen the look he gave me when you asked me for a tour of the place. If looks could kill, I'd be a dead man."

"Are you sure? You're scaring me. What are you thinking?"

"Trust me, Cathy. I know him. Why don't we play a little game?"

"Really? Do you think that's a good idea?"

"Yep. You'll thank me tomorrow. If he lets you leave the room, that is. "

"Okay. Why don't you tell me what you're thinking about?"

10

present

"Wait! Hold the door!"

Running across the marble foyer as fast as I can, I reach the elevator just in time for the last person to hold the doors open for me. I'm breathing heavily, but I manage to thank her and make my way towards the back. When I'm standing against the wall, I begin to fan myself with my hands, trying to cool down. I close my eyes and pray that we don't have to stop on each floor, wasting time. Today would be the worst occasion to be running late since it's Arsen's first day at work under my supervision.

It's been three days since I saw him last.

When I feel hot air hit the back of my neck, a prickle of awareness runs down my body settling in the pit of my stomach. I immediately open my eyes to see Arsen standing next to me. He's watching me with a playful smirk on his lips, and his distinctive blue eyes shine brightly. I can see the light blue colors mixed with green sparks in them.

Um, what is he doing?

"Morning, gorgeous. Ready to teach me how to be a man? You know, break me in?" Sarcasm is dripping off his voice, yet I sense the laughter behind it.

A little flustered and a lot pissed off by his words, I just nod and move away to put some space between us, which isn't possible given that we're crammed in this small elevator. Arsen must know that his greeting rubbed me the wrong way. Maybe it was his purpose all along because he closes the space I just created by standing close to me again.

Crossing my arms in front of my chest in a defensive stance, I'm about to move to the front of the line when I feel his warm hand wrap around my elbow, pulling me back to stand next to him. Heat shoots up my arm, scalding me like boiling water. Stunned for a moment that he would touch me without a care to physical boundaries, I lift my gaze to stare at him.

There's a twinkle in his eyes as he lowers his smiling mouth to whisper in my ear, "Chill, Dimples. I'm just teasing you…"

I want to say something, but nothing comes out. His mouth is so close to my ear that I can feel the fullness of his lower lip graze my earlobe. Annoyed at the reaction of my body, I turn to look at him as I wrench my arm free of his hold. "Keep your hands to yourself, kiddo. Now back off," I hiss back.

He throws his head back as he laughs, so I'm able to observe the thickness of his neck and the way his broad shoulders flex as they shake with laughter. I scowl at him. I want to grab my bag and hit him with it in the head. Maybe he'll stop laughing then. Maybe he'll get a concussion. Maybe that'll erase the stupid smirk off his face. I'm giving the idea some serious thought when the doors open, letting people off. I look up at the number and realize we still have a long way to go. I snake through some people until there are about three or four bodies in between us because I *don't* want to be standing next to him anymore. Take that, pretty boy. Smiling at my success in getting rid of him, I consider possible methods of how to put him in his place once we get to the office. I'm thinking about burying him alive in endless paperwork, assigning him to the most clueless intern we have amongst other painful possibilities, when I feel hot air breathing down my neck again.

"Why, hello there. Fancy meeting you here again," he murmurs in my ear, his voice playful.

You've got to be kidding me!

I close my eyes in frustration, trying to summon all my power to put him in his place once and for all. He said *no* flirting! When I open them, I slowly turn around to face him. The angry words get stuck in my throat, never leaving. Standing behind me in all his blond glory is an innocent looking Arsen with a shit eating grin on his beautiful face and a challenge in his eyes. He wants me to play his silly game with him.

I want to end it, to be the adult and remind him of the pact we made and how he was going to back off and behave. But something inside me tells me this is an Arsen trying to play nice. This is an Arsen trying to be friendly and nothing more. With one hand in his pocket, he props his shoulder on the wall, reclining his body lazily against it.

"What's the matter, Catherine? Cat got your tongue?" He lifts his free hand to run through his hair; it looks so soft. "You know I'm just fucking around, right? I never go back on my word. And like I said the last time I saw you, I can get pussy wherever and whenever I want."

I feel my face burning. Doesn't he realize we're not alone?

"You're stuck with me for however long my father chooses to teach me a lesson, and I like you, so let's try to get along. I think we could be friends if you can forget and move on. Like I said in the car, it's never going to happen again. Trust me,

Dimples. I know when no means no." He moves away from the wall so he can stand in front of me, towering over me. I feel at a disadvantage in this position.

"Stop calling me Dimples. And if you truly mean it, stop calling me gorgeous and invading my personal space. I don't appreciate it," I say as I look up into his amused eyes.

"You have dimples, Dimples. Pretty fucking perfect ones, if I may say so myself. And I like getting in your face. You look very pretty when you're angry," he says softly. "You blush, and it kind of makes me want to do it more."

Okay.

As I process his words, I watch him closely. He's looking at me with this expectant expression on his face, like a kid asking for an extra piece of cake when he knows he shouldn't.

About to answer him, two more passengers get off the elevator muttering to each other, "If Blondie doesn't give up the goods, that piece of fuckable ass better stick around because—"

"Shh, they might hear you. That's Arsen Radcliff! I read somewhere he's never had a girlfriend; he only screws arou—" The doors close before we get to hear the rest of the sentence. I glance at Arsen noticing that he looks pissed. The smile has been replaced by a scowl. Now he looks like the kid who didn't get the cake.

"Um, Arsen…"

"Don't say anything until we get off."

"Okay." Where did funny and teasing Arsen go?

When we get off, I see that as late as I thought I was going to be, we're the first people to arrive. I turn to look at Arsen as I feel his large hand settle in the small of my back, propelling me forward.

"Come with me." There's an authoritative bite in his voice. For a moment, I'm taken aback because he sounds like Ben. Older.

He takes me to the coffee room, not letting go of me until we are inside the room and the door is closed behind us. Running both his hands through his hair, he exhales a frustrated breath.

"Sorry about that. I didn't mean for those women to think I was hitting on you." He smiles ruefully at me. "For once, I was trying to play nice, but what do you know? They all thought I was trying to fuck you. If strangers assume that bull, I can see why you don't believe me. Hell, maybe I don't have it in me to be friends with anyone without fucking them first. Maybe you should tell Amy to find someone who isn't married to replace you, because apparently fucking is all I'm good at."

It's his vulnerability that he's trying to hide so hard behind his playboy façade that finally thaws me out completely towards him. Yes, I can understand why people see him and assume the worst. He is beautiful, perfect even. He is young and affluent, and he sleeps with famous women. I can see why women see him and think fuck-prize.

Most of it is his fault. I mean, I don't think anyone has held a knife to his throat and ordered him to walk out of a nightclub with three models surrounding him as they head back to his apartment. No one told him to screw his way around the socialite phone book. But his words let me catch a glimpse of what's underneath it all. The bad boy who does as society sees him; who gives them what they want.

Trying to lighten the mood, I tease him. "Seriously? You think I'm going to give up the chance at bossing you around? No way. After everything you've put me through, I think I deserve to make you suffer."

His eyes brighten. "You're not pissed off at me anymore? Not even after what those women said?" Disbelief is written on his sweet face.

"Well, I meant what I said before. But I think you tease and flirt with women who you feel comfortable with, who you don't want to sleep with. When w-we met the first time…" Am I really going to go there? I think so. I need to explain the difference in the Arsen from that night and the Arsen standing in front of me.

"You didn't tease me. You didn't flirt with me. You, uh, you just came on to me aggressively, and you didn't apologize. I'm not sure how to explain it, but something has changed. I believe you when you say you want to be friends, so as long as you keep your hands to yourself and don't invade my personal space, we'll be okay."

He shakes his head as his powerful smile sparks the whole room. "Dimples, you are fucking awesome. I mean it. And you're right. I don't usually want to be friends with the girls I fuck. I just fuck them and—"

"Leave them," I finish for him. I should be offended with the way he treats women, but the way the crests of his cheeks are blushing bashfully at the moment make me want to give him a hug instead.

We smile at each other.

Later, when I come back from lunch, I find a box of cupcakes from Magnolia Bakery sitting on my desk. Smiling, because Ben never ceases to surprise me, I open the card lying on top of the box and read the message, expecting to find the handwriting that I know by heart. I find an unknown instead.

A hot redhead told me you love cupcakes.
A.W.R**

"Hey."

Standing in the diner close to work, I turn around when I feel a light tap on my shoulder, coming face to face with a smiling Arsen.

"Hi," I say, returning his very contagious smile.

"What's up, Dimples?" Arsen asks, putting his hands in the back pockets of his pants.

"Uh, I'm here to grab some lunch."

"Cool."

He watches me expectantly. I immediately get the feeling that he wants me to invite him to have lunch with me. Would it be odd if I did? No, I don't think so. We work together after all.

"Would you like to join me?"

Arsen grins. "Only because you asked, Dimples."

"Seriously? What am I supposed to do? Let you eat by yourself?" I ask, incredulity resonating in my voice.

"Nope. I know you're a softie at heart who wouldn't let me eat alone. Now stop whining and let's get a table. I'm fucking starving."

We laugh and make our way to the first empty table we see. I notice the way women stare lustily at him as we walk past their seats, and I can't say that I blame them. The guy is truly gorgeous.

As I watch Arsen, I reminisce about the past month since the elevator incident. I guess you could say that a sort of friendship has started to develop between us, even though he flirts with me all the time. If he was any other man I would be concerned, but the guy seems to do it with anything that has a skirt and a pair of stilettos, so I know not to take him seriously and let myself enjoy some harmless flirting. Besides, I'm always laughing at his silly jokes.

He is truly a nice guy when he isn't trying to get in your pants.

Once we get to the table, Arsen pulls out a chair for me to be seated. After quickly scanning the restaurant, I sit down and watch him make his way to sit across from me.

"So, what's new?" He's watching me closely while he spins a fork on the table.

I grab a napkin and start making shapes with it. "Nothing, really. Ben and I spent the weekend at our summerhouse on Martha's Vineyard with some friends."

While nodding at me in acknowledgement of my answer, Arsen pulls his cell phone out and begins typing on the screen.

"Cool," he says as he continues texting.

"Um, how was yours?"

Looking up with a mischievous smile on his lips, "It was fucktastic. My friend Alec and his band played, so I got lots of groupie ass. Best shit ever. It's crazy what some of those girls will do to get backstage."

"Oh. That sounds like fun," I respond, blushing. I can't figure out why I'm always blushing whenever he talks about his personal life.

It's not like I care.

Arsen stares at his hands and replies softly, "It was fun while it lasted."

At a loss for words, I get the feeling that something is bothering him, and I don't like it. I don't like it at all. I'm about to take his hand in mine when his phone rings.

"Would you mind if I get this?" he asks politely.

"No, go ahead. I'll look at the menu in the meantime."

I open the menu and begin to go over the specials, trying to give him as much privacy as possible. I don't want him to think that I'm eavesdropping, but that proves to be near impossible when he's sitting no more than three feet away from me.

"What's up, baby? I'm at the diner with Dimp-Catherine," he corrects himself.

He waits for a moment, listening to the other person speak.

"Shit. I'm sorry. I completely forgot. Raincheck?"

"Okay…I promise. I'll make it up to you. Anyway, gorgeous, I gotta go. My food just got here. Ciao."

After he hangs up, Arsen throws his phone carelessly on the table and stares at me.

"Sorry about that, Dimples. I guess I was supposed to meet someone for lunch and completely forgot about it."

"You could still go meet her, you know? I won't mind…" And I truly won't. I feel guilty because he's here with me and not with his date.

Lightly rapping his fingers on the table, Arsen randomly changes the subject. "Do you like listening to Muse, Awolnation?"

Taken aback by the abrupt change in topics, I ask him to repeat his question.

"Oh, yes. I love them both. Awolnation's last album is amazing though. Some of my favorite songs are Wake Up, and Burn It Down."

"I think Madness by Muse is fucking genius. I've seen them live a couple times, and they are fucking brilliant," he says, smiling at me and running a hand through his hair.

"You always do that."

"What?"

"Run a hand through your hair. Is it a bad habit, or do you just like touching your hair?" I tease him.

He laughs. "So you've noticed? It's a bad habit of mine. I've tried stopping, but I think I just like getting my hair pulled too much. Especially in the bedroom, ya know?"

"Well, no. I didn't know, and I don't think I needed to know."

"You never know, Dimples…one day that information may come handy to you," he taunts.

"Ha, ha…as if. You forget, I'm happily married."

"Too happily married for some wild fucking with a hot stud like me? You know, I've been called God in the bedroom more than a few times," he jokes, his eyes gleaming devilishly.

I smile. "Modest much? By the way, I can't believe you just called yourself a hot stud. I'm pretty sure that negates how good looking you are."

Arsen grins, making his eyes crinkle. "What? Didn't you know? I'm too hot for my body."

"Are you ever serious or modest?" I say with laughter in my voice.

"Nah. Modesty and I don't get along, baby. I tell it how it is."

"I can't believe we're having this conversation."

Laughing, we both stare at each other, then slowly become silent. The silence makes me uncomfortable, so I look at the time on my watch. Arsen looks at his phone one more time. I feel like I need to break the silence.

"Should we order?"

Arsen nods and calls the waitress over. After she leaves with our orders, Arsen turns to look at me.

"Okay, I have an idea. While we wait for our food to arrive, let's play a game."

"Um, I'm not sure. The look on your face is making me uncomfortable."

"Come on! It'll be fun, and since you're stuck working with me, it will helps us get know each other better."

"Okay, fine. Tell me. I'm not promising anything, though."

With a smug smile on his face, like he just won the Nobel Prize, he says, "Why don't we reveal three things about ourselves to each other?"

Not seeing any harm in it, I agree to play his little game. Besides, I'm curious about him.

"Okay, you start. I need to see what kind of secrets you're willing to divulge first."

"I have a butterfly tattoo on my chest," Arsen says.

"I've seen it! I've meant to ask you about it for the longest time."

Arsen nods, smiling shyly. "When I was seventeen my friends and I went to Cancun for spring break. Needless to say, we ended up at a strip club where we got so fucked up. By the end of the night, I thought I was in love with a stripper named Butterfly, so as soon as the place closed down," he pauses, grinning, "she came with me to get this tattoo. And in my drunken state, I guess I wanted it tattooed over my heart." His eyes sparkle with mirth.

"Why don't you have it removed?" I ask.

"Nah. It's part of me. Besides, Butterfly showed me some very good times," he says, wiggling his eyebrows.

"Well, I'm glad. Okay. My turn." I blush because it's quite embarrassing. "I don't really know how to ride a bicycle."

"What? No way!" He seems truly surprised.

"Yes, I never really learned. Ben tried teaching me a couple times, but I never got the gist of it," I say, remembering Julian's weekend party.

"You don't have to blush like that if you don't know how to ride a bicycle." He grins crookedly before continuing, "I feel bad for your man, though."

I reach and smack him on the shoulder. "Hey!"

Arsen raises his hands in surrender as he laughs. "Hey! You left that one wide open. But I'm sorry. No more teasing, I promise." He lowers his hands and takes a sip of water, "Ready for my second revelation?"

"Sure."

I notice some color growing on the crests of his cheeks, which accentuates his aqua blue eyes.

"I wanted to have my own band when I grew up, but I fucking suck. It's embarrassing."

"No, I don't think it's embarrassing. It's great! Why don't you give it a try?"

"Maybe…nah. It's just something I would've liked to do." Obviously uncomfortable talking about himself, he changes the subject. "Your turn."

For a moment, I stare at him blushing and decide to tell him my deepest secrets. I don't know what makes me want to do it, but I do.

There's an easiness about him that makes me want to trust him.

"Um, I have two. I'm pregnant. But don't. Don't congratulate me yet."

A shadow crosses his eyes, but it's gone before I have a chance to ask him about it.

"Go ahead. I'm listening," he encourages me.

Surprised at his willingness to listen, I can't help but remember the last time I tried speaking to Ben about it a long time ago and how different his reaction was. It's like they are night and day.

Reclining against a tree with Ben's arms wrapped around me, and the smell of late autumn in our local park surrounding us, I feel such yearning as I watch children chasing geese and playing with fallen leaves. They're so beautiful to admire, yet it hurts to even listen to them laugh. I wonder if I'll ever get used to being around them without having to fight the emptiness I carry to take over me completely.

I hope so. I really do.

Ben always tells me that happiness is what you make of your life, but I wonder what happens when your heart's desire keeps being taken away from you over and over again?

Truly. What happens then?

I'm still trying to figure it out.

I admire the lovely children playing and think back to the beginning of the end, to that day when some vital part of me decided it was too much to keep hoping and dreaming. It was the day that hope kept slipping through my fingers no matter how hard I tried to hold it within my hands.

Not wanting to think about it anymore, I turn to look at Ben and see that his eyes are closed while his eternal cocky smirk plays around his lips. I love that grin. It's as if he knows the answers to something you want to know really bad, but he won't tell you just because. And it also happens to remind me of happier days.

The setting sun casts an amber glow to everything in the park including his beautiful tanned face and his dark curls that are flying in reckless abandon. I move from his embrace, then turn to straddle his lap so that we're facing each other. I run my hands through his hair as I watch his smirk turn into an open smile.

"Your hair is getting really long, baby."

"Can't cut it, babe," he answers, keeping his eyes closed.

"How did you know I was going to suggest a trim? And why not?" I ask.

"My hot wife digs it."

"I'm sorry?"

"You heard me, woman." He opens his eyes and stares at me with so much love. "I like the feel of your hands running through my hair." He leans over me, whispering in my ear, "It reminds me of the dirty things you let me do to you when you pull it. Plus the hot interns like it."

"Hot interns?"

Ben laughs when he sees my expression. "Is my woman getting jealous?"

"Jealous?" I ask, frowning. Maybe I am.

"Babe, chill…I'm just teasing you. I don't care about the interns. I only care whether you like it or not, and if I'm being honest, you pull my hair when I am making you come…hard… and it fucking turns me on." He licks my ear.

I can't help the shiver that runs through my body.

"Ben… not here," I protest.

He chuckles.

"Then let's go,"

"You ass. No, we're not going anywhere. We're staying here." I elbow him.

"Cathy…It's been too long. Come on." He wraps his arms around my waist and nuzzles my neck.

Feeling a hint of the intimacy we shared before I became a failure as a woman return, I want to open up to him and just talk to him. Share my inner demons. Maybe if I explain to him how I feel, the emptiness will go away.

I'm about to tell him that we should leave and head home when he kisses me sweetly on the cheek. I slowly turn my face and kiss him on the lips desperately. I need his kiss to hold me here. To this life. To him.

When our lips part, we look at each other as we breathe heavily. Ben's arms are wrapped around me, all of me, and it feels good for the first time in a very long time.

"Babe, what's the matter? I can see something is bothering you. Why don't you tell me? You know I'll do everything and anything you ask of me

as long as it's in my power to do so." He kisses my nose, then moves his hands to cup my ass.

I laugh because as soon as his hands touch my ass, he wiggles his eyebrows and leers at me, looking like a pervert. I decide to come clean to Ben.

"Watching all these children play…it has made me think."

"About what, babe?"

"Um, I'm just so afraid, baby. I-I feel like a failure because I-I haven't—"

"Stop, Cathy. I hate when you do this to yourself. Stop thinking about it. There are so many options that we can try…so many options still available to us."

"No…let me finish, please," I plead. Ben seems annoyed, but he lets me continue. "I want to tell you this. I'm just so afraid that it will never happen. I truly thought the IVF treatment was going to work. I really did." I feel tears gather in the back of my throat, but I can't stop now. "What if we can't…never…"

Ben places a warm finger on my mouth. "Shh…don't be so negative. We could always go back to see the adoption lawyer, you know. I don't mind."

"No, no, no. Ben, that's too much. I'm not sure I could handle it…the not knowing."

"Then why don't you try and be a little bit more positive?"

His words are like a slap to the face. I'm trying to be honest with him for once, and he keeps shutting me down, almost as if my worries aren't important enough.

"Babe, I just think you're going about it all wrong."

"What do you mean?"

"Hell, Cathy, I don't know. I just think you're too negative sometimes. I believe you have this mindset that everything won't work out." He caresses my cheek, but his touch isn't welcome this time. "Babe, don't be

angry. I just think you have to be more positive about it. We'll make it work."

"But—" I want to ask him what happens if it doesn't, but he stops me.

"But nothing. I can see the subject is affecting you. Let's drop it, okay?"

No, it's not okay. But Ben seems to have decided it's time to drop it, so I do. Shrugging my shoulders, I move to stand, but Ben stops me.

"Hey," he cups my cheeks, "Look at me, love. Don't be angry. I just want you to stop blaming yourself and thinking the worst. It's not healthy."

I don't want to look at him anymore. I want to tell him that I'm entitled to think whatever I want, but I don't. Deep down, I know he's right because I know all those things.

My mind knows. However, try telling it to my heart.

Ben stares at me, expecting me to say something, but I don't.

There's nothing else to say.

All I know is that it doesn't matter anymore.

"Catherine? Are you there?" Arsen waves his hand in front of my face. "You were saying?"

"Oh, yes. Sorry." I take a deep breath. "I'm pregnant, but I don't want to get my hopes up. You see, about two years ago I was diagnosed with a condition known as habitual abortion or Recurrent Pregnancy Loss. My case was specifically unexplained RPL. Meaning, I could get pregnant but each pregnancy ended with me miscarrying without a cause. It just kept happening to me, and there was no valid explanation behind it since all the tests came back normal."

Without saying empty words, Arsen reaches for my hand and holds it in his. "Go on."

I look down at our hands, feeling his warm touch in mine, and I realize it makes me feel better.

"After my third miscarriage, it took us forever to get pregnant again. That condition is known as secondary infertility. We tried drugs, acupuncture, IVF, we saw specialists… the whole shebang. But nothing worked. I mean, Ben and I even saw an adoption lawyer, but after he explained to us the whole process of trying to adopt a baby and that even if we went through it all it wasn't a guaranteed thing…" I pause, "I just couldn't do it. It was much too painful, so we kind of gave up. Well, I gave up."

I lick my lips, suddenly they feel dry. "I'm sorry. I don't know why I'm telling you all this." I swallow hard. "I must be boring you to death."

Arsen shakes his head. "No, go ahead, Dimples. I'm listening," he encourages huskily, still holding my hand in his.

Staring at him, feeling the connection between us grow, I tell him what I can't share with Ben. I really have no clue how Arsen is getting me to talk to him about my deepest fears in the middle of the day while sitting in a busy diner. Maybe it's the understanding I see in his eyes, or the supportive grip on my hand, but somehow I know I have found a friend in him. One who won't judge me.

"So now I'm pregnant again, and I'm so scared. I want to have faith and be positive about the pregnancy, but I can't. There's this constant fear that something will go wrong, a fear so powerful sometimes I can't breathe. I look at my stomach and think that it's too good to be true. And if something happens to the baby…I don't know what will happen to me, Arsen. I don't. I want my baby so much it's hard to think of anything else."

Arsen remains quiet for a minute as he studies our hands clasped together.

"If you ever feel like you need to talk to someone…if you ever feel like fear is making it hard for you to breathe…talk to me. I'm here for you, Dimples. I'm here."

I know his words could be empty and that he's just offering his help to be polite, but the powerful gleam in his eyes makes me believe him.

And, I do.

I do.

I do.

"Thank you. I will," I say, letting go of his hand as mine suddenly feels bereft.

"Is there any other big revelation because I didn't think you were expecting, " he says with a grin. I think he's trying to lighten the mood.

Looking down at my barely there bump, I smile. "Yes. I'm not showing yet. As for another secret," I raise my eyes and tap my chin, "Hmm…I'm afraid of elevators and tunnels."

"For real?" His eyes sparkle with curiosity.

"Yep. It's weird. I'm afraid that the elevator will stop working and we'll get stuck in it. And tunnels." I shiver at the thought. "I'm particularly afraid of the ones under water. What if something happens and it collapses when I'm in one?"

"It's okay, Dimples. I'll take pity on you and save you," Arsen says, smiling.

I laugh. "And how do you intend to do that?" I lean forward, "Do you have super powers that I'm not aware of?"

"Baby, wouldn't you love to know?" Arsen teases back as he leans forward, bringing our faces closer together.

"Maybe…but, what if I don't need saving?" I say.

"Even if you didn't, I'd be there for you." He retorts.

"Oh, this is getting interesting." I lean even closer than before. "Arsen, my knight in shining armor."

"Only for you," he answers, but he's not smiling anymore. As a matter of fact, he looks dead serious.

Our faces close, the whisper of his breath hitting my lips…we stare at each other silently for a moment too long. The friendly vibe from before is gone, and instead the air has turned tense…charged with energy.

Slowly, he lowers his gaze and stares at my lips intensely, prompting me to do the same with his. Are they as soft as they look? I can't help but wonder what they would feel like on my skin.

"Excuse me. Your food is ready," the waitress cuts in, breaking the tension filling the small space between us not a moment ago.

"Finally. I'm fucking starving," Arsen says before digging in, back to his usual self.

I grab my fork and run my fingers along the handle, pretending that the awkward moment from before never happened.

After lunch is over, he walks with me to the curb to wait for a cab. It had started raining while we were in the diner, so as we are making our way to the corner a strong wind passes us by, flipping my umbrella inside out. The sudden pull tugs me forward, causing me to stumble blindly into Arsen who immediately wraps his arms around my waist to stop me from falling.

When I look up, embarrassed beyond recognition, he's already staring at me with his piercing eyes. I feel the beginning of a blush stain my checks as I hear the loud thumping of my heart.

I wonder if he can hear it.

I would die.

"I haven't kissed you yet, but I'm already making you weak in the knees?" he teases, tightening his hold on me.

I'm trying to come up with an answer, but my mind is drawing a blank. Instead, I get lost in the warmth of his body so close to mine. His touch feels comfortable and organic as if it belonged there.

"W-what?" I say, swallowing hard.

"However, I think this is where I'm supposed to kiss you," Arsen says as the tips of our noses touch. In a daze, I observe how he brings his lips closer to mine. As he draws nearer, a voice in the back of my head is shouting at me to move because nothing good can come of this. When I think he's about to kiss me, I snap out of my reverie and put my arms in between us, ready to use all my strength to push him away, but Arsen surprises me when he aims for my ear instead.

"I'm just messing with you, Catherine," he whispers before he pulls slightly back, staring at me with laughing eyes.

Relieved because he was teasing me, I begin to push him away and lift a hand to wipe some of the rain off my face. "In your dreams, Arsen," I joke back.

"Fuck, you're getting wet. Let me fix that for you." He lets go of me instantly, grabs my umbrella and fixes it by flipping it back.

"It's all better." He holds it above me, shielding me from the rain.

"Um, yes…thank you."

"Told you. I'm here to save you."

His statement makes me lift my eyes and stare at him as the rain keeps falling around us. The grin plastered on his face sets me at ease. I'm comfortable with friendly and flirty Arsen.

We're standing next to each other while he holds the umbrella over me and not him. He's getting wet, but doesn't seem to mind. "Are you sure you don't want to squeeze under here? I think there's enough room for the two of us."

"Nah. It's okay. A little water won't kill me." He grins, making his eyes crinkle.

As we stand on the corner of Church Street, the noises of the city come alive all around us. I can smell the smokiness of the wet cement and the exotic spices coming from the gyro stand across the street from us. I don't think I've ever noticed all these smells and noises floating in the air before.

"Would you like to share the cab with me?"

Arsen smiles. "Sure."

I'm about to discuss a coming assignment when I hear my phone ringing. I take my cellphone out and see Ben's picture on the screen. "Excuse me for a sec. My husband is calling me, and I need to get this."

Arsen nods stiffly.

After a quick conversation, I say goodbye to Ben. By the time I turn to look at a soaked Arsen, a cab finally pulls to a stop in front of us.

When Arsen opens the door for me, I get in but he doesn't follow me.

"Aren't you coming? I ask, confused.

"No. Actually, I just remembered that I need to run some errands. If you don't mind, can I borrow your umbrella?"

"Um, okay."

Leaning inside, Arsen kisses my cheek goodbye taking me by surprise. And I'm further stunned when he whispers in my ear, "Thank you, Catherine. It was a lot of fun. We should do this more often. You know, just you and me. I know I would like to."

He straightens and shuts the door without saying another word to me.

As the cab pulls into traffic, I turn around so fast I can feel the ends of my hair hitting my face. He's standing under the pouring rain watching the cab drive away.

11

past

Nerves sear through my body, making me feel feverish as I look at the stranger staring back at me in the mirror with eyes that shine brightly.

"Uh, I'm not sure how I feel about this." I tug at the leather skirt, trying to get it to grow a couple of inches without any luck. Turning to look at Morgan who is sitting down on her bed looking perfect, I rub my hands against one another, the sweat making them stick together. "I feel like I should be working a corner or a pole, Morgan. I mean, if I bend down just a little you can probably see my ass."

"Are you kidding me? You look gorgeous. Like the new, improved, and sluttified girl next door. Ben is going to lose his mind when he sees you in that outfit."

Smiling at me, she stands up and makes her way to stand next to me. As she closes the distance between us, I take in her outfit and for a moment wishing I were as tall and as curvy as she is. She's wearing very tight, shiny black leggings with a fitted Rolling Stones t-shirt, and bright pink stilettos. A female version of Julian, she is stunning.

"Seriously, Cathy. Julian gave me a rundown of what's going on between you two, and I know this is going to sound immature, but if you want a guy to stake his claim, make him die of jealousy. Look hot and flirt with hot guys, and he will go all cave man on you. I swear it works like a charm."

I watch her out of the corner of my eye, laughter and disbelief in my voice, "And this has worked for you before, I take?"

"Yep. Always. And let me tell you, the more pissed off you get them, the hotter the make-up sex is after."

I shake my head and continue staring at my reflection in the mirror. "Okay, I get it. But this isn't a skirt. It's more like a scrap of cloth!" I show her the way the skin-tight skirt is hugging my hips. I'm wearing leather glued to my ass, a pretty cream blouse with black lace applications and my black riding boots.

Okay, it actually doesn't look that bad. But I feel naked.

Morgan laughs, making her blue eyes sparkle. "Well, I think you look super hot in that outfit. You're not only going to have Ben drooling after you, but probably Julian and some of the other guys too. You have so much to work with, you know? You're naturally very pretty without any make up, so wait until after I've done your eyes and applied some blush. Poor Ben, I already feel bad for him."

Groaning, I close my eyes and let her play with me like a Barbie doll. I mean she already dressed me and did my hair. Why not let her do my make up? Besides, I have to admit, it's kind of fun.

While she "beautifies" me, I decide that my outfit is the least of my problems. I need to speak to Ben. So, I let the subject drop and stay in her clothes. The girl staring back at me doesn't look like girl next door Cathy at all. She is beautiful in an airy, ethereal kind of way. Opening my eyes wide and closing the space between the mirror and myself, I take a real look at myself.

"Wow, Morgan. I love it! I look so different," I pause, "I look so pretty! Thank you!"

I turn to face her with a big smile on my face. She looks very pleased with herself.

"You're welcome! But I didn't do anything really. All I did was bring out your natural beauty. I told you I had a lot to work with. Anyway, stop looking at yourself. It's you, you hot lil' piece of ass!"

She giggles as she grabs me by the elbow, walking us to the door. "Oh. MAHHHH. GAWWWD! I cannot wait to see Ben and Julian's faces when they see you."

Feeling lots of butterflies in my stomach as we make our way to the main living room, I let fate decide what's in store for me.

I truly hope that Ben is it.

I feel Julian's hands circling my waist as we dance to Santeria by Sublime. Could this grinding of bodies even be called dancing? I'm not sure, so I just play along. Julian told me to trust him, so I am. The closeness of our bodies should bother me, I mean, I'd be surprised if you could see a sliver of light between us as we dance, but the brotherly smile on his face reassures me that this is all for show and nothing more.

After Julian scans the room, nodding to people who are trying to catch his attention, his eyes return to watch me, never leaving mine again. Dancing, we get lost in the music and let the beat of the melody guide our every move. When Caress Me Down starts playing, Julian's hands pull me closer to him as he moves his legs in between mine. Instinctively I wrap my hands around his neck as we sway our hips to the rhythm of the song; our bodies so close that I can feel the heat of his body radiating through his jeans.

Shit.

This feels totally different from the dance before. It's more intimate. I know it must look worse than it is because we're attracting a lot of attention. I'm beginning to feel quite uncomfortable with the way we are dancing.

Damn it.

I look around the room as I put some space between our bodies and try to find the reason why I'm here in the first place. I don't see him anywhere, and I am starting to really freak out now.

Where is Ben?

When I first started dancing with Julian, my gaze landed on an angry pair of brown eyes. Ben was staring at me, unsmiling, but Julian asked me a question, causing me to turn away. After I'd answered him, I glanced over my shoulder, but Ben was no longer staring at me. In fact, he didn't look my way once after that. When the second or third danced ended, I watched Ben disappear with a gorgeous brunette.

Which brings me to this moment.

Where is he?

Imagining him with her is driving me mad with jealousy. I feel sick to my stomach, but I got myself in this situation, didn't I? I can see why Ben won't even come looking for me. Why he's probably hooking up with someone so much prettier than I am. I feel angry tears pooling in my eyes.

He must be disgusted with me.

I hate this.

I deserve whatever is coming my way. I have no one else to blame but my childish behavior.

Shit.

Without giving it another thought, I decide to go in search of Ben and put a stop to this stupid game. I just hope that Ben believes me and I'm not too late. Turning to look at Julian, guilt flowing out of my pores, I stand on my tip-toes to speak in his ear.

"Julian, I'm sorry. I can't do this. If all these people already think something is going on between us or is about to happen, I can only imagine what Ben must be thinking. Please, let me just go look for him."

"Are you sure? I think we're on the right track. He should be coming to beat the living daylights out of me anytime now."

I shake my head. "No, Julian. He left with a tall brunette before."

"What the fuck? I didn't see him leave," he exclaims.

"He left about two or three songs ago." My stomach hurts just thinking about what he could be doing right now.

After a couple seconds, Julian asks, "What did she look like?"

I swallow hard. "A tall brunette, skinny, big boobs, beautiful."

"Fuck!" he pins me down with his stare.

I think I already know who she is, but I still need him to confirm it. "I-Is that Ashley?" I ask, breathlessly.

Julian clenches his jaw and nods once.

Feeling like the air is knocked out of my lungs, I stare at the dance floor before I meet his gaze once more. "This is enough. I can't do this anymore."

"Hey. He's going to come back. You'll see."

I shake my head, "I know it's just dancing, but I feel sick to my stomach. I don't want him to get the wrong idea. Please," I beg, "I just need to go find him and try to explain everything. I just can't do this. I just can't."

Julian immediately lets my body go, a tender expression in his eyes. "It's okay. Go. Or would you like me to go find him for you? Try to talk some sense in him?"

"No. This is my battle to fight. I got myself in this mess, and I've already dragged you deep enough. I'm not sure if I'll still be here after tomorrow, but truly, thank you for caring and for listening to me. Ben is so lucky to have you as a friend." I kiss him on the cheek, then turn away from him.

Julian pulls me back. "He's very lucky. You know, I wasn't joking about poaching before, but damn if I'm not tempted at this moment. I like you. I hope you both work it out because I have a good feeling about the two of you together."

Smiling, I nod.

"Cathy…"

"Yes?"

"If things with Ben don't work out, you know where to find me." Julian smiles, making his blue eyes sparkle.

Breaking into a laugh, we hug each other one last time before I make my way to find what I hope is forgiveness and my future.

Even if I have to beg on my knees.

For Ben, I would do that and more.

As soon as I'm standing in the empty hallway, I feel a pair of large hands wrap around my waist.

"Mmmhmm…bored with Julian already?"

Ben's voice sends shivers running down my spine.

"No. You know I'm not interested in anyone but you..." I try to move away from his hold, but he tightens his grasp, making me wince in pain.

"Bullshit. I saw the way you were dancing with him, and the only reason I didn't beat the shit out of him is because—"

"Stop! Let go of me so I can explain to you what happened."

When Ben does as I say, I spin around to look at him. He looks raving mad, but he's here. I throw myself at his chest. I don't think I can hold him any closer without crawling into his skin. I'm filled with so much love and relief that I don't immediately notice how his hands are trying to push me away instead of hugging me back.

The minute I realize what this means, I let go of him and turn away as I hear Ben curse under his breath. I want to say that I understand and that I'm okay, but the words get stuck in my throat. I take five or six steps when he grabs me by the elbow and pulls me right back, slamming me against his chest.

"For fuck's sake, Cathy. Where do you think you're going?" he asks harshly.

Looking up at his face, I feel the tears running down my cheeks. "I-I'm really sorry. I've got to get my suitcase and leave tonight. I'm sorry, Ben. It was my fault."

Ben shakes his head as the scowl on his face deepens. "Where the hell do you think you're going?" He groans in frustration. "You know what? Never mind. Don't answer that question. You have a lot of explaining to do, but not here."

"But you don't want me anymore."

"You must be joking, right? Of course I want you. You're my girl."

The music, the people walking in and out of the room, the laughter, the shouting, everything becomes a blur. All I can see is the guy standing in front of me.

Only him.

He's gritting his teeth so hard that it makes his perfect square jaw even more pronounced. The expression on his face tells me he wants to murder me, but it's his eyes that hold me enthralled. I see tenderness and possession swirling like a vanilla and chocolate ice cream cone. I see something that I can't believe.

I see my future.

You are my girl.

With his words bouncing in my head, etching themselves in my soul, I try to close the distance between us, but I don't get a chance.

Ben's strong arms are wrapped around me in the blink of an eye. He's hugging me so tight that I don't think I can feel my ribs anymore. Nestled in the curve of my neck, I can feel the light stubble of his chin tickle my skin as he whispers in my ear, "I need you now, fuck my damn conscience. I can't take it anymore. I need to be inside you right now. I want you naked beneath me. No more games."

I feel chills running all over my body as the heat of desire pools in between my legs, and the butterflies of anticipation flutter in my stomach.

Nodding, I close my hand around his as he pulls me in front of him. Fully clothed and in public, he slams his hips into mine.

"I want you," he whispers in my ear.

I do, too.

As we make our way to our suite on the second floor, we keep stopping to make out against the diamond-paned windows and the paintings hanging on the walls, Ben's hand under my skirt and inside my panties.

"Fuck, Cat, you're so wet."

Ben lifts me up in his arms. Or did I climb him? My hands lock around his neck, and my legs straddle his waist. We groan when our bodies rub against each other intimately. I have a feeling we're not going to make it to the bed."

Ben scoops his hands under my ass, lifting me higher and burying his head in my neck. "You're going to be the death of me."

Blindly entering the dark room, too busy kissing as we try to rip our clothes off, we walk straight into a piece of furniture. Laughing, the two of us break apart just long enough for Ben to whisper in my ear, "Cathy, babe, we may need the lights on if we don't want to break every piece of furniture in this room."

"Mmhhmmm…hurry up. I'm dying here, and I don't think I can't wait any longer."

He flicks the tip of my nose. "My horny little minx."

I nod my head as he lets go of me because, yes.

That's not a lie.

I want him.

All of him.

So badly.

When his body untangles from mine, he makes his way in the darkness to the entrance of the room in search of a light switch. I give props to whoever came up with the idea to always place them by the door. Brilliant.

The minute the lights come on, I don't bother to admire the décor and the lavishness of the suite. All I want to see is Ben. All I see is Ben.

As he walks back to me, I shamelessly drink him in. I take in the perfection of his tall and muscular body, the size of his hands, the beauty of his face, and the need in his eyes. The craving. Under his gaze, my breasts tingle as my body, feverish with desire, feels swollen where I want him, where I need him the most.

A teasing smile on his lips, Ben slowly approaches me as I move backwards. By the time my ass hits the edge of a dresser, I'm trembling from head to toe with anticipation. As Ben draws nearer, closing the space between us, the expression on his face makes my heart beat hard and fast.

When he's standing in front of me, I reach for him, and the world around us disappears. All I can feel is his hot mouth on my skin, kissing me so roughly I know it will leave marks. Not stopping him because I want to be branded by Ben, I pull him closer to me. Our frantic hands help us discard what little clothing we have left on. When we are completely naked, Ben grabs me by the shoulders and stops kissing me.

"We have to stop…" he says painfully. "I wasn't expecting this to happen, so I'm not prepared."

"Oh, you mean protection?"

Ben nods as he rubs the back of his neck.

"It's okay. I'm on the pill a-and this would be my first time without a-a, you know…condom," I say as I feel my face burning.

Ben cups my face in his hands, letting his fingers caress my cheeks. "It would be my first time too, you know. Are you sure, babe?"

"Yes. Oh yes," I beg. "I can't wait any longer."

Without a moment of hesitation, Ben lets go of my face, grips my shoulders once again, and turns me around to face the mirror propped on the dressing table.

"Watch," he demands, his voice husky with passion, "Watch us."

When our eyes meet in the mirror, an unsmiling Ben lowers his finger to the vee of my body. I feel his finger slip inside me, stroking me once. I whimper, about to beg for more when he removes his hand completely. I stare at his reflection in the mirror as he brings his finger to his mouth, his tongue darting out to lick it before he lowers it again. Sliding his finger, he spreads my wetness mixed with his own on my clit. I'm on the brink of exploding when he withdraws his finger once more.

Ben reaches for my hand and curls my fingers around his dick as we stroke him to full erection together. I can't see anything, but I can feel the hardness and the smoothness of his skin covering his dick as he grips my hand tighter in his. Letting go, I take the base of his dick in my hand, but I don't put him inside me. Instead, I try to savor the moment. I'm breathing slow and easy, making the moment last. I love how free and uninhibited Ben makes me feel. He makes me feel beautiful and powerful.

When his hand lands on the small of my back, bending me at the waist and pushing me forward, I grip the edge of the dressing table. Nudging my thighs to open wider, I moan when I feel Ben guiding the tip of his arousal inside me. With a tense jaw, he impales me in one hard, deep thrust that makes the mirror rattle. Lifting his eyes from where we are connected, we stare at each other as he begins to slowly pull back, bringing his free hand around to stroke me. When he's almost all the way out, he aggressively thrusts forward again, groaning and rubbing me as he pounds harder and faster each time. Ben grabs my hair in his fist, giving it a not so gentle tug as I lift my ass higher up to give him better access into me.

"Oh, yes…" I groan with each thrust.

"Fuuuuck, baby…you're so damn tight…fuck."

He wants to take, he wants to demand, he wants to dominate.

I let him. I let him because I feel wanted. So wanted.

I give him everything.

As our rhythm becomes more desperate, Ben lets go of my hair to grip my hips roughly in both hands as he thrusts deeper, fucking harder into me. I feel him inside me, outside me, everywhere and beyond. I feel him in my soul.

Feeling so close to the edge, I lift my eyes to look at his reflection in the mirror. I want to see him when he comes inside me. Ben is watching me already. I don't think he ever stopped.

"So close, Cathy… I need to pull—"

"No. Don't…it's okay."

"Shit…so close."

As our bodies continue to slam against each other, I can feel the muscles of my body tighten around him. Ben's fingers rub me faster, and faster until I come undone. A scream escapes my mouth as a rainbow of colors explodes inside me, heightening the sweet emotions flowing through my body.

I observe Ben close his eyes and tip his head back as a ragged groan escapes his mouth when he climaxes. When I feel the warm rush inside me, his arms wrap around my waist as he lays his head on my back, thrusting and shuddering one last time

Warm and fuzzy feelings are running through my blood vessels as he kisses my sweaty back.

"Wow," his raspy voice mumbles as he tightens his embrace around me.

"Um, yes. Wow."

"Cathy…."

"Yes?"

I feel him nudge me once more. "Why did we wait so damn long?"

I want to smack him for making such a stupid joke, but when I turn my face sideways to look at him and protest, the tender smile on his lips robs me of logical thought.

"I hope this proves to you how much I want you. You belong to me. Only me."

At a loss for words, I nod.

I'm his girl.

I'm lying in bed with Ben, spooning. His arms are wrapped around my chest and waist, pulling my back tightly against his front. In the safe haven of his embrace, I sigh contently as I feel his soft breath hit the back of my ear.

I knew it. I just did.

I knew that if we slept together, if I let him own me physically with his hands, with his mouth, with his body, the intimacy of the act was going to push me over the brink, that I was going to free fall into an unknown abyss. Well, I'm on the other side. And if I felt like I could soar before, now I'm skyrocketing through the air.

My body sated but deliciously tender and sore, lips bruised, heart complete, I want to get up and jump on the bed. Shouting to the world how happy he makes me. Ben makes colors seem brighter when he walks into a room, he makes my heart feel as if it wants out of my chest every time I see him or think of him. He makes my world spin.

I smile into the pillow and snuggle closer to his warmth, thinking that Ben was right. I don't understand why we waited this long. Ashley who? I don't care. Now I know that Ben feels something for me. Maybe it's not love for him yet, but I have hope that someday it will be.

"Mmm, stop doing that, baby. Unless you want another go…"

Laughing because I feel so happy, I tease, "I wouldn't mind another one. I feel like I've been robbed."

"Woman, you're going to kill me. Aren't you sore? I don't want to hurt you. And fuck that shit, robbed, my ass! I felt you spasm around my dick. And babe, trust me, I deliver."

"Seriously, cocky much?" His smugness is such a turn on.

"Yes, I'm cocky alright," he says, nudging me with a huge erection.

"What the hell? How can you be…"

"Babe, I'm a guy. Alone with his girl who has her sweet naked ass plastered against his dick. So yes, I'm going to want to fuck again, and again."

"Wait! No! Before we do anything, I-I want to know…I need to know. Was it good for you? Did you like it?"

Letting me go, he lifts his body to lie on top of mine. His arms are around my head, and his legs and upper body cage me under his. He stares at me with fire burning in his eyes. "Cathy, please. Stop this shit. I don't like it when you doubt yourself. It's just me, babe. And I—"

He stops himself, checking his words. Ben lifts one of his hands, caressing my cheek lovingly. "I think you're perfect.

From the way your green eyes look like deep forests, to your dimples that make me want to do stupid shit. Everything about you is perfect. Everything you do is perfect. So stop that, Cathy. And to answer your question, it was fucking amazing. You're amazing."

"Oh."

As a blush as hot as an iron covers my face, all I can do is lay there trying to let his words sink in. He thinks I'm perfect.

"That's right. Oh all you want. Now, not to sound like a horndog, which I am and proud of it, can we um, get to it?"

I smack him on his chest as I'm about to protest, but Ben grabs my hand in his. Bringing it to his lips, he kisses it once. "Gosh, why am I even dating you? You are such an ass!"

Ben's face softens as he murmurs, "Because," kiss, " I am the most tender," kiss, "affectionate," kiss, "sweetest," kiss, "and horniest person," kiss, "you'll ever meet." Lifting his face, his eyes pin me on the spot. "So, what do you say? Want to be my girlfriend?"

My hands sweating, my chest bursting fiercely like fireworks, I nod. "Yes…if you want to."

He grins boyishly. "Yes, I want to."

When Ben lowers his mouth, his lips touch mine very softly, very carefully…opening my mouth to him, his tongue caresses my own as his hands go to my legs, spreading me open once more. As I feel the tip of his erection about to enter me, I break the kiss. Breathing heavily, my body screaming for him, "Wait. I need to know something else."

He groans, moves off my body and lies on his back, throwing an arm over his eyes. "Go ahead."

Sexual frustration is seeping out of his pores. Man, does he want me that bad?

"Hey, you said you wanted to talk. So I'm talking."

"Touché, baby, touché. Go ahead. We are all ears."

"We?"

"Yes, my dick and I. He's awake, after all."

"You're bad."

"Only for you, babe, only for you. Now go ahead. I don't want to rush you, but we're waiting."

"I wanted to tell you that nothing happened between Julian and me. And before you go there, I left with him, and we danced a bit too close to each other, but it was all for show. I was angry with you and I didn't think, so I left with him. I didn't want to hurt you, and I most certainly don't want you to get into a fight with Julian over me. He was very sweet in trying to help me out."

Lifting the arm covering his eyes, he looks at me as he speaks with a scowl on his face, "Julian sweet my ass! He was fucking testing the waters. He wanted you. I saw it. He has some explaining to do, but don't worry about it for now, babe. He enjoyed it, but he's never getting that close to you again, and he knows it too. So don't apologize for that."

"Please don't be too mean. He seriously was being sweet."

"Don't worry about it. Let me deal with my best friend. And I'm not pissed anymore."

"Okay, next."

"There's more?"

"One more. Where did you go when you disappeared?"

"I couldn't stand watching you dancing with someone else, so I went to get a beer. I was so mad. I was just getting ready to come find you and put a stop to that loser's game when I saw you leaving. That's when I caught up to you outside in the hallway."

"Are you sure? You weren't, you know…with someone else? You were gone for a couple of songs." Why isn't he telling me about Ashley? I should tell him that I saw them speaking, but I don't want her to ruin our moment. Maybe I'll talk to him about it tomorrow.

Ben decides he's had enough of talking because as he's answering my question, his hand goes between my legs again. I feel as he dips not two but three of his fingers inside me, stroking me lightly. "Babe, how many times do I have to tell you tonight? I only want you." Without removing his fingers, he lifts his body with one shoulder watching what he is doing to me. "Only you."

I feel him remove his fingers and watch him move on top of me. Opening my legs with his hands, he enters me slowly, taking his time, making the moment last. When he's all the way in, he pauses as we stare at each other, both of us breathing heavily. Slowly, he brings a hand to caress my naked shoulder. "I've wanted to do this since the moment I kissed you on the street."

"Have sex with me?" I ask.

"No." He bites my lower lip. "Make you mine."

This time he makes love to me. There is no roughness in his treatment of my body, and I don't miss it. This feels as if he is telling me with his body what he cannot voice yet. This feels like we are imprinting each other to our bodies and to our hearts. Moaning, I grab the back of his neck and pull him down for a kiss, getting lost in the moment.

Later, as the room is illuminated with soft purples and pinks of the early morning, we're on the brink of falling asleep after a long night of making love. When my eyes are closing from deep and exquisite exhaustion, I feel him move closer to me, his nose nuzzling my neck as he murmurs in my ear, "I'll never get tired of you…of this." He holds my hands in his, twining out fingers together. "I just want to touch you. So fucking badly. So fucking much. You are mine now. Only mine."

Before falling into an abyss of dreams, I hear myself replying.

"I'm yours."

The truth reverberates within me until it is etched in my soul.

I wake up, opening my eyes as I stretch my body. Uh oh. Now I feel sore. Very sore. I have red marks everywhere on my body. Smiling, I don't feel shocked or scared because they remind me of our night together, our first night together, and of everything that happened between us. Those bruises and red marks are a visual memory of what it means to be branded. I was branded physically by Ben with each hard thrust of his hips into me, and with each kiss and every soft word whispered, he branded himself in my heart.

As I extend my arms above my head, trying to shake the sleep induced haze off my mind; I notice that Ben is not in bed. Not giving it a thought, I flip on my stomach and reach for his pillow, bringing it close to my face. I bury my nose in the fluffy case as I try to absorb his essence, inhaling his unique peppermint scent mixed with sweat and the musky aroma of sex.

Geezz…I remember now. This pillow was under my stomach last night when he drove into me from behind. Feeling warm moisture settle in my core, I groan and move the pillow to my chest and hug it as if it were Ben. After a couple minutes of lying idly, I decide I should take a shower before he returns when I hear the door open. I prop myself on my elbows as I watch a freshly showered and dressed Ben enter the room. His smile is so big when he sees me that you can see the beginning of laugh lines around his eyes and mouth.

He is gorgeous.

And he is mine.

"You're up. I'm glad. I want to teach you how to ride a bicycle."

"Seriously, Ben? I told you when we had this conversation weeks ago that I wasn't interested in learning."

As Ben gets closer to the bed, the smell of his aftershave and his shampoo holds me enthralled. "I know, babe, but I want to teach you. It's fun. And during the summer we can go to New Hampshire or Vermont and go mountain biking. It's awesome. And I want you to do those things with me."

"Okay, fine." When he's standing in front of me, I notice the writing on his tee. "I don't get your t-shirt."

"What?" Ben asks.

"It says "Liquor on the front."

A sexy smirk appears on his face. "Read the back, babe, and say it quick."

When he turns around, I see the rest of the saying. Well. "Poker on the back?" Enunciating the words aloud, I get it. Seriously?

While Ben laughs, he reaches the edge of the bed and kneels next to me. "Gladly, baby. But not now. Now, I want to do this."

"Ben, take that shirt off! Seriously, that's—"

"It's the shit. Now get your delicious ass out of bed. I'm teaching you how to ride a bicycle."

"Thought I did that last night…"

"You did, baby, and you almost gave me a fucking heart attack. But this is different. Come on, no more buts."

"Fine," I groan and get out of bed.

Freshly showered and feeling not so sore anymore, I make my way to the spacious breakfast room. The maid who I stopped to ask for directions referred to it as a breakfast parlor. I giggle. Parlor. My secret guilty pleasure is to read regency novels, and the word parlor reminds me of them. Ben definitely could be the hero in one. He definitely looks the part. Ruggedly handsome and masculine.

When I arrive at the room, my eyes immediately scan the area looking for Ben. It doesn't take me long to locate him. He's talking to the same beautiful brunette from last night whose exotic features make mine look boring and plain. She is supermodel tall with a Victoria's Secret model body. They are standing by a window deep in conversation, but that's not what bothers me.

What punches me in the gut, leaving me breathless, is the way she's holding his hand in hers. I see the glimmer of tears in her eyes as she talks to him. It looks like she's pleading with him. Ben looks annoyed, but I can see the softening in his eyes as he lifts a hand to wipe a tear off her face tenderly.

Shit.

Watching him touch her face so gently is a blow to my heart. I'm breaking into a thousand tiny pieces. Walking backwards without looking, I crash into the housekeeper who was holding a tray filled with glassware. It falls and breaks, just like me. Everyone turns in my direction and I apologize to the room, making my way to the front door as fast as I can.

I feel the cool air hit my wet cheeks the moment I begin to run. I don't care. I just want to get away from that house. I knew this was going to happen. I let myself be fooled by my own wishful thinking. I thought I could make Ben fall in love with me like I had with him.

Yes, I love him. And it hurts. But Ben was never mine to begin with, so I can't be angry with him if he wants to end whatever we have.

I knew it.

I knew it.

I hear someone shouting my name, but I don't stop running. I don't even know where I'm going. My blonde hair keeps getting in the way as I try to escape, partially blinding me until I hit a human wall. A warm wall whose arms wrap around me tightly.

How did he get ahead of me? Whatever. It doesn't matter.

I try to get away from his strong grasp, but he won't let me. Ben leans down and speaks into my ear, "Cathy. Stop fighting me. It wasn't what you think."

When I'm about to protest, he puts a finger on my mouth. "Shhh. Let me explain. That was Ashley. She wants me back, but what you saw wasn't us getting back together. It was me letting her go. I don't want her anymore, Cathy. I've just explained to her that…that I have fallen in love with someone else and that I don't love her anymore. I love you, Cathy. Only you. So, please…stop."

The fight leaves my body, and I lift my eyes as hope is reborn, spreading like a wild fire inside of me. "Y-you love me?"

Nodding, his eyes are luminous with fervor. "Yes, Cathy, I love you. I love you so fucking much."

"I love you, too. So much."

Ben

Love can destroy you.
Love can erase you.
Love can heal you.
Love can reinvent you,
And, if you are lucky enough,
Love can make you whole again.

That's what Cathy has done to me.

I cover her hand in mine as we make our way to the house. The need to be alone with her is driving me fucking insane. I need to show her with my body what words are not enough to describe. Show her that she owns me, body and soul. Not even Ashley, whom I thought was my future before she cheated on me, had ever reached inside me the way Cathy and her innocent green eyes did. She changed the biological makeup of my broken body, embedding herself into my DNA, slowly healing me with her smile, gluing me whole again with her love.

Fuck.

I have it bad.

And I love it.

I love her.

So fucking much.

I look down at the small hand in mine, feeling her sweet warmth all the way to my dick, and I realize that this tiny package of perfection has the power to completely destroy me, to annihilate me if she ever chose to. The funny thing is that I don't give a damn about it. If it means that I get to be with her, to hold her in my arms, to call her my own for however long I have.

And it better be a shitload of time because at this rate forever might not be long enough.

When our gazes meet, a shiver of awareness runs down my spine, settling where I need to feel her wet and warm and pulsating around me. I remember the way her body welcomed mine, giving herself so freely to me.

As we walk back to the house, I let go of her hand and wrap an arm around her shoulder, pulling her closer to me. I feel her arms wrap around my waist.

"Ben…"

"Yes, babe?"

"Are we going back to our room?"

"Yep. We need to clear up some stuff."

"Okay. Could we avoid going through the main entrance? I kind of don't want to run into anyone after the show I put on, and I must look like a raccoon from crying," Cathy asks, her voice muffled from my chest and raspy from tears.

Leaning down to kiss the top of her head, I close my eyes for a brief moment as I inhale the flowery scent of her shampoo. "Whatever you want, babe."

And I mean it.

We are now lying on the bed facing each other. I want her naked and on top of me, but I know it can't happen yet. I need to explain some things and make her understand that the past is the past and it better stay there, once and for all.

When a strong urge to touch her comes over me, to have her body next to mine, I pull her closer.

"Much better."

"Ben…I'm sorry for jumping to conclusions when I saw you with Ashley. It's just that last night I saw you walking out with her, but when I asked you about it, you didn't mention her."

"I was going to tell you about her, but I didn't want to talk about it just then. I wanted it to be just about the two of us. Just you and me and nothing else."

"After last night I shouldn't have doubted you. It's just…when I saw the way you touched her face, the way she was holding your hands and how perfect she was, I was so jealous. I knew I could never compete against—"

I put a finger under her chin and lift her face to make her look at me. "Let me explain. You're not going to like parts of what I have to say, but it's the truth and you deserve the truth. And knowing the truth is the only way you'll see that there's no need to give Ashley a thought."

"Okay."

I can hear the fear in her voice, but I know this is what we both need.

"Ashley and I have known each other for a long time. We both went to St. Patrick's Prep. I was a junior, and she was a freshman. I guess you could say I was popular because I was already the starting quarterback and because of my last name. No big deal. I enjoyed the perks. I was very young and an idiot. Julian and I slept with pretty much every hot girl that caught our attention. And there were quite a few, Cathy.

"I remember the day like it was yesterday. Julian and I were getting shit faced in our dorm, when Oscar, who you haven't met, came to tell us about this new hot transfer. That she was a freshman and fresh pussy." When she winces in my arms, I squeeze her hip, knowing that this is nothing and only gets worse. "He decided he was going to screw her sooner rather than later. Julian and I didn't give a fuck because, frankly, we didn't care. Oscar was good looking, but Julian and I got the most attention from the girls in school, so if she was that hot we knew she'd eventually sleep with one, or both of us," I pause. "We were kind of assholes back then.

"It didn't work out that way because the next day I ran into her, and I mean body slammed into her. She dropped her folder and some books, I think, but I couldn't tell you exactly what because the moment I saw her, I kind of fell in love with her. After we began dating…I mean, I was so crazy about her that I was afraid to hook up with her and have her think I was a man whore or something like that, so I asked her to be my girl. It wasn't long after that we—" Hell, this is hard to say. I can feel how tense Cathy is, but I continue, "I was her first, and she was my last. We dated all through my junior and senior year at St. Patrick's, and for half my time in college. I thought I loved her, and I was planning to propose to her once I was done with college and start Law School at Columbia. I figured my parents and her parents could help us out while we were both finishing school."

I have to take a deep breath, but as I exhale I realize that I don't feel any pain. I'm about to tell her what happened next, how Ashley took my heart and ripped it to pieces. Before Cathy came into my life, just the memory alone had the power to make it hard to breathe, but as I stare into pools of rich green, I know I don't feel anything anymore.

I feel no pain.

I feel no tightening in my chest.

I feel healed.

I feel whole.

I feel love.

"Go ahead." She takes my hand in hers and brings it to her mouth, kissing it slowly.

"We did the whole long distance relationship for two years. And it worked. I guess because she was still in high school and I was popular Ben playing college level football, and we were in love. Once she finished high school, I begged her to go to school with me, but she didn't want to. She said she hated Florida and its hot weather. She chose NYU because she wanted to stay close to home. It made sense to me, you know.

"Things went to hell half way through my junior year, her freshman year at NYU. On my way home for spring break, I decided to propose to her. As soon as I got home, I spoke to my parents. They were hesitant at first, but after I presented them a sound plan, they agreed. I spoke to Ashley's father and he agreed. That same day, my dad took me to Van Cleef and Arpels on Fifth and I bought her an engagement ring. Since I was in the city already, I decided to surprise Ashley. I knew she had already made plans with a friend from out of town, but I didn't care, I wanted to see her that day."

"Oh, Ben…"

I can hear the hurt in her voice. Shit, she is hurting for me even when I'm telling her about another woman. I love her.

"She had her own place in Gramercy Park, and I decided to surprise her with her favorite pink roses. I was twenty years old, stupid and idealistic." I take a deep breath. "I was in the kitchen, opening a bottle of champagne, when I heard the door open. Hearing her giggles, I turned around just in time to see her jump

Oscar. They had no idea I was standing there like a fucking asshole watching. Oscar walked them to her bedroom while they continued to make out. The room was across from the kitchen, so I saw the moment…the moment when he threw her body on the bed, scattering rose petals all over the room. That's when they realized something was wrong. Ashley stood up immediately, turning to look at the fucking joke on the bed."

When Cathy gasps, I lean down and kiss her wet cheeks. She is crying for me.

"I don't remember exactly what happened after. All I know is that the security guards of the building were pulling me off of an unconscious Oscar. Everything after that is a blur…Ashley crying and asking me to forgive her…the police interrogating me…the lawyers…my mom crying…my dad threatening to sue Oscar's parents…his parents threatening to sue me and end my career. I was broken. I was numb. And it hurt so much."

"Eventually, I got over it. I learned to forget, I guess, but I never forgave Ashley. We had been done for over two years the day I met you. You know, I thought I was doing better. I thought I was in a good place. Random hook ups here or there. Never a serious girlfriend after that. But the day I met you, something changed in me. I don't believe in love at first sight anymore, but I can tell you that from the moment we kissed, I felt as if I had been awakened from a numbing stupor." I link our fingers and stare at her creamy skin. "For the first time, in a very long time I felt alive."

I lean down as I bring my hand to the back of her neck, pulling her lips towards mine. Kissing, we lose track of time, our mouths sometimes gentle, sometimes brutal, but always with want.

I'm now brushing soft kisses on her eyelids while I feel them tremble against my mouth. "My beautiful girl, you healed me. You made me believe in love again, and I love you. So fucking much. After a week of knowing you and spending time with you, I knew I was over Ashley. Completely. There was no doubt that you were my only, my reason to be. But seeing Ashley today, I was able to forgive her. To close that chapter in my life. What you saw was me letting go of the past, finally. There is no Ashley left in me, no part that wants her. I want you. All of you. And no one else."

Cathy moves on top of me. She grabs my face in between her hands as she kisses my lips once, twice…not enough times. Her touch lights up a match inside of me, making me burn brightly.

Her kiss incinerates me.

"Oh, Ben."

"You remind me of a bunny when…you know…"

Feeling a smile tug at my lips, I watch as a happy and very naked Cathy opens her eyes, turning her face in my direction. With my head propped on the heel of my hand, I admire everything that is mine. I've spent the majority of the last half hour drawing shapes on her skin and tracing the goosebumps my touch rises on her skin.

"Come again. You get it? Come again?"

"You're so silly. And, yes. I'm going to call you Benny The Bunny."

"What the hell?" I laugh.

"Well, you're cute like one and…"

"And?"

I can hear the laughter in her voice. "And you can keep going, and going, and going, and going…"

"Ha. Wanna give my carrot a taste? They tell me they are good for your eyes," I tease.

I move on top of her, pinning her arms above her head, and watch the way her breasts rise and fall as her breathing accelerates. She's so beautiful.

With my need for her returning, I lower my fingers until I find my sweet spot. The spot I own. Guiding a finger inside her, I discover that she's already wet and ready for me. Between moans, she tells me what she wants me to do, but where's the fun in that? In a playful mood, I want to taunt her, so I tease her as I lower my head to lick her pink nipple. The tight bud feels like silk against my tongue. As my finger keeps moving inside her, going deeper and deeper, the heel of my palm applies pressure to her clit. Her moans get louder, and it makes my dick rock hard.

"Ben, please…I need you…now. I-I can't…"

"What is it, baby? What can't you do?"

"I c-can't wait any longer. I need…"

"What do you need? Tell me."

"I need you."

"What do you need, baby? Say it."

"I-I…" Hearing her hesitation makes me want to push her over the cliff. And being the son of a bitch that I am, I do. I'm about to move off her, when she wraps her arms and legs around my shoulders and hips.

Looking down at her, her shiny blonde hair making a golden halo on my pillow, I admire the full lips that have driven me to fucking distraction every time I feel them on me. I also see the green eyes that make me lose my mind with desperation. I see perfection. I see beauty. I see my girl.

I lift my body on one arm, taking the head of my dick and bring it to her warm core. "What do you need, Cathy? I want to hear you say it."

"I want you inside me, Ben. I need you inside me."

With one swift thrust, I'm deep inside her. The moment I feel her tighten around me, I don't move. I can't. I try to control every inch of my body that wants to go fucking wild and pound her hard.

"Are you mine, Cathy?"

Her face flushed, she nods. That's not enough. I need to hear her say it.

Pulling back just enough to leave the tip of my cock inside of her, I thrust into her, hard, almost as if I can push the words out of her mouth. "No. Say it. I want to hear you say it."

Dazed with passion, she looks at me with such open tenderness, making my throat tighten with emotion. "I'm yours. Only yours, Ben."

I slam into her. "Say it again. I want to hear you say it."

"I'm yours, Ben. I'm yours."

I can hear the bed frame rattle against the wall from the force of my thrusts, but I can't stop. Her legs and arms pull me closer as if she's trying to bring me inside of her. I move a hand to cup her where my dick is. "This belongs to me. Only me. You hear me? This is mine." I can hear my voice hoarse from exertion.

"Yes, Ben. Oh my God…"

"Jesus, Cathy, so sweet. So fucking beautiful. I'm so close."

Slowing down, and then coming to a stop, we stare at each other as blinding awareness passes between our connected bodies.

I know at this moment that there is no going back for me.

I belong to her as much as she belongs to me.

"I love you, Cathy."

"I love you."

I'm wearing a helmet and trying to find my balance on the stupid bicycle, but Ben isn't helping at all. Instead, he just watches me with a stupid grin on his face.

"Hello?" I exclaim. "Are you going to teach me, or are you just going to stand there watching me try to not to fall on my ass on this stupid thing?"

He clears his throat. "Hell yes. I'll teach you." As he makes his way towards me, I adjust my ass, trying to find a good spot on the seat that makes the soreness in between my legs hurt less.

"Jesus, Cathy."

"What? I can't get myself comfy. The seat hurts me right there." I groan. "This is so hard."

"Yes…something is getting hard alright."

"Stop it! You kept nagging me about learning to ride this stupid bicycle, but it's not working. And now it looks like it's going to start raining soon. We're going to get wet," I say frustrated with myself.

"Yes, babe. You're supposed to ride it wet."

"Are you seriously making dirty jokes at this moment?"

"It's not my fault! You keep wiggling that sweet ass of yours, and I'm only human."

The sky decides to open up at that moment, pouring rain

falling down on us.

Ben lifts his shoulders as he gives me an apologetic grin. "Sorry, Cathy. I tried."

"Come on, sicko, let's go. You can teach me tomorrow."

We leave the bicycles in the shed where we found them. As we make a run for the house, Ben grabs me by the waist and lifts me up, spinning us as the rain falls. Laughing, we play in the rain, chasing each other, rolling on wet grass, being silly.

So this is what being in love feels like. I can see why people think love is like a drug. You can't get enough of it. You need more.

When we are cold to the bone, Ben takes my hand in his and walks me back to the house. Our feet are making squashing sounds on the wet grass, and I probably look like a drowned rat, but I don't care. I'm with him.

"Hey, I have an idea." Lifting my hand, he plants a kiss on it.

"Yes?"

"So that the day isn't completely wasted because of the rain, maybe you could ride something else…" He grins at me as his maple brown eyes let me know exactly what he means.

"Um…yes. Maybe."

"Christ, why the fuck are we still here and not in bed already?"

"Not sure?" I laugh. I can't really help myself around him. He makes me so damn happy.

"I fucking love you, you know that? You stole my heart."

"Yes? Well, do you want it back?"

"Fuck no!"

"Let's get out of here then."

"How the hell did I get so lucky?" he asks huskily.

"Well, if you keep talking you won't be getting lucky," I tease him.

Immediately, Ben lifts me up, throwing me over his shoulder as he starts to run towards the mansion. Once in the room, I proceed to show Ben that I may not know how to ride a bike, but I do know how to ride…

Him.

12

present

"Don't do that, Dimples. It's turning me on."

Dropping the pencil I was chewing not a minute ago, I look up from my seat behind the desk. Ah, Arsen. The tips of his blond hair still look damp from his shower. He's wearing a crisp white shirt with no tie and an unbuttoned black suit jacket. As I look at Arsen and the way his clothes fit so effortlessly, I think he should be the poster boy for careless elegance. When I let my eyes roam over his body, I cannot picture my perfect Ben showing up to work dressed like this; he's always clothed impeccably. However, Arsen makes it work.

He really does.

To hide my smile, I bend under the table to retrieve my pencil and hear him mutter something that I can't quite catch. It makes me smile bigger. Some people would call what we're doing flirting, but Arsen flirts with everyone and his off color jokes are really one of the highlights of my day.

Once I sit back in my seat, his eyes soften when they land on my face.

"How are you feeling, Dimples? Baby kicking yet?" Arsen asks as he half sits on the corner of my desk that's closest to him, blue sincerity sparkling through his eyes.

With my first trimester almost over, my barely there bump has begun to show a little. Really, if you weren't paying close attention you wouldn't be able to see it, but I can, and what's even better is that I can feel it.

I love it.

I touch my belly for a moment and feel my smile grow wider as I remember Ben's words this morning while we were in bed.

Kiss, kiss, kiss.

As I lie on my back pretending to be asleep, I feel Ben spreading soft kisses on my belly. I smile and open my eyes to observe my husband as he admires the small bump growing in me. Tingly and warm fuzzy feelings crowd my heart. There's so much love in those eyes of his. So much hope.

I watch him as he gently lowers his hand to touch it. "Hello there, little princess. This is your daddy wishing his beautiful girls a good morning." His voice is husky from sleep and deep emotion.

"How do you know it's a girl? What if he's a boy? Will you be disappointed?" I move my free hand to cover his.

"Hmm. Good question. I don't know why I think she's a girl. I just do. Maybe I want to be surrounded by beautiful girls for the rest of my life." He grins and moves to lie down next to me, kissing my shoulder as he pulls me within his embrace. "But I would never be disappointed if the baby is a boy because it's part of you, part of me. It's our baby. Your gift to me."

"I'm feeling great, thank you for asking, and it's still too early to feel the baby kick. According to Dr. Pajaree, I won't feel the baby move until I'm close to eighteen weeks." I take a deep breath as I try to bury the panic and fear I feel every time I think about how close we are to the end of the first trimester. "I'm only ten weeks, so I still have a ways to go." The light mood is gone, replaced by a gloomy silence. I don't want to smile and tease Arsen anymore. I actually don't want to talk to anyone.

I hate this fear.

This uncertainty.

I look away and stare at the computer screen. "Uh, Arsen, I think you should go back to your cubicle. The day just started, and we have a lot of work to do. Amy needs to go over some paperwork with me before she leaves on her trip next week. Would you mind getting back to work?" I say, rudely dismissing him.

I don't bother to look in his direction, so I assume that he has already left when he startles me by sitting on his hunches next to my seat. Spinning my chair to face him, he puts his hands on the armrests, blocking my exit.

"Hey, hey. Catherine. Here, look at me. Talk to me."

I shake my head and stare down at my lap. "Arsen, please. Leave. I don't want to talk to you, okay?"

"No, it's not fucking okay. Something is obviously bothering you. I want to know what it is so I can help. Want me to call Amy?" He pauses for a moment while he considers his next word carefully. "Ben?"

"No. It's nothing, and I am fine. Please, just get your work done."

He seems to accept my answer, and I'm about to breathe a sigh of relief thinking that he's given up.

"No. I know you. I won't leave this place until you tell me what's the matter."

Looking up, I notice the stubborn expression in his face. It reminds me of a determined young boy trying to build his first tower of Legos. I lower my gaze to my lap once more to avoid staring at him.

"Just back off, okay?" My voice is desperate now. I'm trying to hold back the angry tears I feel growing at the back of my throat. I don't know if it's the hormones, or if I've just lost my mind. At times I can be so happy, then something triggers a memory of my past miscarriages to resurface, and I'm enveloped in darkness once more. Anger is always there, waiting to bring me down with heavy chains of fear.

"Look at me, Catherine. Please look at me—"

"Good morning! Oh, Arsen…I didn't see you there. Cathy?" Arsen and I turn to face Amy at the same time. She's standing there, holding two cups of Starbucks coffee in her hands. The odd expression in her face lets me know that whatever was going on between Arsen and me must look worse than it actually is. I disregard Arsen, push his hands off the armrests, and stand.

After I've made my way around the desk, I grab the coffee that Amy brought for me and guide her towards her office. She shoots me a look loaded with questions, but I ignore them. I don't want to talk about it.

It's not what she thinks.

As we are about to cross the threshold of her office, I hear a frustrated groan escape Arsen. I turn around and watch him stand up, shaking the dust off his clothes and straightening his pants. When our eyes meet, I don't know if I see compassion in his eyes or sympathy, but it makes me feel like shit for treating him so badly. Quickly, I tell Amy to go ahead because I forgot to get something from my desk. Halfway there, Arsen makes his way to stand in front of me.

"I'm sorry, you didn't deserve that," I say.

"This isn't over, Dimples. I'm taking you out for lunch, and you're going to tell me what the fuck is going on with you. One moment you're happy, smiling and looking so damn pretty. The next, we talk about your baby and you're gone, replaced by a bitch, and I don't like it. You're going to tell me what is the matter. I thought that was our deal, you talk, I listen, no bullshit. And I won't take no for an answer, so don't even think about it."

His eyes…

The way they are looking at me now makes me want to tell him all my fears. They make me believe that he can be a friend who will listen to me and not tell me that everything will be fine. That he'll understand what it's like to have such consuming fear that it will destroy you; what I can't share with Ben. I feel my heartbeat speed up as I nod.

I'll take a chance on Arsen.

"It's the baby…I'm so scared. The date is coming up, a-and what if something happens again?" I whisper.

"Fucking hell. We gotta talk about this. Meet me for lunch?" he asks as he rubs my arms tenderly.

"I can't. I'm meeting Ben for lunch, but we could talk after work?"

"Tell him you're busy. Say that a lunch meeting came up."

"I don't think—"

"Dimples, it's just lunch. It won't kill him to eat on his own."

"No, no, no. It's not that. I just don't feel comfortable lying to him."

I don't. I have never lied to him.

"Then forget it," he says as he begins to walk away from me.

As I watch Arsen leave, I realize that I don't want him to. I want to talk to him. I need to talk to him. He's the only person I can do that with.

"Wait!"

Arsen turns around. "Yes, Dimples?"

"I'll call Ben…"

"So we have a date?" A slow grin appears on his face, blinding me with his beauty.

"Not a date. Lunch," I clarify.

"Fucking awesome. I have the best place to take you to."

"Nowhere fancy, please. I-I just want to talk…"

"No worries, beautiful. I can eat for the two of us." A winsome smile appears on his face, making him appear so much younger than he is.

"Whatever. Get your ass to work now. Or I will tell your father that you flirt with the interns and old married ladies like me."

He pins me down with blue liquid fire again. "They love it. And so do you, but watch it. Smiling at me like that may give you more wrinkles than you already have."

"Asshole."

"Only for you, Dimples," he says, grinning.

Inside Amy's office, I close the door behind me and watch her going over some paperwork. It's not until I make my way to her desk that I realize that I'm still smiling.

When Amy looks up from her seat, she watches me as I sit in one of the free chairs facing her desk.

I smile at her. "Good morning, dear. Thank you for the coffee."

After a pause, Amy decides to go for the kill. "Cathy, what is going on between you and Arsen? I hope I didn't walk in on anything that I would so do with that boy. You know, because I'm not married and you are…" She lets the last words hang in the air.

As if I didn't know that.

As if I would cheat on Ben.

"Seriously, Amy? You really think I would do something like that? Cheat on my husband, a husband who I love? Arsen and I are only friends. And he's younger than me on top of everything. Besides, you forget that he's been dating that actress from that t.v. show. Melissa something."

Amy listens to me while considering her answer. "I know you wouldn't. At least, I hope you wouldn't. Ben adores you. It's just that…I don't know. The way Arsen was looking at you made me feel very uncomfortable. He was looking at you as if…well, I'm not sure, but let me tell you something. It did not look friendly at all. And he is not that young, Cathy. He is twenty five."

"Twenty four," I interrupt her.

She shoots me a questioning glance. "Whatever. He could be eighteen and still be very dangerous. He's just so fuckable and gorgeous. An excellent combination to find in a man when you're single. Listen, Cathy, I don't want to sound accusatory or anything. Just be careful with him, okay? I've been there and done that. It always starts as a fun way to pass the time, light banter, innocent flirting…until it is *not*."

I'm about to protest when Amy lifts a staying hand, not letting me continue. "No, Cathy. It's not my business, so you don't have to explain yourself to me. I'm your friend, and because of that I'm warning you…just in case."

As much as I want to disregard her words as nonsense and throw them back in her face, I know she's not totally unfounded. Remembering the restaurant incident, I can't deny she's somehow right. It happened, but it's all in the past. Arsen hasn't made a move on me since he told me he wouldn't. And he flirts and teases every woman in the office.

No, she's wrong.

"I know I don't owe you any explanations, but I don't want you to think badly of him either. He's a good guy. What you saw earlier in the morning was Arsen trying to comfort me, to get me to talk to him." I twist my fingers. "He was asking me about the baby, and something he said, or maybe I said it, but it made me realize how close I am to the end of my first trimester. A-And it always happens right around this time. Talking about it with Arsen brought on one of my dark moods. He was just trying to figure out what happened."

As the words leave my mouth, I know they are true. Nothing more than a concerned friend comforting another friend.

"Oh, Cathy! I'm such a cow. I'm sorry. I didn't think about it. I just saw Arsen practically caging you in your seat looking at you with such intensity that I jumped to conclusions." She stands up, makes her way to my seat, and hugs me.

"It's okay, you silly woman. I knew you wouldn't be able to hold your tongue. It was a matter of time. And I wouldn't explain myself to you if I had something to hide. Besides, Arsen doesn't deserve your suspicions. He's a good guy."

Amy lets go and moves to sit next to me. She reaches over our seats to hold my hand in hers. "I know he's a good guy. He's actually quite sweet, but I just don't trust him. Sometimes, when he thinks no one is watching him I notice the way he looks at you."

"What do you mean? He doesn't look at me any differently that he looks at you," I say.

She grows quiet before speaking once more. "You know what? Forget I said anything…I must be imagining things."

"But."

"But nothing. Enough about him. I'm sure it's all in my imagination. Tell me, love, how are you feeling? I bet Ben is over the moon!"

With one of my hands in hers, I cover my stomach with my free hand, tenderly stroking the small piece of heaven inside me. "We're okay. Ben is, as always, the rock I need to lean on when the going gets rough. I mean, so far this pregnancy has been super easy, but there are times when this choking fear that I will lose the baby paralyzes me. And it comes out of nowhere most of the time.

"Amy, sometimes, I get these panic attacks and I cry. I can't stop crying. I'm so afraid, but Ben is always there to clean my tears, hold me in his arms and tell me everything is going to be okay. I couldn't ask for a more perfect husband. I don't know what I would do without him. I love him so much." My chest tightens at the thought of his support. How can someone be worthy of such a man as my husband? I don't think I will ever be.

"I'm glad you have Ben, babe. I'm glad you're at a better place in your marriage."

Amy is silent for a moment. "Cathy, I don't want to be negative, and I know what Dr. Pajaree has told you, but have you, um, considered what will happen if you, um, have another miscarriage?"

I have. It would destroy me.

Completely.

"Yes. We'll be okay. Dr. Pajaree told us not to think about baby names yet, so in a way I'm kind of prepared if it happens again," I lie.

I'm not prepared for it to happen a fourth time.

I am not.

It would be the end.

While I wait for Arsen to finish up with work, I give Ben a quick call. To be honest, I waited until the last minute because I wasn't sure whether I was going to go through with it. I know it's just lunch, but lying to Ben about Arsen makes me uncomfortable. It's like I'm hiding something from him, which I'm not. But the nagging feeling is there.

After one ringtone, Ben answers.

"Babe."

I swallow hard as I rub my free hand on my black skirt, wiping the sweat away. "Ben, baby, I-I have to cancel lunch today. Amy said that Bruno wants to have a lunch meeting with the two of us."

"That's perfect. I was about to give you a call to let you know that I wasn't going to make it. Micky needs me to go over some files with him. Raincheck, wife?"

"Oh, yes. That's great. I don't feel so bad anymore." And I don't. "I thought you were going to get stuck eating by yourself."

"I planned on having my wife for lunch, but…"

"Ben!" I exclaim.

Ben chuckles. "It's alright, babe. Kerry is bringing us lunch."

"Is she the new intern you always talk about?" I ask.

I'm curious because about two weeks ago when I met Ben at his office, I saw a beautiful auburn haired girl talking to him, and the way she was looking at him implied deep admiration. I kind of got the feeling that she had a crush on him.

"Yes. Graduated from Columbia Law as well. I like her. She's a nice girl and learns fast. Anyway, how about I take you to our Thai place for dinner to make it up to you?"

"Sure."

"Oh, before I forget. I heard from Julian."

"That's lovely! How is he doing? Is LA treating him well?"

"He told me he met someone and—"

"Are you ready to go?" I hear Arsen ask.

I look up from my desk to see Arsen standing in front of me without his suit jacket, the sleeves of his white shirt rolled up at the elbows. His blond hair, a mess, is pointing in all directions. It looks like he's been tugging it.

"Who is that?" Ben asks on the other line.

"Oh, that's Arsen, Bruno's son. He's here to let me know that the meeting is about to begin. I-I've got to go." The lie rolls off my tongue.

"I've got to go as well. I'll see you later."

"Wait!" I say, stopping Ben from hanging up. I turn to look at Arsen as he slowly lifts the frame with my wedding picture in it and holds it in his hand, an indecipherable air surrounding him as he examines the picture.

"Yes?" Ben asks.

I want to tell him that there's no lunch meeting, but I don't. "I love you."

"I love you too, babe. Always."

After I hang up, I watch Arsen tracing the photograph with his thumb.

"Please tell me this isn't your husband. You're too beautiful for him," Arsen says as he puts the picture back on my desk.

Dismissing his commentary as a joke, I ask, "So where are you taking me?"

"It's a surprise. I told Amy that we need the whole afternoon off, though."

"What? No! I have so much work to do."

"It's fine. I kinda told her you had an appointment with your doctor and that I was going to take you there."

"Arsen! Those are more lies!"

"Chill. It'll be fun. It's just one afternoon. It won't kill anyone."

"What am I going to tell Ben?"

"He doesn't have to know. And what the fuck? I'm just taking you out to eat. You can go home after we're done. No harm done."

"Yes, I guess you're right."

And really, what's the harm in it?

13

"Your apartment is empty, Arsen. Do you ever do anything else other than sleep in here?" I say as I sit down in his black leather couch.

At first, when I found out he was bringing me back to his place, I was uncomfortable with the idea. But upon closer examination, I didn't think this

was any different from spending time with him alone in his apartment than in my office after everyone had already left for the day while we worked on projects. And it wasn't like he was some random stranger. He was Arsen. My friend. And I needed to talk to him before this fear made me lose my mind completely.

"Nah, no point." Since he has forbidden me to go to the kitchen with him and watch him cook, I wait in his living room. He wants it to be a surprise.

"Hey, are you still seeing Melissa Stewart?"

He laughs. "Yes and no. We're fucking, but I'm not sure about how serious she is, though. I kinda get the feeling that she's cheating on me."

"Arsen, you're cheating on her too. I saw that beautiful brunette come and meet you after work yesterday." Seriously. I think I've seen more girls parade through our lobby since Arsen began working there than ever before.

"Melissa can be cool sometimes. She knows she's gorgeous and," he opens the oven door and inserts the surprise meal, "In all honesty, she could probably do much better than me."

"I don't think so," I say, offended for Arsen. "I think you could be a great catch if you decided to settle on someone."

Quiet for a second, Arsen grabs a bottled water and a beer, then makes his way to the couch. After handing me the drink, he watches me carefully. "I was serious about someone a long time ago. It didn't work out."

"Really?"

"Yes. Her name was Jessica. I thought she was the love of my life."

"What happened?"

"Real life happened," Arsen shrugs, taking a swig of his beer.

"What do you mean?" I ask as I play with the cool plastic in my hands.

"She died." A shadow crosses his eyes, and for a moment he looks lost and sad. I don't think I've ever seen him like that.

"I'm so sorry…"

"It's cool. Let's not talk about it anymore, okay?" he asks dismissively.

"Okay."

"So, tell me, what was that back at the office? You seriously threw some crazy mixed signals. One moment you were laughing and talking about the baby, and the next you turned into this cold person. Not my Dimples."

I want to say that I'm not his Dimples, but I let it go.

"It's just…the first trimester is almost over, and that's when bad things happen." I open the bottle and take a small sip of water. "It's just too much. Sometimes I get these panic attacks. That's what you saw today."

"Jesus." Arsen puts the beer bottle on his coffee table and sits next to me. "Listen, Dimples…I've been through hell and back. I know what it's like to lose what you love the most, but life goes on, and you must not lose hope, you know? Without hope, living can become a fucking nightmare. So, be positive that this pregnancy will work out. And if it doesn't, well, maybe it wasn't supposed to be."

"What are you trying to say? That I'm not meant to be a mother?" I ask hurt.

"Fuck, no. You deserve the same kind of happiness as every woman. But what I'm trying to say is that life has a way to sort itself out. Just have faith."

Sighing, I rest my head on his shoulder. Suddenly I'm so tired. "It's more easily said than done, Arsen. It's just so hard. And…I'm not—"

"Yes?" Arsen prompts me.

"I'm not sure my marriage can handle anything going wrong. It's been very tough on us. I can't talk to Ben about it because he just dismisses it and," I pause when I feel his arm wrap around my own shoulders, "sometimes it's just hard."

Arsen leans down and rests his head on top of mine. I want to move away, but I'm too tired and I like his warmth. It's comforting.

"Go on. I'm listening."

I sigh. "It's been better between us, don't get me wrong, but I'm just worried about the baby. It's overwhelming not being able to be at peace. To be constantly worrying." I rub my hands on my skirt. "I have nightmares that I lose the baby and I wake up crying in the middle of the night."

"Ben doesn't wake up?" Arsen sounds angry.

"No. I mean, he could, but I usually just go to the bathroom and shut myself inside until I've calmed down."

"Fuck, Catherine, that's bullshit. You should tell Ben. You shouldn't suffer in silence like that. It can't be good for the baby or you."

"No, it's okay. And I would rather not bother Ben. I've tried talking to him before, but he thinks I'm being too negative, so I just don't talk to him about it anymore."

"That's fucking stupid."

"Hey, don't be angry. I'm seriously okay. Besides, it's my fault if Ben doesn't know what's going on with me. I don't tell him anything. I've learned to hide it."

"I don't give a shit about that. I'm just your co-worker, your friend, and I knew something was up. He's your husband. He should be able to tell."

"No. Please, stop that. Ben is perfect, he's the best husband a woman could ask for."

Arsen laughs bitterly. "If he's so fucking perfect, how come you're talking to me and not him?"

I don't like where this is going. Arsen shouldn't blame Ben about my issues at all. They are mine. Ben has no fault in this mess.

"I-I think I should go." I begin to move away from him, but Arsen stops me, grabbing me by the elbow.

"Hey…sorry. Don't go. I didn't mean to upset you. I'm sorry if I got carried away."

We stare at each other for a moment.

"Stay." He lets go of my elbow and grabs my hand, intertwining our fingers. "I promise I won't say anything about your perfect husband anymore."

I'm still debating when Arsen lifts our hands and plants a kiss on mine. "Please, I'll behave. No more Ben bashing." A smirk appears on his lips.

"Okay. But please don't talk about Ben like that. I don't like it. He's not to blame at all."

"Boy Scout promise. I'm here for you, Dimples," he says as he caresses my cheek softly with his free hand.

I can't help laughing. "Are you sure of that? We're already fighting, and this is our first heart to heart."

"Nah. I like feisty. And your eyes look like nothing I've ever seen when you're angry. They are so beautiful."

"Thank you," I say as we smile at each other. I can feel heat radiating my face.

Arsen gazes at me quietly. "I fucking love that I can do this to you." He softly touches the crest of my right cheek, "Ben is so damn lucky."

"I—"

The timer of his stove goes off alerting us that whatever he's preparing is done cooking, and breaking the intensity and intimate moment we're sharing. I can't say that I'm not glad.

Without letting go of my face, Arsen shakes his head and smiles ruefully at me. "Guess it's time to eat. Ready to be blown away by my culinary skills?"

"I'm starving. At this point, cardboard sounds pretty appetizing," I say, grinning.

Arsen grins back. "Nah, I can do better than that."

And just like that, Arsen is back to his usual self.

After he lets go of my hand, he makes his way to the kitchen.

"I hope you're not allergic to Nutella," he says, opening and shutting drawers and shelves.

"Nope. I'm not allergic to anything," I answer as I make my way to the counter that serves as a table and sit down on a high stool.

Arsen places a handmade flat pizza covered in Nutella and slices of banana. It looks and smells delicious. "My specialty."

"Oh my God. Arsen, this smells so good!" I inhale the sweet aroma of baked bananas and hazelnut.

When I'm finished eating three slices of the delicious pizza, I notice that Arsen hasn't touched his. "What's the matter? You haven't touched your food."

He's staring at me with that funny look of his that raises the small hair on my back. "I'm just watching you eat."

"Um, sorry. I'm starving, and it tastes so good."

Arsen smiles playfully. "Not as good as you do, I'm sure."

He pushes his plate to the side, moves forward, and lightly strokes my cheek.

"Maybe I should try," he states simply.

Suddenly, none of this seems friendly. Being alone with him, the flirty banter, his touch…it feels like we're hanging on by a very thin thread of what's allowed and innocent, and what's not.

With an uneasy feeling in the pit of my stomach, I move away from him and stand. "Um, this has been great, but I've got to go home." I make my way to his living room where my coat and handbag are. "Thank you so much for having me over and listening to me. You have no idea how good it has made me feel."

"Dimples…" He puts his arms on my shoulders, turning me to face him. "I was just teasing. Don't be scared of me."

"Um…I-I'm not."

I lie because what just happened there freaked the hell out of me.

"Cool. So I guess I'll see you tomorrow at work," he says as he lets go of my shoulders.

After saying goodbye to Arsen, I make my way home. Taking my cellphone out, I notice it's almost six in the evening. I can't believe I was in his apartment for almost five hours and didn't think once to check the time. Ben hasn't called which means he's probably still busy with work.

As I ride the train home, I decide not to tell Ben about my day if he doesn't ask me for specifics. I don't want to lie to him again, yet somehow, for the first time since I've met Arsen, I feel like I've done something wrong.

But how can that be?

We're just friends, right?

14

Walking towards the exit of the building, I give Ben a call to let him know that I'm on my way to the bar to meet Arsen for drinks, even though I won't be drinking any alcohol. I stayed behind because I needed to get in touch with Beth, Mr. Radcliff's personal assistant in England.

"I can wait for you. I have to make some phone calls myself. Melissa left me a voicemail telling me she needs me to fly to Paris next weekend with her. Apparently it's her movie premiere, and she needs me there holding her fucking hand like a kid while she ignores me for the photogs." He throws his body on the couch, laying flat on his back. His white shirt is now partly unbuttoned, revealing a glimpse of his muscular chest and the outline of his butterfly tattoo.

"That's incredible! I can't believe you didn't know. Her movie has been all over magazines and gossip blogs. You know this is a really big deal, right? People would kill to be there."

"Well, I'm so damn over her. I don't know what I was thinking when I got involved with an actress. They are full of shit and drama. The sex is

fucking amazing, and she is hot as hell, but I can get that anywhere else. Now, a model may be—"

"Stop! Stop, Arsen," I laugh. "Too much information. Just last week you said you were trying."

"Fuck, I did. Didn't I?" he says, groaning.

"Yep."

"It isn't working anymore."

I grab a pencil and twirl it in my fingers. "Well, whatever you do about Melissa, please don't do it here. I really need to get in touch with Beth. Why don't you head over to the bar without me? You can talk to her on your way there."

Groaning, Arsen gets up from the couch. "Fine. But I would much rather watch you make phone calls than deal with a prima donna. And that's saying a lot."

"Go!"

Grudgingly he leaves.

Silly boy.

After the uncomfortable incident in his apartment two days ago, I was worried that things were going to be different between us, but I'm glad they haven't changed. The next day, Arsen showed up as if nothing happened and continued to be his usual flirty self. It's great having a friend that you can tell all your secrets without feeling guilty about them. Besides Amy, he's the only other person who knows how scared I am with the pregnancy.

I stop at the front desk of the building to say good night to Carlos and Frank, the security guards on duty.

"Good evening, gentlemen," I say.

"Good evening, Mrs. Stanwood," Carlos says in a heavy Spanish accent.

"You look lovely as always, Missus. How is Mr. Stanwood? On your way to meet him for dinner?" Frank asks. Sometimes I find Ben shooting the breeze with Frank down in the lobby when he comes to pick me up. I think they bonded over their love for the New York Mets, or something.

I smile when I see the expectant look in Frank's eyes. "Not tonight. I'm going to meet Mr. Radcliff's son for drinks. I'm hoping that Ben will join me there."

Once I say my goodbyes to the two men, I walk out into the street and immediately get hit with hot and humid air. The kind that makes you break into a sweat without moving a muscle. A typical Manhattan summer night. With my skin feeling clammy with the heat, I decide to take a cab instead of walking to the bar. After getting one and giving the driver the name and address of the bar, I can finally call Ben.

After one ring, I hear my husband's deep voice on the other line, "Hello wife. I was just about to call you."

"Hi, babe. I'm sorry to call you so late, but I just left the office. I'm heading to meet Arsen for drinks. Are you working late tonight? I think you should to meet me there so I can finally introduce you to Arsen. We can have a drink and then head over to our favorite Thai place for dinner?"

Ben chuckles. "Babe, anything else?"

I smile into the receiver, tightening my grip on my phone. "I'm doing it again, huh? Sorry. I can't shut down Bossy Cathy so soon after work."

"Don't apologize. I'm teasing you, my sweet darling. I love Bossy Cathy. She and I have a fine relationship. I particularly recall this one morning while the two of us were in the shower and she proceeded to tell me what kind of pressure and speed she liked best in her shower head."

Oh my God. I do remember that. How could I forget? I can still see Ben's wet dark form kneeling down on the floor with one of my legs wrapped around his shoulder as he pulled my ass closer to him and…

"I'll be there around eight. I have one more conference, and then I'll meet your famous protégé."

Swallowing hard, I protest. "He's not my protégé! And that's perfect. I can't wait to see you."

"Yes. I've missed you too. How are you feeling?"

"Great, baby. Today was a good day."

"Perfect. I have some plans of my own for us."

"Really? May ask what kind of plans, Mr. Stanwood? Will I like them?" I say flirtatiously.

"You really want to know?" he growls back.

"Yes, I'm dying to know. Maybe it's not that interesting." I know I'm teasing him, and he loves it. It gets us both hot and bothered.

"I want to throw you on the bed face down, rip your panties off, and fuck you with my fingers until you are begging me to fuck you with my dick. Then I'll climb on top of you and kiss you from the nape of your neck down your spine, licking away the sweat of your skin until my tongue tastes what's mine. Only mine," he says roughly.

"Oh. Is that i-it?" I stutter back. Desire gathers between my legs as my nipples harden.

A satisfied Ben chuckles once more. "Yes. That's it. Anyway, babe, Kerry just walked in to let me know it's time for my next conference. Text me the address and name of the bar. Expect me to be there around eight." His voice is businesslike now.

"O-okay." I obviously can't think straight yet.

"Babe?"

"Yes?"

"Tonight," he growls.

Still thinking about Ben, I wait in line to use the bathroom before making my way back to the bar to meet Arsen. Taking my cell phone out, I check for messages to pass the time.

I have two messages. One is from Ben telling me other sorts of naughty things he'd like to do to me tonight, and the second one is from Arsen asking me where I am. I smile and decide not to reply to any of them and put my phone back in my Ferragamo leather bag. Leaning against the wall, I listen to the conversation between the two girls in front of me.

"I cannot believe he blew Brooke off like that! I mean, she is way hotter than Melissa Stewart!"

"Duh! Brooke is a nobody! Melissa is a freaking actress and perfect to boot! But oh my God! Did you see how gorgeous he is? Pictures don't do him any justice!"

"Melissa may be an actress or whatever, but no one ever says no to Brooke. She is pissed! She told me she was going to call Stalker Magazine and snitch on Arsen's whereabouts saying that Melissa is here with him."

"Get out! That's so messed up! We can't let her do that! But what did she expect? I read an article in Vogue about him and his family. The reporter specifically noted that Arsen never dates regular girls, and even said that almost every girl that he's been involved with has been on the cover of a magazine. I wonder if he's actually waiting for Melissa or some other famous person to show up?"

"I'm not sure. Brooke said that Arsen told her he was expecting a friend. Oh my gosh! Do you think it can be one of his trust fund friends? They are all hot! If I can't get Arsen, I will totally sleep with one of them!"

"Shut up, Ally. You'll never sleep with Arsen. None of us ever will. Though, I gotta say that I don't even need to speak to him. He looks like a douche, but I would totally do him. I've heard he's huuuuge."

Appalled, I step away. I can't stand there and listen to them objectify Arsen as if he is just a fuck toy. He is so much more than that.

In the months that we've known each other, I've come to see a sweet, fun, and naughty side of him that I'm pretty sure not many people know. He always brings me cupcakes because he knows I love them, he flirts with pretty and plain girls alike, and most importantly, he's trying really hard to prove his father wrong.

I'm so angry; my body is shaking. I'm halfway to the bar when I see Arsen sitting on a leather couch. He looks his usual casual and relaxed handsome self, but the way his eyes keep traveling around the room, not making eye contact with the bunch of vultures staring at him, and the way he's clenching his jaw lets me know he is uncomfortable with the attention he's attracting. I watch as another drop dead gorgeous woman makes her way towards him only to be rebuffed. That's it. That's the last straw for me. Angry at every single woman in this room for making Arsen feel hunted, I turn around and make my way back to those airheads in the bathroom line.

I'm ready to battle stupidity and big boobs.

I tap the redhead on the shoulder. When she turns around she looks down her nose at me with an empty look on her pretty face. "Yes?"

Oh, I'm so going to wipe the pretty off that whore's face.

Trying to control my temper, I take a deep breath and slowly exhale it as I pull my blonde waves behind an ear. Well, here goes nothing. "I couldn't help but overhear you talking about Arsen Radcliff. I was going to let it go since you seem quite young and immature, but I can't. So I'm going to give you a piece of information. Arsen is a real person with real feelings. Just because magazines and gossip columnists are infatuated with him, doesn't make it all right for you guys to harass him in person. It's not okay." I put my hands on my hips, "And, if your friend Brooke calls a magazine, I'll call the cops and say that you offered to sleep with him for money. Yes, like an escort."

The girls' eyes get as big as saucers. I love it.

"Oh, and by the way, he's here with me. Now, back off girls." As the last words exit my mouth, a crazy idea fills my head with excitement. I know what will shut them up once and for all.

Turning around, I make my way towards Arsen. If my body was shaking because of anger before, now it's shaking with excitement. I'm not sure I can go through with my plan. When Arsen sees me walking towards him, a magnifying smile appears on his lips. How can a guy manage to look so damn sexy and sweet at the same time?

Yes. He is more than a playboy. He is my friend.

I speed up the pace, trying to get to him before my conscience changes my mind. I can feel the eyes of the girls on my back as awareness vibrates through my body like a low grade earthquake.

When I'm standing in front of him, he runs a hand over his blond hair, making a loose strand fall on his forehead. "Hey, Dimples. I thought you ditched me," he says, leaning down to kiss me on the cheek. I close my eyes, and pray that Ben never finds out about this because he'll kill me.

I'm doing this for a friend.

My mind made up, I open my eyes. Quickly, before Arsen realizes what I'm about to do, I move my face so his kiss lands on my lips.

Soft lips against soft lips.

Heat.

Heart beating wildly.

It feels natural.

Stunned, Arsen's eyes widen in shock. I don't think a peck on the lips is enough to shut those girls up, so as I sense Arsen getting ready to push me away, I move my hand to the back of his neck and pull him closer towards me. With our lips glued to one another, I try to mutter, "Tilt your head to the side. For goodness sake, pretend that you are enjoying this!"

With my hands on his shoulders and standing on my tiptoes, I maneuver Arsen's body in a direction so I can see if the girls are still watching us. They are. With mouths hanging wide open.

Take that, bitches.

Once the girls leave, I push him away. Maybe more forcefully than is needed. Arsen, who is breathing heavily, looks seriously angry. Like he wants my head on a platter.

He brings the heel of his palm to rub his lips as if he were cleansing them from my kiss. I'm not bothered by it, really. I still can't believe I just kissed him.

The jokes that life can play at you.

"What the fuck was that for? You better have a good fucking reason for that kiss becau—"

Pissed off at him because I was trying to help and I'm getting shit for it, I smack him on the shoulder.

"You're such an asshole! I kissed you because I was trying to make a point to a pair of groupies of yours."

"What? Groupies? What the fuck are you talking about?" A scowl settles on his brow. Crossing his arms over his chest, you can see the outline of his muscles through his white shirt.

Frustrated, I stamp my foot. "Are you even listening to me? I kissed you because some girls were talking shit about you. About how much they wanted to sleep with you, and pretty much how that's all you're good for."

Slowly a smirk appears, replacing the angry look on his face. "But why kiss me?"

I groan. "Because I was trying to make a point!"

I watch as Arsen, tentatively at first, lifts his hand, bringing it close to my face. When he's sure that I won't protest to his touch, a confident Arsen stares back at me. Transfixed, I think he's going to touch my cheek, but instead he pulls a strand of my blonde hair that had been stuck on my lipgloss behind my ear. His pinky finger touches the skin of my neck, sending a shiver running down my spine as aqua-blue fire burns me to the ground.

"I fucking *love* when you make points." The smirk turns into a heart stopping smile.

An Arsen smile.

A smile that snaps me out of my Arsen daze.

Suddenly I feel like I need to put some space between us, so I move to sit down on the couch. Arsen follows my lead and sits next to me. Too near. His thigh is touching mine, and I can feel the warmth radiating off his body. With one of his arms spread along the couch behind my back, I feel him everywhere. He's everywhere.

It feels comfortable.

It feels organic.

But should it?

I'm not sure.

"In the moment, I thought the kiss would teach them a lesson. Not sure why." Turning to face him, I smile deviously at him. "Maybe I just wanted to shut them up. I shouldn't have, though. If Ben ever kissed someone else, I would kill him, but it's okay. I wouldn't call that a kiss. The way you reacted, it was more like kissing a dead fish."

"Are you fucking kidding me? My very married friend had her damn lips on my mouth…fuck. Give me another chance and I'll show you how much of a dead fish I'm not, Dimples. "

"Are you serious? Whatever." I shake my head disapprovingly. "You digress. You need to get your act together, kiddo."

"Wait, what? What are you taking about? And, Dimples, kids don't fuck like I do."

"You really need to stop cursing so much. I'm talking about the fact that I had to excuse your slutty behavior to that pair of nitwits and as I was doing it I realized it's no one's fault but yours! If you don't enjoy being objectified, stop airing your dirty laundry for the whole world to see."

Flashing a roguish smile, he removes his arm from behind me and sits up straighter.

"And stop grinning like an idiot. I'm trying to be serious here. I know your game. I can tell it bothers you when people only want to know the fake you. You know, the playboy, the womanizer, the rich boy; instead of trying to get to know the real you. So stop acting like an asshole and start acting like an adult. Prove people wrong, that you're not just some kind of loser living off his daddy's money. Show them the real Arsen. The one I know. The one who understands the company better than his own dad. The one who takes time to bring a pregnant lady cupcakes because she likes them. The one who never ignores the plain girls. Then maybe people will stop publishing all that trash about you, and I won't have to excuse you to strangers and kiss you in front of them to make a point!"

The smile gone, Arsen glides himself closer to me if that's even possible, and takes my hand in his. The gesture is not sexual, yet it feels intimate. The heat of his palm imprints itself onto my skin.

"Fuck, Catherine. Is that why? You did that for me?" His voice is raspy.

"Yes, of course. You're my friend."

Silently, he watches me with eyes that shine so bright they look feverish.

Does he always watch people with such intensity?

After a moment, he murmurs, "Like I said before, Ben is a fucking lucky guy."

I ignore his comment and ask him, "Arsen, I know it bothers you. Why not do something about it?"

Without letting go of my hand, he lifts his shoulder in a careless manner.

"I—"

"Hi. I'm sorry to be so late."

Looking up from my place on the couch, I see Ben standing in front of us in all his tall and dark glory. When I'm about to greet him, I notice the hard expression on his face, a frown settling on his brow. His eyes aren't devouring my face, and his lips aren't smiling back at me as usual. No. Instead he seems to be intensely studying my lap. Odd. Lowering my gaze I see what's caught his attention.

Arsen's hand covering mine.

All of a sudden, what felt like a harmless gesture between friends not a moment ago now seems immoral.

Improper.

Offensive.

I try to come up with an innocuous excuse to let go of Arsen's hand without simultaneously hurting his feeling and appearing guilty to Ben.

"Baby! You're here," I say as I stand up to greet him, removing my hand from under Arsen's as naturally as possible. Walking up to Ben, I stand on my tip toes to hug him hello. Before I know it, the muscles of his arms are around my small frame, tightly embracing me and lifting me off the floor as he kisses me possessively. Claiming me. Still suspended in the air and in his strong hold, I lift my gaze to meet his after the kiss ends. He isn't watching me. He is looking past my shoulders. He is staring straight at Arsen.

I know it.

Without bothering to turn around and have my suspicions confirmed, I place both my hands on either side of his face and guide him back to look at me. When his warm brown eyes are boring deeply into mine, I finally smile.

"Hi."

"Hi." The scowl begins to recede, and his eyes immediately soften.

"You finally came. I was beginning to worry that you weren't going to show up."

Liar.

My stomach tightens with guilt as I realize I had forgotten he was supposed to meet me here.

At last, when he slowly and intimately slides me down the front of his body, a smile appears on his handsome face, making the corners of his eyes crinkle. "I'm sorry. The meeting ran a bit longer than expected, but I'm here now. Ready to meet…" Ben lets the last word hang in the air.

Once I'm safely deposited on the floor, I let go of Ben's embrace. Grabbing his hand in mine, I turn around guiding him back to the couch where Arsen is sitting. He's observing us like a hawk with a blank expression on his face. The roguish smile is gone, the fire extinguished from his eyes.

I clear my throat because all of a sudden it feels as if I have swallowed cotton balls. "Ben, this is Arsen Radcliff. Arsen, this is my husband, Ben Stanwood." The two men stare at each other without saying a word. The tension is so palpable in the small space between us that I can feel the hair on my neck rising. Arsen doesn't make any move to stand up. He just stays rudely sitting on the couch while Ben and I stand over him. I'm about to drag Arsen's ass off the couch so that the two men can shake hands or something, when Ben stretches his own. "Nice to meet you, Arsen. Cathy has spoken very highly of you. She seems to like having you around."

As they shake hands, I notice that the knuckles in Arsen and Ben's hands are turning white.

Men.

A fake smile that makes Arsen look almost ugly taints his features as he replies, "Yeah?" Turning to look at me, his eyes warm for a second before turning cold again. "I like being around Dimples. She's nice to look at," he sneers.

What the hell?

Where did that come from?

Flattening his lips, Ben ends the handshake abruptly. With the greeting over, I'm about to walk around the table to sit back on the couch when I feel Ben's hand wrap around my elbow possessively, halting me mid-step. Puzzled, I turn to look at him.

He takes a step closer to me and leans down to whisper in my ear, "One drink and we are out of here, got it?"

My eyes widen at the sharp tone of his voice and his words. His jaw set, I know there's no room for a rebuttal.

I guess one drink it is.

I nod as I free myself from his hold and make my way to the couch. Ben seems to have other ideas about seating arrangements because he pulls a chair out for me right in front of Arsen so that the table is in between us.

What the hell is going on?

An unsmiling Ben looks as hard as a rock as he waits for me to be seated. On the other hand, Arsen, with eyes so cold they look like shards of ice, flashes a hard smile at us. One that reminds me of the night we met. With a sinking feeling in my stomach, all I can do is stand there and hope that tonight doesn't turn into a big ugly mess.

Arsen spreads his arm in an inviting gesture, his voice dripping with sarcasm, "Please, do be seated. I can't fucking wait to hear what else Dimples has said about me. I hope it's all good." He leans forward and looks me straight in the eye before continuing, "Because we're good together…very good together. Aren't we, Catherine?"

What is Arsen trying to do? More importantly, what is he hinting at?

When Ben is seated, he reaches for my hand and brings it to his lips, kissing it once before lowering it to his lap. Our fingers intertwined, I stare into his scorching eyes for a moment longer before facing Arsen once more. There's an indecipherable air surrounding him. I feel like I don't know this Arsen.

This Arsen is a stranger to me.

After the waiter leaves with our order, we sit in a triangle of tension without saying a word. If it weren't for the music playing in the background, you'd probably be able to hear a pin drop. My attention is focused on Arsen's long finger tapping the table-top in between the couch and chairs.

Tap.

Tap.

Tap.

After a few seconds, I can't take the silence anymore. Swallowing hard, I tuck some hair behind my ear; the silky threads running between my fingers calm me down.

"Uh, so, babe…" A flash of anger crosses Arsen's eyes but it's gone in a second, replaced with a nonchalant one. "I'm so jealous of Arsen. There's a possibility that he'll be attending the premiere of Melissa Stewart's new movie as her date! Are you dying of jealousy?" I bump his shoulder in a teasing manner. I want to pretend that I brought Melissa up just because it was the first topic to pop in my head, but it isn't.

I brought her up so that Ben knows Arsen is with someone.

His muscles relaxing, Ben smiles at me for the first time since he arrived to the bar. "I could never be jealous of anyone. I have you," he says as he squeezes my hand in his before addressing Arsen. "That's awesome, man. She's gorgeous, and the movie looks good. Cathy has a sick obsession with gossip magazines, so the trash they publish tends to rub off on me."

As he leans carelessly on the back on the couch, he stares at us for what feels like forever. It's like he's memorizing the way Ben and I look together. "Save it. We're over. I won't be surprised if tomorrow she is photographed with some other unsuspecting fucking loser."

When I hear this piece of information, I don't feel sorry. I'm happy. The realization stuns me.

"Anyway, I've just remembered a previous engagement. Sorry, but I've got to jet." Arsen takes his wallet out to pay when Ben stops him.

"No, please. Let me get the bill. It's the least I can do."

He raises an eyebrow. "Are you fucking shitting me? I can take—"

"No. I'd like to get the bill. You've done so much for Cathy already. I want to get this."

Arsen stares at Ben with dislike in his narrowed eyes. Just when I think he's going to reject his offer once more, he tilts his head to the side and pins me down with his gaze. Slowly, a smile appears on his face. "You know what? Go ahead. It was a pleasure to meet you, Ben. Cathy," he runs a hand through his hair, "I'll see ya around."

Standing up, he grabs his suit jacket that was lying on his side of the couch and says his last goodbye. He doesn't shake hands with Ben, and he doesn't even turn to look at me as he walks away.

It hurts.

I don't know why, but his indifference hurts. It shouldn't because he's nothing to me, but it still does.

I'm about to excuse myself to Ben saying that I need to use the restroom, when I feel a tap on my shoulder. I turn around in my seat to find Arsen standing behind my chair. Ready to stand up and ask him what the matter is, he leans down and plants a lingering kiss on my cheek. His warm lips make my skin tingle.

"I'm sorry, Dimples," he ruefully whispers in my ear, then moves away. I lift a hand to my cheek to rub the exact spot where he kissed me, not sure if I'm rubbing the tingling sensation away, or if I'm trying to seal the kiss within my skin.

He walks up to the bar to say something to the bartender, a model perfect Asian woman who smiles and writes something on the palm of his hand. When she walks away to serve other clients, a smiling Arsen turns to look at a group of young women sitting together, admiring him. He hands them what looks like a business card and kisses each one of them on the cheek. The flirting doesn't bother me, but when he kisses them on the same spot where he kissed me, it feels as if he is punching me in the gut.

It feels like betrayal.

I'm still watching his retreating figure when he reaches the entrance to the bar. Inside me, a strong voice is begging him to turn back around once more, to let me see him one last time.

And then everything becomes a blur.

Ben lets go of my hand.

Arsen turns around.

Our eyes connect for a moment.

I see something in his eyes that resonates deep inside me, but I don't understand it.

I don't think I'm ready to understand it.

Then he is gone.

I feel bereft. As if some basic living part of me has gone with him, leaving me incomplete, lacking. Perplexed and uncomfortable with my own feelings, I remember that Ben is here with me. Turning to look at my husband whose presence I completely forgot about, I feel shame scorching my skin an angry red.

"I think we should go," he says tonelessly.

15

The ride home is quiet.

No hands are held, no laughs, no questions about how our day went…maybe everything has already been said, or nothing needs to be said at all. When we get home, our cat is the only living thing there to welcome us.

I take my jacket off and lower myself on my knees to pet Mimi as I coo, "Hi, pretty girl. Did you miss your mommy and daddy?" Purring, she lets me pick her up in my arms. I kiss the top of her head, stalling for time. I'm not sure why, but I feel like I have some explaining to do as if I'm guilty of a major crime.

Maybe you are.

No, I'm not.

No, I am not.

"Would you like another beer before going to bed?" Hesitation echoes in my voice. I let Mimi jump down and move to the kitchen looking for food.

I watch as Ben removes his pinstriped navy blue Brooks Brothers suit jacket, the outline of the thick muscles on his back visible through the white shirt. He turns to look at me as he starts to tug at his tie. Forcefully.

I love that tie.

I bought it for him.

Looking past me, he talks cooly to his reflection in the mirror behind me, "Not tonight. On our way here, I remembered some paperwork that needs my attention. I'm going to head to the office and," he glances at me sideways, "Work."

His words feel like a bucket full of ice-cold water thrown in my face. "Oh, okay. I just…you, um…okay. I guess. Should I wait up for you?" I look down at my watch and see that it's only 10:00 p.m.

"No."

Ben closes the space between us, wraps his hands around my shoulders and leans down to kiss me. I close my eyes and wait for his kiss. A kiss that I hope will clear the stiffness in the air. Seconds pass and nothing.

Opening my eyes, brown ones meet my stare. Slowly, I watch as Ben lets go of my shoulder, his hand making its way to my face. Cupping my cheek, his thumb softly rubs the spot where Arsen kissed me as if cleaning a stain off my skin.

Silently, we stare at each other as time stands still.

"Go to bed, Cathy," he whispers huskily.

And he is gone.

I toss and turn for what seems like hours. Images of Ben and Arsen keep swirling in my head, disrupting me from falling asleep. I give up and turn on the lamp on my nightstand as my eyes land on the alarm clock.

1:11 a.m.

And no Ben.

My gaze lands on my cellphone, a crazy idea settling in my head. Before I lose courage, I reach for it and type a message.

C: What was that about?

I wait for ten minutes which turns into a half hour. Giving up the hope that he'll text me back, I put my phone down on the nightstand when it buzzes.

A: Go fuck your husband, Dimples. I'm busy.

His message is like a stinging slap on the face. Perplexed by his answer and hurt by his words, I decide he doesn't deserve an answering text.

I wonder who is keeping him busy? The answer shouldn't matter to me, but it does.

When I lie back on my pillow, turning on my side and pulling the covers around my shoulders, I close my eyes tightly and try to fall asleep. I try to push Arsen's message out of my mind.

It shouldn't bother me. It shouldn't hurt me. He is nothing to me.

But, it does.

I don't know why,

And I don't think I want to know why.

As I'm drifting into sweet oblivion, the last image to cross my mind is of a pair of saddened brown eyes.

Ben.

Hearing my alarm going off, I groan as I reach blindly to shut it off. In the early morning, even the most melodious tune can sound like an aggressive battle cry to start the day. I hate it. After I shut off the annoying sound, I lie flat on my back and stretch my arms and legs, shaking the sleep away. Turning to my left, I open my eyes, expecting to find a sleepy Ben snoozing.

He isn't there.

His pillow looks fluffy and perfect, like he didn't sleep on it. My skin prickling, I sit up and look around. Ben is nowhere to be seen. Even the bathroom door remains closed. He has a bad habit of always leaving the door open whenever he takes a shower, letting the steam escape purposefully. He says too much steam makes him sweat.

"Ben?" I ask, my voice groggy from sleep.

No answer.

Once I'm standing, the chilly air touches the skin that isn't covered by my silky top and shorts, raising goosebumps all over my body. I rub my arms to warm myself up as I reach the bathroom door and open it slowly. Ben is not here.

I notice something stuck between the glass and the wooden frame on the mirror above my dresser. Biting my lip, I reach for the note and read it. My hand covers my mouth as I feel my breath catch in the back of my throat.

Hope you don't mind driving yourself to work this morning. I forgot to tell you last night that I needed to go to the office earlier than usual this morning. Big lawsuit. Don't expect me for dinner.

Ben.

He didn't wake me up to say good-bye.

He left without saying a word.

With a tight chest and a churning stomach, I make it to work. I hope the way my day started isn't a sign of things to come because I might not be able to make it through without breaking down and crying. On my drive into the city, I tried calling Ben three times, but each time Carla excused him, saying that he was in meetings. Ben has never not answered my phone calls and he has never left home without first kissing me goodbye.

Until today.

On the short walk from the parking garage to my office, I notice the dark sky with its ominous gray clouds heralding showers any moment now.

Great, that's just great.

The humid air makes my body feel clammy with sweat, causing my clothes to stick to my skin, and the constant honking of busy traffic in the middle of rush hour in Manhattan feels like a nail being pounded into my head with each blare of a horn. I make it to the office without getting rained on, say hello to the security guards, and head to the office.

Once I'm sitting behind my desk, I reach for my black leather Gucci satchel and pull out my phone and a small pocket size mirror. Feeling a tight knot form in my stomach after I confirm that Ben hasn't called me back, I wonder if I should give him another call.

But my pride won't let me.

I didn't do anything wrong. If he would only speak to me, I would know what was the matter. *Arsen*, the small voice inside my head whispers. No. Why would Ben be upset about Arsen? There is nothing there.

We are friends. Good friends.

Or so I thought.

After yesterday, I'm not sure anymore. *Ben knows, he suspects.* Shaking my head like a mad woman, I try to dispel the insinuating thoughts roaring through my mind.

No, no, *no!*

With a trembling hand, I put my cellphone back in my bag and reach for my mirror on the desk. I take a look at myself, and I'm appalled to see the black bags under my eyes. The tight bun holding my blonde hair in place only accentuates how tired and pale I look, almost like a ghost. And not even the small amount of makeup I have can hide the fact that today I don't look my best.

Whatever.

I'm allowed to have a bad day, right? After I apply some much-needed lipstick and blush, I'm ready to officially start the day.

"There you are! Cathy, I'm going through a major crisis in my life."

"Morning, Amy. You're looking well this morning." I smile at her, even if it's the last thing I want to do at the moment. She looks breathtaking with her hair blown out in thick curls and the tight grey pantsuit she's wearing.

"Thank you, love. You look great as well. Black suits you with your coloring. Anyway, as I was saying…major crisis, Hello!"

"Well, tell me about it. We have a couple minutes to waste." I feel the first sincere smile on my face since yesterday evening.

Amy grabs a fiery red wave between her fingers and observes it for a moment before lifting her gaze to meet mine.

"Catherine, Cathy, Cat…the sad truth is that I need a good screwing. I have forgotten what it feels like to have an orgasm without my rabbit."

I feel my cheeks blush. "Um," How do you answer that? "I thought you, uh, weren't you seeing that guy with the yacht? What was his name? Nigel?"

Amy moves to sit on the corner of my desk, exactly where Arsen sat yesterday. The moment feeling like a déjà vu. "Yes…but he wasn't good in bed. At all. Like, sex with Nigel was one, two, ooooh baby, baby, you're so tight, so wet, and he was done." Snapping her fingers, she motions the quickness of the act itself before continuing, "I'm totally under-fucked. Which reminds me, I need you to introduce me to Charles. What? Don't look at me with those big and pretty green eyes of yours. I'm a straight woman, they don't work on me. You know which Charles I'm talking about. Girl, I need him in my bed. Now. And you're going to make it happen."

Oh boy.

"Amy, um, he is Bruno's closest friend. You remember who Bruno is, right? Your boss? My boss? How the hell am I going to introduce you two if I'm not friends with him?"

She waves her hand in the air, as if that small detail has no bearing on the conversation. "I'm not sure. I noticed him at the cocktail party that Bruno held when he first got in town. I saw him talking to you and Ben, and he was checking me out. So make it happen, Cathy. I have faith in you and your planning abilities. Invite him to dinner or something. I'm serious, Cathy. I want him."

"What makes you think he is, you know, good in bed? I mean he's good looking but—"

"Darling, dahhhling…the man has been around. Don't let him fool you by his girly job. If half the things that are said about him are true, I might be bowlegged for a couple days," Amy devilishly smirks, wiggling her elegant eyebrows at me, and causing us to laugh.

Amy and I are still laughing when an angry Bruno storms into my office. Without saying a word to us, he throws a newspaper on my desk.

"Look at this!" He shouts. Puzzled, we lean over my desk to have a better look at the front page of the publication.

The picture erases all traces of mirth off my face.

Swallowing hard, I reach for the newspaper and bring it closer so that I can see the image clearer. When I'm holding it between my hands, I can feel Amy move closer to me. "Oh, no."

My stomach recoils as I scrutinize the picture. Plastered on the front page is a picture of Arsen sniffing coke off a girl's breasts. The white shirt he wore yesterday is mostly open, revealing his beautiful and perfect tanned chest. His blond hair looks messy, but it's his flat stare that breaks me. His eyes look cold. So cold. Arsen is high on alcohol or drugs, maybe both, and he appears not to care that he's being photographed. This guy is the old Arsen, not the sweet guy that I've grown to care for in the past months. It looks like they are at someone's house and the girl is the same bartender from last night. The same one.

I know I'm to blame for this.

My throat dry, I'm having some difficulty swallowing as I remember the way he looked at me before leaving. When our eyes connected for an instant that felt like an eternity, I remember seeing emotions reflected in them that I pushed to the back of my mind, pretending that they didn't exist.

Betrayal.

Hurt.

Anger.

Bruno's harsh words break me from my reverie. "As you can see, my pride and joy of a son has decided to stop playing the silly charade of a reformed man. He's gone back to being himself, a waste. Cathy, don't expect him back. You should start looking for someone else to replace his position. Consider that picture his two-week notice, only that he won't be back at all. I won't allow it. Have a good day ladies."

Astonished, I observe Bruno's abrupt departure. His angry strides long and purposeful.

After he disappears, Amy snatches the newspaper away from me. Bringing it close to her face, she murmurs the headline, "Arsen Radcliff, a cokehead?"

The words wrap a thin coat of fog around me, numbing me a little, numbing me a lot, but in the end…they numb me.

Arsen.

I won't see him ever again.

The thought causes my heart to skip a beat, contract…

The thought makes me want to throw up.

16

It's been a week since I last saw him.

Since I last heard from him.

It happened last Thursday evening.

Today is Thursday.

Seven days have passed,

And nothing is the same.

Nothing ever is, though.

Right. When I told Ben that Arsen had been fired, it was like blasting an ice-sculpture with a fire torch, watching it speedily melt in front of my eyes. His icy demeanor that began the night we left the bar and carried through the next day until Ben got home and I was able to impart the news, finally thawed. There was no more stiffness in the air.

Life went back to normal.

Back to the way it was before Arsen started working in the office.

According to the article I'm currently reading, Arsen is back with Melissa Stewart. However, he was photographed on Sunday morning exiting the hotel where a very famous pop star is said to be staying. The magazine alludes to the fact that Arsen is two-timing Melissa, America's next sweetheart, with this dark haired singer. I wouldn't be surprised if he were. That's Arsen in a nutshell.

I'm numb as I stare at the picture for a while longer until the colors of the image begin to blur, blending together. My beating heart remains calm. It must mean that I don't care, right? At least not anymore. It's not even that I miss his flirting or his charisma. No, I miss my friend. I miss talking to him and laughing about everything and nothing at all.

I miss him.

Putting down my magazine on the kitchen counter, I look around the room from my seat. Everything looks so perfect and so neat. I wonder how many cracks lay hidden underneath all the shiny and expensive accessories. Probably many.

Just like me.

"Babe, can you pick up dinner tonight? I may be running late. Amy needs me to stay with her and go over some clients' demands," I say, trying to shake the gloom that settles over me every time I think about Arsen.

Ben lifts his brown eyes from a folder filled with paperwork. "Sure, no problem." He puts the folder down and removes his glasses, rubbing his eyes with the heels of his hands. He looks tired and stressed. The realization hits me that since Arsen came around, I seem to have stopped paying attention to Ben.

I push all thoughts of Arsen out of my mind and focus on my beautiful husband sitting in front of me.

"Cathy?" Ben asks.

Trying to clear my thoughts, I shake my head. "Sorry, babe…what were you saying?"

"The baby, babe. I'm just reminding you to make sure you have Monday off. We have our twelve week checkup."

Oh.

My heart begins to race. "Oh, yes. Of course," I say as I grab my bag and shove away the first things I see without a care whether I need them or not. "How could I forget? I've got to run." I stand up, tripping on my own feet as the same old crippling fear makes me clumsy.

Slowly, I make my way to my husband who is sitting across from me and bend down to kiss him on the cheek. I need to get out of here before I breakdown in front of him, and he sees how scared I am.

"Wait, babe. What's the matter?" He grabs the back of my neck to hold me in place as we stare at each other, his free hand caressing my cheek. If he's doing this because he noticed something in my face, and he's trying to distract me, make me forget, it's not working.

"Nothing. Truly, I've got to go."

I break free from his hold and make my way to the counter to put my plate and mug in the sink. My back is facing the room, so I don't notice when Ben stands up and comes to stand behind me. With his large frame hovering over me, he grabs me by the hand, turns me around, and pulls me in for an embrace, kissing me on the lips. Just when I think he's going to let go of me, he tips my chin up so that I'm looking into his eyes.

"Cathy, it's going to be okay. We've made it this far without any complications. Have some faith."

Nodding, I feel my eyes begin to fill with traitorous tears that let him know exactly how anxious and frightened I am.

"I have faith in you, Ben. T-That's all."

He pinches his lips together. "No, Cathy. You can't live your life that way. Have faith in life, in what's in store for you, for the two of us. Whatever it is, no matter what, you've got me. But you have to learn to not be afraid, to trust life." He lets go of me as his other hand sneaks between us, covering my barely there bump. "This is part of our future. And if it's not…if it's not in the cards for us, maybe it's time we look into adoption one more time."

I'm about to protest, but Ben stops me.

"I wouldn't mind. It'll be our baby no matter what. And, as long as you're there with me, as long as we do it together. Don't cry, my darling." He wipes my tears away with his thumb. "Remember, I love you. No matter what."

"I love you too," I murmur with an aching heart, guilt whipping me in the face. I have a wonderful husband who's always been there for me and loves me like no other, while I've been pining to hear from an asshole.

I'm done.

Ben's words are what I need to hear for me to shake off the numbing fog that has enveloped me in a thick cloak of yearning, not letting me breathe since he left.

I'm free.

I wrap my arms around his waist and stand on my tiptoes to kiss him on the lips.

Gently…

Lovingly…

Softly…

I show him what he means to me. I'm so lost in the moment that I'm taken by surprise when I feel his hand in between my legs, his fingers stroking and circling me slowly. I break the kiss as I hear Ben groan.

"Seriously, Ben?"

My husband winks at me. "You started it, wife. Now go before I change my mind and bring you back to our bedroom and show you how fucking serious am I," he growls, bending down to bite my lower lip.

As I watch his retreating figure, wiping some of the remaining tears away from my face, I can't help smiling a little. I don't want to think about the future because it scares me, but of one thing I'm sure.

I love this man.

So much.

Feeling my belly, I speak to the room and to our baby, "We are very lucky to have him, you know."

Monday it will be twelve weeks. Can we make it past?

I hope so.

"Please, don't leave me little one. Don't leave us."

We need you.

There's nothing more delicious than waking up in the arms of your husband after a good night's sleep. The luscious comfort of his skin against yours rubbing intimately together, feeling your flesh awaken by his possessive touch while your own gentle one drives him to perdition. Your body and his body fitting together like two pieces in a carnal puzzle.

Warm steel-like arms tighten around my midsection, shackling me to him. Turning around within his embrace, I push my body closer to the human wall, snuggling closer to him. Softly, I spread kisses on his naked chest, letting my tongue trace the outer ring of his nipple, lingering between the ripples of his muscles. As I taste the salty sweetness of his skin, I'm falling in love all over again with his flavor. I feel Ben's arms letting go of me as his hands lift my silky nightshirt, and remove it completely. With only my panties on, and nothing on him, we gaze at one another, our breathing the only sound you can hear in the room.

Ben caresses the length of my curves with the back of his hand as he tenderly smiles. "Morning."

I reach out to brush a brown lock off his forehead. "Morning, handsome."

"What's this?" His hand goes in between my legs, rubbing me gently outside my panties until I can feel the moisture seeping through the material.

"I want you." My hand reaches for his length, feeling it thicken and grow in the palm of my hand as I wrap my fingers around it. Warm steel. Raising my body higher on the bed, I nuzzle his neck with my nose. And then, after slightly licking my lips, I begin to kiss him under his chin, behind his ear, the thick veins of his neck…my tongue tasting the flavor of arousal.

"Um, Cathy…if you start kissing my neck like that, there is a 110% chance that I'm going to jump you like a fucking starved man and rip this pretty little thing you have on." His fingers continue to tease me, rubbing me in small circles, pushing in through the fabric. My body is a bomb about to explode by the magic of his fingers.

"Good."

I tease him with my tongue because I want to drive him mad with desire.

"Fuck." Groaning, I feel his free hand wrap around mine as we work him, faster and rougher.

"Mhhmmm, I like this, Ben. I need you inside me right now." My voice is husky with lust.

"Well…"

I let go of his embrace, push him to lie on his back and straddle him. Moving my panties to the side, I take him in my hand and lower myself until I'm fully seated on him and I feel him throbbing inside me.

"Damn…Cathy…"

Propelling myself on my knees, I begin to move in and out of him, his hands cup my ass and pull me closer to him. Our bodies this closely connected, I can feel him in my soul with every single thrust of his hips into mine.

I love it.

I tip my head back as I laugh and let the rhythm of our bodies set the pace of our lovemaking. On the verge of explosion, my body starting to tighten around his dick, Ben grabs fistfuls of my hair in his hands and pulls me down for a kiss. A fiery kiss that blazes through me, burning me from the inside out.

Ashes.

His kiss turns me into ashes.

When the kiss is over, he lets go of my face just enough to whisper against my mouth, "I love your dimples when you laugh."

Dimples.

Dimples.

Fuck.

Arsen.

Sick to my stomach, I don't think I can finish it, but Ben is so far gone that he doesn't notice my sudden withdrawal.

"Shit, Cathy…"

Ben lets go of my hair to grip my hips as he picks up the pace, my ass slapping against his thighs faster and faster. Harder and harder.

"CATHY!" he shouts as he comes inside me.

I don't.

I can't.

I look down at him lying on the bed, feeling the warm liquid spreading inside me as he thrusts a few more times. And all I want to do is cry because he just tainted my memory of Arsen.

Dimples.

The words sound amiss on Ben's lips. They don't belong there.

With a flush covering the crests of his cheeks, Ben begins to sit up with me on his lap, still connected to one another. Wrapping me in his arms and grinning like a cute little boy on Christmas morning, he buries his nose in my neck and kisses me softly behind the ear.

"Damn, Cathy, how did I get so lucky?" He lifts his face, pecking me on the nose. "You're so damn perfect." His voice is hoarse with emotion.

Not bothering to answer him, I kiss him on the shoulder and untangle myself from his embrace. Once I'm standing, I remove the stretched panties and throw them in the garbage bin. Turning around, I take in all of my husband.

And for a moment…

A tiny fraction of time…

I wish I were staring at aqua blue eyes instead of brown.

After I'm done with my shower, Ben jumps in to get ready for work.

When I hear the water running, and an unsuspecting Ben humming a familiar melody, I sit on my bed as stray droplets of water wet my back, the edge of the towel, and my comforter. I grab my phone and make the biggest mistake of my life.

My hands are shaking, and I feel sick to my stomach because of nerves, but I do it anyway.

I text him.

C: I miss you.

Ben and I are driving home from work when I hear my phone ringing. I pick up without looking at the caller I.D.

"Is this Catherine?" an annoyed woman asks.

"Hi, yes. This is she. May I ask who's calling?"

"My name is Sali. We don't know each other, but I'm friends with Arsen. Listen, I don't know what's the deal between the two of you. I mean, it's not like you're famous or anything, but he's been drinking for almost four days straight. My boyfriend, Alec, has kept him company for the duration of his freaking drinking binge, and I'm done. I want my boyfriend back. Besides I can't stand watching Arsen drink himself to oblivion."

Stunned by her words, I swallow hard before responding. "Okay. And what does this have to do with me?" Feeling Ben grab my hand, I turn to look at his profile in the darkness and watch him drive.

"Uh, everything or nothing. One never knows with Arsen. All I know is that he hasn't shut up about you. He's in really bad shape tonight and I was wondering if you could come here and talk some sense into him. Maybe get him to go home and sleep the alcohol off. He's not well."

I clutch my cellphone tighter in my hand. "Okay. I'm with my husband. So it'll be the two of us. Tell me the address and we'll be there."

"Uh, you're married? I can't believe this." My answer seems to stun her, but only momentarily. "Whatever. Not my problem. Just get here as soon as possible, please. My boyfriend's band, MOMO, is about to start playing, and I don't want to witness another one of Arsen's drunk performances."

I end the phone call after she gives me the address. My insides are churning with anxiety.

I'm going to see him again.

"Ben, um, that was a girl named Sali. She's friends with Arsen."

When he glances my way, our eyes locking for a nanosecond, his expression turns guarded. "Why was she calling you? What does she want with you? Did that boy make her call you?" His voice is accusatory.

Bothered by his harsh tone and the way he refers to Arsen, I snap back at him as I let go of his hand. "He is not a boy, Ben. He is twenty-four years old. And he doesn't know she called me."

I cross my arms then turn in my seat to look at him. "Apparently he's very drunk, and she needs me to go talk to him. Maybe get him to leave with us."

Ben frowns. "No way. You aren't his mother." The word mother makes me flinch.

"We are not going. I won't do it, Cathy. Let his friends take care of him. He's nothing to you but a past employee."

The light changes to red, making us stop. Frustrated and hurt by his words, I don't want to look at him anymore, so I gaze out the window. I'm considering getting out of the car to flag a cab and go see Arsen by myself, when I feel Ben's cool fingers wrap around my chin, turning my face so that we're eye to eye. Ready to shake my chin to get out of his hold, his countenance paralyzes me.

Love.

I see love.

I feel love.

A love that makes his eyes burn as fiercely, and as brightly, as a wildfire.

Guilt placates me.

Guilt paints my skin red.

Placated, I try to explain to Ben why I need to do this for Arsen, and maybe at the same time I try to explain it to myself. I grab his hand and let the words fly out of my mouth before the light turns green and I lose him.

"Ben. Please…Arsen is my friend. H-He made me laugh and kept me entertained at work, and he, um, was there for me when I needed someone to talk to about the pregnancy."

Yes, that sounds true enough.

"What about your pregnancy? You haven't mentioned anything to m—"

"Never mind, it was a one-time thing," I lie to him, "But that's not the point. The point is that he's my friend and apparently his friends think I can talk some sense into him. I don't know why they seem to be under that illusion, but I have to at least try Ben. I have to."

He stares at me intensely, appearing to consider his answer. After a small pause, he lets go of my chin and wraps his fingers on the steering wheel. He's clutching it so tightly you can see the veins in his hands pop. Nodding once, his voice is filled with calm wrath, "Fine. But, Cathy, this will be the first and last time. I don't like it, and I'm sure you wouldn't like it either if I had to go get a woman you barely knew randomly. I'm going to let it slide because, well, I don't have a choice, and because you say he's your friend. And that's the only reason why we're going."

He turns to look at me one last time as the light turns green. "Because he's your friend. That's all."

I softly murmur back, "Yes, my friend."

The words tighten my chest.

After driving for fifteen minutes, trying to find a parking spot on a Friday night in Manhattan, Ben drops me off at the entrance of the bar. He tells me to go in first while he goes in search of a garage.

Once I wave Ben goodbye from the street, I turn on my feet until I'm met with the ratty and dilapidated front façade of what I think is the bar. Glancing to my left and right, I search for something nicer looking, but with everything closed, this seems to be the right place.

Talk about a dive bar.

I never expected to find spoiled, attention seeking Arsen in a place like this. When I cross the threshold to the shabby locale, I'm greeted with the smell of stale beer and cigarette smoke. Distaste making my nose scrunch up and eyes squint momentarily. Once I get used to the surroundings I browse the bar, looking for the familiar head of golden blond hair I've missed so much. Not finding him anywhere, my eyes land on a stick thin tan black haired beauty. Her big brown eyes are taking me in as she leans over a tall, good looking guy and whispers in his ear, nodding my way. When he turns around, I notice the tattoos covering his arms and neck. He grasps the girl by the hand and walk towards me, only stopping when they're standing a foot away from me.

Wow.

The guy standing in front of me is beautiful in a Euro-Asian kind of way. His body is lanky but well defined, his eyes are sky light blue and his jet black hair makes the white milkiness of his skin stand out. The girl is just as gorgeous. Petite and thin, her big brown eyes make me think of warmth.

"You must be Catherine. I think you got here a little too late. Now we must sit through another one of his drunken performances. But as soon as he's done, please get Arsen the fuck out of here. The man is going to have tabloids hunting the place down, and people are going to lose their shit. We hate notoriety," he says in a sexy raspy voice.

"Hi. Yes, I'm Cathy. And you are?"

"You're such an asshole sometimes, Alec. Move over, baby." Pushing him to the side, the petite girl takes my hand in hers. "You're as pretty as I imagined, but older. Anyway, hi, I'm Sali. It was me who called you before. And this is Alec, my boyfriend. His band is playing tonight and, well, Arsen decided he wants to be a fucking rock star and play with them. I wanted you to get here before he went on stage and made a fool of himself in front of all those people, but it's too late. As you can see, he's about to perform."

When she moves her small frame out of the way, my eyes land on the stage where there's a man sitting on a wooden stool behind the microphone. He's staring down at the floor, seemingly lost in thought.

Heart beating wildly.

Dry mouth.

Palms sweating.

The fog that wrapped itself around me like an anesthetic cocoon in the past week begins to slowly dissipate as I drink in his ravaged beauty with eyes so thirsty they feel dry. His cheeks appear sunken and hollow, it looks like he has lost weight, and his clothes, usually so pristine, look worn and dirty.

Arsen.

Finally.

When a stranger shouts something at him, Arsen lifts his face, but his gaze doesn't land on the audience. It lands on me. My heart seizes to beat when our eyes first connect, but his blue gaze is like a defibrillator to my chest, sending warm electric shocks bringing me back to life.

Empty eyes explore and study me closely as a potent shiver travels down my spine, leaving me cold in its wake. I watch Arsen close his eyes as he lifts a shaky palm to push some of his blond hair off his face, highlighting the contours of his perfect arms and chest. After a moment of respite, he shakes his head once and lifts his eyes to stare at the audience, avoiding looking in my direction.

Completely ignoring me.

I feel an intense pain in the back of my throat, making it hard to swallow as I watch him stand up, walk to the edge of the stage, and lean over the crowd to say something to a group of girls standing closest to him. Giggling, they nudge each other until one of them, the one wearing the shortest skirt, shimmies out of her thong and hands it to him. His eyes empty, he smiles charmingly and puts the disgusting item in the front pocket of his shirt. Once he's done flirting, or whatever you want to call it, Arsen makes his way back to the stool and sits down. When a young guy with a guitar approaches him, Arsen turns his back to the audience, the girls forgotten, and begins to talk to him.

Feeling a small hand wrap around my upper arm, I tear my gaze away from the stage to stare at Sali who's currently scrutinizing me with her big pretty brown eyes.

"Don't mind that. He's just fucking with everyone. On a good note, he doesn't look as drunk as before, but I'm still afraid he's going to make a fool of himself. When he's done with the song, Alec is going to get him off the stage, and that's your opportunity to make him leave with you. Oh wait! Where is your husband? Did he go home because that would be totally cool. Maybe you could drive Alec's Porsche?"

I get the feeling that Sali doesn't want Ben here.

"Yes. Ben, my husband, is here with me. Well, he should be here any moment now. We couldn't find a parking spot."

"Oh. Well, never mind. Just get him out of here, 'kay?"

"Babe, I gotta go to the stage. I don't know what Arsen wants to do, but I gotta be there. You cool?"

After a quick peck on the lips, Sali tells Alec to go and kill it, and to make sure Arsen doesn't make the biggest mistake of his life. I don't understand why singing a song would be such a terrible thing. As a matter of fact, it makes me feel proud of him.

"Um, Is Arsen any good?" I hate how shaky my voice sounds.

"Fuck, yeah! He's awesome! Alec has been trying to get him to join the band, but he won't do it. I personally think he doesn't want to deal with the fame. I mean, look at the guy! He's popular enough without being in a band."

"Is Momo popular?"

"They do okay." She smiles at me, pride shining through her eyes. "Anyway, look! They're starting. Let's hope Arsen is able to sing after the alcohol binge he's been on since last Thursday night."

I steal a glance in his direction and see him talking to Alec as his hand covers the microphone. Alec seems to be trying to talk some sense into Arsen who is shaking his head mulishly at him, then Alec throws his hands in the air and walks away from Arsen, leaving him all alone. A smile so cruel it could be a sneer crosses his lips as he stares at his feet. When he lifts his eyes to look at the audience, I feel the small hairs lift on the back of my neck.

Slurring his words a little, I hear the voice I thought I would never hear again and it makes me happy.

So happy.

"I'm not going to introduce myself because there's no fucking point. According to my father I'm a fucking nobody, and it's cool." He runs his hand through his hair and lets it settle on his nape. "I agree with him. Anyway, my friend Alec, who likes to pretend he's a struggling musician when he could probably buy a damn record label himself, has allowed me to grace you all with my shitty and worthless talent. Hope you enjoy it. Oh, yeah, I forgot. I dedicate this song to a friend of mine."

Oh no. Don't.

Arsen laughs into the microphone at his own private joke, but his next words destroy me. "You see, she's this pretty little thing. Fucking beautiful, really. And she has dimples, the prettiest fucking dimples you've ever seen. But she's married, loves her man, and that doesn't work for me because I want her. Really fucking bad." The crowd goes crazy with his words, but I can't hear anything.

I'm deaf to the loud sounds around me.

His words are all I can hear.

All I want to hear.

In a few sentences, he has shattered all my foolish illusions that we were friends, just friends. He has spoken the final truth that I cannot deny anymore.

And it hurts.

It hurts so much because I did this. I allowed it to happen.

"Anyway, this is for her." As the words leave his mouth, he lifts his gaze from the audience until it lands on me.

When our eyes connect, we stare as if the world didn't exist around us. As if it was only the two of us.

Fire and Ice.

Clutching myself tighter in my arms, I want to run and escape this room. I want to leave him behind, but I can't. My feet are stuck to my spot on the dirty and wet floor, watching him about to crash and burn, bringing me down with him.

Without breaking eye contact, he shatters my heart with his lyrics.

In the shadows of the other man, in the shadows of the other man.

In the shadows of the other man, I can hear your voice calling for me, calling for me.

Green-eyed beauty with a heart of steel, heart of steel.

Open your eyes, open your eyes and see me, see me.

Witch, you hypnotize me with your wicked ways and with your body of white chocolate temptation. Let me taste you before I rip my brains out, my brains out.

I wander aimlessly through the pages of my broken love story trying to find my way back to you.

In the shadows of the other man, in the shadows of the other man.

In the shadows of the other man, I can hear my soul crying out for you, crying out for you.

Soul catcher, soul stealer, give me back my soul. Without my soul, I am nothing, Without you I am nothing, I am nothing.

In the shadows of the other man, in the shadows of the other man.

In the shadows of the other man, I am nothing.

I am nothing.

I feel chills run over my body. I feel hot and cold…so cold. I'm shaking, and so hot my cheeks are burning. Arsen's words are spinning in my head, making me dizzy.

I can't.

I can't do this.

Excusing myself, I try to walk calmly toward the washroom without breaking into a run. My steps shaky, I feel eyes on me. Everywhere. A nagging voice in my head tells me that I should worry about Ben. What if he saw the whole performance and connects the dots? But I can't. I have to get out of here and deal with the consequences later.

I need to be alone.

Once in the restroom, I give up attempting to cool myself with a wet paper towel, and splash my face with water instead. It works a little, but I still feel my face burning. Lifting my eyes to the mirror, I panic at the emotions painted on my face. I look flushed, almost feverish, and my eyes are shining again, a euphoric sparkle that shouldn't be there.

No, no, no, no.

But it's true, right? I knew it all along. Selfish me wanted Arsen, so I labeled him a friend when we were anything but. His teasing, his smiles, his touch…

It was never the same with anyone else. And I liked it.

No, I loved it.

I loved the attention he paid to me and the way he made me feel. Alive. Happy. He made me forget. Ignorance is bliss, right? Well, knowledge is misery. And the truth hurts.

Because it can't ever be, it will never be.

Walking out of the bathroom, I don't notice the people waiting to use the facilities. Therefore, I am taken by surprise when I feel a hand close around my upper arm, stopping me in my tracks. Before I have a chance to dislodge myself from his hold, he opens the men's restroom, guides us in, and locks the door behind us.

Scared, because I don't know what he has in his mind, I shout at him, "What the hell do you think you are doing? Let me out this moment." As I try to push him away from the door, he grabs me by the shoulders and pins me against the door. I wince at the strength of his hold. I'm waiting for him to do something, anything.

But he doesn't.

All he does is stare at me. He's watching me with such thirst and hunger in his eyes.

How could I not have noticed this before?

Oh, you knew, you knew.

Heat pulsates in my core with each caress of his eyes on my face. Roaming my features, he stares at my mouth, my neck, my cheeks, my eyes…

Arsen leans forward as his cheek touches my temple and stays there. I can smell a mixture of beer and cigarettes on him, but I don't care. It's him. I smell underneath it all. Arsen. His skin on my skin.

Explosion.

Fire.

I am about to speak, when I feel the tip of his nose tracing the edge of my jaw. Slowly, Arsen moves down to my neck, his nose following the path of my collarbone. I need to do something. Get him to stop but I can't, I am stunned. And if I'm honest with myself, I am relishing his touch.

I missed it.

When I feel his tongue replacing the tip of his nose as he continues to trace my neck, I can't stop the moan that escapes my mouth. I'm lost in sensation when he stops. Out of nowhere he straightens his body and lets go of me. He moves to stand in front of me, huge and imposing. His breathing is hard and fast. I can see the bulge tenting the front of his pants, goading me, making me wonder what it would feel like if I touched him right now. If I unzipped his pants and grabbed his dick. Hard. I know he would like me to.

Looking at each other without saying a word, it's Arsen who breaks the silence, "Go ahead. Touch my cock. I know you want to. I can see it in your eyes."

I shake my head. "No. Stop it, Arsen. You're delusional."

"You do. I've seen the way you look at me. You want me, Catherine. So stop fucking lying to yourself. Shit, even when your perfect husband was sitting right next to you at the bar, you could not stop staring at me."

"A-Are you crazy? I don't want to. We are—"

"Say it. I dare you. What are we, Dimples? Why don't you fucking tell me what we are?"

"Why are you doing this?" Tears burn my eyes.

"Why did you bring him?"

"Who?"

"Your husband!" he shouts.

"H-He wasn't here."

"Yes, he was. He saw the whole fucking thing. And I gotta say, I'm fucking glad he did."

"Oh, Arsen. What have you done? Does that make you feel any better?"

"No, it doesn't make me feel better, but I can't fucking get you out of my head. And I've tried. Trust me, I've tried so fucking hard. But seeing you here," he pushes his body against mine, "I know one thing. And I'm fucking done pretending, Catherine. Hell, I fucking missed you. I need you."

I shake my head vigorously, denying his words and the way they make me feel. "No. You're crazy."

As his breathing slows down, he smiles. "Your eyes betray you, Cathy, and I can practically smell your pussy getting wet for me. I gotta say, Dimples, it's fucking turning me on."

I feel shame and anger rising inside of me. He is right.

"I don't want you. Get off your high horse, buddy. You are good looking, yes, but I'm married and not interested. You're my friend, and that is all, Arsen. You're a child to me."

I'm lying, lying, lying.

The smile is wiped clean off his face. I'm glad.

"A fucking child? A friend?" The hurt in his eyes is like death to me.

"Please, let me go. You're imagining things, Arsen." Turning around, my back to him, I reach for the doorknob when I feel the whole front of his body press against my back. I close my eyes as I feel a shiver running through my entire body. He pushes me forward until my front is against the door, and my back is glued to his. I feel him everywhere, from his hot breath hitting behind my ear and neck, to his bulging erection on the small of my back.

"Please, Arsen. Don't do this. I'm married," I beg with all my heart.

"What if I told you that I don't care that you're married? I don't mind sharing. What if I told you that I'll settle for fucking you once? Just once where I'll make you come so hard on my cock that you'll forget that you're married and beg me for more? And if you're a good girl, Dimples, you may get it again before I let you go back to your husband, sore between your legs because I fucked you so good."

I'm shocked and aroused.

What the hell is wrong with me? Why am I so turned on when he basically just insulted me and my marriage. "I-I think you're drunk, Arsen, and you need to sleep. You're not attracted to me. You think you are, but you aren't."

Immediately pushing his hips forward, I feel the ruthless pressure of his erection on my back again. Arsen brings his mouth close to my ear to whisper words that make my stomach tighten with excitement and fear.

"Does this feel like I'm not attracted to you? You're fucking gorgeous, Catherine. And I've wanted you since I first laid eyes on you. Fuck, all I could think that night every time I watched you take a sip of wine was that I wanted your lips wrapped around my cock, sucking me hard and fast. And whenever you uncrossed your legs, I could only imagine what it would feel like to spread them open for my cock to get inside of your tight pussy and fuck you right on the table. It's been fucking hell wanting you and not being able to have you, not being able to do anything about it," he pauses, "I want you, Catherine."

When the word pussy left his mouth, he touches me there, slowly rubbing me over my skirt, his hand sliding in and out, his fingers trying to go as deep and close to my clit as my skirt will allow him.

"Mmmhmmm…yes, you are so fucking hot. Feel how hard your wet pussy is making my cock…I bet I could slide your panties to the side and fuck you nice and hard right against this door, right now."

His words snap me out of my haze.

What the hell am I doing? I get it together, slap his hand away and turn around to face him one more time. The last time.

"Get your fucking hands off me. Who do you think you are to speak to me like that? Does it work with other women? You tell them you're going to fuck them, and they just spread their legs for you? You're too pretty for me. I like real men. And my husband is everything you are not. A man."

I see anger replacing disbelief in his handsome features. I lied when I said that he was too pretty and not a real man. He is beautiful. Before I lose steam and my own anger is replaced by fear, I forge on, "You picked the wrong woman to mess with. I'm happily married to a great man whom I love so very much. A-And I'm not interested in fucking you. My hand would probably do a better job."

So not true.

He looks so angry. And baffled. Just as I think I have put him in his place, Arsen gets himself under control. There is a mean, almost cruel smile that doesn't reach his eyes on his face. "Baby, you may say no to me tonight and pretend that you're above all this," He grabs my hand, guiding it towards his dick as he makes me rub him over his jeans, "But you'll beg me to let you suck my cock one of these days, mark my words. You're so fucking wet right now. I can smell it."

"You're disgusting."

"But you want me," he says flatly.

"I'm pregnant with another man's child!" I yell.

As I remind him and myself of my state, I feel Arsen wince as his hand goes immediately slack. Good. I'm repulsed by the reaction his touch awakens in me and I want to make him feel just as sick.

"Fucking hell. I-I…" he mutters.

I take advantage of his momentary shock and manage to snatch my hand free of his hold. The air feels saturated by the powerful currents of electricity flowing between us as we stare at each other. It's tangible. Realizing that this is my chance to escape before he says something else, I move as fast as I can, unlocking the door and fleeing. Not looking back, I leave him and his bittersweet words behind—where they belong.

On my way back to the bar, I see Sali talking to Ben. He looks so familiar and formidable, so different from Arsen. Day and Night. How did she know that was my husband?

"Hi, babe. When did you get here?" I'm surprised my voice sounds so calm when there's utter turmoil inside me.

"I've been here for a while. I even saw Arsen perform, but I couldn't find you, so I stayed at the back, " Ben says without looking at me.

I reach out for his hand and make him look my way. "Oh. T-That performance was great."

Sali cuts in, and I silently thank her with all my heart. "Whoa. And what a performance that was! You know, it's upsetting to see he's still so hung up on that woman he was seeing back in Paris. Such a waste. But you know how those bored married socialites like to play around with young meat. Mind you, it was totally shitty for him to get involved with one, but that's Arsen. He likes to play with fire. Cathy, I think you should go. I mean, I think I overreacted when I called you. He's actually much better. Not as drunk as I suspected. So yes, thanks guys! Ben, it was great meeting you! And Cathy, before I forget, come with me to the bar so I can borrow a pen and take down the info of your hairdresser. I love your highlights!"

Confused, I stare at her beseeching eyes. What is she talking about? I nod and follow her after she says goodbye to Ben. As I follow her to the bar, I turn around just as Ben lifts his hands to his face, the palms roughly rubbing his eyes as if trying to expunge images from them.

When we get to the bar after the crowd opens up to let us through, a sober Sali addresses me. "I don't know what's going on between you and Arsen, but that was fucking messed up. You need to back off. I didn't know you were married and when I found out you were I still didn't care. Arsen likes pussy and he fucks whatever he wants and whenever it's offered to him. But that," she points at the stage, "Is not cool. That's my friend hurting. So you better drop your innocent act and get the fuck out of here. Go back to your husband who seems to be a really nice guy and don't contact Arsen again. He'll get over you. He always does. Now, get lost, bitch."

And she's gone.

What have I done?

Numb, I walk back to Ben and pretend that what just happened in the bathroom between Arsen and me never actually occurred. That Sali never uttered those horrible things to me and that the whole performance never happened. As we're getting ready to leave, my stomach drops when I see Arsen making his way towards us. Ben must spot him as well because all of a sudden he wraps his arm around my waist so tightly that it feels like my bones are going to break.

When Arsen is standing in front of us, he doesn't ignore me like I thought he would. He continues to behave as flirtatious as before, but now when I look at his eyes they appear cold and empty.

"Ben. Fucking great to see you again. Hope you enjoyed the show." He aims his blank stare at me, hissing, "Hope you're not missing me too much at work. Anyway, I wanted to thank you both for listening to my shitty friends and coming to my rescue but as you can see, there's no need. They are assholes who think I need saving…fuck that shit. I need more alcohol and pussy."

His words are like punishing lashes to my body, making me flinch in pain.

When I get home, I feel dirty and guilty. I know I didn't ask for Arsen to follow me to the bathroom, to touch me and say all those things to me. I did not. At all. But I can't get him out of my mind. And worst of all, I wanted them to be true at that moment.

Ben was quiet and pensive on the drive home, but he didn't seem to withdraw from me like the last time we saw Arsen. He asked me what I thought of Arsen's song, and I was able to give him an honest answer when I told him that it was good. After that, he dropped the subject and asked me about my day.

Nothing else.

Was he ignoring what happened back at the bar? Or was he in denial like I was?

After I take a shower, I put on a silk babydoll, apply cream to my face, and make my way to bed. I'm exhausted, and I just want to close my eyes and put the day behind me. I need respite from my thoughts for a couple hours.

I'm awakened when I feel the bed depress next to me. Ben. My sweet, sweet husband. Without thinking, I reach for him. Maybe if I touch him, I won't crave someone else. Pushing myself closer to his front, I begin to kiss him all over his chest. I shower small kisses around his hard chest and over the ripples of his abdomen. I'm using his body to distract me, but it works because suddenly I want Ben to touch me. To make love to me.

"Jesus, Cathy…what are you trying to do to me?" He whispers huskily into the dark room as he lets me explore him.

"Let me show you…" I say breathlessly.

As soon as my hand wraps around his growing erection, he pulls me on top of him and lifts my baby doll dress, growling when his eyes narrow on my nakedness. Slowly, he turns my body around, guiding his dick to my lips as he brings my hips closer to his mouth. His fingers gently spread me open and I feel his tongue inside of me, tasting my arousal. I'm losing my sanity and dying of pleasure. As I moan, I let the sweet traction of his tongue, and the gentle pressure of his stroking fingers give me what I need, what I want. Craving more of Ben, I push his now hard dick all the way inside my mouth until I feel tears in my eyes. He is so large and thick, but I like the choking sensation I get as if I can't breathe.

Minutes pass, the room is permeated with the smell of sex, we're all hands, mouths, skin against skin, sweat is everywhere, helping us move, helping our bodies glide. Climax within our reach, I close my eyes and give in, getting lost to the magic of his satiny tongue. My body explodes as I taste his cum land on my tongue. Ben raises his hips, the tip of his dick hitting the roof of my mouth as my name crosses his lips branded with my flavor. Shutting my eyes tighter, I swallow him clean.

When I'm climaxing, it is Arsen who I think about.

Now I know why I felt so guilty.

He was right.

Arsen was right.

I did want him.

I still do.

I feel so filthy because I want his touch and his hot breath on my skin once more. I feel so fucking polluted because just thinking about his hands on me still makes me so wet. I feel ashamed and disgusted with myself because Ben hasn't been able to turn me on like this for a very long time.

I can't believe it.

And what is worst of it all?

I want it to happen again.

So badly.

After tossing in bed for another hour, I give up my fight with insomnia and go in search of a glass of water. Flushed and hot, my mouth feels parched with thirst, but the water doesn't help at all. Screw it. I need to cool down. I open the freezer and stick my head in while getting blasted in the face by cool air. It feels delicious. Calmer, I make my way back to bed.

As my head hits the white, fluffy pillow, I turn to look at the clock. Its neon light lets me know that it's close to three in the morning. Groaning, I flip on my side and begin to fall asleep when the vibration of my cell phone startles me, waking me up. Blindly, I reach for my phone and stare at the letters that together form a name that has engraved itself in the deepest recesses of my mind.

Looking over my shoulder to the man sleeping next to me, I watch an unsuspecting Ben, oblivious in his sleep. A nervous energy runs through me that causing my hands to shake.

Should I answer?

What if I wake Ben up?

I want to answer.

I need to speak to him.

I need to hear his voice.

You shouldn't.

Wavering, hesitating, vacillating.

Good intentions lose the battle as I feel an overwhelming panic consume me at the thought of not speaking to him ever again because somehow, call it a hunch, I know that if I don't answer this phone call he'll be lost to me.

I begin to laugh. That's all we've done since my last box made it into his apartment.

Ben laughs. "Don't say it! I know, I know. But—"

"But what? Please tell me. I need to hear this," I tease him, nudging him in his stomach.

"Well, I'm pretty damn sure we managed to squeeze in a word here and there."

"Oh, yes. Totally." In a manly voice, I repeat his greeting, "Babe, how about you slip into something more comfortable say, like, me? Those were the first words you said to me as soon as I walked in. Is that having a conversation? Because you weren't even done putting my box down before I was thrown over your shoulder and on my way to your bedroom."

Ben smirks. "Our bedroom. And I think we had quite an awesome conversation in my bed. I remember hearing you say, harder, please, God, yes…"

I smack him on the shoulder as I feel a blush covering every surface of my skin. His words bring back memories of last night and this morning.

"Oh, God…baby…don't stop! Don't! Yes! Yes!" He keeps teasing me. Giving up, Ben and I burst out laughing so hard until we have tears in our eyes and it's hard to breathe.

When we stop, I grab his face in my hands, lean down, and kiss him. I try to demonstrate to him with my tongue, my lips, my hands, my body, how much he means to me. He's the everything to my nothing.

"I love you so much," I whisper against his lips.

Ben groans, "Say it again."

"I love you."

"Again."

"I love you, I love you, I love you, I love you," I say, giggling.

"Man, it's like fucking music to my ears every time you say that."

Ben's hands begin to pull my boy shorts down, but I stop him. I stare at him for a moment, taking him in. This boy of mine is a force of nature. His energy revives me. He fills my life with all sorts of beautiful colors. He makes me so damn happy.

"Um, Ben?"

"Yes?" He sits up and begins to plant kisses on my neck.

"I-I thought we were going to do something today. You know, maybe go for a walk in the park?"

Ben stops kissing me and lies down on his back once more, but his fingers continue to caress the exposed contours of my body.

"You're right. We need to leave the apartment and go food shopping. I've waited to go with you so you can pick whatever you like."

"Aww, baby. That's so sweet."

"Yes. I'm sweet alright, want a taste?"

"Oh my God. Okay. I'm going to take a shower. Want to join me?" I ask. I kind of hope he does. Shower sex with Ben is a favorite of mine.

"You know I do, but you're right. We need to get moving. And I need to call Julian, Micky and his girl, Megan to see if they want to join us for drinks tonight."

"That sounds great." I get off the bed and make my way to the shower. When I'm almost there, I turn to look at him once more.

Ben is biting his lip while he watches my body with such desire. Smirking, I shake my ass seductively as I make my way into the bathroom. I hear him groan, and I can't stop myself from laughing out loud.

This is happiness.

There's a pet shop two blocks away from Ben's apartment and every time we walk past it I make him stop and wait for me until I'm done drooling over the cute kittens and puppies displayed in the window.

Today, however, it's him who stops walking when we reach the shop.

Curious as to why he's suddenly not moving, I ask, "What's the matter, baby? Do you have a rock in your shoe?"

He shakes his head as I feel his hand tremble in mine.

"No. No rock in my shoe. Actually, I was thinking…um, would you like to go inside for once? Maybe we could get a turtle or a hamster? You know, our first pet?" he asks, his voice wobbly.

I let go of him and clasp my hands to my chest. "Yes! I would love to."

I can't believe he wants to adopt a pet with me. I don't care if it's a turtle or a bird, it will be our first pet together. It's like we're becoming a family, and that's all I've ever wanted. To have a family of my own with him. To be a mother.

"Well, what are you waiting for? Let's go inside then. Maybe we can get a cool snake or something?"

"No way. I'll kill you. No snakes allowed in the apartment."

Ben leans down and whispers in my ear, "Too late for that."

"You're such a horndog. Come on, let's go. I want a cute hamster," I say, shaking my head.

I laugh when I hear him mutter something about snakes and not complaining about it last night. Seriously, my boyfriend is such a sicko.

As soon as we walk into the store, I separate myself from Ben and begin browsing the aisles, admiring all the cute fish, birds, puppies, and everything in between.

I'm gushing over a very cute puppy when I feel the softest of scratches on my leg. I lower my gaze and notice a very cute kitten with a red ribbon tied around his neck staring at me. I get down on my knees to pick him up in my arms and make my way to the counter, thinking that it must have gotten out of her cage.

When I get there, I see Ben watching me carefully, almost as if he expects me to run out of the store with the cat in my arms.

Weird.

The owner also has an expectant look on his face.

"Hey, I found this cute little thing on the other side of the store. Here you go."

And that's when it happens. The moment I hand the kitten back to the owner, I see what I thought was a bell dangling from the ribbon sparkle like…oh.

Oh!

I swallow hard. "Um…what's that?"

Ben removes the kitten from the owner's grasp and steps away from the counter, coming to stand in front of me. Without saying anything, I watch him as he unties the red ribbon from the cat's neck, sliding off one of the most beautiful rings I've ever seen in my life.

I hate crying, but at this moment I can't do anything to stop the tears flowing from my eyes. When the ring is free from the ribbon, Ben takes my right hand in his and stares at me with loving eyes.

What? Wait a minute. He has the wrong hand!

"Um, Ben…I think you have the wrong hand," I manage to whisper.

Ben looks down, curses under his breath, lets go and takes my left one this time.

Much better.

He clears his throat. "Cathy, meeting you was chance, falling in love with you was destiny, and loving you is my reason to exist. I could tell you all the different ways I love you, but words are cheap. Instead, if you accept to be mine, if you let me be yours, I'll show you for the rest of our lives how much you mean to me. Babe, I want to grow old with you. I want you to be the mother of our children, and I want you to be the last person I see before I take my last breath on this earth. I love you. Will you marry me and let my love for you make me the best man that I can be?"

"Y-yes. Yes. Yes!" I watch him as he slides the beautiful diamond ring all the way on. Not waiting for him to say anything else, I throw myself at him. I grab the back of his neck, pull him down towards me and kiss him hard on the lips.

When we break away, Ben cups my face in his hands, and stares at me. "That's it, babe. You're stuck with me and the kitten for life now," he says huskily.

"The kitten is part of the deal?"

Ben nods as he smiles.

"Well, when you put it that way, there was really no need to ask."

Laughing, Ben pulls me closer to his body and kisses the top of my head.

As we leave the pet shop, my gaze lands on Ben holding the kitten close to his chest. An easy smile adorns his handsome face while his long dark brown curls flutter in the air with the soft breeze blowing in the early afternoon.

I lower my eyes to stare at the huge diamond decorating my left hand. Apparently it's an heirloom and very valuable, but Ben didn't choose to give it to me for that purpose. His grandmother gave it to him before she passed away and told him to only give it to the woman who made him feel like he could conquer the world because that's what true love does to you. It makes you feel invincible and capable of doing anything you set your mind to.

He told me I was that woman.

I look up into the sky and watch the sun shining brightly down on us. I don't know what tomorrow will bring, but one thing I know for sure is that as long as he's next to me, and as long as he's part of my life, I will be okay.

Everything will be okay.

If only I had known that years later we would suffer three miscarriages within a year, and then nothing, I think I would have questioned my words.

But I was young and in love, and like his grandmother told him, I felt like I could conquer the world with his love.

I felt invincible.

If only I had known that it takes a lot more than love to make a marriage work, then maybe our story would be different.

If only.

18

present

Saturday was a blur.

Sunday was a blur.

Today is Monday, and it already feels like a blur.

Just another day.

Just another day.

Just another day like the day before.

I feel restless. I feel lacking. I feel half empty, half full.

Ben has been his perfect sweet self. He whispers the right words in my ear, kisses me at the right moments, and always holds me close.

So why do I feel like this?

Has the bubble been burst already?

I'm standing in front of the mirror getting ready for work, looking at my pretty reflection. I don't recognize myself this morning. I can't. Where has the magic gone? Where is the sparkle in my eyes?

I feel like my world has been infected with darkness. I have a loving husband, a beautiful home, financially stable…we even got our second chance at complete happiness with the small miracle growing inside me.

My life is good.

So why do I feel hollow?

Maybe it's because in the short period of time that he was a part of my life, I discovered something that I didn't know existed; something I didn't know I could have. Something I may want?

I don't know.

Without realizing it, Arsen wrapped me so tightly in a web spun by his sweet deceit that I don't think I can break free even if I want to.

Green eyes stare back at me in the mirror. My eyes. The eyes of a stranger. I lift a hand to fix my hair, watching my reflection. The waves cascade down my shoulders as I run my fingers through the soft golden mass. Hair in place, I reach for my perfume, tilt my head to the side, and expose my neck for the mist to come. When my finger is on the pump ready to press down, I feel a familiar tug in my lower abdomen.

Oh, no…

Oh, no…

Not this time.

Not again.

Numb with fear, my hand automatically drops the perfume, letting it fall on the carpeted floor. I shut my eyes tightly and try to breathe in through my nose and exhale through my mouth as I attempt to calm myself down, but I can't.

Just breathing hurts.

Fighting to escape the dark cloud of panic settling over me, I wait for the next blow of pain to come and hope that it never does even as despair begins to dig itself within my heart. I wait because there's nothing else to do.

Again.

It hits me.

Still I watch my reflection and register that my eyes don't look opaque anymore. They shimmer brightly. They shimmer with tears of sorrow, of grief, of what will never be. But this was never meant to be, was it?

Oh, God.

It was never meant to be.

I feel painful cramps strike me over and over again, each one more intense than the last. Each blow killing me softly. With nothing to do but wait for the inevitable to come, I wrap my arms tightly around my belly. I don't want to move, afraid that it will make my baby leave my body sooner, faster.

I need to feel her inside me for just a little longer. I need to hold onto that small miracle for just…

Slowly, I lower myself to the floor and lean against the mirror. I close my legs as strongly as possible and pull them up against my chest, not allowing the baby to leave my body just yet. I wrap my legs in the illusionary safe cocoon of my arms as I start to rock back and forth, forbidding the truth sink in. My body is trembling, my hands are shaking, and I'm so afraid.

I'm so fucking afraid.

I can hear a broken voice mumble unintelligible words into my ear as I rock myself like a mad woman.

"Why me?"

"…body broken…"

"…not woman enough…"

I look around the room, realizing I'm alone. All alone.

The crazed voice I keep hearing is mine.

Minutes pass as I fight my body, pleading with it, pleading with God to let me keep my baby this time. Refusing to believe that life would be so cruel to tease me for a fourth time after such a long period of heartbreaking yearning and wishing just to take it all away once more. I continue to sway, oblivious to the world outside, when I feel a pain so intense in my lower back that it snaps me out of my mad daydream. The excruciating pain feels like someone took a heel and dug it in my lower back, twisting it mercilessly. As it passes, I'm left struggling to catch my breath.

When I feel something moist between my legs, I cautiously pull them apart to see bright red blood soaking my tan trousers. Death is spreading through my clothing like a disease.

It looks so red.

So vivid and bright.

It is exactly in this moment, when I'm looking at life slowly seeping out of me, that I willingly jump into the dark abyss of hopelessness. Misery welcomes me with its dead arms, despair freezing my heart.

A crazy urge comes over me. I need to feel the blood on my hands to know it's real. Reaching to touch myself, I let my fingers linger there until they are covered with my blood. When I pull my hand away and raise it to my eyes so I can take a better look, I rub the red liquid between my fingers and let it stain my skin. My body trembling hard, fingers red, something inside me snaps, cutting loose. I grasp my head between my hands, close my eyes and scream.

Anguish, anger, and sadness are carried in that never-ending shriek.

"Cathy! What's this? Oh, Cathy!" I hear Ben shout as he comes barreling through the door into our bedroom.

"Oh, Ben…please forgive…" Looking up from the floor, I can see Ben's horrified expression. "Please forgive me." My voice is hoarse from crying and having screamed so loud.

"I couldn't do it…I couldn't…I couldn't keep our baby safe."

I watch as Ben lowers himself to sit down next to me. He lifts me off the floor and sits me on his lap. I can feel the tremors running through his body, the way his arms wrap me so tightly in his warm embrace.

But I feel nothing.

I'm dead on the inside.

I'm cold.

"I couldn't…"

"Oh, Cathy…please…" his voice is hoarse with pain.

"No. I couldn't. It's happening." Swallowing hard, I continue, "It already has. It's over."

Everything is a blur as Ben stands up, holding me in his arms and takes me to the bed. He calls Dr. Pajaree, then lays down next to me, holding me in a powerful embrace and grieving with me for what was never going to be.

"Stay with me, Cathy. Stay with me," he cries.

19

Garbage.

I'm throwing everything away. I'm cleaning the attic. I'm getting rid of any item that reminds me of what I will never have, of what Ben and I will never have. Is it a cleanse or a purge?

Who cares.

I lift my hand to wipe the sweat off my forehead as I glance around the nearly empty room. I can almost begin to feel at peace. I don't ever want to see another baby item in my house. I want all hellish reminders removed once and for all. I want an empty attic.

Just like me.

God made me a woman to punish me. I hate my body. I wish I could erase my memory. Maybe if I couldn't remember one thing, it would stop hurting so much.

I've lost all hope.

Wishing…

Wishing…

Wishing…

My dreams and hopes are shattered.

Like my heart.

My body.

And my soul.

I want to scream.

My body is a ticking bomb.

Tick. Tick. Tick. Tick.

Everything dies inside me.

Nothing survives.

The placenta didn't implant properly. The placenta didn't implant properly. The placenta didn't implant properly. The placenta didn't implant properly. The placenta didn't implant properly. The placenta didn't implant properly.

It has been three weeks since the incident, since my life completely changed. I don't care about anything. I don't care about Ben. I don't care about work. And I most certainly don't care what happens to me. My life leads nowhere, so why should I keep trying and trying?

I'm done.

I've given up. And it feels so fucking good. Living in an emotionless stupor suits me quite well because it helps me forget and not feel. And I want that. I want to not feel.

Not one thing.

When the last of the baby items is wrapped in a garbage bag, I move to the top of the stairs and throw it down with the others. I watch as the bag lands in a mountain of shiny black plastic. That's better.

Relieved, I walk to the center of the airy, and now empty room and let my eyes roam the bare wooden walls. There's nothing left. No furniture or boxes filled with memories of my marriage throughout the years, not one bitter memento. I got rid of it all because each picture, each rickety chair, each item resurfaced a pain so deep, so crippling within me that it made it hard to breathe.

Yep, this is much better.

As I scan the place, I'm overcome by a desire to twirl. I want to let my body move freely in any direction it wants to take me. Closing my eyes, I tip my head back, and twirl with my arms outstretched, feeling free, unburdened. Faster and faster I'm blindly spinning as tears soak my cheeks. Unhinged by grief, I laugh so hard that it makes my stomach hurt. Or am I sobbing? Maybe a little bit of both.

"Cathy, stop that right now. You're going to make yourself sick," I hear Ben say. His voice ringing with sadness. Why? Isn't he supposed to be perfect fucking Ben? Never sad and always happy. Always ready to catch me when I fall.

Ben. Ben. Ben. Ben. Ben. Ben. Ben.

The space between us grows each day. Can we stop it? I don't know. I don't know. I don't know.

"Go away, Ben. Or join me! But don't tell me what to do," I manage to say between laughs. "This is so much fun!" Really. He should give it a try.

"Don't make me force you to stop."

Well, that doesn't work for me. With my eyes closed, I continue to twirl and ignore his warning. "What are you going to do, huh? Stop me with your big and strong hands?" I taunt him because I really don't care, "Maybe—"

I'm cut short when I feel his very strong hands on my forearms, stopping me like he said he would. "Stop it! Stop it!" He yells at me. "Open your eyes, Cathy! Look at yourself. I can't do this anymore. I can't continue to watch my wife driving herself to an early grave. You're killing yourself, Cathy! Open your fucking eyes and look at me!" Swallowing hard, Ben shakes me as the choked words leave his mouth. "Look at me, Cathy. Look at me. Please."

And I do.

His pleading brown eyes are wet with unshed tears. "Well, what do you want? I'm looking at you now. Tell me what do you want from me, Ben?"

His grip on my arms grows tighter. I'm sure I'll have bruises by tonight. The pain feels good, though. It makes me feel alive.

I hear him groan as he lets go of my arms and pulls me close to his body. He wraps his tense arms around me in a constricted embrace. It's a desperate call for help, and one I don't care for. I don't return the hug. My lifeless hands remain on my sides as Ben tips my chin up, making me look at him.

Clenching his jaw tautly, Ben stares at me for a moment before speaking. "I want you to stop hurting yourself. You're not eating, you haven't showered in days, and all you do when you're not sleeping is clean this attic. There's nothing else left here to throw away, so please, Cathy…please. Come downstairs with me. Let me bathe you…feed you…whatever you want, baby. Just let me back in. I can't take seeing you like this and not being able to do anything about it."

"Let me be. It will pass…" I whisper.

"How, Cathy? You won't speak to anyone. You won't return Amy's phone calls, not even your dad's. Hell, you won't even speak to me. It's like you're here in my arms, but you really aren't. The real Cathy has already checked out and I'm left only with the shell of my wife. You need help, babe, and it's okay to ask for it. I'm here."

"I don't need saving."

"Yes, you do. And I wish I could save you, Cathy. Take the pain away; erase it from your body. I wish I could hurt for you, but I can't. You have to save yourself. All I can do is love you. Through it all, just love you. But you need to let me back in."

"Are you even hurting, Ben? Do you even realize what happened? I fucking lost a fourth baby, Ben. A fourth beautiful baby. What kind of woman am I that I cannot even carry full-term? My body is poisoned. It kills them, Ben."

My voice is rising, but I don't care. I can't stand Ben's poise, his perfection…the way he seems to always look at the fucking bright side of things. Life is a fucking joke. And he needs to realize that.

"You keep saying that we will be okay. That we'll get through this shit." Lifting my arms, I push him away until we're standing in front of each other not touching, a gulf between us. "That there are other options. Well, dear Ben, I'm fucking done with it all. I'm fucking done. I don't want to try anymore. I don't want to look at another baby item in this house. I don't ever want to hear you talk about us having a baby, about the different options available to us. I don't want to fucking hear it coming from your mouth. I'm done. I'm done. I'm done! Do you understand me? I don't want it anymore!"

My body is shaking from anger.

Or is it despair?

"It hurts, Ben. Do you understand? No, you can't understand it! Why am I even asking you? Asking Ben who has answers for everything. You want to know my answer? I'm not woman enough, Ben!" I begin to angrily hit myself, my hands attacking my empty womb as I sob irrational words. I want to feel as much physical pain as possible. "I'm a joke. And that's the sad truth. So, please, please, please! Stop it! Just fucking stop. Let me grieve however I want. I need to…"

"Babe, let me try—"

"STOP IT! STOP IT! STOP TREATING ME AS IF I AM A FUCKING PORCELAIN DOLL! I'M BROKEN, DO YOU HEAR ME! I. AM. BROKEN."

He reaches out for me with an entreating hand, but I don't let him. Shaking my head, I turn on my feet and flee the attic as fast as my feet will allow me. I turn my back on him and maybe on our marriage, but when I said to him that I was done. I meant it.

I meant every single word.

And he's right. Ben is right.

I've checked out.

A month later.

A: Catherine, I need to see you.

C: Why? I thought you were done with me.

A: I went into the office to see my father. I ran into Amy. She told me what happened…

C: So? It's in the past.

A: I want to be there for you…

C: What a joke. And no. I don't need you. I don't need anyone.

A: Dimples, please. I know you must be hurting. Before shit went down between us, before I got fucking drunk and ruined everything, we were friends. I want to be there for you.

A: Answer me please.

A: Are you there?

A: Don't shut me out of your life, Cathy.

C: Fine. But don't tell anyone. I don't want anyone to know.

Later that morning, I call Ben at his office to let him know that I'm going into town to meet Amy for drinks. At first he's taken aback and surprised. I can't say that I blame him. I haven't spoken to anyone in close to two months. But when the black lie rolls off my tongue, I realize that I would like to see her, to speak to her again. I've missed her. But before today, I wasn't ready to face anyone. I need to heal at my own speed, under my own terms.

My heart is broken, my dreams and hopes shattered alongside it. Even though the healing process has begun, and I know I will heal eventually, I will never be the same. I will never be the Cathy I used to be.

She's gone.

And in her stead, there's me.

The leftover.

The burnt ruins.

I'm a woman with so many inner scars that Dorian Gray's twisted reflection could be mine. But they are my scars. My hellish reminders. They make me who I am, who I'm left to live life with. And I would never change that.

"Would you like me to come with you?" Ben asks.

"No. It's okay. I need a girl's night out. I think it would be good for me." I wonder why lying comes so naturally to me now. Have I always lied to myself? Maybe.

After some silence, he continues, "I think it would be good for you. I'm glad you're speaking to her again. Maybe you could try giving your dad a call…"

"No. One step at a time. This is good. Anyway, I've got to go. I need to run some errands. I'll leave dinner ready for you since I won't be here by the time you get home."

"Cathy, don't hang up just yet. I need to say something. I'm happy you're getting out. I really am. Maybe this means—"

"Ben. It doesn't mean anything. All I'm doing is going to meet a friend for drinks and maybe dinner."

Which I am…kind of.

"Okay, babe. I'm just glad. Have fun and say hello to Amy for me."

I hang up without saying good-bye. I won't be made to feel guilty for this. I won't.

Besides, why should I? If I'm in ruins, I wouldn't even know how to describe the state of our marriage.

I hate when Ben reaches for me at night.

I want to throw up every time he makes love to me.

I've grown to hate looking at his beautiful face and everything that makes him so perfect.

I hate the fucking joke that our marriage has become.

And I hate myself because I seem to have lost all care for everything.

Valentino Red. Bright red lips.

A body fitting dress that shows off my petite figure.

Blonde curls falling down my back.

Champagne flute in hand.

Tangy bubbles on my tongue tickling my throat.

I wait for him. Sitting on a stool next to the bar, I scan the room looking for Arsen as the loud dance music pounds in my ears. He's running late, or maybe I'm just early. Either way, it doesn't matter because I'm out of the house, out of my self-imposed jail.

Calm.

I know I should feel nervous, but I don't feel one thing.

I'm just cold.

"Excuse me, I noticed that you're alone. Would you let me buy you another drink?" a dark haired man asks. Upon close examination, I note that he's very handsome and he looks like Ben, though he appears to be a bit older than my husband.

"Thank you but no. I'm waiting for a friend. And he should be here at any moment." I turn in my seat, completely dismissing him.

"You don't have to be such a cold bitch, you know." The man leans down to whisper viciously in my ear.

"You have less than a minute to apologize to her and back the fuck off, dude." Ah. A ferocious chill snakes down my spine as I hear his sweet, sweet voice.

Arsen.

Out of the corner of my eye, I see the guy mutter something to Arsen, maybe an apology, but I don't really care. All I want, all I need at this moment, is standing in front of me. And for the first time in a very long time, I don't feel so lost anymore. Not so cold.

I watch Arsen and the way his eyes shine like blue fire when they land on me, a burning fire that gradually melts the chronic sheet of ice covering my body. With one look, Arsen provides the warmth I didn't know I needed until this very moment.

"Oh, Dimples."

That's all it takes. With those two words, I come undone. Not caring that we're in the middle of a busy bar with loads of people watching us, I throw myself at him, bury my face in his chest, and let myself cry.

Oh, how I missed his smell.

How I missed him.

With me wrapped in the security of his arms, Arsen throws some bills on the bar and guides us to a corner booth, away from all the people watching us closely. He sits down first and then pulls me on top of his lap, never letting go of me. He begins to rock us both in a soothing motion as he tries to console me. One of his hands is on the back of my neck; my hair tightly wrapped in his fist as the other one gently caresses my back. Up and down. His touch is not sexual…it's soothing. Arsen, a friend gone wrong, is comforting me. His are the first arms I am able to find solace in.

"I-I'm…so…soorryy."

My words get mixed between tears.

"It's okay beautiful. It's okay. I'm here. We'll talk later."

After a while, when I'm all cried out, I begin my tale of sorrow, my trip down memory lane. Recounting how my life has been since the last day I saw him makes it feel as if a heavy weight has been lifted off my chest. It allows me to breathe painlessly again. With Arsen, I can finally grieve and not pretend that everything is all right. With Arsen, I can let my emotions take over me and not be ashamed by them.

With Arsen, I can be me.

Sniffling, I take the napkin that Arsen handed me before and wipe my eyes and nose. "I must look like a mess."

"Nah. You look like the cutest raccoon I've ever seen." I watch as he lifts his hand and slowly brings it to caress my cheek. Closing my eyes, I get lost in the sensation of his warm palm against my skin, and his light touch makes my body tingle. When I gaze at him again, his eyes are hooded with want, and he watches me while his thumb gently strokes my skin. I notice his breathing begins to accelerate as we continue eyeing each other. The loud background music has changed to hip-hop, but it's the silence between us that makes me instantly aware of his hands on my body.

Sluggishly, I get off his lap and move to sit next to him. The distance between us provides me with a chance to clear my mind and slow down the crazy beating of my heart.

"So, basically, I've given up. I don't want to ever try again, Arsen. It hurts to just think about it. I don't know if it's because th-the miscarriage is still too fresh in my memory. I really don't know. I mean, try to put yourself in my shoes. Wishing, hoping, and praying for that one thing that you want and need the most to be finally yours just to have destiny, or life, or karma, or whatever the hell you want to call it, snatch it out of your hands over and over again. I can't go through it again. I just can't."

His eyes pierce me.

"I know exactly how that feels. More than you know." Letting his words hang in the air for a moment, I get the feeling that he's trying to tell me something. "But listen to me, and listen carefully…I've been there. You know about Jessica." He grips my thigh, "I'm not going to go into details, but there was a time when I wanted to give up on life. Shit went down that made me who I am and I can't, I won't, ever change that. Fuck, just thinking about it still hurts, but along the way to finding myself again, I discovered an innate truth."

"Yes?" I whisper.

"Life without love, without chasing your dreams, is nothing. It means nothing. It's a sad fucking empty shell, Catherine. It's so easy to drown in darkness, to let it smother you, swallow you whole, to be blinded by it. But you gotta fight. You gotta fucking fight."

"That's so easy for you to say. I hate it when people tell me that things will get better…that one day it won't hurt so much…to not give up and fight! Well, show me how. Show me a way to—"

"Stop. I don't know what I'm doing either, Catherine." He takes my hand in his. "Life is full of surprises and challenges at every turn, but I won't let them stop me. I'm trying to improvise as I go. It's the only way to survive. You need to look the fucking sick joke that is life straight in the eye and tell it to bring its fucking A game because you shouldn't go down without a fight." He kisses my hand and turns his tall frame towards me as he encases me with his body.

"I won't let you give up. You gotta fight. So cry all you need, get drunk to forget, but don't let the shittiness of life get to you. You're better than that. And maybe you should speak to Ben. Open up to him." The words are forced out of his mouth.

"No. I don't want to speak to him. He always tells me the same thing. That it'll be okay. That we'll be okay, but it won't be. It never is."

"Dimples, I'm telling you pretty much the same fucking thing. And Ben is right. You need to let him help you. Together, the two of you could probably overcome all this fucking bullshit," he says.

"No. You're not trying to reassure me with false promises." He opens his mouth to speak, but I stop him before he says anything else I don't want to hear. "No, Arsen. Thank you, but leave it at that. I don't want to talk about him, or the poor state that my marriage is in."

The bar is getting busier by the hour. I'm wondering how long we've been here when I notice that we are still holding hands. I'm staring at them when I feel him move closer to me, leaning down to whisper in my ear, "He's a good guy, Dimples. I'm sure he means well. And maybe you shouldn't be here with me when you can be with him."

Annoyed, I push his hand away. The truth can always be a damn bother. "Yes. But I don't want to. I want to be here. If you want to leave, leave. I don't care. I like you, Arsen, but I'm not going to take relationship advice from a man whore who can't open up or settle down long enough with the same woman because he's scared shitless. Sorry."

He pins me with furious eyes as he crosses his arms. "You know what? Fuck you. I'm trying to help you. And FYI, I don't give a fuck about your marriage and—"

"Yes. Go ahead! Say it! I dare you. Say that you don't give a fuck about me. And why should you? I don't even like myself."

With angry tears beginning to burn my eyes, I stand up and leave him sitting there. This is not what I signed up for when I agreed to meet up with him behind Ben's back. I'm not sure what I was expecting, but definitely not this.

Outside the bar, I walk towards the curb to try and catch a cab. When I lift my bare arm in the air, I remember too late that

I left my jacket back in the coat check. Whatever. The cold air is a welcome relief as it cools down my heated skin.

When a yellow cab pulls in front of me, I'm about to get in, but Arsen's voice stops me.

"Fuck. Cathy, wait!" He grabs my arm and spins me around until we're staring at each other. Out of the corner of my eye, I notice that we are attracting unwanted attention, but I don't care.

"Let go of me, you asshole!"

My anger takes him by surprise, making his hand go slack. I snatch my arm away and leave him standing there as I run blindly for a couple of streets before Arsen catches up to me. He grabs my hand forcefully, making me follow him to an empty alleyway that hides us from pedestrians as I start hitting him and yelling for him to let me go. One of his free hands tries to cover my mouth to stop me from screaming, but I don't let him. I viciously bite him, feeling my teeth break through his skin. I can taste his blood. And it's fucking sweet.

"Fuck you, Arsen. Leave me alone. I hate you! I hate you! I hate you!"

"Would you please listen? FUCK! Stop it Catherine! Look at me! Calm down!"

Crying and defeated, I let him lower us to the dirty ground. As I sit on his lap, Arsen murmurs, desperation in his voice.

"Shhhh…Cathy. You've got it wrong. You've got it all wrong. I care…I care a lot." There's hopelessness and yearning in his voice and in his hold of me.

When I lift my eyes and meet his, I finally understand everything. The song, the phone call, tonight…I get it. I do.

And I'm not sure if it's the desperation and sadness I feel, the look of want in his eyes, or the attraction I've been fighting all along, but I decide that I don't care anymore. I'm done with doing the right thing. It's at this moment, when I feel Arsen's hot breath on my face and his arms wrapped around me, that I decide to throw everything away. Ben, my marriage, my future.

I need to feel him inside me.

I need Arsen to burn me to ashes with the fire roaring inside his blue eyes.

I need to kiss him.

So I do.

When our lips meet, it's not a tender moment. It's fierce.

Passionate.

Cannibalistic.

Teeth clashing.

Hair pulling.

Like this is the last kiss we will ever taste.

Arsen breaks away first. With his chest rising heavily, he stares at me with a desire so powerful that warmth gathers between my legs.

"Let's get out of here," he says as his hands settle on my shoulders, letting the tips of his thumbs caress my skin, brandishing me with his fingerprints.

Silent for a moment, I let myself drink in his beauty. The color of his eyes, his strong jaw, the golden stubble adorning his face, his full lips…

I'm not naïve. I'm aware that if I leave with him right now, we're going to do more than just hold hands.

We are going to fuck.

If I leave with Arsen, I will be turning my back on my marriage and Ben once and for all. If I leave with this man with the blue inferno in his eyes, I will burn until there's nothing left of me.

20

Once Arsen shuts the door behind us, he immediately pushes me against it and begins to kiss me desperately. He kisses me from the mouth, to the neck, all the way down. A sheen of sweat covers my cheeks, my chest…desire pulsating through my veins. Moaning, I reach for his head and pull him up, face to face. I need to feel his lips on mine once more.

When we break apart, we study each other as we let the reality of what we're about to do sink in. As silence fills the room, all I can do is stare at him while he watches me with hunger in his eyes. He is so different from Ben. Arsen's golden beauty is the perfect foil to Ben's dark looks.

"Dimples, what I wouldn't give to know the thoughts inside that little head of yours," he says, a small smile playing on his lips.

"Arsen, I'm not here to chat."

The smile is wiped clean of his face. "What are you here for, Catherine?"

I shake my head. I don't think I can actually voice what I want him to do but Arsen seems to know exactly what I want.

"Show me your tits," a voice as rough as sandpaper orders.

"What? No. Why?"

I'm taken aback by the crudeness of his words. But what did I expect? A love poem?

"You want to fuck, well, lets fuck. I want to see your tits. I need to feel them in my hands. You have no idea how long I've waited for this. Fuck, Dimples…" he murmurs as he tugs the neckline down, causing my small breasts to flow out of my dress. I close my eyes out of shame or possibly excitement when I feel Arsen's large hands cupping my breasts. His thumbs rub my nipples awake.

"Are they sensitive?" Arsen asks huskily, pinching them.

"Are they sensitive?" he repeats his question when I don't answer.

"Yes," I croak.

Arsen squeezes harder once more before letting go of them. As soon as his hands are off my body, I miss his touch.

"Turn around and show me your ass." I'm so far gone, I just follow his instructions without protesting. "Yes, like that. Now, lean against the wall and push your ass out. I want to see your pussy."

Arsen doesn't waver. He just orders and I follow.

With my back facing him, I can feel his hands on me slowly lowering my thong mid-thigh. With my underwear out of the way, he spreads my ass between his hands, massaging it as one of his fingers enters me from behind, feeling how wet I am, how wet he makes me.

Moaning, I push my ass harder against his hand. "Oh, sweet fuck. Feel how wet you are…you must like it, don't you?"

I want him inside of me, so I begin to move away from the door when he pulls my hair, bending my neck backwards.

"Don't move. Want me to fuck you right here like this?" Nodding like a crazy woman, I say yes.

"Want it rough?"

I swallow hard. "Whatever you want. I just want you now." I want him to make me numb, take away the fucking pain for just a little while.

"Push your ass towards me, baby. I am going to fuck you now." He pauses. "This is your last chance to say no. Are you sure you want to do this because once we do this, there's no turning back."

I close my eyes and make a decision.

"Yes. God, yes. I'm sure."

Arsen leans down, and whispers in my ear, "You will not regret this."

I feel Arsen's arms around me as he lifts me up in the air and carries me towards his kitchen. "What the he—"

I don't finish the sentence because his mouth is on mine. His tongue battles with mine. The kiss is aggressive, possessive, and needy. When I feel the counter under my ass, he lets go of my body and leans back to look down at me. Slowly, he removes my red dress and my bra, leaving my breasts bare. Completely naked, I begin to unbutton his shirt.

"Fuck…you make me lose my mind." He leans down and nibbles my lower lip as he wraps both of his arms around me, lending my back support.

With his white shirt open, his naked chest grazes my breasts, my nipples already tender from his teeth, pebble so hard it hurts. I close my eyes and let his mouth wander my body only to open them when I feel his tongue grazing the valley of my breasts. I see him tracing a path with his tongue all the way to my neck, never taking his eyes off of mine. Maintaining eye contact, he lowers his mouth to one of my breasts and rolls the nipple with his tongue.

When Arsen lets go of my back, I put my arms out behind me to hold myself in place. Arsen then grabs my ass roughly and pulls me closer to him. I can feel his erection through his pants as he grinds himself against my clit. And just as I'm about to get lost in the fucking sensation, I feel him moving to stand between my knees. His fingers curl around them and urge them wide apart. I offer no resistance as he stands between my thighs, breathing over my mouth, and then bending down to bite my lower lip.

I can taste my blood.

My stomach tightens and the beating of my heart fills my ears. I watch him closely, and what I see in his eyes frightens me because it's a reflection of what I want. But Cathy came to play, right?

I'm a big girl.

I know what I want.

We watch each other as I feel his thumb brush over my clit. Sucking in a deep breath of air, I ask him, "Why are we doing this, Arsen? Why do you want me? You could have anyone you want."

Arsen runs three fingers over my clit, then presses them deep inside me. Arousal flies through my body. My hands go to his hair, pulling his face closer to mine as I hear myself cry out. I spread my legs wider and lift my hips as an invitation for his merciless touch. I whimper when Arsen starts to rub one spot faster. Harder. Beautifully brutal. After a few moments, I'm already so close to coming when he stops.

"Stand up. Turn around and bend over," he orders.

I am so lost in pleasure that I don't freaking care what his words mean.

What he is about to do.

What we are about to do.

Until now, Arsen and I have only fooled ourselves into pretending that we are friends and nothing else. In my mental haze, I know that if we go further today my marriage will be over. The jaded side of me, the one that rules my life, is telling me to go ahead and fuck Arsen. To throw everything away just to feel alive once more, to just feel.

On the other hand, there is a big part of me, the one I have been ignoring pretty much since I agreed to meet Arsen, telling me, urging me not to do it. Not to do this to Ben. Not to do this to myself. That I am cheating myself; that I am better than this. That part of me is also saying that I love Ben and that without him, I will be nothing.

Well, screw that.

And screw the guilt I am feeling, and screw what my fickle heart is telling me.

Like I've said before, I want to forget.

And Arsen…

He's my kryptonite.

So I turn around and bend over the kitchen counter. I hear the sounds of his zipper opening and of foil paper being ripped. When I feel his hands grab my hips, I grip the edge of the counter for support. Bent forward as I am, offering myself to him, my eyes land on an object that sparkles brightly when light falls on my hand. It's my engagement ring and diamond wedding band. Dispassionately, I admire the beauty of the rings…the simplicity of the design…the way it seems to be flashing like a warning signal.

Ben.

He gave me these rings as a promise to be mine forever. We said our wedding vows as he put that wedding band on my finger.

Ben.

I close my eyes to the reminder of what I am about to do, of what I am about to throw away. What I want to do.

"You want this, huh?" he asks hoarsely.

"Yes! Yes! Yes! Shut up and fuck me, Arsen. Just fuck me," I whimper and plead. "Make me forget. Please, make me forget."

"Shit, Catherine." He slowly caresses my naked back, making me tremble under his tender touch. "I will."

It all happens at once. I close my eyes, my cell goes off, and Arsen slides all the way in, pushing me forward with the force of his thrust. A cry escapes my throat. Is it pain? Is it pleasure? Is it guilt? Maybe all three.

When I feel his dick inside me, my body instantly recognizes the difference. The thickness…the length…it's not the same, but it feels just as good. Maybe even better because it's not Ben. I shut my eyes and silence the voice screaming in my head that this is wrong. In this moment, nothing exists but Arsen and me.

Not even Ben.

"Do you like it, Dimples? Do you like my cock fucking your pussy?" he hisses as he begins to move.

I feel my arousal covering him as he thrusts with slow and easy care. My swollen body embraces him, welcomes him, and takes all of him.

And my cell phone keeps ringing.

I hold my breath and ignore the annoying ringtone and its reminder. I don't want to think. On the brink of having an orgasm, I push my body back against him. I can hear the sound of our bodies clashing…slapping…and the phone ringing.

Arsen groans as he clutches my hips harder, his fingers leaving indentations on my skin, savagely filling me, erasing every single memory of Ben off my body. I hear my moans getting louder as he brings one of his hands to rub my clit incessantly.

I'm close, so close.

The phone rings again, and again, and again…

Never stopping. Taunting me with its music.

I don't open my eyes. I don't want to lose the rhythm, but my body has other ideas. Arsen grips my hands in his as he leans over me, his front pushing me all the way down so that I'm flat on my stomach, and regains the lost rhythm.

There are no words of love being whispered in his kitchen. No laughs. The noises filling this room are the frantic slapping of our bodies, his groans, and my moans.

And the fucking cellphone that won't stop ringing.

He fucks into me smoothly as his fingers find my clit, this time rubbing me without mercy. I can feel my climax hovering above me, just waiting for that final push. I open my eyes and put my head down and look under my body where he's pumping into me. His cock huge and glistening makes me want to take him in my mouth and suck him, but I don't. Instead, I lift my ass in the air and push harder against his dick, forcing him to slam his body into mine. I'm giving him everything I have. Arsen begins to thrust harder, and harder, and harder. I feel light headed. I am so close. The pain becomes unbearable but I can't stop myself from enjoying the aggression of his hips. It's driving me closer to my climax. Behind me, Arsen slams into me one last time shoving me forward.

We come together hard.

"Fuuuuuck!" he shouts.

I moan.

After a lengthy silence, our heavy breathing the only sound in the room, Arsen finally answers my earlier question.

"Because we can't help ourselves. We can't keep avoiding this."

When Arsen pulls out of me, my eyes land on my phone peeking out of my bag. The image staring back at me.

Ben holding Mimi and smiling into the camera.

Sometime later, after another round, I'm lying naked on top of Arsen. Our bodies sweaty from screwing, his hand gently caressing my back, a crystal clear thought suddenly forms in my head. With my chest pounding frantically, I realize I haven't felt like this for a very long time. ALIVE.

And I want more.

A lot more.

Crying.

My eyes are tired.

Scrubbing.

My body is raw.

God, give me strength. I want to go back. I need to go back, but could I?

Could I go back to Arsen and let him fuck me again until he erases the pain away? Until he pulls me out of the deep ocean of remorse I'm drowning in?

Those waves. They keep pulling me down. And I need to break through. I must. But he made it all go away. He made me forget, even if it was just for a couple of hours. He made me forget, and I want to forget.

I must forget.

Scorching. The water falling down on my skin is burning me and it feels so very good. The pain is a sweet punishment for having tasted the deliciously forbidden.

Foamy soap covers me as I continue to scrub my body down, washing him away. I don't want to, but I must. I cannot go to bed smelling like another man, smelling like the musky scent of Arsen's cum, so I coat my body with jasmine scented soap over and over again. Ignoring the swollen redness in between my legs, the rug burn on my knees, the bruise growing on my left breast close to my nipple…I erase all traces of him off my body.

After I'm finished showering and patting myself dry, I apply lotion on my body and face and head to bed. My hair still damp from the shower wets my pillow as I lie down, pretending to be asleep before Ben comes to bed. I don't know how I will face him, kiss his lips, taste him in my mouth, when all I want is to taste someone else. Rubbing my legs together and feeling the soreness in between them is a reminder that I should feel remorseful. And I do, I feel remorse, but I don't think it will stop me from repeating what happened tonight. No. I want to be selfish. For the first time in a very long time, I was able to forget about the pain and the memories.

I lost myself in the sweet oblivion of Arsen's body.

I felt alive.

I felt high in the freedom of walking away from my shitty life and pretending for a brief moment that I was just Catherine. A woman. A sensual woman who isn't a failure.

When Arsen touched me, I didn't feel a visceral reaction to his touch.

When he went deep inside me with each thrust of his hips, I didn't feel like it was sex to get pregnant, I didn't feel the lack of romance.

When he fucked my brains out on the carpeted floor for a second time, it didn't feel like work or a task. It was pure raw passion, and I want more.

I crave more.

But can I go through with it again?

I don't know.

The guilty tears have dried, my body is clean, and my conscience is garbage, so why am I so confused? The answer should be simple; walk away, come clean with Ben, apologize and hope that he has it in him to forgive and forget. The thing is, I'm ashamed, but I'm not sorry. I'm not. It's funny, really. Thinking about the way he came inside me, on me, everywhere, makes me sick to my stomach, guilt twisting it so tightly. Yet, the memories make my heart flutter as fast as a hummingbird's wings. Control and restraint gone, being with him was pure bliss.

Sometimes not being in control, not being able to think, just losing yourself in the moment, is the greatest feeling in the world. It's liberating. It's addicting. It's the most powerful high you'll ever get. It's a kind of freedom that tastes so sweet on your palate that you can't help but want more each time you have it.

Ben joins me in bed not too long after, and I wish he hadn't. It's only when I feel his warm hand on my hip, when I'm lying next to my unsuspecting husband that the realization of what I've done finally sinks in. Massive revulsion roars inside me, making me nauseous. Dirty. I feel dirty.

I'm a cheater.

I'm scum.

I can't stand his touch, so I turn away and lay on my side. With my back facing him, I can pretend that this is like every other night. I can lie to myself and ignore the remorse that festers inside me, not allowing me to fall asleep. But the minute I close my eyes, I realize what a big mistake it was as my mind begins to replay what happened back in Arsen's apartment.

With a tight chest, I recall every single vivid detail…

Touch yourself.

I want to watch as you make yourself come.

Yes…rub those fingers on your clit.

Fuck.

Look at me when you do that.

Yes. Like that.

Imagine that my cock is inside your pussy as my fingers fuck that sweet ass of yours.

Can you feel it?

I watch him as he takes his dick in his hand and starts to pump it slowly.

Up and down…

Up and down…

I rub my clit faster as I watch him stroking himself.

Stop.

Fuck your pussy with your fingers.

Yes…Deeper. I want to watch them disappear inside you.

Take them out. Stand up. Come here.

Good girl. Now put them inside my mouth and pump my cock with your free hand.

Hissing, he grounds his erection against my hand as he whispers for me to do it harder.

I watch as he sucks my fingers. The way Arsen's tongue slides across them. And I continue to watch him as he pulls them out of his mouth.

Yes.

Pull Harder…

Harder…

God, Dimples. I need you now.

Get on your hands and knees.

I am going to fuck that sweet pussy now.

Hard.

So fucking hard.

Yes, I'm on my knees feeling a man, who's not my husband, inside me. I can feel the way his hands spread me open, wider so he can go in deeper, thrust deeper.

His fingers invade me.

Everywhere.

Feeling my body tremble, I even remember the way a groan torn out from his chest as he pulled out and came over my back, spreading himself on me.

Yes. I need to apologize to Ben for everything. I need to apologize for loving Arsen's taste on my tongue because of the simple fact that it wasn't his. I need to apologize because for the first time in a very long while I was able to orgasm without closing my eyes and picturing blue instead of brown. Because tonight, with eyes wide open, I climaxed as I got lost in a sea of blue.

Could he forgive me? I'm not sure I want him to. No. I do. I do. I love Ben. I love my Ben.

What have I done?

What have I done?

A restricting panic begins to rise inside me when I feel Ben's stubbled chin tickle the back of my shoulder. With his nose buried in the curve of my neck, he inhales deeply, making my breath accelerate. When I'm about to turn around to let him know that I am awake, he wraps his arms around me.

"I am sorry. I am so fucking sorry for not being able to give you…but you are enough. You are more than enough for me. You're my fucking world, babe. And I need you back. Please stop shutting me out, I can't take it anymore." He tightens his grip, bringing our bodies closer together as he continues to whisper fiercely in my ear, "Own me, fill me, break me, repair me, complete me. Do whatever you want to me. Just stay with me. I need you. I need to be able to live. I need my life back, I need you back."

I die a slow death with every word he whispers in my ear. His words are like daggers to my heart. They cut me. They tear me open. His words destroy me.

Not knowing what to say, and feeling like shit, I continue to pretend I'm sleeping. After a few minutes, I hear Ben's breathing deepen, letting me know that he's finally asleep.

I want to scream.

I want to cry.

I want to apologize.

I want to be alone.

I want to die.

I close my eyes tighter and make a promise with myself. I won't go near Arsen ever again. I will not tell Ben because it was a one-time thing, and some things are better left unsaid.

And it will never happen again. It will not. I know it. We will get through this. It will be as if it never happened. My love for Ben will be enough.

I love him.

I love him.

I love him.

That is what I keep telling myself as I begin to fall asleep, but the last thing I remember is picturing brilliant aqua eyes staring down at me.

And just like that, I know that my words are empty, my promises fickle.

I will see Arsen again.

I will…

Until I can't anymore.

21

People say that if you play with fire, you'll get burned. Well, when it comes to Arsen, I not only want to get burned, I want to be incinerated.

He's my chance to be unguarded and content. To be wildly, incredibly, fiercely happy. With one kiss, he awoke something inside me that had laid dormant for a very long time—the will to live. And I am going to embrace it, even if it's at the cost of my values and marriage.

Three weeks have passed since our affair began. Three weeks of living in a sullied heaven. A place where the taste of him, the smell of him, the feel of him are all I care about, all that makes my heart beat faster. A place where he's my only reality. Three weeks of ignoring thoughts of Ben during the day, and avoiding his touch at night. I love him, I still do. But he's not what I need, not what I hunger for.

Crazed, I need to be with Arsen to feel at peace, to feel calmed and centered. To feel claimed. Owned. I'm losing my mind over this man, and I can't stop myself from letting it happen. I can't do anything but wait and watch for the wreck to happen. And it will. It will leave me broken.

Destroyed.

In pieces.

On the rare occasions when Ben and I have dinner together, it has become extremely difficult to watch him eat, or talk to him as if everything is normal because nothing is. Sometimes, small things from the way he holds his fork or puts food in his mouth remind me of Arsen. I watch Ben's dark hair and imagine Arsen's blond locks in between my legs. I stare at his fingers gripping the fork and think back to the forbidden place where Arsen's fingers were the other day. How much it hurt at first, but how good it felt when Arsen fucked me there right after.

It's awful to sit in front of my husband and relive my day with my lover. The worst is when Ben makes love to me, and I imagine he's Arsen.

But such is my reality. No one said cheating was pretty but hell, it's downright disgusting.

Yet, I can't stop myself from doing it.

Today, Ben is under the impression that I'm going shopping in the city and maybe staying to have dinner with Amy. Really, lies are so easy to tell when you don't care anymore, or when you have lost all shame.

That is my truth.

Arsen picks me up in his white sports car from Grand Central and begins to drive seemingly to nowhere. "Where are you taking me?"

He takes my hand in his as he glances my way. "To my apartment. I feel that's the only place where we get to be private without having to worry whether we'll run into someone who knows us."

"But we're in Manhattan. I'm sure we can have privacy if we choose to." I lean over and run my hands through his hair.

"I guess. But if I want you, I won't be able to stop myself from taking you no matter where we are." He lets go of my hand to let his fingers roam over my exposed legs, his caressing touch warming my skin like the sun.

I smile and think of the last time I saw him.

We were at an underground nightclub. Arsen had chosen this place because we could blend in with the crowd easily and go unnoticed. The music was fast and hard, but as the crowd moved around us, bouncing and grinding, Arsen and I remained in our own little bubble. I could smell his delicious cologne and if I wanted, taste his sweat with my tongue. Arsen bent his head to rest his forehead against mine, grabbed my ass and pulled me flush against him, instantly igniting my ache for him. And like rolling waves, we danced together as one. Slowly. Sensually. Carnally.

The heat of the club, the sweat of our skin, the feel of his body so close to mine, yet not close enough, made me feel euphoric. Nothing seemed important but Arsen.

Nudging me gently, then not so gently, I started to laugh when I felt exactly what had nudged me. A smirking Arsen closed the space between our faces and kissed me open mouthed while our bodies kept writhing against each other.

I loved it.

We should have felt awkward by making out to this extent in the middle of the dance floor, but Arsen and I seemed to be in a different world where the passion that was making me incredibly wet and Arsen extremely hard, made everything trivial. I didn't even care if pictures of this night made it on the newspaper. I was that far gone in ecstasy.

When the song changed to something even louder and faster than the one before, Arsen seemed to realize where we were. He let go of my ass, and cupped my chin in his hand while his fingers ran through my hair.

He moved his mouth close to my ear and whispered, "What is it about you that makes me fucking lose my mind?"

Before I had a chance to react, Arsen grabbed my hand and made me follow him to a dark and empty corner. By the time we made it to there, he backed me up against the wall. Arsen grabbed the hem of his shirt to wipe the perspiration off my face, revealing part of his six-pack. I wanted to lean down and trace my tongue through every ripple covered in his sweat.

After he releases his shirt, Arsen took me by surprise when he used the front of his body to pin me against the wall. He put his hands on the wall encasing my head, and then he leaned down to run his nose through my hair, my throat, behind my ear.

"The feel of you..." he whispered in my ear, "I want you so damn much. I don't think I have ever wanted someone as much as I want you."

It was in these moments when I was out with Arsen, so full of him, that not a thought of Ben crossed my mind. When I was able to bury my feelings for him deep in my heart and ignore the guilt festering inside me.

When I could ignore reality and pretend that Arsen was mine.

And in that moment I was drunk and high of him.

He was all I wanted.

He made me want to throw my head back and laugh.

He made me forget.

When Arsen voiced how much he wanted me, I felt powerful and inebriated with excitement. I wanted to show him how much he meant to me. He watched me closely as I lowered my eyes to where our bodies were connected, my hand coasting over the lean sides of his waist, the muscles of his chest, and his tense abdomen. Our need for each other so palpable in the air around us.

I wanted to touch him, to feel him in my hands, to make him feel as excited as he made me. I wanted him down on his knees with want. For me.

Without giving much thought to what I was about to do, I slid my fingers inside his jeans and boxer briefs until they curved over his erection.

I saw him close his eyes and take a deep breath as my hand felt how hard he was for me. Wanting to give him as much pleasure as possible, I slowly caressed his length, my thumb lightly rubbing the head of his dick.

Up and down…

Up and down…

I contracted my fingers boldly around him until I heard him hiss.

Arsen lowered his head and began whispering kisses all over my face with such tenderness it made me want to cry. It was as if he were worshiping me with his mouth and his touch. His searching lips lingered in the corners of mine, across my nose, then made their way back to my mouth. Urgently, I turned my face to kiss him, wanting his lips, his tongue, his mouth on mine, and he gave me what I wanted. He kissed me slowly, owning me by excruciating degrees, making me moan and open my mouth fully to the penetration of his tongue. Arsen led the kiss, setting the pace, not letting me pull away even when I felt overpowered by him.

He removed his hands from the wall and pulled me even closer to him than before. Arsen then hunched his shoulders over me and brought one of his hands to cup my ass, lifting me so that I stood on my tip-toes. I let go of his erection and brought my hands to his hair. I twisted and pulled it until I made him groan. He moved his mouth to my throat, to the top of my breasts peeking out of my tank top and licked the sweat off.

By that point, I had lost my fucking mind with need for him, so I brought one of my legs up to wrap around his waist, bringing us closer than before. In this new position, I was open to him, open to his wandering hand.

He caressed the inside of my thigh as his fingers under my skirt inched up, and up, and up until I was sure he could feel how wet I was. His possessive hand stroked me outside my panties.

I knew we should have been paying more attention to what was going on around us, after all we were in a very public place and people could snap a picture, but honest to God…

I couldn't care less, and Arsen seemed less concerned than me.

Arsen lips parted, and his eyes widened ever so slightly as he felt how close I was to getting off; his fingers teased and caressed me until I shattered.

My pulse pounded in my ears and throat while I felt spasms come over me, each beat of bliss pulling low moans from my throat. If not for the support of his hand on my ass, I'd have stumbled forward. His erection pressed hard against my belly while he watched my face, my mouth, the fast rise and fall of my breasts, with an expression of awe. Once I was coherent again, I noticed his flushed face and the way his jaw was set so tight, conveying how tense and in pain he was.

A smiling Arsen put a finger under my chin and lifted it until I looked up into his beautiful eyes. He bent to kiss me once more, but this kiss was short and sweet.

"Only…so…much…self…control." I heard him say through the music. Then he helped me lower my leg and set our clothes in order, wincing as he adjusted his erection. When he was ready to lead us back to our table, he made sure my clothes were in place. He leaned down to whisper, "I don't know how it's possible, but you look more beautiful than before."

I looked at him feeling my already flushed face turn hotter and mumbled, "Ummm…thank you."

Arsen gazed down at me for a moment longer, then throwing his head back, he laughed. When he was done laughing, he said, "Best fucking dancing experience ever. Maybe I should do it more often?"

I wanted to smack him on the shoulder, but I laughed instead. He looked so adorable, all flushed. "Which reminds me…about your situation."

Arsen wrapped his arms around my waist. "Don't give it a thought, Dimples. I am very satisfied. Just keep your sweet ass in front of me when we get to the table and we'll be okay."

"What's that smile for?" Arsen asks.

"Oh, nothing. Just thinking about your moves."

"The club?" he asks, a cocky smile on his lips.

"Yep."

"Shit, that was fucking incredible."

And I agree. It was incredible, but it was because of him.

When we arrive at his apartment, I take in the minimalistic décor. I've only been here twice before today. We usually meet in a hotel in Queens, but Arsen figures his apartment can be just as private as long as we pretend not to know each other when we walk in.

The last time I was here my whole attention had been on Arsen, so as I make my way to his master bedroom, I take in my surroundings. Everything looks so empty and lifeless.

"How come you don't have any pictures hanging on your walls?" I ask, glancing over my shoulder to stare at Arsen who is stripping me naked with his eyes.

Arsen shrugs his shoulders and follows me.

"There's no point. All I want to look at is standing in front of me," he says hoarsely.

"Oh. Um…" I stutter.

"Wait, come here."

Curious, I turn around and approach him. Arsen surprises me by picking me up and wrapping my legs around him. Our bodies connect intimately with our clothing as the only barrier between us.

"Better," he says as he squeezes my butt. "I've missed you." He leans down and kisses me, his tongue seeking and tangling with mine.

After kissing for a couple minutes, I break away with the need for air.

"I've missed you too," I murmur against his lips.

Arsen carries me to his bedroom and puts me down in front of a floor length mirror next to his bed. As I look at my reflection, I begin to take the pins out of my hair and let it flow over my shoulders.

I want Arsen. He makes me feel free. His mere presence buries a side of me that I hate, one that makes me vulnerable by reminding me of all the pain. A pain I want to forget. And Arsen does that for me. Maybe that's why I feel this obsession with him.

"What are you thinking?" he asks.

I watch Arsen in the mirror as he begins to remove his clothing. He pulls his gray cotton t-shirt over his head and drops it on the floor, removing his pants and boxer briefs next. The powerful muscles on his torso and his arms give me the impression that he could lift me with one hand without any effort.

"Nothing. Just admiring you," I say, warmth settling in my core as I observe his naked body.

Arsen chuckles and closes the distance between us. Placing his arms on my shoulders, he leans down, buries his nose in my hair, and takes a deep breath, drinking in the smell. He's so close to me that it would be extremely easy to get down on my knees and take him in my mouth. The image and the memory of his taste makes me tremble from head to toe.

"Strip down for me, Catherine," he orders roughly.

When I begin to remove my jacket, he moves away and sits on the edge of the bed. He observes me carefully as if he is the hunter and I, his prey.

My hands tremble as I take off my clothes until I'm down to my black lace bra and thong, showcasing my slim body. I can see my pebbled pink nipples and the vee of the most intimate part of my body through the lace work.

I lift my eyes from the perusal of my body and observe Arsen doing the same while he strokes his erection in his hand. There's a sexy smile adorning his face as he drinks me in.

"Come here." The order, though softly said, makes me shiver in excitement.

Arsen makes a dark side of me, one that is uninhibited, come out and want to be just as bad as he is. Maybe it's because he sets me free, I don't know, but when I'm with him I don't care about anything other than him.

Slowly, I straddle him until the only thing separating us is the thin silk of my thong. It would be so easy to screw each other. All he would have to do is slide the fabric to the side and push inside me. But we don't move. We gaze intensely at each other instead.

"You drive me fucking crazy," he says before he licks the valley between my breasts, lightly running his hands over my back. I tilt my neck back as I offer myself to him.

"I want to fuck you so bad, Dimples. I haven't been able to think of anything else since the last time I saw you." He lifts his hips, grinding his erection against my sex. The carnal friction makes me groan as I feel the humid warmth of my body seeping through the material separating us.

"Can you feel how much I fucking want you?" he asks roughly.

I meet his gaze and stare at his feverish bright eyes. "I want you too," I whisper softly against his mouth. I want this. I want him. He's everything I need in this moment.

Arsen remains silent for a second, "You know, when I saw you for the first time, I remember noticing how sad your eyes looked." He runs his finger along the edge of my jaw, "But it was nothing compared to how lost they were three weeks ago," he adds huskily.

"And how do they look now?" I ask as I rub myself on his dick.

He smiles tenderly at me as he rubs his thumb across my lips. "Not so lost."

I nod. Like a beacon, this man's inner light illuminates all the darkness surrounding me.

Arsen sobers up. "Dimples, I want to make that fucking sadness in them disappear completely."

"Oh." I don't think that's possible. I'm truly past remedy. And If I wasn't before, I am now. "I don't know if that will ever happen. I-I don't think it's feasible," I say.

"Fuck feasible." He kisses me on the lips. "For you, I'll fucking make the impossible happen. There's no room for fucking sadness in such a pretty face as yours."

I want to smile as I take in the earnest expression on his face, but instead I shake my head once more as tears pool in my eyes. I'm falling for him, and I don't want to. I dismiss the thought and let the thrill of the moment take over my mind.

Arsen begins to kiss my neck, letting his tongue trace the goosebumps awakened on my skin by his touch. Skillfully he removes my bra, tosses it on the floor, and then palms my breasts until my nipples are a bright red.

I lift myself on my knees, about to remove my thong, when he puts a staying hand on mine.

"No," he orders. "Leave it on."

Arsen grabs his hard dick in one hand while the other pushes aside the thin fabric of my thong, twisting the string so tightly around his palm you can see its red imprint on his skin.

"You're so beautiful, so fucking sweet," he murmurs.

I begin to lower myself onto his erection when my phone begins to ring.

It's him.

This is the fourth or fifth time he's called.

"Don't answer." Arsen pushes his dick inside me, then out again, and begins to rub the head of his dick across my clit. "Let it go to voicemail. If it's him, he knows you're busy with friends." He chuckles when the word friends rolls off his tongue.

Arsen's cruel mocking snaps me out of my haze. Sobering me on the spot. I feel torn by what we are about to do, but the wetness between my legs betrays me. My body knows what it wants.

"No. I need to get this. He's going to worry. I haven't spoken to him since he left this morning." I remove his hands from my underwear, get off his lap, and make my way to my bag. Covering my breasts with one arm, I fish for my phone with the other, wishing I could ignore Ben and extinguish the guilt beginning to fester inside me.

When I finally find my phone, I answer.

"Hello?"

"Babe."

"Hi, baby. What's going on? I can't talk for too long. The store is getting busier and I still have to try on the clothes I found," I say, sounding breathless.

Ben laughs. "You can buy whatever you want as long as you don't buy more of those frilly things you wear to bed that I always end up taking off, or shredding with my fingers." I look down at the set I'm wearing and notice how stretched they are.

Feeling sweltering shame burn my face, I slide them off my legs and toss them on the floor. Now I'm completely naked. Clean on the outside yet so, so dirty on the inside.

"Um, Ben…I—"

"It's alright. I've got to go. I was just calling to let you know I won't be home for dinner. I have to go over some paperwork. Kerry is staying and helping me out, so we'll probably just order take out."

At the mention of Kerry's name, my senses begin to tingle but I smother them right away. I have no right to question anything. I was just sitting on Arsen's dick.

"Oh, okay." I'm about to say that I have to hang up when I feel Arsen's hand in between my legs, his fingers finding and invading my pulsating core.

He leans down and whispers in my ear, "Tell him you're busy and that you have to let him go." He pushes harder inside me. "I want to fuck you now."

"Is that Arsen?" There's disbelief in his voice.

Arsen chuckles as he keeps stroking me. I want to whimper because of the things his wicked hand is doing to my body, desire flooding my senses. Arsen steps closer to me until his erection is wedged in between my ass and his stomach.

"Y-yes, baby. That's Arsen." My voice is shaky.

I try to move away from him, but he won't let me. His free arm snakes around my waist tightly, holding me in place.

"Don't you fucking dare, Catherine. You're mine for now," he whispers harshly before nipping me in the ear. The sweet man from a couple minutes ago is gone and in his place is the old Arsen, cold and crude. His thumb furiously rubs my clit as his fingers continue to slide in and out of me.

"What the hell are you doing with him? I thought you were shopping." He sounds angry.

Suppressing a whimper, I try to come up with a valid excuse as to why I'm with Arsen. I try to find the right lie to deliver to the man on the other line. The man that I supposedly love so much, my faithful and steadfast husband.

"I-I ran into him. He's here with his mother."

I know he doesn't believe me. Ben is quiet for a minute. A minute too long. "I've got to go. Bye," he says frostily.

The coldness in his voice scares me, prompting me to stop him from hanging up. "Wait!" I use all my force to push Arsen away. This time it works because he lets me go as I step into the middle of the room.

"Yes?" I hear Ben ask.

My body and mind are at odds because I'm still aroused by Arsen's touch, yet I'm sick with disgust for allowing it to happen. But I can't stop. I can't.

I stall for time, not really sure what to say.

Meanwhile, my lover is standing in front of me, watching me with stormy eyes as his chest contracts from his heavy breathing. His raging erection is tantalizing and beautiful.

"I guess I'll see you at home," I say.

The muscles in Arsen's chest tense, but I ignore it. Ben is silent, and I think he's going to hang up before replying, but he surprises me with his next words and how deep they cut. "Yes." Ben pauses, "I love you. Don't forget that. Always."

The line goes dead, leaving me drowning in shame.

Arsen must notice a change in my demeanor because he doesn't give me a chance to say or do anything before he pounces on me. Lifting me up in his arms, he brings me back to his bed.

As soon as I'm lying down, he begins to spread kisses all over my body, almost as if he were trying to brand me with his lips. The instant I feel his skin on mine, I can go back to pretending that nothing exists beyond the walls of his room. I know I should be angry with him and sickened by what he just did, but I can still hear Ben in my head, and I don't want to. I can't. I'll go mad with guilt.

So I use Arsen.

"Arsen…"

His lips land on mine. "Yes…" he murmurs between kisses as his hands explore the curves of my body.

"I need you. Now," I beg.

Make me feel nothing but your body inside mine.

Let me lose myself in pleasure.

Bury the truth so I don't have to hurt because of it.

Lifting himself on his elbows, he hovers above me. I notice his lips are red and puffy from mine. "What do you think I'm trying to do here?"

"I don't want to kiss anymore. I-I—"

"You want me to just fuck you?" He pushes the tip of his erection inside me. "Like this?"

I spread my legs wider to welcome him, grab him by the shoulders, and lift my hips. "Yes, please. I don't want to think anymore," I beg.

As soon as the words leave my mouth, I know I made a mistake.

Arsen's body stiffens instantaneously. "Is this about his phone call? Because if you want me to fuck you so you don't have to think about him, I won't. Fuck that," Arsen spits at me as he rolls away from me, landing on his back.

"What do you mean? I…you don't want me?" I sit up, grab the silky white sheet, and cover my exposed chest as I stare at his golden frame. The swollen tip of his dick gleams with the proof of my desire for him.

We stare at each other without speaking. I'm blushing of embarrassment, and Arsen is openly eyeing me with anger written on his face.

"No," he says flatly, nostrils flaring.

I'm humiliated and mortified beyond words. What was I thinking? Of course he doesn't want me. I'm worthless.

"I understand."

I move to stand, but Arsen blocks me. Kneeling in front of me, he cups my face in his hands. "Fuck, Catherine. Stop. Look at me, please."

I raise my eyes and stare at him. He's like the sun. Blinding. I can't tear my gaze away, even as I'm being blinded by him.

"Why is it always like this with us?" Groaning, he runs a hand through his hair. "One moment it's like we're flying, and the next I want to fucking hurt someone." He pauses, lust and some feeling I don't understand warring in his eyes, "I want you. So damn much. You know that. But I can't do this. Not when it's him you're thinking about."

"B-but I want you." It's not a lie. I do, so much.

Whenever I'm with him, I don't feel cold, or empty, or broken. He makes it all go away.

"No. Not like this. I'm a worthless piece of shit for taking what's not mine, but I won't let him in here." He points at his bed. "Not here. This is where I don't have to share you. This is where you're mine," he says gently.

"Oh, Arsen. You aren't…and he—"

"Shh, beautiful. Enough about him. Come here, let me kiss you. I need that fucking sweet mouth of yours on mine," he says softly.

When Arsen lets go of my face, he leans down and kisses me on the lips once more. It's short, but I can't stop the reaction of my body the moment our mouths come together. His kiss invades my senses, inebriating me with its sweet flavor.

"You're right. I was trying to…I'm sorry. So sorry," I say guiltily as we lie together on his bed.

He looks up from his slow examination of our intertwined hands. "It's fine. I understand what you were trying to do. I've been there. I've used sex to bury thoughts and emotions." He kisses my forehead before continuing, "Sometimes it works, sometimes it doesn't, but I don't want to fuck you while you think about him."

"I'm sorry."

"Forget it. Besides, I like this." He lets go of my hand and wraps his arms around me as he chuckles. "Cuddling. Who the hell would've imagined that? You're turning me into a pussy. Saying no to getting laid and cuddling instead," he says, a boyish grin appearing on his face.

"Are you sure you don't want me to take care of it?" I nod in the direction of his erection.

"Nah, it'll go away."

"But aren't you in pain?"

"Nothing I can't handle. Now be quiet and fucking kiss me again."

And we get lost in sweet moments of oblivion. Our breaths filling each other's lungs, Arsen slowly becoming part of me.

Hours later, before I leave his apartment, Arsen hugs me fiercely. He kisses the top of my head and every surface of my face. When he lets go of me, he raises a hand and cups my chin. "Is it like this with him?"

I'm taken aback by his question.

"No, don't answer. I don't want to know," he says as he plants another quick peck on my lips.

As I make my way to the train station, I realize I should call Ben, but I choose not to. I want to think of Arsen for a little bit longer. For the first time since our affair began Arsen and I weren't intimate, but somehow I feel closer to him than ever before.

When I arrive home later that night, I'm greeted by the smell of garlic and tomato sauce.

"Ben?" I ask loudly as I begin to remove my diamond studs, feeling my hair graze the top of my fingers.

"In here!" he shouts.

I want to change out of my clothes and brush my teeth, but instead I go in search of Ben. Faltering in my step, I'm not exactly sure what I'm going to say when I see him. I'm pretty sure he didn't buy my excuse that I ran into Arsen while I was out shopping.

As soon as I reach the kitchen, I find Ben standing by the counter eating spaghetti from a floral bowl. He looks his usual preppy self even in washed out jeans and an old plain gray tee. He's watching Mimi purr as she brushes herself against his leg, a sad expression on his face. When he hears me come in, he raises his gaze and examines my appearance. A bleak look flashes in his eyes, but it's gone in an instant. And just like that, I'm reminded of everything I want to forget so badly and why. He's a daily reminder of what will never be.

"Hi. I thought you were going to be working late tonight?" I ask as I put some shopping bags on the floor. Arsen picked up some stuff for me so I could come home and continue with my charade.

"I was supposed to, but decided to come home in the end. I thought you would be here…"

"Um, yes. I decided to have dinner with Arsen since I hadn't seen him in ages." As I lie, I'm overcome by repugnance at my own behavior. Not knowing what to do to get rid of it, I push all thoughts of Arsen out of my mind and focus on Ben.

"Did you just leave him?" Ben asks, carefully placing his bowl on the white marble countertop.

I reach for a napkin, wipe the corners of his mouth, and let my fingers hover above his lips. Lifting my eyes, I stare at his familiar eyes and the way they watch me with so much love.

"Yes, he wanted to go for drinks after dinner. I didn't feel like having a drink, so I came home early."

He circles his arms around my waist a little more forcefully than I'm used to. Silently we gaze at each other as Ben lifts a hand, then lets his thumb rub my lower lip, mirroring what Arsen had done not two hours ago.

I wonder if he can tell how swollen my lips are…

"I find it interesting that he was gone for so long and all of a sudden he seems to be everywhere," he says quietly, still rubbing my lip. It's beginning to hurt.

"What do you mean? I haven't heard or seen him since that night at the bar," I say as a cold shiver runs along my spine.

"How could I forget the bar? It was a fucking show. However…"

"Yes?"

"I say that he's popping up everywhere because not three days ago I read on Page Six that he has been seen with an unknown blonde around town a couple times now."

I feel like my stomach has dropped to the floor. "R-really? Do they k-know who she is?"

"Yes, really." Ben grips my waist harder. "And no, they don't know. You know how Manhattan is. If you want to be anonymous, it's the place to be."

"Yes," I say, lifting my hand and placing it on top of Ben's; stopping him because his touch has turned painful.

"As I was saying, they don't know the identity of the woman, but they don't seem too concerned. They called her the flavor of the week," he chuckles.

I feel like Ben just kicked me in the gut. "Well, if she's the flavor of the week, then why do they mind?"

"No fucking clue. Anyway, not my point. My point is that even you ran into him. How funny is that?" he asks bitingly.

"Um, yes. Well, I…we didn't speak about his dating life. It was just…um…you know, life. Anyway, shopping wore me out." I begin to pull away from him, but his hand remains planted on my waist, "Ben, let go. I want to take a shower and go to bed."

"Why, babe? Are you tired?" he asks with a hint of sarcasm.

"Yes. Please, could you let go?" I say as I try to push away from him, but I'm met with resistance once more.

Suddenly his touch makes me uncomfortable. There's something in the way he's staring at me, and the tension I sense emanating from his body that lets me know how angry he is. Angrier than I have ever seen him.

"Too tired to spend some time with me?" Ben asks, grabbing me by the hips and turning us around, backing me up against the countertop.

"Ben, no. Not tonight. I'm tired. Please, stop." I feel sick to my stomach.

"Babe...I've missed you." When he leans down to nuzzle my neck, I sense desperation in him. His hands close around my wrists, moving them to wrap around his neck. He then grabs my ass, lifting me on the countertop.

"No. I really don't feel like it tonight."

"I need you, babe. So fucking much. It's been so long," he says hoarsely as he lifts my skirt and begins to pull down my panties.

"No!" I exclaim, pushing him away with all my strength.

I hear Ben curse, but he doesn't approach me anymore. With our chests rising heavily, I get down off the counter and fix my skirt without looking at him. "I said no, Ben." I want to cry and throw up, but do neither. "I-I need to go lie down."

"Jesus Christ," he mutters, "Just fucking go." He runs his hands over his hair, his frustration blasting me in the face. "I can't win with you. Forget it. I'm going to the office." He turns around and leaves me standing in the middle of our empty kitchen.

It's not until I watch him walk out of the room that I break down and cry. *What have I done to Ben?*

I look down, noticing that my hands are shaking violently as I feel revulsion turn my stomach upside down by my own actions. I want to scream, I want to throw up, I want to die. I'm repulsed by me, but that's a price I'm willing to pay to be with Arsen.

I shut down the voice inside my head that tells me that this is the beginning of the end.

22

I'm currently in Barneys looking for an evening gown to wear to one of Ben's black tie affairs tomorrow night. I wish I didn't have to go so that I could spend the night with Arsen in his bed while Ben is out schmoozing people I don't care for. As I wait for Arsen to arrive, I can't stop the smile tugging at my lips when I recall his words on the phone just an hour before.

"What do you feel like eating?"

"You."

"Stop it. I'm serious."

"Me too."

"Whatever. How about you meet me at Barney's first, then we can decide where to go from there?"

"Yes. Back to my place. Where I'll show you how hungry I am."

Feeling warmth saturate the apex of my legs, I decide to get serious in my endeavor to find the right dress before I explode with need. I settle for a J. Mendel strapless gown with a tonal mesh one-shoulder panel. It's black and not in your face sexy with its slit wrap skirt. Looking for shoes, I get lucky when a very cute guy approaches me right away, asking me if I need help for the day. After I point out the pair of purple Manolos I liked and give him my shoe size, I sit down and wait for him to come back. In the meantime, I take my phone out to see if I have any missed calls from Arsen. There's only one text message from Ben. I feel a pang of pain in my chest, but I ignore his message and text Arsen to let him know my whereabouts.

When the cute blond guy comes back with the pair of shoes, he kneels in front of me, taking my bare foot in his hand and propping it on his knee. "I hope you don't mind if I help you with this. It's one of the few perks of my job."

An answering smile on my lips, I can't help to joke back. He's that cute. "Oh, really? I'm sure women don't mind it at all."

He smiles, then points at my wedding rings. "Sadly it appears that I'm already too late. Should I go beat him up? Would that make you give him up for me?"

I look down at my left hand and see Ben's big diamond and my wedding band. I want to take them off. They suddenly feel so very tight. Cut off circulation tight.

Cute guy must notice the change in my expression. "I'm sorry, ma'am. I didn't mean to—"

"It's nice to see that you're having such a blast when trying on a fucking pair of shoes, Catherine."

He releases my foot right away and stands up. I raise my head and let my eyes land on a very pissed off Arsen. If looks could kill, poor cute guy would probably be dead by now.

Angry at his accusative tone, I shrug my shoulders in a blasé manner and pretend I don't care what his words are implying.

"We are, well, that is, I was until a moment ago. If you don't mind, Arsen—"

Arsen pushes him aside, kneels down in front of me and puts my Ferragamo's sling-back on, then stands up. Turning to look at sales attendant, he hands him his black American Express and tells him to charge whatever I want on it. After the bill is settled, and without saying a word to me, he grabs me by the elbow and makes me follow him to a dressing room.

We stare at each other in angry silence for a moment. I'm so irritated at how rude he was that my hands are shaking. "What the fuck was that?" I yell, not caring that people might hear us. "He was just doing his job!"

Spearing me with his blue eyes, Arsen's calm voice is more potent that the loudest of shouts and his quiet demeanor quenches my anger. "I don't give a fuck. He touched you, and you are mine. Only mine. Only I get to touch you."

"I am not yours. You are being foolish," I whisper.

"What the fuck are you trying to say? You wanted him to touch you? Want him to be your next boy toy? What, my cock is not enough for you?" Arsen hisses, knowing that he's hurting me.

"No! Stop it, Arsen! Are you even listening to what you are saying?"

He pulls away from me to sit on the bench. "In all honesty, Cathy…you have a history."

"How dare you?" Shame and anger resurface.

"Well, you're here with me, aren't you? While your husband is at work?"

"I hate you."

Arsen smiles coldly. "You only hate me because you know it's the truth."

"I'm leaving. Goodbye, Arsen. Call me when you grow up."

As I turn to leave, he grabs my hand. I try to push him away, but his hands are everywhere on my body, pulling me back to him. "I'm sorry, Dimples. I didn't mean it. Don't go," Arsen murmurs.

"Arsen!" My protests become halfhearted as his touch ignites the passion that only he can create in me. His deft fingers unzip my dress until it falls on the floor leaving me partially naked. Arsen then reaches inside my panties and discovers the evidence of my arousal.

"No, you're not leaving. You're so fucking wet. You're going to fuck me right here, right now."

"I don't want you."

"Keep saying that you don't want me, but feel yourself…you're soaked." He withdraws his finger from my flesh and brings it to my mouth. "Taste yourself. Don't you dare lie to me. You want me," he growls.

And I do. I can taste the sweet saltiness of my body on his fingers.

"Dimples, say you want me. Say it," he commands as he brings his wet finger inside me once more—circling, playing with me, lighting fireworks throughout my body.

"Say it!"

"Yes! Arsen, I want you!" I hiss as my world becomes dazed with pleasure and lust. Need and want.

"Can you see me touching you?" he whispers hoarsely in my ear.

"Yes."

"Watch this."

And how couldn't I? We're in a room surrounded by mirrors; I can see our reflection everywhere I look and it sets my body ablaze.

I watch as he unzips his pants and lowers his boxer briefs, letting his erection spring free. I watch as he slowly removes my panties, spreading my ass open for him. And I continue to watch him as he pushes my body down, so I'm bending at the waist, my hands on the bench for support, offering myself fully to him.

"Push that sweet ass against my cock." He slides his dick along my entrance, rubbing himself against me. "You definitely wanted to fuck, my pretty Dimples." His voice is cocky, yet there is a sense of wonder in it. "Fuck. That ass…bend down lower for me…yeah…keep going."

And I do. I'm floating on a cloud of lust from which I never want to descend.

"Nice, Dimples. Now watch this."

I watch as he slides his dick all the way inside me. His thrusts are slow. Arsen is taking his time, enjoying watching us. I cover my mouth with my hand. I bite it hard as I try to stop myself from moaning out loud.

When he pulls out, I can see in the mirror the way his dick glistens, I know that if I put him in my mouth I'd be able to taste myself on him. He orders huskily, "Turn around. Sit on the bench. I want see you, all of you. Spread your legs open for me, and show me my sweet pussy."

"Arsen, maybe we shouldn't. I'm scared of being caught," I croak as he pulls my panties off my legs with one hand while the other rubs me mercilessly. I can hear the wet sounds his fingers are making as he begins to pump in and out of me. Raw. So fucking raw. So fucking beautiful.

I laugh because only Arsen can make me go from pissed off in one moment to exhilarated in the next. "I've never done this."

"What? Fuck in public? This is nothing, babe." There's a sexy smirk on his face that highlights how beautiful he is. Golden beauty. Letting go of me, a desperate moan escapes my mouth as I grab his hand and guide it back to my body.

"No…Arsen, please…finish this."

"I'm going to lie down. I want to watch you riding my cock."

I can't help giggling as I watch Arsen's large figure struggling to fit on the floor of the small dressing room. A playful smile touches his lips. "The things that you and your body make me do, Catherine. Now, fuck me."

As I lower myself on top of him, I grab his arms and hold them above his head. Watching him like this, with him inside me, feeling him throb. I feel so alive.

"You make me…"

I don't finish my sentence. His mouth covers mine as his hand, wrapped in my hair, pulls me down for a wonderful kiss filled with promises.

As we walk out of Barneys holding hands, without a care that someone will see us on this side of town and take a picture, Arsen tells me he wants to make a quick stop at Barnes & Noble. Nodding, I let go of his hand and wrap my arms around his mid-section. I bury my nose on the left side of his chest and inhale the smell of his cologne as I let the softness of his cotton t-shirt rub against my cheek. Being with Arsen like this, just the two of us in the middle of the day with nothing to do but enjoy each other's company, makes me feel content, happy, satisfied. If only life could always be like this.

As I sigh contently, I tighten my grip around him and let him guide our step.

"What is it, Dimples? Are you too sore to walk? Think I might have gotten a bit carried away back in the dressing room," he chuckles as he grabs my ass and gives it a squeeze.

I laugh. The teasing gleam in his eyes makes him look like such a naughty boy. "Maybe you did-Wait! What are you doing? Put me down this moment, Arsen!" Arsen lifts me off the ground, throws me over his shoulder, and bites my ass!

"Put me down this minute, Arsen!" I laugh and wiggle on his shoulder as he continues to take small bites of my ass. "What the hell do you think you're doing, you silly man! No, no, don't bite it again! It tickles!"

But Arsen doesn't listen to me; he just keeps on laughing along with me. I want to get back at him, even if I'm hanging upside down, so I pinch his ass which only makes him bark with laughter.

"Hell, no. Save your energy for later, Dimples. I plan on keeping that pretty mouth of yours busy, don't you worry," He teases.

"Arsen, seriously! Stop it this instant! Put me down!" I'm laughing so hard it makes my stomach hurt.

"Nope."

Mortified because we are attracting attention, I cover my face with my hands as I try to get down. "Oh, my God! This is so embarrassing!"

"Let them watch. Poor people need some excitement in their boring lives once in a while, Dimples. Besides, I like this," he says smugly.

And then the asshole bites my butt once again.

In the cab on our way to the nearest Barnes and Noble located in the Citigroup Center building, all Arsen and I do is make out like teenagers. Kissing, feeling, touching, we can't get enough of each other. With Arsen's hand under my shirt, rubbing my nipple erect, my hands on his blond hair pulling him closer to me, we are in the middle of a very heated lip lock when the voice of the cabdriver breaks through our kissing induced stupor.

"Yo, man. We here. Either you pay now, or I'm gonna keep driving around the block and make you pay for it!"

I feel a blush creeping across my cheeks, so I hide my face on Arsen's neck as I try to fight a mixture between embarrassment and giddiness for having been caught like a pair of horny teens.

Eyes twinkling and offering a bemused smile, Arsen tips my chin up and pecks my nose with a kiss. "Want to keep driving? Or should we get out?"

"It's okay. Let's get out." I say as happiness brims all over me.

"Good choice. I'd go broke if I let the meter run because I could do this all day," he says, the back of his hand grazing my cheek lightly.

I leave Arsen browsing through shelves of fiction novels and make my way to the romance section. Historical romances are a guilty pleasure of mine. I discovered them at the age of fifteen, and I have never been able to shake them off. When I find a winner, a sexy cover with a shirtless guy with smoldering eyes, I grab the book and sit on the floor. With my back against the shelves and my legs tucked under my butt, I begin to read the synopsis. It sounds good, so I flip the pages until I reach the last one, then read the closing line just to make sure it has a happy ending. Sadly, this one doesn't end well, so I stand up and place it back where I found it and go look for Arsen.

By the time I reach him, he's holding a plastic bag in his hand filled with books.

"What did you buy? Let me see." I grab the bag and pull the books out to read the titles. Surprised that he would be into this kind of literature, I look up and stare at him. Running his hand over his hair, there is a blush covering his cheeks as he tries to justify his purchase.

"Yes, well…I saw the movies and…Harry Potter got to me. So, I want to give them a chance."

"Arsen! Don't be embarrassed! It's cute. And the books are amazing. I've read them all, and I loved every single one of them. Want me to read them with you?" I grin.

"Really? You would do that?" he asks, disbelief in his voice.

"Yes! Bellatrix and Snape are my favorite characters."

"Is Bellatrix the one played by Helena Bonham-Carter?"

I nod.

"She was fucking awesome. But then again, everything she does is pretty fucking genius." There's a hint of a smile on his lips. Watching his enthusiasm is endearing.

We smile at each other and enjoy the moment of having found something else we have in common.

"Alright, let's go. I'm starving," I say.

Pulling me close as he wraps me in his arms, Arsen lowers his mouth and plants a kiss behind my ear. With a Harry Potter book in one hand, and a heavy plastic bag in the other, my stomach tightens when he whispers, "Me too…"

I hand Arsen the shopping bag and tell him I need to use the restroom. On my way to the bathroom, I notice the children's section that is filled with comfortable couches, toys for sale, and bright and colorful book covers. There're strollers parked here and there, moms telling their kids not to touch this or that, babysitters gossiping amongst themselves, kids running and throwing books off the shelves with their small hands while others sit nicely and browse through pages filled with pictures. Feeling a familiar pang in my chest, I pick up the pace and try to get away from there as quickly as possible. After I use the restroom and wash my hands, I head to the entrance, avoiding the area that makes my nightmares reappear at all costs.

When I get to the entrance, Arsen is nowhere to be found. After a few minutes of walking around the sections closest to the front of the store, I begin to think that maybe he went looking for me. Begrudgingly, I go find him, though I really don't want to go near the back again. Just knowing that I'm approaching that area makes my heart beat faster, my steps feel heavier and my palms sweaty.

In the months since my last miscarriage, I've been able to avoid coming in close contact with children, particularly toddlers and babies, and I would like to keep it that way. I swallow hard. I'm not sure I'm ready for my lucky streak to end. I can't even look at a pregnant woman without feeling envy and anger.

Where the hell is Arsen?

"Jaime! Come back here this minute!" A woman calls after a small boy who comes barreling through the narrow pathway between tables filled with books, zooming right past me. Moving out of the way just in time, I barely avoid him crashing against me. With a hand on my chest trying to slow down my breathing, I look around for Arsen. I don't think I can stay here for much longer. Panic is starting to work its dark magic around me.

I lean against a bookshelf taller than me and close my eyes for a moment.

It doesn't matter.

It doesn't matter.

You don't care, remember?

You're over them.

You're over it.

Chanting these words as if they were a litany in my head, I fight the usual darkness attempting to swallow me whole when strong arms that feel like a lifeline pull me out, bringing me back to reality where there's light. His light.

I keep my eyes closed and let him wrap me in a soothing embrace. With his arms around me, smelling his spicy smell, listening to the calm beating of his heart, the haunting ghosts begin to fade. The wonder of the moment is that Arsen isn't embarrassed by my manic outburst. If anything, it's as if he is trying to help me through it.

"Catherine, I'm here. It's okay," he whispers softly.

When I can form a coherent thought and feel more calm, I speak into his chest. "We need to leave, Arsen. I-I'm not sure I can do this…not yet."

Arsen is silent for a moment. "I don't think so. I think we should stay here, Catherine."

His words are a slap on the face.

Hurt, I begin to pull away, but he stops me when he tightens his grip around me. "No. Please, Dimples, hear me out."

"You have one minute, Arsen. After that I'm out of here." Opening my eyes, I raise them to look at him straight in the eye. "With you or without you."

He lifts a hand and tugs the front of his hair. "You can't keep running away from your nightmares. They'll eventually catch up to you. They always do. I wasn't there for you when that fucked up shit went down, and not a day goes by that I don't regret it, but today I can help you. I can be there for you. You don't need to do anything. Just go in there, face those fucking demons, and show them what you're made of. You're stronger than you give yourself credit for. You're standing here with me after all. You're laughing and living life again. So fight, Dimples. Fucking fight it."

"Oh, Arsen…"

His words break me and heal me all at once. A blow to the stomach and a comforting caress in one swift movement.

"Listen to me. There's no way to correct your present without confronting your past. Let's just go in there, sit down for a few minutes, and then we can leave. I won't push you to do anything else, just this one small thing. Please, let me be there for you." There's a fierce entreaty in his voice, in his eyes, in his hold of me.

I laugh because he makes it sound so easy. "Just this one small thing?"

"Hell yeah. I know you can do it," Arsen says.

I shake my head because I can't believe I'm actually going to listen to this nutcase and go through with his idiotic idea of healing.

"Fine. I can't believe you're making me do this."

Feeling a light tap on the side of my leg, I lower my gaze to find a small child standing in front of me holding *Where The Wild Things Are* in her hands. Her big, innocent, brown eyes are stripping me naked with their intensity as she watches me.

"My brahther is mean. He don't want to read me a 'tory and I can't read yet. I want a 'tory. I want a 'tory."

With a tight knot in the back of my throat, I let go of Arsen and kneel down. "Um…where is your mommy or your babysitter? Do you want me to find them for you?"

"Nu-uh. Lilah is with her friends."

"Do you want me to go get Lilah for you? Is she your older sister?"

"Nu-uh. Silly! Lilah is my nanny. I want you to read me my 'tory." She scrunches up her nose when she sees me shaking my head no. It's horrible, I know. Denying this beautiful girl what she wants breaks my heart, but I can't do it. I just can't.

I'm about to stand up when she grabs my shoulder, her face brightening like the sun. "Pleeeasse? My mommy told me that if I say please and thank you I can get whatever I want. Pleassee?"

I silently curse and turn to look at Arsen, pleading with my eyes for an out. His hands in the front pockets of his jeans and a lazy smile on his lips, he shrugs his shoulders carelessly, mouthing, "She asked you."

I know he's pretending to not care, but his eyes give him up, they contradict his blasé demeanor. His eyes are willing me to be brave.

Swallowing hard as my heart beats as fast and hard as a stampede of wild animals, I nod to the small child. "Sure. Why not?"

And it's at this moment with Arsen smiling down at me that I decide to fight back. Maybe it doesn't have anything to do with him, but his support has everything to do with it.

When the little girl sits on my lap right on the carpeted floor, with books around us and the noise of people talking, I feel the comfortable heat of her body on my lap, warming me, warming my heart, and I know I am on my way to recovery. Closing my eyes for a moment, I lean down and inhale the sweet smell of strawberries and chocolate emanating from her hair. After a few minutes, I lift my eyes and see the blue fire that I love so much staring back at me with such tenderness.

That's when I know a painful chapter has been closed.

He was right. Even when the horizon seems to be bleak and full of pain, we must learn to fight and persevere because the rewards of those tears of struggle mean that you get to live your life once more.

Arsen taught me that.

Staring at him, a blinding fog disperses away from my heart as the truth stares back at me in those misty eyes.

I love him.

I've fallen in love with another man.

But can you love two men at the same time?

Because I think I do.

23

Arsen

I can feel again.
I can see her face.
I can touch her body next to mine.
I can bury my nose in her hair and breathe her in.
I can close my eyes and feel her sweet lips
tracing my face with lingering kisses.
I can feast on her body as if it were my last meal.
I can feel again.

The afternoon sun is shining through the naked windows of my apartment as I open my eyes and find Catherine here, watching me sleep. She is lying on her side, facing me with both hands tucked under her right cheek, the sun bathing her face in light. She hasn't left yet. I notice the small smile playing on her lips, and I can't help but smile back. She makes me so damn happy.

There are still moments when I can't quite believe that she's finally in my arms. You would think that spending almost every day together while her husband is at work, laughing over stupid shit and having lots of fuck-tastic sex, would have grown old by now, but it hasn't. I live for these moments when she's with me; when the world is left outside this room and the only person that matters is right here next to me.

She's wearing one of my old t-shirts. Hmm…I wonder if that's all she is wearing. Sweet. Her blonde hair is down and framing her face, but her eyes look puffy and red as if she had been crying. I want to ask her what made her cry, what has brought that sad look in her eyes again, but I touch her instead. When we are together, that sad and lost look leaves her eyes.

I remember the first time I met her. As we shook hands and I gazed into the deep green depths of her eyes, I could see her damn soul through them, and it was broken, calling for me. Dimples, though beautiful on the outside, was hiding something shattered, something hard, something that I very much wanted to fix. I also got the feeling, one I can't seem to shake to this day, that she would change everything as I knew it.

I want her to be free of whatever still haunts her.

I want to be the temple that she seeks solace in.

I want to be her damn savior.

I want to help her heal.

"Tell me about Jessica," Catherine asks, touching the tattoo on my chest.

At first I don't answer, allowing myself to just enjoy the burning sensation her fingers leave behind as they trace the outline of the butterfly.

"Arsen?"

I take her small hand in mine, bringing it to my lips, and placing a kiss in her palm. How can mere words adequately describe how guilty I still feel over Jessica's death?

Clearing my throat, I decide to be as honest with Catherine as possible. I can't look at her perfect eyes and tell her that I killed someone, so instead I focus on our intertwined fingers lying against my chest.

"She died. She died because of me."

"Arsen, look at me. What do you mean?"

"I killed her. I was drunk…we were drunk…she was driving." Pausing for a moment, I take a deep breath before continuing, "I shouldn't have let her drive, but I was just as fucked up as she was. We were supposed to sleep over, but we got high and decided to take a drive in her new Ferrari. I walked away with only two broken ribs, but she died."

"Oh, Arsen. I'm so sorry…"

We are silent for a while before she speaks again.

"D-did you love her?"

"Yes. I thought she was the moon to my starless night."

"Oh."

"How old were you? I mean, how long ago was this?" she asks hesitantly.

"I was twenty, and she was eighteen."

I shut my eyes tightly. Fuck. Even after all this time it still hurts.

"I'm so sorry, Arsen. "

"Yeah, me too," I pause, "The women, the drugs, the alcohol…they all helped me to forget and numb the pain. But eventually you have to deal with your demons because you're never truly free until you've faced them. And I have."

"Do you…do you still love her?"

"I do. I think some part of me will always love her. Yes, we were young when we met, but she was my first love."

"You have to stop blaming yourself for her death, Arsen. It wasn't your fault."

"I know it wasn't my fault, but I could've prevented it. I still blame myself…I just don't let the guilt eat me alive anymore. I don't let it destroy me. I know Jessica wouldn't want that."

"Why don't you try to meet someone else? Fall in love again?" she asks, staring directly into my eyes.

Putting Jessica back in the recesses of my heart, where she'll always be, I watch Catherine for a very long time. I take in the feverish color covering her cheeks, her stormy green eyes, and the way she seems to light up the whole room, my whole world.

"You know, I didn't think I could fall in love again but—"

"Why are you wasting your time with me? This…this…" Without finishing her sentence, she stares at me as if I were a fortune teller, but it's her question and the pain I see reflected in her beautiful face that take me by surprise.

"What's the matter, Dimples?" Needing to feel the warmth of her skin against mine, I raise a hand to trace her cheek, the curve of her cheekbone, her lips.

"How can something so wrong feel this right? Like it was meant to be?" she asks throatily.

"Maybe we were meant to be together…"

But were we? Or did we force our hand?

Catherine is silent as she gazes at me with so much fucking feeling that it makes my shitty heart sing. It's at times like this, when she's stripped of makeup, her lips swollen from my kisses and her hair is lying on my pillow, that I can't help but be glad that I pursued her, that I didn't give a damn that she was married, that I took advantage of the situation like the son of a bitch that I am.

I need her.

"Why do you want me? I'm so screwed up. And to top it all off, I'm a cheater, and a liar," she asks.

"I want you. Simple as that. No explanations are needed. No whys, no hows, I just do. You are perfect to me, Catherine. Completely. Make no mistake about that. And if you are a cheater, what the fuck does that make me?"

"But, what about Ben? This isn't fair to him. He doesn't deserve this."

"I don't know. Let me ask you something. Would you be able to walk away from this, from us, right now—without once looking back?" I ask.

"I don't know…"

Questions left unanswered, Catherine closes her eyes and pushes herself against me.

"Kiss me, Arsen. Make me forget," she whispers softly against my mouth.

I keep my eyes open at first, watching how her lips part to welcome my kiss, only closing them when I taste her sweetness on my tongue. Kissing Catherine is fucking perfect.

Slowly, breaking the kiss momentarily, I take her t-shirt off and unhook her bra, then pull her closer to me until I can feel her breasts against my bare chest. Growing hard, one of my hands goes to the small of her back pushing her against me and hold her closer. I want her to feel how much I want her, how much I need her. It's never close enough. She owns me. And I'd like to think that I own her too, even if it's for a couple of hours each day.

I'll take whatever I can get.

With our hands wrapped around our hair, we kiss for a long time. Both of us naked, Catherine lies down on her back and opens her legs invitingly for me. Christ, how the fuck do you say no to that?

I settle between her legs, but I don't thrust into her right away. No, I like to have fun and get her moaning first. Kissing her temple, then her nose, eyelids, the pretty beauty mark next to her mouth, I make my way down to her collarbone. When I reach her breasts, I let my tongue play with her nipples, sucking them gently and biting them hard until I can hear her moan.

By the time I reach her belly, my fingers have been stroking her clit to prepare her for me. Sitting back on my knees without breaking eye contact, I bring my soaked fingers into my mouth and lick them clean. With her taste in my mouth, I smile when I see her blush like that. Catherine is so damn beautiful, and she has no idea of the power she holds over me. I lean down and run my tongue along her clit before she has a chance to move. So sweet, I breathe in her scent as if it were the last bout of air my lungs would inhale in this life.

"Put your legs over my shoulders," I order, breathing between her thighs and watching her body tremble.

Never breaking eye contact, she rests her calves and heels on my back. She's so damn perfect. I lower my mouth one more time and let myself go fucking wild on her pussy.

When I feel her gripping my hair, I look up and watch her as she tosses her head back into the pillow, thrusting her hips against my mouth again and again as I lick, slide, and suck.

"Fuck, Arsen! I'm…I'm…" she gasps.

I grip her ass with my hands and push her harder against my mouth. The essence of her drives me fucking insane because there's nothing as sweet as the taste of your woman on your tongue.

In this moment, she is mine.

I put two fingers inside her and stroke her fast and hard until she comes undone, screaming my name into the room. I grin because I love making her come with my name of her lips.

After her body quiets down I move in between her legs once more. Spreading her open for me with one hand, I grab my cock in the other and thrust in.

Finally…

Home sweet fucking home.

Excruciating need making my body tremble. I wrap both my hands in her hair and make her look at me as I start moving inside her. I want to watch her face while we fuck. I move slowly at first, letting her body take as much of me as possible, but when I feel her tightening around my cock again I pull out. Gently, I turn her to lie down on her stomach as my hands grab her hips, and fuck smoothly into her from behind. I enjoy seeing the red marks that my strong hold leaves on her white skin, wishing for a moment that her fucking husband paid more attention and noticed them.

Jealousy fills me as I pick up the pace, fucking her harder, owning her harder, erasing him from her body. Feeling close, I fist her hair in my hands, tilting her head backwards and let loose. I can see how wet she is making my cock as I take her and I fucking love it. I rub her clit faster and start pounding her ass. In and out of her body. My body.

I own it.

Catherine cranes her neck to look at me as we move closer to the edge together. I shout her name as she screams mine and just like that we come together, as one entity, one body, one soul. I look into her excited eyes, and my mind finally acknowledges what my heart has known all along as the truth—I'm hers. I belong to Catherine. And I want her to be mine, only mine.

After I thrust a few more times, our bodies shiver and go slack. I wrap my arms around her tightly and pull her closer to my chest, moving us to lay down sideways. With our limbs tangled together, and my cock still inside her, I feel like I can fly. I nuzzle her neck and lick the salty sweat with my tongue, lingering on the spot behind her ear, and chuckling when I feel her tremble. I can't help it. She is so damn sweet.

I murmur in her ear, "Well, hello there stranger. Fancy meeting you here." I thrust my softening cock gently inside her. Lying on her side with my front covering her back and one of her hands pillowing her cheek, Catherine brings her free hand to link with mine.

"Do you ever get tired?" Laughter rings in her voice.

"Nope." I let go of her hand and tickle her under her armpits. I can't help laughing as she squirms under my arms like a fish out of water. She's so ticklish. As we laugh, I slide my cock out of her. I don't want to, but this is about to turn into a major war and I don't want to lose. I hate losing. Catherine distracts me when she runs her tongue along my nipple and sucks it into her mouth, knowing full well it will screw with my mind. A moment later, she's straddling me with both my wrists locked in her firm grasp above my head. I could break free of her hold in the blink of an eye, but I like this playful side of my Dimples so I let her get away with it. Her blonde hair cascades down her shoulders, showcasing the creamy whiteness of her skin, and her body is perfect to fucking feast on it. Her pretty green eyes don't look like shards of ice anymore. They are shining brightly with excitement and hopefully with love.

She owns me.

She lowers her lips to mine, and as we kiss, I don't notice that her hands have let go of mine until it's too late. Her hands may be small, but those fingers can tickle!

I lock her legs with mine and flip her on her ass. Better. The sight of her mouth is driving me mental, so I kiss her again. I want to eat her. I want to devour her. Suddenly, I can't move.

I can't breathe.

I love her.

This woman is it for me. I thought Jessica was the love of my life, and maybe she was, but I can't keep denying that I've fallen in love with Catherine. The truth paralyzes me, humbles me, yet it sets me free. And it makes me feel powerful, too.

Superhero fucking powerful.

"Thank you, Arsen. Thank you for making me forget, for making me laugh again, for what you did back at the bookstore," Catherine whispers. I half groan, half growl, and pull her up on my lap. As she straddles me, she wraps her arms around my neck, winding her fingers through my hair and giving it a slight tug. I tuck an arm under her delicious ass and the other around her waist, pulling her as close to me as possible.

Feeling like a girl with butterflies in my stomach, I close my eyes and nuzzle her neck, licking her ear. "I want you to be happy again, Catherine. I really do. And I want to be part of the reason that you are."

Catherine closes her eyes for a moment and seems to consider her next words carefully. When she opens them, gloom stares back at me, prickling my skin. A bad feeling settles in the pit of my stomach.

"Please, don't go there. Don't ask me for more. I-I can't…"

Fuck, that hurts.

"Why the hell not?" I ask because I'm a masochist and I know her answer will be a punch to the gut.

"Because I'm married. And I love him."

Fuck. Fuck. Fuck. I did ask, though.

I sneer. "It didn't look like you loved anything but my cock when you were blowing me before."

My words make her flinch. Well, hers make me sick.

"Oh, Arsen. Don't say that…don't be cruel. You knew I was married."

"Are you fucking shitting me? Of course I knew it! I just had no fucking idea that it was going to hu—"

I stop myself before I say words that I will regret. Letting her go, I sit up on the edge of the bed, turning away from her.

"You know what? Forget I said anything. Never mind. It doesn't matter, right? We're just having fun. Screwing on the down low when you're not pretending to be Perfect Cathy, the wife of the mighty Benjamin Stanwood."

"Arsen…" Her voice breaks.

"Nah. It's okay, Cathy. I fucking get it. I get it. I'm your mid-life-fucking-crisis ten years too early. Instead of asking Ben to buy you a diamond necklace, you chose to fuck me. And why the hell not? Diamonds won't make you scream and come as hard as you do when you're riding my fucking cock."

Grinding my teeth, my body shakes as I try to control my temper. I don't want the venom brewing inside me to poison us beyond remedy, but I do want to hurt her. I want to break her, shatter her.

Quid pro quo, quid pro quo, bitch.

I'm breathing hard as I clench my hands into tight fists because if I don't, I may tear the place apart. Christ, this hurts.

As I'm trying to get myself under control, I feel Catherine move and get off the bed. Maybe she's had enough? Good riddance. I'm done. Closing my eyes, I bring my hand to the back of my neck and rub it. Soft, warm hands cover my knees.

"You don't understand. You can't. I-I don't understand it either, but this thing between us was never supposed to be. It wasn't supposed to happen. It's wrong, so very wrong. I lo—"

Catherine checks herself. "What do you want me to say to you? What do you want me to do? You-you say pretty words,

Arsen, but they don't mean a thing. They are just empty words. You make love to me, you fuck me, you do everything you want to me, and I let you because I love it. I love being with you."

She looks down at her hands, then meets my gaze once more. "You make me forget. You make me feel happy, you make me smile and giggle like a teenager…but what you don't realize is that my marriage was exactly the same way before it got tough, before it started to hurt me, before every single miscarriage tore a bigger hole inside me.

"My marriage was not just good, Arsen. It was amazing. And it's not Ben's fault at all that I'm here lying naked with you. Ben is still the same man. It's me who changed. It's me who chose to cheat on my husband of six years. It's me who chooses to answer your every call and drive myself here. No one is forcing me to take my clothes off and get on my knees in front of you…it's me. It's all me."

"Catherine…"

"No. Let me finish. So what makes you think that you're any different than me? Than Ben? What makes you think that you have what it takes? Do you want me to leave Ben and be with you? YOU are the one having fun, Arsen. So when you claim th-that I think you're only my fuck toy and nothing else…I don't know what you want me to tell you. I don't know what you want from me."

I look into her brilliant eyes and I lose it. I begin to beg like a fucking child.

"I don't know. I don't know. Just don't go tonight. Stay with me…tell him that you're spending the night at Amy's. Don't go back tonight."

She shakes her head. "Are you even listening to me?" she protests, her voice rising. "No. You know that's impossible. I can't. I must go home. Ben is starting to suspect something is going on. I need to—"

"Leave and play the role of the fucking perfect wife, huh?" Anger replaces my need for her. I spit the words as if they are acid on my tongue.

"Yes," she states simply.

"Let me ask you something. Do you play it at night too? When you leave my apartment after having been with me, do you go back to your perfect three million dollar home in the suburbs of Westchester and fuck your husband?"

I watch her blush as she lets go of my knees. Kneeling on the floor with only the sheet wrapped around her body, Catherine speaks. "That's none of your business."

"Are you fucking kidding me? Yes, it's my business. You're mine!" I shout, anger flowing through my veins, making me burn on the inside.

"No. I'm not. I'm Ben's. I'm married to him. Not to you," she speaks quietly to the floor.

"You know what? Fuck you!" My head is throbbing, and it feels like it's ready to explode. Standing up, I try to get away from her as quickly as possible.

"No. No. No. Please, Arsen…don't go," she pleads desperately. I look down at her on the floor and see the pain expressed vividly on her face. Fuck. I can't see her hurting like this and not do anything about it.

Sitting down on the floor, I pull her naked body next to mine. With her slight figure wrapped in my arms, the situation doesn't seem as hopeless as it truly is. It doesn't hurt as much either. When I feel like I can breathe once more, I listen to her speak as I rock us back and forth.

"Please, Arsen, don't be upset. Let me think. Give me time to make sense of the mess I've made of everything. Please, understand that I can't just up and leave Ben. I-I…he doesn't deserve it. I need time to think, Arsen. I need time. Please don't force my hand like that. Please, I beg you. I-I mean…does this even mean something to you? How do I know that you're just not playing around?"

"What the fuck, Cathy? Does it feel like I'm playing around? Like I don't give a shit? I'm at your constant beck and call!" I shout. After taking a deep breath and calming myself down, I continue, "Do you care for me? Do you care for me at all?"

The words are torn out of my chest.

Ripped from my soul.

"Yes. So much, Arsen. So much. B-But that doesn't change one thing. Not one thing," she repeats.

There are no tears shed, no blood spilled.

Nothing.

Just the truth between us. And it hurts. It hurts so fucking much because there's nothing I can do to change it. Nothing I can do to make her not love her husband and love me instead. Nothing I can do to make her leave him and take me instead.

Nothing.

I'm bleeding out for her.

The afternoon glow has disappeared from the room, and in its place a cold darkness has settled around us. As I rock our bodies, not sure who's trying to comfort whom, something strikes me as pretty damn hilarious. Not fifteen minutes ago, I felt like I was in fucking nirvana. Laughing, falling in love, not feeling like such a failure for the first time in my life because of her.

And now this.

Yes.

I'm bleeding out.

24

Cathy

I told him.
I told him not to go there.
What am I supposed to do now?
I keep saying that I never thought this
was going to become what it has. But it has.
You cannot expect to play with fire and not get burned.
I did, and now I'm incinerated.
The thing is I wanted to be.
I still do.

Every action has a consequence. It doesn't matter if you try to run or hide. It eventually it catches up to you. Call it karma if you must, but said karma can totally kick you in the ass.

I wish I could make myself believe that I had no idea what I was doing, or what I was getting myself into, but I did. I was well aware the moment we kissed, and I asked him to bring me back to his apartment that there was no going back. I made a choice that night, and continue to do so every time I meet with Arsen behind Ben's back, and every time I lie to Ben. I am responsible for every deceitful word I have uttered, and every dishonest action I have committed.

I am.

And now I have to face the music. I have to make a choice once again. And it doesn't matter what choice I make. Which path I choose to follow. Either way, I will break my own heart. I will lose a part of myself.

But I think I already have.

I love two men.

And this time, the monster that I am, the one I've become, will bring someone else down with me. It's the darkness in me, I tell you…it follows me everywhere I go, spreading like spilled black ink on white paper.

I curl up in his arms; my head resting on his chest as I let the beat of his heart soothe me, filling me with bittersweet hope.

Can I really do it?

With the smell of sex around us, I look up and meet his fiery gaze and one thought becomes obvious; Arsen has to be in my life. I can't let him go. I need him. I want him. He's become a vital part of me. He's the air I need to breathe.

And I think it's time.

But can I?

I decide to take a shower before I head back home. Lifting my hand, I sniff the inside of my wrist. It's smells like Arsen—a delicious mixture of cologne, sweat and the musky scent of sex. After a few minutes under the water, I give up any expectation that he'll join me as he usually does. When I'm finished and dressed, I come out to an empty room. Arsen is nowhere to be seen. The bed still unmade with its silk sheets twisted to the left, looks bereft and cold.

With my Ferragamo slingbacks in one hand and my leather satchel in the other, I'm about to head to the kitchen in search of him, when an unsmiling Arsen walks into the room already showered and dressed. His wet blond hair is pulled back from his forehead, making his young face look harsh and older.

"Oh…you took a shower in the guest bathroom?" I ask clumsily. I don't recognize the solemn man staring back at me.

"Yeah, I actually gotta jet. Alec called me while you were in the shower. He needs me to come over to his studio."

"Oh. Okay. I guess I-I'll call you."

"Whatever you want. I'll be around." He shrugs his shoulder, his voice dismissive.

"Um…uh…about before," I'm ready to tell him that I need a couple days to mull over my decision, but the flat look in his eyes freezes me on the spot.

"Dimples, forget I said anything. I thought about it while I was in the shower. It's cool, this arrangement we have. I'm okay with it as long as you are."

Flinching at the coldness in his voice, I watch him as he turns around and walks out of the room, leaving me all alone. Suddenly I feel very cold.

"Okay," I whisper into the empty space.

As I'm driving back home, I decide I need to unload. I need to speak to someone about what feels like the biggest decision or mistake I'll ever make in my entire life

Arsen. My chest tightens and my stomach feels funny just thinking about him. Something doesn't sit well when I think of the way he looked at me before he left. I shake my head, dismissing the thought, and decide to call Amy. She's the most open-minded person I know. And she's been through it all. If anyone can listen to me without judging or playing devil's advocate, it will be her. Pressing the hands free button, I say her name and wait for the system to connect the call.

"Oh my God. Is this Cathy Stanwood calling? I thought you fell off the face of the earth, my dear."

I chuckle at the sarcasm in her voice. "Yes. It's me. I need to speak to you, and according to my navigation system we have about forty minutes to talk before I get home." I take a deep breath. "I'm cheating on Ben…with Arsen."

"I knew it. I just knew it. I told you…that boy looked like he wanted to fuck the shit out of you every time you both were in the same room. I knew it was a matter of time before you finally gave in. I tol—"

"Stop it, Amy. I didn't call you so you could tell me what you knew or thought about Arsen. It's irrelevant. I'm calling you because…because I think I'm going to leave Ben." I tighten my hands around the steering wheel when I say the words that I never thought would be possible.

"Cathy, are you sure? Listen. I know you called me because I've been there. Twice. But listen to me, girl. Listen to me carefully. My first husband was a pig who slept with his best friend's wife and I will never regret leaving him. It was the best decision I've ever made. But Matt was a sweet and really nice guy. I was just at the wrong place in my life when I thought marrying him would save me. So when I realized it wasn't going anywhere, I cheated on him. I cheated and served him with the divorce papers. And let me tell you, he's my biggest regret. I miss him everyday, and not a day goes by where I haven't regretted the way I ended things with him. He didn't deserve it."

"I don't think Ben deserves my cheating on him with Arsen, but it's too late. It's already done a-and I don't think I can stop. Not now." Swallowing hard, I choke with my next words, "Arsen makes me feel alive, Amy. He makes me feel again. When I'm with him, I feel total freedom…I feel like my heart—"

"Let me stop you right there, babe, and call your bullshit. I don't think your heart has anything to do with it. Truth of the matter is that you like it when a gorgeous twenty-four year old guy fucks your brains out. And I can't say that I blame you. I've been there, done that—fucked the energizer bunny. So, please…let's be honest here. You want to leave Ben, an amazing guy who kisses the ground you walk on because you are bored with married life and you would prefer to beca—"

I grind my teeth before I interrupt her. "You know what? I thought you were going to be the last person who was going to judge me. I didn't call you so you could tell me everything I've done is wrong. I knew that, I still do. I wanted someone to listen to me, and maybe offer me some advice, instead of just saying that I'm cheating on my husband because I'm bored."

"So tell me, Cathy. Tell me why you're cheating? And, what's the purpose of calling me when it appears you've already made up your mind? Did you expect me to say, Shucks! Life got tough, so it's okay to cheat? You know, I used to be very jealous of you. So much so that it took a lot of work to be in the same room watching the way Ben looked at you, with so much love pouring out of his eyes and not hate you a little. So yes. I'm pissed. I haven't heard from you since the baby, and then out of the blue you call me telling me that you're thinking about leaving your husband?" She pauses, "Honey, I don't know what you're expecting from me, but I think you're making the biggest mistake of your life. There. I've said it. Is that what you wanted to hear?"

Shame makes heat run through my body. "You know what, Amy? You're such a hypocrite. And you can go to hell. I-I know what I did is horrible—"

"Sucks to hear the truth, huh?"

"Ben doesn't deserve it. Hell, I live with the man. I'm married to him. I know he's the last person to ever deserve this kind of betrayal, but it happened and I haven't been able to stop it. I can't, do you hear me? I can't. I don't know why I called you. I'm sorry if my call pissed you off, but I never thought that you would judge me so harshly because you've been there. Sometimes these things just happen…" My voice breaks and I start crying.

Shit.

"Yes…but they are avoidable."

"I can't! I'm so sorry," I sob.

After a few hesitant moments, Amy finally speaks. "Oh, honey. I'm sorry. I'm just so angry. And the way you dismissed it as if it were not important because it was already done…" She groans into the speaker, "Forget about it. Let me give you one piece of advice and that's all I'll say because each marriage is different and people cheat for so many different reasons. Some people cheat because they can, because they know they won't get caught, because of boredom or lust, because it's their way to reach out, show that they need help—to ask for help. Whatever your reasons, before you end your marriage, make sure you're aware that there's no going back. No time machine that will let you undo your mistakes if you and Arsen don't work out. And chances are, babe, that it won't work out. It never does. Who knows? Maybe someone new, younger and prettier girl with perkier breasts will come along and Arsen will leave you for her. He's young, Cathy. What makes you think he's serious and not just playing around? That you're not just the flavor of the week? Or the month?"

"I don't know," I sniffle, "All I know is that I can't keep doing this to Ben. And I can't stop seeing Arsen. I need him. So the only choice left, the only solution really, is to leave Ben."

"But what if—"

"And if things with Arsen don't work out, well, at least Ben is free to find someone more deserving of him than me. I know it sounds like a pathetic excuse, but it's true. I don't deserve him anymore. At this point in my life, I want Arsen so much that I'm willing to throw everything away. Besides, I can't keep lying to Ben…going to bed and let-letting him touch me after I've been with Arsen. It's not fair. It's not fair."

Silent for a moment, I can almost picture Amy battling with herself. "Babe, do whatever you think is right. Just keep in mind that there's no going back, love. That's all. And if it backfires, you'll be divorced and alone. Of course, I'll be there for you, but…"

"I know. It won't be the same."

"Do you have feelings for the kid?"

"Yes, I do. Amy, I think I'm in love with him."

"Girl! Oh my God. That is so not the answer I was expecting. I mean…are you sure it's love and not lust mixed with like?

"I don't know, Amy," I sigh. "I think it's love. It feels like love. It looks like love."

"Just because it feels like love doesn't mean it is. It could be infatuation, newness…but tell me, what about Ben? Do you not love him anymore? Don't you care what this is going to do to him?"

"I care, I care a lot. That's why I can't keep doing this to him. I need to set him free, Amy. To let him go, even if in the process I break his heart…and mine. He'll heal…we all do. I love him, but I'm not sure I'm in love with him anymore."

And I do. I love Ben. So much. But he doesn't make my heart flutter. He doesn't fill me with butterflies. Being with Ben doesn't give me that high anymore…No. All those feelings have been transferred to him. To Arsen. So I guess that's the answer to my own question.

After I ask Amy how she's doing, we say goodbye and hang up. The streets of Manhattan long gone, I drive the remaining tree lined distance to my house in silence. Pulling up into the driveway, I notice that Ben's black Maybach is missing. Wondering if he's working late, I take my phone out and check for any missed calls or text messages. I only have one from earlier in the day, asking me if I wanted to take a trip down into the city and meet him for lunch. A text message I obviously ignored since I was too busy texting and waiting for Arsen to show up.

After I park the car in the garage, I make my way to the foyer, turning the lights on as I walk through the hallways. Once I'm sure that Ben isn't home, I stand under the large crystal chandelier hanging from the cathedral ceilings and consider my next move. I tap a finger on my chin, make up a quick excuse as to why he didn't hear from me all day, and give him a call. His phone rings five or six times before it goes to voicemail.

Odd.

Looking at my cell, I make sure of the time—yes, he should have been done with work hours ago. After two more unsuccessful attempts, I leave a message telling him that I'm home but heading straight to bed and that I will speak to him in the morning. This is how my days and nights have been for the past three weeks. I ignore his calls during the day and avoid him at night. With a chest full of guilt, I look around the big house, our home, and wonder what will happen to all of this if I go ahead with what I think will be my final decision.

I groan as tears begin to fill my eyes. *Since when did I become such a watering pot?*

I lift the Barneys garment bag that I put down on the floor when I first walked in and make my way to the master bedroom. I need to rest. Yes, that's it. All the lying, cheating, and sneaking around has finally caught up to me. I'm exhausted. I'm emotionally and mentally wrung out.

Seeking solace in sleep, I never hear from Ben.

The next morning when I open my eyes, I notice that Ben's pillow looks untouched. Wondering if he slept in his office, I get up and go in search of him, not exactly sure why I'm suddenly consumed by this…this necessity to see him, to touch him, to feel his warm skin against mine, to make sure he's real.

The moment I stand outside his office, I can't help but notice the way my hands are trembling. After a few seconds of taking calming breaths, I knock once, turn the knob, and open the door.

What greets my eyes shocks me to the core.

I survey the unrecognizable room.

What the hell happened here? It looks like a tornado hit Ben's pristine office.

There are papers and articles scattered all over his desk and on the floor. His clothes are thrown in one corner. Th-the couch…the love couch is gone and in its place sits a new dark wine colored leather one.

Brand new.

With shaky legs, I approach the alien piece of furniture that doesn't belong here. That shouldn't be here. Slowly…tentatively…I kneel down in front of it and let my fingers caress the smooth surface. The coolness of the leather is a welcoming sensation. Funny, I didn't realize until now how warm I felt. Tugging the neckline of my robe away from my neck, the room suddenly feels oppressive, constricting—I can't breathe. I need to get out of here.

"How do you like it? It was delivered yesterday," Ben says flatly.

I turn around when I hear his unexpected voice, my hands flying to my chest. "Ben! Babe. You scared me!" Ben is reclining his shoulder against the doorframe, watching me. His suit jacket swung over his shoulder carelessly. Briefly, I observe he's still wearing the same clothes from yesterday.

"I'm sorry. I didn't mean to startle you."

Moving away from the door, Ben approaches me carefully as my pulse begins to accelerate. When he's a foot away from me, he extends his hand and offers me his help to stand. I take his hand in mine, letting the strength of his pull help me up, bringing our bodies flush against each other. Unsteady on my feet, I hold onto his hard chest for support as I look up and stare into his eyes, eyes that usually sparkle with so much light, but today appear to be as flat and rough as unpolished gemstones. They watch me intensely. His gaze robs me of breath, strips me naked, and sends my heart beating into a wild frenzy. Ben lifts his hand and lets the back of his fingers caress my cheek. Not closing my eyes for once, we stare at each other as if trying to memorize our features. And I do. I memorize his rugged beauty until it's imprinted in every crevice of my soul. Ben is the first one to break the silence.

"The couch was delivered yesterday. I like it."

"Oh. B-But who…"

"I did. I came home since you weren't here." There's no suspicion or accusation in his voice. Just cold-hearted resignation. "Anyway, I've got to shower." Ben lets go of me, "Remember, tonight is Alan's masquerade party. I hope you didn't make other plans," he says coldly.

"No. Of course not. I bought a dress yesterday."

"Just making sure."

Ben walks out of the room, not once glancing back.

25

After a short drive to Greenwich, we arrive to the home of Alan Vanderhall. The beautiful estate is located off the very private and coveted Round Hill Road. There are two majestic gated entrances that lead us into the private gravel drive to the main house. As the car makes its way through the property, I see lush grounds with both ardent lawns and formal gardens. The road is illuminated with Japanese paper lanterns and the trees are wrapped in winter twinkling lights. The lights are a magical contrast against the darkness of the night, and I can't help being awed by the beauty and the feeling of electricity and magic in the air.

As I look at the lights twinkling, I try not to think about Arsen. Earlier today, when Ben left the office to go take a shower, I'd called Arsen to let him know that I couldn't meet him today, but he didn't answer. He hadn't even texted me back. Suddenly cold, I begin to rub my arms. Ben glances my way and shakes his head wearily.

I feel panic settling in the pit of my stomach.

I'm afraid.

Has my indecision cost me Arsen?

No.

He was just busy. That's all.

Dismissing my negative thoughts, I watch as we continue to drive through the lit pathway until we reach the main house, an extraordinary larger than life Georgian stone mansion. After Ben parks the car to the side and dismisses a valet attendant who comes to help us, he utters the first words he's said to me all night without even glancing my way.

"Would it kill you to smile and not look so miserable for once, Cathy? I know my presence is repugnant to you, but please, could you give it a try? Alan is a very important client of the firm."

Disbelief in my eyes, I'm stunned by the harshness of his words. "I beg your pardon?"

"Nothing, Cathy. Forget I said anything. Just pretend that you want to be here with me and not somewhere else." A dark look crosses Ben's eyes, but it's gone before I get a chance to fully understand it.

I grab his hand and make him turn to look at me as I frown. "Hey…babe, Ben. I want to be here. I want to be with you." The truth flows out of me as pain gathers in the back of my throat, but I mean it. No matter what tomorrow brings, no matter what my final decision is, I want to be here with Ben tonight. I want to pretend for one last time that I'm Cathy Stanwood. His wife. And, that he's mine.

Without once looking at me, I wince when Ben reaches for his domino cape and a black leather half mask depicting a panther and begins to put them on in silence. When he's finished tying the mask behind his head, he turns around to look at me. I can only see his dark eyes through the slits of the mask shining like black marbles, his full lower lip, and the strong lines of his jaw covered in a slight stubble. Dressed in a crisp black tuxedo and with most of his face covered, he appears to be as dangerous, graceful, and beautiful as the feline he's pretending to be for tonight.

"If you say so, Cathy. Would you like me to help you with yours?" He points at the mask sitting on my lap.

"Yes, please," I say quietly.

I watch as his large and strong hands slowly caress each side of my collarbone. His touch as gentle as a butterfly's wing makes me want to close my eyes and lean my head against his shoulder, not caring that there's a stick shift between us, but I don't. Instead, I continue to watch him as one of his hands reaches for an elegant silver half mask covered in black lace and brings it to my face. After he's finished tying the black ribbon under my French bun and making sure that my hair isn't ruined, he places his hands on my shoulders. As my body trembles from the warmth of his touch spreading through me, I'm about to thank him, but the manner in which he's watching me so closely, so absorbingly, arrests all thought.

My gentle Ben is watching me like he wants to fuck the shit out of me. As if he wants to own me with his dick and the strong muscles of his body; mark me with his seed, crush me with the might of his powerful arms, and strangle me with his bare hands while he thrusts so hard into me that the headboard of the bed makes the wall behind it shake.

This is not him.

And it's my fault.

An angry stranger has replaced my sweet husband, and somehow I can't make myself look away from his dark gaze. I continue to stare at him as he lowers one of his hands towards my knee that's exposed by the slit of my gown. His fingers pull the fabric further away from my knee, and when his hand makes contact with my bare skin, arousal spreads through me. His hand begins to trace an upward path on my leg, closer and closer to my pulsating core, not caring that the silk of my dress may rip. He stops when he reaches the outside of my silk panties.

Ben's eyes don't leave me as he cups me, his palm feeling the moisture gathering in between my legs through the soaked silk. Ben hooks his finger and pulls the thong to the side, baring me to him. And only then does he enter me with one finger, sliding it slowly, yet assuredly. I want to close my eyes, but I can't. After slowly pumping it in and out of me, he withdraws his finger and brings it inside his mouth, washing my taste with his own. Bringing his hand back to my core, he enters me with two fingers this time, stretching me as his saliva lubricates me some more. Throwing my head back, I can't help groaning as his movements become more forceful.

Everything becomes a blur of heady sensations as I get lost in the feel of his hand, the sound of wetness my body makes, the smell. Yes, my husband is hand fucking me and it is heaven. There's a feverish brightness sparkling in his eyes, the stick shift in between us, my legs spread open for him, and that's all that matters. As his breathing accelerates, I can hear myself panting louder and louder.

I feel close, so close.

I'm about to come when he withdraws his fingers from me, leaving me bereft. With his touch gone, I feel empty, aching, and wanting his hand inside me again. He lifts his wet fingers, tracing a path along my lips, inviting me to take him in. Shocked with Ben's reckless behavior, I don't move.

"Open your mouth, Cathy. I want you to taste yourself…taste what I can do to you," he growls.

Feeling color stain my cheeks, I open my mouth as he dips his fingers inside.

"Now close your mouth and suck them, Cathy."

So I suck, hard. Even as the motion reminds me of Arsen and what happened in Barneys.

By the time he removes his fingers from my mouth, I think he's going to allow us to pull ourselves together, but he surprises me once more when he leans down and kisses me on the lips. We get lost in the sweet oblivion of his kiss sealed with my taste. It's demanding. Needy. It's a kiss that wants to engrave itself on our lips—our souls.

When he pulls away, Ben is breathing heavily and appears to be as discomposed as I feel. "I want you to remember that once we get to the party…I now have you branded on my lips." He leans towards me and whispers roughly in my ear, "You are mine."

I watch him righting his mask and attire, before getting out of the Maybach and making his way towards the passenger door. Still feeling breathless and aching everywhere, I'm about to touch up the red on my lips when he opens the door for me.

"You look breathtaking in that dress, by the way. I'll wait for you out here while you touch up your make up." His voice is cool and detached once more, so unlike my Ben.

Inside the car, I'm alone, uncomfortable, needing to orgasm, and looking at myself in the passenger's visor mirror. I look at my reflection, and all I see are lies…but at this moment, when I'm sore between my legs because of Ben's rough yet divine handling, one truth becomes apparent.

I feel like I've just cheated on Arsen with my own husband.

After I exit the car, we make our way to the brightly lit majestic entrance as orchestra music floats through the air, surrounding us. Climbing the stairs with one hand lifting the front part of my gown to avoid tripping over it, and the other on Ben's forearm as it lends me support, I take in the scenery.

At first I'm blinded by the potent lights emanating in all directions from the house but as I grow accustomed to the splendor of the environment, my first thought is how dazzling everything looks wrapped in a golden blanket of light.

After handing our capes to an attendant, I glance around the splendid home and let myself be enraptured by the beauty. There are majestic crystal chandeliers sparkling like little diamonds in the air, candles glowing its amber light, white orchids by the hundreds, thousands maybe, surrounded by green moss. It's enchanting.

Against the muted color of the walls, hundreds of colors in the form of evening gowns move like a kaleidoscope, floating around the room, as men become the perfect background in their black tuxedos, allowing the women to shine.

Careless and free, there's a sort of reckless atmosphere enveloping us as every person wearing a mask pretends to be someone else for tonight.

There's electricity in the air. A kind of magic.

And it's freaking me out because, call it intuition, but I can sense that he's here.

All eyes on us, we make our way to a large group of people standing by a grand piano, where a very famous virtuoso is currently playing an achingly beautiful melody. With Ben's arm encircling my waist, I feel the exact moment when he tenses up, his grip growing stronger, almost hurting me.

"Ah. I see Alan and his wife, Loretta, with their daughter. Let's go greet them. I need to have a word with him before we can make our way to the bar."

"How do you know who Alan and his wife are when everyone's wearing masks? I can't recognize anyone. Will Megan and Micky be here?" I stare into his eyes as I ask.

"I could recognize Alan and his wife anywhere and at any time. They're both very tall people with a very distinctive blonde hair color."

I glance at the group parting to welcome us amongst them, and notice three people with hair so blonde that it's almost white. "Oh. I guess, you are right. I do see how unique their—"

Oh, God. No.

I want to stop walking. Completely.

I can't.

I can't take another step.

Oh, no, no, no.

However, Ben seems to have other ideas. Not letting go of my waist, he pulls me forward as he continues to walk.

I manage to whisper accusingly, "No-o, Ben…p-please. You…you knew."

I see Ben's eyes through the mask, and the anger reflected in them. "No, I didn't know that he was going to be here. I wasn't sure anyway. And it doesn't matter. It's about time that he saw you with me, your husband. Now, keep moving Cathy, or do you want me to drag you toward him?"

"No, no, no, no. Please, Ben, not like this. Not like this."

Vile rising in my throat, I want to vomit. My stomach hurts, and I can feel tears in my eyes. No, I don't want Arsen to see me like this. Not after the way we parted last night…not with Ben.

"Yes, Cathy. Maybe by doing this you will finally understand how much you—"

"Well, well…look who decided to finally grace us with his presence. The mighty Benjamin Stanwood and his beautiful wife Catherine, correct?" I flinch when Alan says my name. Ben never calls me Catherine.

No. Only Arsen calls me by that name.

I avoid looking at the man wearing a full mask of what looks to be a cross between the sun and fire with flames or rays pointing in every direction. I can't. Instead, my eyes land on the beautiful female standing next to him. She's wearing an exquisite white princess gown. The bustier is filled with white Swarovsky crystals, and her mask depicts a swan with silver and white feathers adorning one corner. Her lips are as full as mine, and her neck is long, thin, and elegant. Her blonde hair, swept back in a simple ballerina bun, allows me to see her perfect bone structure. She is breathtaking, and she's holding Arsen's hand in hers.

Do you hear that? That's karma shouting in my ear, "Eat it, you bitch," as I watch Arsen with another woman.

Jealousy is such a potent threatening emotion. It doesn't just eat you alive—it eats you from within. It's venom that spreads in your bloodstream, polluting you, killing you. It corrodes you until there's nothing left. And right now, I'm being suffocated by it. I hate her. I hate her.

Feeling faint as sweat breaks in the small of my back and my temples, I can hear Alan speaking, "Ladies and gentlemen, let me introduce you to Ben Stanwood and his—"

Ben interrupts Alan. "My wife, Cathy Stanwood."

That's when I finally lift my eyes to stare at Arsen, and I just know. As I stand next to Ben in a room full of people, I watch and yearn for the man standing in front of me, and I know there's no going back for me.

I choose Arsen.

I choose him.

26

The blonde girl extends her long and pretty hand first. How I hate her hand.

"Hi! My name is Jillian, but you can call me Jill. And this," her free hand settles in the center of Arsen's solid chest, "is Arsen Radcliff. A close family friend." Her stupid face lights up when Arsen smiles down at her. Fisting my hands so hard I can feel my nails breaking through skin, I fight a visceral reaction taking over me. I want to slap the smile clean off her face.

He is mine.

Mine. Mine. Mine.

Ben's grip is now so painful, I can feel myself growing numb around my waist.

"Jill, it's alright. I already know the Stanwood's. Catherine," Arsen's raspy voice emphasizes my name, "worked for my dad. I trained under her tutelage until I decided I didn't give a shit anymore." Blushing by his words, I observe as Arsen addresses Alan and Loretta, a smirk on his lips. "I hope I haven't offended you, Uncle Al." He turns to look at the regal woman standing next to him. "And Aunt Lo, you know I mean no disrespect. Ahh…I hear the band playing in the ballroom."

Lifting Jillian's hand to his lips, he places a soft kiss on her palm and drops it in the air. "Gorgeous, would you mind if I took a turn around the dance floor with the lovely Mrs. Stanwood? It's been a while since I saw her last," Arsen says sarcastically.

Arsen addresses Ben, without looking at me. "Would you mind if I stole your wife, Ben? You know, for just a little while?"

I wince when I listen to his blatant lies and innuendos, blushing with the color of shame. Ben's jaw tightens as the thick veins on his neck appear before answering Arsen. "If Cathy wants to, I don't mind."

When he pins me with his pleading gaze, Ben's cool façade chips a fraction, allowing me see the vulnerability behind his act tonight. His eyes beg me not to go. Not to leave with Arsen. To stay with him.

Please. Please. Please, don't go with him. Stay with me.

The thing about being selfish is that you don't care if someone is at your feet begging you to stay with him, offering you the world, his heart and soul. It doesn't matter. You'll do whatever you want to do. What you need to do for yourself. Nothing matters but what you want. What you think you need.

I want to be selfish.

I want to be careless.

I'm past feeling guilty.

I'm completely and utterly out of my mind because of a man and I don't care. I'm like a heroine addict going through withdrawals. I must have Arsen.

And I'm angry.

I'm angry because that slut is here with him and not me.

Without looking at Ben, I pull myself away from his hold and take Arsen's hand in mine, accepting his offer to dance.

Slipping.

I'm slipping away slowly from Ben and his hold on me.

"Yes. I would love to."

Odd. Somehow my voice sounds clear and calm, not giving away the raging storm brewing inside me.

I let go of Arsen's hand once we begin to move away from the group and head towards the ballroom. I never look back, even though a big part of me wants to, the part that knows how much I still love Ben, the part that hasn't allowed fucking to cloud her judgment.

But I don't.

And I know I should have.

Arsen leans down to murmur angrily in my ear. The breath escaping through his mask makes the flyaway hair on my neck tickle my exposed skin as his voice sends shivers running down my spine. The closeness of our bodies ignites my body with need once more.

"Is Ben in some kind of fucking denial? You just eye fucked me in front of him and a shitload of people, then agreed to walk away with me for a dance, and he still doesn't do anything. Is the guy fucking blind?" he growls.

"How dare you?" I hiss.

"How dare I what? Speak the truth? Insult your husband? Ignore your pathetic calls and then show my fucking face at this party with a date? What is it, Dimples? Give me your fucking best."

I can't continue listening to him without either breaking down and crying in the middle of the dance floor or slapping him across the face, gathering unwanted attention towards us. I push his hand away forcefully, leaving Arsen at the entrance of the ballroom as I go in search of a place where I can be alone and calm down.

Finding a small room that is clearly not intended for guests' use, I walk in and when I'm about to shut the door behind me Arsen appears out of nowhere, pushing me further into the unlit room as he shuts us both inside.

"What the hell are you doing here? Someone may have seen you follow me. There will be gossip!" I protest.

"It hurts, doesn't it?" he taunts me. "Seeing me with someone else? Ignoring your phone calls because I'm too fucking busy with real life to deal with a fuck buddy? Now you know what it's like to not be wanted."

"I never said I didn't want you!" I yell.

"Yes, you did." Taking his mask off and throwing it on the floor, I watch him run a hand through his blond hair. "You told me not to push you. That you love your husband, and you gave me the sorriest excuse that I've ever heard…to give you fucking time. But you know what, Catherine?" he says, an ugly smile plastered on his achingly perfect face, "I'm okay with your shit, but don't expect me to wait back at my apartment for you to call me whenever you're bored. You get to go back to your husband and play house with him, so why the fuck shouldn't I enjoy some pussy on the side? Oh, wait, no…I've got it." He smacks his forehead, "You're the pussy on the side, right?"

I slap him across the face. My stinging hand hurts just as much as I hurt on the inside. His cruel words are like a dagger to my heart because they are true.

"H-how dare you!" I'm trembling in anger.

Laughing Arsen, shrugs.

"I hate you. I hate you. Do you hear me?" The words are torn from my chest, but I can't stop myself from repeating them. "I hate you, I hate you, I hate you!" Fisting my hands on my sides, I want to kick him, scratch him, bite him; whatever I can do to cause him pain. I want him to feel my pain. I want him to hurt just as he's making me hurt.

"So what?" he asks nonchalantly.

As I watch Arsen shrug his shoulder carelessly once more, something inside me snaps. I lunge toward him and start slapping, biting, kicking…whatever I can do to hurt him.

"YOU'RE SUCH A FUCKING ASS—"

"SHUT THE FUCK UP!" He yells back at me as he grabs my hands forcefully and turns our bodies, pushing me against the wall.

Our chests rise and fall, breathing heavily as we stare at each other. The want, anger, and need reflected in his eyes make me want to fuck him, right here, right now. But instead, I murmur defeated, "Let go of me…I need to get back to Ben. We're done."

Arsen lets go of my arms to urgently lift my ass in his hands, pushing our bodies closer against each other as he growls in my ear, "No. Never. You're mine. All fucking mine."

As panic rises inside me, a surge of desire so strong, I can't do anything but feel, rushes over me. I need Arsen in my body. I need to feel his dick sliding in and out of me. I want him to fuck me hard. Surrendering, I wrap my legs around his waist and let him do whatever he wants with me.

I am his.

He kisses my neck as my body pulses with want for him.

"Please…" I whimper as I tilt my head back not caring that we could get caught. Not caring that Ben could be looking for me at this moment.

His mouth crushes mine as waves of desire crash down over us, washing the despair and shame I feel away. As our tongues tangle, I open my legs wider for him. I can feel his erection as he grinds himself against me. Losing myself in the depths of his eyes, I hear the sound of his zipper sliding down, and of silk being torn.

One hard thrust and he's inside me. Entering me deeply, roughly, yet gently, filling me completely. Lifting my ass higher with his hands, he leans his forehead against mine as sweat begins to cover our bodies.

"I can't, I can't. I thought I could share you, but I can't. Please…leave him. I need you, and I know you need me too. You need me. Be mine…" he says gruffly.

Thrust.

"I'm yours. I'm yours," I reverberate.

Thrust.

"I can't share you. Seeing you with him is fucking breaking me. It's breaking me." His voice is husky with passion.

Thrust.

"Leave him. I can't keep doing this anymore. I can't keep sharing you."

Thrust.

"Yes, I'll do it."

Thrust.

"When?"

Thrust.

"Tonight."

Arsen increases the tempo of his thrusts making them faster, harder, driving us closer to our climax.

"I can feel you shaking…fuck…your pussy is so fucking tight…hell, you're so close. Look at me, Dimples. I want to watch your eyes when you come."

He puts his lips next to my ear and whispers hoarsely, "Come for me, Catherine, come for me. Now."

I explode, losing myself in the blue sea of his eyes. Arsen kisses me as he pushes himself deeper into me, coming inside as his large body vibrates fiercely with the power of his climax.

After a couple minutes pass and our breathing evens out, Arsen pulls out of me, making me flinch as his softening erection leaves my sore body. He zips his pants up while staring at me.

Without saying a word, Arsen hands me a tissue to clean myself up as the skirt of my dress falls from my waist down to the floor in a river of black silk. In a daze, I can barely manage to look at him as I clean the sticky liquid in between my thighs.

Once I'm done, Arsen takes the tissue from my hand, walks to the garbage can and throws it away for me. As he makes his way back, he spots my thong on the floor. Thinking that he's going to discard it himself, I'm surprised when Arsen picks it up and tucks it inside his jacket instead.

"Let's go back before people start wondering where the fuck we are. But, Dimples, as you walk back to meet Ben I want you to remember what you said to me." Stepping closer to me, he wraps my hair in his hand, giving it a tug so that I'm staring at him. "When you go back to him, remember that I am inside you…that you belong to me."

I leave before him while he waits inside the room so that we don't raise any suspicion. My legs are shaking from the hard grip I had on his hips as I make my way back to Ben. I am trembling and so ashamed. I can't believe I just let Arsen screw me against someone's door while my husband is in the same building, and not once did I think about him. Not once. Not even as I was coming and saw fucking stars. As guilt tries to take over me, I try not to think of what just happened, pretending like it never did.

When I return to the main room, Ben immediately spots me walking towards him. At first he looks angry as he scans my countenance from afar, but by the time I reach him all I can see is sadness in his eyes.

Such despairing sadness.

The eyes that used to shine so bright with love now look empty and drained. Lifeless.

When Ben lifts a hand, I instantly assume that he's going to take mine in his, but instead, it goes to his front pocket. Retrieving a handkerchief, he hands it to me.

"Your lipstick is smudged," Ben says quietly.

27

As I look at Ben's eyes filled with such raw pain, I think that I shouldn't be here. Not after what happened last night. I should have gone to a hotel and spent the night there.

My mind is a cluster fuck of thoughts, so many of them swimming through my head not letting me be at peace. But I guess I don't deserve peace, right? A lying, cheating, and deceitful woman like me should suffer.

Oh my God. What have I done?

This is over.

But it has been for a while.

Since the first time I went back to Arsen's place.

Oh, Ben.

Ben and I are over.

My marriage is over.

I did this.

I did.

Can you be physically ill from a broken heart?

Because it hurts. So much.

I feel dirty.

Worthless.

I don't deserve to feel pain, though. I don't deserve the tears that are beginning to form in my eyes. I don't deserve him. But after today he will be free of me. He will be free of me once he knows the truth.

What have I done? Shortly after I return from having fucked Arsen against the wall, the soreness between my legs proof enough, Ben decides he's had enough of the party and that it's time to leave. As we are saying our goodbyes, someone disguised as a lion approaches us needing to speak to him about work. Excusing himself, Ben follows lion man and gets lost in a sea of masked strangers.

Feeling a strong hand wrap around my elbow, Arsen whispers in my ear, "Don't go back with him. End it now. Come back with me. Call him on our way to my apartment. Just don't go back with him," he pleads with ferocity.

I shake my head and pull myself away from his hold. "I have to. I need to end it the right way, Arsen. Not that there's a right way to do this. Now, please, stop it. I told you already that I'm leaving him, but you've got to let me do this in my own way. I'll call you tomorrow."

If Arsen in his jealousy thinks that my going back home with Ben means that something is going to happen, he is insane. I can still smell him on my skin, on my clothes, taste the cigarette he had smoked before…Arsen is everywhere.

He is on me.

Inside me.

Around me.

I know I have to go home and somehow manage to come clean with Ben. My sweet, sweet husband. He deserves to know the truth. He deserves to know how the woman he claims to know and love, has been fucking a younger man for a while now, loves it, and doesn't plan on stopping.

I need to get out of here.

When Ben sees me walking towards him, he stands up. Frowning, he watches my clothes, my hair, my every move. It makes me think that he already knows.

Good. I want to get things over with.

I'm about to ask if he is ready to leave, but his empty eyes rob me of words. I wonder how much he knows, and if he will hate me once he learns the truth.

There are two warring parts of me in this whole fiasco. The one who wants to do right by Ben, and the selfish one who just doesn't care anymore. The Cathy who loves him wants to take him in her arms and beg for forgiveness, promising him that it meant nothing.

But that's the thing…

It isn't about the thrill anymore, the high Arsen makes me feel whenever he makes me come, or the numbness he provides me. Now it means something.

We ride together in the car in silence. He has an arm around my shoulders for the entire ride, sometimes leaning his cheek on top of my head, sometimes kissing my hair, inhaling the smell of it…I want to drown in the current of tenderness flowing between us, but what if he can smell Arsen on me?

I keep my head reclined on his shoulders with our hands linked together. It is uncomfortable with the console between us, but that is the last thing on my mind—I just need to feel him close. Looking at our hands intertwined makes me feel as if I am being sucked into a black hole of sorrow and pain. I know with certainty that this is going to be the last time Ben and I ride in his car together like this.

I lift my head and look out the window for a moment. The moon looks red tonight. Beautiful.

By the time we are home, our masks long gone, I'm about to tell Ben that I am going to take a shower, when he takes my hand in his and makes me follow him to the kitchen without saying one word. After turning the lights on, he lowers his body and embraces me in a hug so fierce in its nature that it leaves me breathless and a little shaken. When he opens his eyes to look down at me, he shatters me.

"How about a glass of wine?" he asks softly, smiling sadly at me.

I can't do this tonight. I can't do this to Ben. But I already have. Returning the hug, I stand on my tip-toes and kiss his chin as I feel a full blown panic attack coming on. I can do this. Just don't think about it. Talk to him tomorrow.

"Would you mind if I shower first?" I need to take a shower and wash Arsen off. Will the guilt of what I have done wash off too? I doubt it.

When I'm out of the shower, Ben has changed into sweats and a Columbia t-shirt and is cooking something.

"Dinner?" I ask.

"Yes, I'm starving. I don't understand how people expect men my size to be satisfied with hors d'oeuvres. It boggles my mind."

Ben and I hardly speak through our late meal, but I don't mind the silence. The last thing I want to do in what will be our last night together is make small talk. I don't want to eat. I don't want to drink the wine he served me. I just want to watch him. Memorize the patterns of his dark stubble, the way his dimple peeks at me every time he chews, begging me to kiss it.

After I help Ben remove the dishes from the table, I start to wash them. The hot water burning my hands is a welcome relief. Nothing like physical pain to numb you. The haunting voice of a man singing about how he can't take his eyes off of his lover envelops the whole kitchen. I close my eyes and get lost in the singer's melancholy voice telling his lover that without love there is no glory.

With a knot in the back of my throat, I feel Ben's warm arms wrap around my waist from behind. Letting go of the dish, and wiping the soap on my yoga pants, I bring one hand behind his neck, pulling his face closer to the curve of my neck as my other hand rests on top of his on my stomach. With my back against his front, we sway to the gentle rhythm of the music…slowly…tenderly. Ben kisses my neck, my hair, behind my ear, showering me with kisses that feel final.

The knot in my throat keeps getting bigger and bigger until tears fall down my cheeks. Treacherous tears. I don't know if Ben sees them. I don't care. I just want to get lost in his touch, in his warmth, in him for one last time.

When the song ends, I turn around as Ben lets go of my body. Bending down, he lifts me with ease into his arms. Saying nothing to each other, I put my arms around his neck, and rest my head on his shoulder as I inhale deeply into my lungs, trying to absorb his smell. As he carries me, I can hear his breathing accelerating, becoming strained, and somehow I know it isn't because of my weight.

He can feel it too.

Our last night.

Our grand finale.

I want to say something, but I can't find the right words.

It isn't until we make it to our bedroom, and he places me tenderly on the bed, that I know I have to stop whatever is about to happen.

But I can't…

And not because I care that Ben may erase Arsen from my body. I don't fucking care about Arsen at this moment. I can't do it because I don't want to sully Ben with my body. I don't want our last time together to be the day I let someone else come inside me while panting his name in an empty room.

Slowly, Ben removes our clothes until there's nothing left between us.

"So beautiful…" he whispers hoarsely as he runs a hand over my breasts. "You're so damn beautiful."

I'm about to stop Ben when he leans over me. What I see punches me in the gut, leaving me speechless. Taking my hands in his hold and looking down at me, I see the glimmer of tears in his eyes as he whispers against my mouth, "Please, Cathy…not tonight. Not tonight. Let us…let me just kiss you."

He kisses my tears away, licking them off my face and swallowing them as if they are his own.

"It's always been you, Ben…" I choke as deep emotion overpowers me. I want to tell him that it will continue to be him forever, but that would be a lie.

Ben lowers his forehead to press against mine. I feel the moisture from his tears, my tears, our tears. Together.

"I don't want tomorrow to fucking come, Cathy. I'm afraid." His voice is hoarse with pain as he pleads. He bends down to kiss my lips, my eyes, my temples, my nose. I try doing the same as my arms and legs wrap fiercely around his body. I want to consume him, absorb his body in mine and keep him that way. Just the two of us, filling each other, surrounding each other.

Holding both my hands over my head, he looks down at me as he slowly and gently slides inside me. He looks so lost, so hurt, so vulnerable…it is so tender, so sweet, and so painful. Our emotions guide us through the dance of two bodies trying to communicate at their most honest, vulnerable, basic, and raw moments together what they can't with words.

I love you.

Please forgive me.

Don't leave me.

How could you.

I hate you.

I love you.

I will fucking die without you.

You are mine.

Only mine.

I belong to you.

Only you.

It is beautiful. It is soul shattering. It is good-bye.

Late Sunday morning. I watch as my husband's large and powerful body falls to the ground in surrender.

Broken…by me.

"I fucked Arsen," I tell him quietly.

Earlier that morning.

After taking a shower, I wrap a towel around my waist and make my way to bed where an exhausted Cathy is currently sleeping.

Cathy.

My past, my present, and my future—my forever.

Or so I thought.

Watching her sleep with messy hair and no makeup in the aftermath of having fucked all night long, she can still manage to rob me of breath. I bend down and kiss her lips, lips that look red and swollen, and this time I know that I'm the reason behind it and not him. Cherishing the moment, I let my mouth linger on hers as I close my eyes and inhale the smell of jasmine and sex branded on her skin deeply into my lungs, savoring that, for once, she doesn't smell like him. I grind my teeth and think back to all the times she's come home, pretending to be too tired to stay awake and keep me company. Or on the few occasions when I've reached for her at night, and she turns away from my touch because she doesn't feel like fucking, all the while smelling like a different man.

I wonder…

I wonder how many times have I been fooled by her? By them?

Sometimes the need to know consumes me, driving me mad with jealousy. Yet other times, when I stare at her pretty face smiling at me, telling me that she loves me, letting me fuck her, I want to smother that need. I want to believe every single lie of hers so I can gladly continue living in denial. I love her that fucking much.

But this love, this madness has become the cross I bear on my back, pulling me down to my knees. My living purgatory. I can't keep living a life where I question every word, every action of the person I should trust unconditionally. The constant doubting and the unanswered questions running through my head are fucking with my peace of mind. I can't.

Is she with him?

Did she just fuck him?

Was she on the phone with him?

Where is she?

Why is she not answering my calls?

Is she thinking of him as I make love to her?

I can't do this anymore.

It's fucking killing me.

I really can't keep fooling myself. I can't. Watching her disappear with Arsen last night is the last blow my poor fucking heart…my pride…can take from her.

I'm fucking done.

I straighten and grab the sheet wrapped around her naked waist and pull it up, covering her shoulders with it. Her shiny blonde hair is spread over our pillows, surrounding her in a pool of gold. My Cathy.

I move away from her, get dressed, and head to the door. As I stand on the threshold, I take a last look at the room, my eyes scanning the perimeter and stopping on picture frames, pillows, furniture—all of our memories together. I don't feel anything as I take in the room filled with so much happiness, heartache, love, hate.

I feel nothing.

I'm numb.

My eyes land on the bed and admire an unsuspecting Cathy. Her face, her rosy breasts…I memorize every single fucking curve of her body. They were once mine, but not anymore.

Love is never supposed to hurt. Love is supposed to heal, to be your haven from misery, to make living fucking worthwhile. But as I stare at my wife, I know it's all fucking bullshit.

Love has the power to destroy you.

Love has the power to bury you alive in a coffin full of pain and despair, robbing you of air, of the will to live.

I close my eyes and bring the heel of my hands to rub my eyes. I suddenly feel so tired. My whole body hurts—my head hurts, my eyes hurt, my chest hurts. As I sit in my office, waiting for Cathy to wake up and join me, I realize what a fucking mistake last night was; the worst decision I've ever made. I knew I was going to pay dearly for it today, but I'd needed it. I'd needed her. I'd needed to spend one last night with my wife. I'd wanted to smell her hair, kiss the tip of her shoulder and hold her in my arms as if it were any other night, pretending that she was still mine. And I'd wanted to say goodbye to her—to our small family of two.

But as I wait for her, I'm sinking in a quicksand of guilt that threatens to swallow me whole. Here I am, waiting to face Cathy, demanding the truth from her when I'm guilty as well.

In search of emotional respite from the nightmare my fucking life has turned into, I've stooped to their level, and I can't say that I feel any better from it. If anything, I'm disgusted with myself because I let weakness get the best of me.

I open my eyes as I recline my head on the back of my leather chair, looking up at the ceiling. Feeling sick to my stomach, I recall what happened Friday night. The night I didn't come home.

After leaving work so I could come back here to receive the delivery of the new couch since Cathy decided she had better things to do than answering my calls, I stayed home for a couple of hours. But just being here while she was out and probably fucking Arsen filled me with so much anger. I knew that if I were here by the time she came home, I wasn't going to be able to control myself around her, so I went back to the office to drown myself in work. It helped me to forget.

I was planning to stay and go over more cases when Micky and the interns asked if I was interested in joining them for drinks.

I didn't refuse this time.

One drink turned into two, two turned into four.

In my alcohol-induced haze, I remember thinking that the interns, Clara and Kerry, were so fucking gorgeous. Both girls were trying to get me to dance with them, so I did. Why not? Soon it wasn't going to matter…
As we danced, I felt Kerry's arms snake around my chest and I liked it. I

liked feeling the warm touch of a woman, of someone wanting me. Looking down, I saw her smile provocatively at me.

Yes.

She wanted me.

And at that moment, I wanted her, too.

I watch as Ben's lifeless body slides to the ground. When he looks up from the floor, he watches me with warm maple eyes that sparkle with unshed tears.

"How long has this been going on?" his voice breaks, "How many times have you fucked him, Cathy?"

"I-I…" I take a deep breath. I can't stop now. I must go on. "It's been going on for a while now."

"I knew it. I knew it. I fucking knew it."

Ben lowers his head in between his knees and starts pulling his hair with both hands, almost as if he wants to rip it out. When he looks back up, his eyes pierce my soul. "Do you screw him before or after you're with me because you haven't stopped fucking me."

Silence.

Speechless by the hurt and betrayal I see in his eyes, I'm not able to form a coherent response. When Ben realizes that I won't answer the questions or accusations he's throwing in my face, he snaps.

"Answer the fucking question!" Anger makes the veins of his neck protrude, looking like they are ready to explode.

I can't answer.

I can't.

He will hate me.

The intensity of anger directed at me, anger that he's entitled to feel, startles me, catching me by surprise. I have never seen Ben this angry before.

"Fucking answer me! I deserve a fucking answer, you cheating whore!"

Both of us flinch at his words.

"Both," I croak.

The tears that are glossing his eyes spill over, and all I can do is watch them fall down his beautiful face. I want to go to him and apologize, ask for his forgiveness, but I can't. I lost that privilege a long time ago. I deserve his fury, his disgust, his hatred.

As we stare at each other, letting the truth sink in, I face a stranger. Ben doesn't look like the carefree boy I fell in love with. He looks like a ravaged man. A man who knows pain, the kind that can kill you, destroy you, drown you in a sea of darkness and hatred. I wonder if he will ever break through and heal?

"Do you love him?" He lets his words hang in the silence of the room. Lowering my gaze, I stare at my trembling hands. "For Christ's sake, Cathy! Would you answer the damn question! Do you fucking love him? Yes, no? What is it going to be?"

"I…"

His body trembles as he groans.

"Yes. No…I don't know. It feels like love when I'm with him. It feels…I'm happy when I'm with him, Ben. And that's the truth."

Ben gazes at me from the floor. I can see the tears in his eyes, hanging on his lashes, running down his cheeks. Licking some with his tongue as he wipes his face with the back of his hand, his stare never wavers.

"Do you love me? Do you still love me? And be fucking honest for once in your life." Clenching his hands into fists, he murmurs to himself, "I fucking deserve it. This is bullshit. I can't…I can't."

Well, here it goes. Maybe this will make him hate me, destroying all the love he has left for me. I don't deserve it anyway. I need to destroy it so he can move on. And he deserves my honesty.

"I love you, Ben. I'm just not sure I am still in love with you."

I see him flinch. Good. I'm glad. This is the only way for him to be free of me. For a moment, I wonder if there's something essentially wrong with me. How can I hurt someone that I claim to love so much? Why am I doing this? How did we get to this point?

Because you took the easy way out when things got tough, Cathy. You didn't fight.

"Why?"

"Why what?"

"Why did you do it? Why did you fucking cheat, Cathy? And why did you continue to cheat? Was the sex that fucking good? Don't you think that I hurt just as badly when you had the last miscarriage? Don't you think that I wanted that baby just as badly as you did?"

I want to tell him it is because of the miscarriage. It has always been about them. The miscarriages were the oil, and Arsen was the fire. Together it scorched my crumbling marriage, burning it to the ground. I want to tell him that I am so confused and that my emotions are all over the place. That I have doubted our marriage for a while now. That I thought the baby was our second chance, but that is gone now too. I want to be honest, but his cruel questions are the morphine I need to numb myself so I can answer without feeling any remorse.

"I slept with him for the first time the night I told you I was going to meet Amy for drinks. He called me and said he wanted to speak to me about th-the miscarriage…he wanted to be there for me. I was so numb to everything. I couldn't stand seeing your face, being around you. Your perfection was driving me insane. I met up with him, never thinking that I was going to sleep with him."

"But you were attracted to him. I saw it. You must have known…that fucking song—it was for you."

"Yes." Sitting down next to him, I continue, "It didn't start like that, Ben. We were just friends. But somewhere along the line, it changed. The first time it happened made me feel so good, so alive that I knew right then and there that I wasn't going to stop. He f-fucked me, Ben. He didn't make love to me. He made me forget, he made the numbness go away, he made me feel wanted, needed. I don't know…I felt young and beautiful again—not so broken."

I stare into his eyes. "With him, it didn't feel like work. With Arsen, I was able to cry, be angry, hateful even, and not care about hurting his feelings like I did with you. H-he didn't treat me like a china doll; he treated me like a person. Every time I tried telling you how I felt, how fucked up I was, all you said was that everything was going to be okay and that we were going to get through it.

"It was just too much, Ben. Too fucking much. Your perfection was asphyxiating me, and I couldn't handle it. I think I grew to hate you, resent you, and Arsen made it all go away. With him, it was just me, Cathy. No wife, no failure, no nothing. Just me. And it felt so good. It was like a drug. I needed more, craved more, and the more I had, the more I wanted. The more I wanted him."

I swallow hard because my next words are the hardest to admit, even to myself. "It started as sex, Ben, as an escape, but it's not anymore. As everything was happening…I-I think I fell in love with him."

Silence.

"D-Don't think I'm trying to excuse my behavior because I am not. I know I was wrong, very wrong, b-but I'm trying to answer your questions as truthfully as possible." I lower my voice to a soft murmur, "You deserve it."

He begins to bang his head against the wall.

Thump.

Thump.

Thump.

The constant thumping is driving me crazy.

Sitting there, I watch him hurt himself until I can't take it anymore. I'm about to touch him when he swats my hand away as you would do to an annoying mosquito.

It hurts.

But I did this. I did this to Ben and to myself. I can't complain that he's repulsed by my touch.

When he finally looks up, he grabs me by the shoulders and shakes me aggressively. "Were you fucking careful?" he utters with disgust and fear etched in every syllable.

At first I don't understand what he means.

Oh.

Shaking my head no, the look in his eyes says it all. He wants to kill me. Or Arsen. Or both of us.

"So, let me get this straight. He fucks you, comes inside you, and then you let me do the same? Now I understand the constant showering. You must be shitting me." Silent, I watch his face as sudden realization dawns on him. Pinning me with furious eyes, his breathing accelerates. "Last night…you fucking needed to wash him off, didn't you?"

Nodding, I begin to cry.

"You make me sick."

Ben lets go of me harshly and stands up, almost as if close contact with my body will cause him physical pain. The release of his strong grip causes me to fall back with just enough time to put my arms behind me to cushion the fall. Turning around, he begins to shout angrily at me, his face red with anger and tears, "Did you ever think what this would do to me? Do you even," he curses under his breath, "Do you even fucking care?"

My stomach tightens as he shouts at me. Each word is a punishing blow to the gut, robbing me of air, but I owe him the chance to get it all out—to punch me with his words, and break me with his anger. Call it atonement, but I must pay for what I've done. I just didn't expect that honesty could hurt so much. That witnessing the consequences of your behavior and the mess you've made could be so painful. I alone should suffer the consequences of those choices. Not him. But sadly, he's paying for them too.

"I did at first…b-but I stopped eventually."

Ben is breathing heavily, and his stormy eyes are filled with anguish. "You need to leave. I can't…I can't…I can't keep doing this to myself. I-," He groans as he puts his hands around his head and begins to rock back and forth on his feet. In silence, I watch him for what seems an eternity, trying to give him space. After a few minutes, Ben looks at me.

"When you were broken, I loved you for the two of us, Cathy. For the two of us and I didn't fucking care…I didn't. I thought my love would be enough, I loved you that much. If you had asked me to cut my own arm off for you, I would have. I would have given you my whole fucking body, Cathy. Only for you. I should've never had to share you, Cathy. Never. I thought you were mine, like I'm yours. Or was. Fuck. Fuck. Fuck. This is so fucking unbelievable.

"You know what? Let's have the fucking truth. I've heard your pathetic excuses, how about you hear me out now? Let me tell you something, Cathy, I hope you're happy because Arsen may own your heart, your body, but you'll always be empty because I own your fucking soul. Your soul is part of mine and it always will be. I will heal, I will learn to love again, but you…I pity you.

"You say that you're walking away from me and our marriage because of the strain the miscarriages put on our relationship." He hits his chest painfully, "What about me? You think I wasn't hurting just as much as you? Every fucking time I close my eyes, I can still hear the blood-curdling scream from that day. Sometimes I'm afraid to fall asleep because images of you covered in your own blood haunt me even in my dreams. You miscarried and lost the babies, Cathy. Well, I lost those babies too and I also lost my wife. I was left with nothing but memories."

He pauses and wipes some tears off his face before continuing, "I wanted that fucking family too. You were able to retreat into your own head, hiding from everyone and anyone that cared for you. You stopped caring and I was okay with it. I was able to handle it because I kept fucking hoping that things would get better, that with time I'd get my wife back. Do you think you were the only one to ever doubt us? To want to give up on us? To want to hide? To wonder about other people? I've wanted to fuck other women too, Cathy, just so I could forget about you and remember what it feels like to be wanted, needed, again. But I didn't. I loved you too much, and sadly, I still do, and I had more respect for our marriage, for you.

"All I really wanted was…I just wanted to hold you in my arms for as long as I could. I wanted that second or third or fourth chance for us to be whole again. That was all. So if you think you'll be happy with Arsen, well good luck. But honestly, I don't think you'll be able to. You need to take a closer look at yourself first before you can be with anyone else, see why you couldn't just open up to me and let me help you. But that's not my problem anymore. I'm done. Just remember, Karma is a bitch."

His painful words light an angry fire inside me, and I want to burn him with it. How dare he! Life has been hell for me since my last miscarriage, hell since the beginning of this whole mess. I haven't been able to think straight since that day, not that it excuses my behavior. He wanted to know the truth, so I was giving him my own version of it, not once was I trying to justify my actions. I knew it was wrong the first time it happened, and I continued to know through the entire affair that it was more than wrong—It was unforgivable. But sometimes all the righteous reasoning in the world won't stop you from making a mistake. Sometimes even holding onto someone as you're falling won't stop you from falling. Sometimes you just have to fall.

I am so angry at him, at myself. So guilty, so sorry, and so ashamed. But feeling shame suddenly makes me want to yell and scream and hurt him again and again. Shame makes me want to hurl things at him instead of apologizing.

Looking up from my spot on the floor, with tears falling down my face blurring my view, I answer him with the best that I've got. "Karma may be a bitch, but when he came inside me I didn't care because I came so fucking hard that I saw stars!"

He stares at me, and the love I've seen in his eyes so many times before is gone. "You fucking whore…get out…get out!"

I did it.

I made him hate me just as much as I hate myself.

Now he can be free.

I stand up from the cold wooden floor of his office and walk to our bedroom. I need to go to Amy's. I can't stay here anymore. My marriage is over. Finished. Arsen was the fuel needed to burn my marriage to the ground, but I was the one who held the match in my hands the entire time.

Wiping my nose with my sleeve, I throw away as many of my belongings in the garbage as possible. I'm erasing my existence from his home. When I'm done, I leave the bathroom. Ben is standing by the large window facing our front yard, his back to me. With his head hung low in defeat, he's gripping his hair so hard with his hands; I can see the muscles of his arms bunch up.

As I walk towards him, I notice his body slightly shaking. I want to pull him close to me and kiss his tears, tell him that I love him and that I meant the words I said last night, but what good would it do? It's over between us.

My back now to him, I grab my coat and start putting it on when I hear him whisper, his voice raspy with tears, "The other night, when I didn't come home…"

"Yes?"

"I almost fucked Kerry." He takes a deep breath. "I want a divorce."

Not turning around, I let the meaning of what he just said sink in. I poisoned Ben. I deserve it. With the fight drained out of me, I whisper, "I understand. I'll come back tomorrow when you're at work to get the rest of my things."

With these words fresh on my tongue, I leave.

Walking out of the door.

Walking out of his life.

Leaving my sunshine behind and letting the darkness, disguised as freedom, welcome me in.

When I'm standing outside the house, I look up from the driveway to our bedroom window and see that the curtains are drawn. As I turn and start to walk towards the garage, it finally starts to rain, wetting my face. Licking my lips, I can taste a mixture of salt and rain. Funny, I didn't realize I was still crying.

The agonizing pain begins to gather inside my chest, ready to explode with grief. I take a few steps but stop dead on my tracks and stare at the wet cement. Rain keeps falling around me, droplets of fresh water making the asphalt under my feet glitter like stars.

I want to go back.

I've made a terrible mistake.

It feels as if I left my whole heart, my whole being back in that house with him. Standing here lost in the past, the truth comes crashing down on me. I do love him with all my heart, and I have lost him. Forever.

But I also love Arsen.

I can't wait to go back to Arsen's apartment. I need his kisses to erase the pain away like only he can. He's my numbness.

Minutes pass and I want to move, but my body won't listen. My feet are glued to the ground. I want the rain to cleanse me. I feel so dirty and so cold.

Empty.

Oh, Ben.

What have I done?

30

Arsen.

I need him.

I need to see him and make sure I've made the right choice, even though deep down I know the answer.

I'm driving and trying to hold myself together. I can't lose it just yet. I need to get to his apartment first. Then I can bury this crushing pain engulfing me in the deep corners of my heart and ignore reality. But the pain is too powerful to contain as it takes over me. I throw my phone on the passenger's seat and wipe the tears off my face as deep gut wrenching sobs are torn from my chest. When I can't stop crying, the tears preventing me from seeing ahead, I pull off to the side of the road and park the car.

As excruciating pain hits me from within, making me bend over at the waist, I wrap my arms around my stomach, attempting to shield myself from the pain. Shutting my eyes tightly, I fight the nausea brewing inside me as despair sucks the air out of me.

I can't breathe.

I can't breathe.

I can't breathe.

I'm drowning in pain.

He is gone.

Gone.

Gone.

The love of my life is gone.

And it's my fault.

I open the car door and throw up viciously on the ground. After there is nothing left inside me but bile, I rest my forehead against the cold glass of the driver's window. My eyes ache with all the tears I've shed since this morning. The realization of what I had—and lost—begins to register in my mind, and in my heart.

How am I going to live a life without Ben in it?

He's all I've ever known. He's been my world, my truth, and my reality since I was eighteen years old. He's the other half of me. Is there even a Cathy without him?

Tough shit. You did this, now you deal with it.

Even if I wanted to get Ben back, it's too late for us. Too damn late.

I close my eyes for a moment, too exhausted to fight the memories. I let them take over, enfolding me in a bittersweet cloak made of yesterdays. The first time we kissed in the rain, the first time we said I love you, the day he proposed to me, the time he held me as I bled…these memories are all I have left of Ben, of our love, and they belong to me. And nothing will ever take them away from me. Nothing—not even my lying, cheating, deceitful heart.

As I start to drive again, my phone keeps ringing, but I ignore it.

Like I ignored it last night and all day today.

Arsen.

I need him. I need to see him. He'll be able to take the pain away, make me forget like he always does with his numbing kisses and morphine-like touch. He's the beautiful painkiller that my broken body and my shattered heart demand to stop hurting. I laugh like a crazed woman because I truly have no shame left and I don't give a shit about it as long as I can make the agonizing ache of losing Ben disappear.

After I park the car in the garage of his building, I take the elevator to Arsen's apartment. I glance around the square space and I'm able to see myself reflected on the mirrored walls; my eyes are puffy from crying, my skin pale from throwing up, and my lips still swollen from last night. As I look at the deranged woman staring back at me, I try to push thoughts of Ben away from my conscience.

By the time I make my way to his apartment, my body is shaking violently from nerves. I don't know where we will go from here. What happens now? I love Ben, yet I'm standing in front of someone else's door, waiting for him to fuck the pain and memories out of my head.

I happen to love this man too.

I gulp as I stand outside his apartment trying not to think about anything other than the physical release that my body requires from Arsen. I ignore the shouting voice inside my head telling me that Arsen is the wrong choice. If he is the wrong choice, why does it feel so good when I'm with him?

After ringing the doorbell, Arsen opens the door immediately and lets me in without saying a word. He looks like hell, maybe even worse than I do. Wearing only his Armani boxer briefs and nothing else, I can see the contours of his perfect body and the way his golden skin accentuates every groove and plain of his muscles. Whenever I see the dimples right above his ass and the deep vee peeking out of his underwear, an urge to lick him there takes over me.

I look up and absorb his achingly beautiful features. His eyes are bloodshot, his blond hair is a mess, and the dark shadows of his stubble give his face a menacing quality. Yes, I want him to fuck me raw. I want him to leave scratches, bruises, and red marks on me as proof of what I have done. I want him to fuck me until the physical pain numbs my entire being and my orgasms numb my mind.

In silence, we stare at each other for a long time. Arsen is the first one to speak. "Where have you been?" he asks shortly. "How come you haven't answered my fucking phone calls? I've been trying to get in touch with you since last night." He drags his hands through his hair repeatedly. "You said you were going back to your house to end things with him. How long could that have taken you?"

Watching his anger surface is like watching a tornado about to hit an unsuspecting town. Powerful. Breathtaking. Devastating.

"What the fuck is going on? Why are you standing there saying nothing?" Arsen walks towards me and grabs me by the shoulders just like Ben did not two hours ago, shaking me forcefully, desperately. "You were with him, weren't you? You spent the night with him," he asks repugnantly.

Nodding, I hear him curse under his breath.

"Did you fuck him?"

"Yes," I whisper.

"How many times?"

I shake my head and try to move away from him, but Arsen tightens his grip on me, stopping me. "Look at me when I speak to you and answer my question." His voice wavers, "How many fucking times, Catherine?" Once he realizes that I won't answer him, he shakes me once more, almost as if the action will push the truth out. "Fucking answer!"

"Three times," I say as I watch him flinch.

"Did you come?" he asks, swallowing hard.

"Yes." I did. Every time.

"How?"

"What do you mean how?"

"How did he make you come? Did he fuck you from behind? Did he eat your pussy? Did he—"

"Stop! Stop!" I shout as I cover my ears. His words are making me sick. The truth makes me sick.

"Answer the fucking questions. How did he make you come? I want to know."

"The first time he made love to me, he was on top of me. W-we came as we stared at each other. The second time, I sucked his dick until he came in my mouth as he a-ate my p-p-pussy. The third time, he fucked me from behind on the edge of our bed."

"Did you think about me?" he asks hoarsely.

"No."

Arsen lets go of me. Fisting his hands, he closes his eyes as his breathing accelerates. When he stares at me once more, the harsh look in his eyes makes me take a few steps back.

"Catherine, go to my room, get naked, and wait for me there. Do not ask fucking questions and do what I tell you." He burns me with his blue gaze, "Go. Now." He turns around and heads to his kitchen, leaving me alone.

In his bathroom, I take my Burberry trench coat off, my cream-colored cashmere sweater and skinny jeans next. My black-lace bra and panties are last. When I'm nude I walk out of his bathroom, expecting an empty room, but Arsen is already there, naked and slowly pumping his erection in his hand. As he watches me walk towards him with preying eyes, I can feel myself getting wet. A foot away from him, I'm about to reach for him and kiss him, but Arsen lifts a staying hand.

"Get on your knees," he angrily commands. "I want you to get on your fucking knees. Now."

Stunned, I try to process his words.

"I SAID NOW, YOU FUCKING SLUT! GET ON YOUR FUCKING KNEES!"

Wincing as if he has slapped me, I get on my knees in front of him. I want to be angry that he called me a slut, but I am one. I'm a whore who cheated on her husband and now I'm back in my lover's apartment.

I am a slut.

I can feel the coolness of the marble floor seeping into my skin. I raise my eyes to stare at him standing above me, his raging erection so close to my face.

"Now open your mouth for me."

As I open my mouth, I can feel a shameful flush covering me from the top of my head to the tips of my toes. Mortified, I close my eyes as he grabs his dick in his hand and begins to push it inside my mouth.

"Open your eyes. I want to watch them as I fuck your face."

When I do, we stare at each other as he fills my mouth with his throbbing erection. I wrap a hand around his dick and begin to lick the head, swallowing the pre cum that makes the tip glisten. My body is instantly aroused, and my nipples pebble under his gaze.

"Bite it," Arsen orders, his breathing coming fast and short. "Let me feel your teeth around my cock."

I shake my head no and I'm about to let go of him.

His hips push forward until I feel him hit the back of my throat. I'm kneeling and trying not to gag with his thrusts. Tears of shame burning my eyes, my vision is blurry as I look at his enraged face.

"I said to fucking bite it!"

He's doing this on purpose.

Hurting me.

Humiliating me.

"Fuuuck!" he exclaims as I bite him. The sick and twisted side of me actually enjoys it. Physically hurting him.

His hands go to the back of my head, fisting my hair as he pulls me closer to him. Picking up the punishing pace, he thrusts into my mouth painfully and without mercy.

Faster.

Faster.

Trying to breathe through my nose, I fight my gag reflexes as my own saliva and tears cover my chin and face.

"This mouth,"

He thrusts deeper.

"is,"

He thrusts harder.

"mine."

He explodes inside my mouth as he pumps a few more times until I have swallowed him clean. Arsen shivers and pulls himself out of my mouth with a popping sound. His shoulders and chest contracting with deep and heavy breathing, he looks down at me still kneeling on the floor with stormy eyes. "Remember that the next time you fuck your husband," he states and leaves his bedroom.

I'm naked and sitting on the tile floor of his shower stall with my arms wrapped around my legs as scalding hot water pours down on me, stinging my skin and turning it a bright red.

I'm so numb.

So lost.

I shut my eyes tightly as I try to make the images of what happened back in the bedroom disappear. When I lean my head on my knees, feeling the boiling water burn my back, I hear Arsen opening the door to the bathroom. Not wanting to face him, I turn to look at the wall.

"Catherine…" he whispers huskily.

I ignore him as I feel a knot on the back of my throat. I can't cry in front of him, he doesn't deserve my tears, so I shut my eyes tighter and scoot closer to the wall.

I sense the moment Arsen kneels in front of me, his cool hands touching both of my knees. I open my eyes as he grabs my hand and moves to lie down on the floor, bringing me down with him and climbing on top of me, shielding me from the scalding water as it pours down on us. Face to face, chest to chest, beating heart against beating heart, both of his hands cupping my cheeks as we stare at each other.

Never this close.

Never this far.

I put my arms in between us to push him away, but he stops me when he begins to desperately kiss my lips. Between broken murmurs, Arsen whispers frantically against my lips. "I'm sorry.

I'm sorry. Please, stop. Don't cry anymore. Don't cry…I'm so sorry. I'm not worthy of your tears. Fuck. Fuck."

Sitting on the floor, Arsen lifts me on top of him and holds me in his arms. My legs wrapped around his hips, I cannot bring myself to reciprocate the embrace, so I stare at his golden beauty as water drips down his face. I cry harder when I see the mistiness in his eyes.

"Oh, Arsen…" I whisper against his mouth. "Don't you understand? I feel you on my skin, I feel your taste in my tongue, I feel your hardness inside me, and it's never enough."

"Fuck, Catherine. Please forgive me, forgive me, forgive me," he repeats brokenly. He points to his chest with a closed fist, "This belongs to you. Only you, Catherine. It's been yours since the day I met you, and it will be yours until you don't want it anymore." Growling, he pulls me closer to him, "I just want your hands on my body, your lips on my mouth, and your heart to be mine. Only mine."

Lost in his words, we kiss, and then we fuck. But for once, it feels like he is making love to me.

Taste.

Sweat.

Feel.

Wetness.

Warmth.

Hardness.

Thrusts.

Fingers.

Slap…

Slap…

Slap…

Skin against skin.

Legs trembling.

Hair pulling.

Nails breaking through skin.

Arsen moving inside me.

My hands and legs wrapped around him.

His eyes boring into mine.

Aqua-blue fire burning me to ashes.

Nothing exists.

Nothing matters, but him.

It's just Arsen.

And me.

Moving to the aggressive rhythm of his forceful thrusts.

Raw.

So Raw.

It hurts.

But I love it.

I love him.

His roughness feels like love.

His love is like a numbing drug.

He is my drug.

My numbness.

He whispers in my ear, "You belong to me…only me…I need you…we need each other."

I close my eyes and get lost in mind numbing release, not hearing the last words he whispers in my ear as he comes inside me once more.

Sitting with my arms wrapped around my knees next to Arsen, I watch him sleep, looking so boyish and content. But even his perfection can't stop the pain, the guilt, and shame from resurfacing. I'm disgusted by how low I've brought myself. I hate myself because I can't let go of Arsen. And I hate myself for all the pain I've caused.

I lift a hand to caress his cheek feeling the stubble of his chin. Yes, I do love him. I love Arsen because he taught me to move on, live life, and forget. I love him because he makes me laugh. I love him because he opened my eyes to life and helped me heal. And I love him because he's Arsen.

But he just isn't my Ben.

The memory of Ben and the way we parted is pure agony. It hurts to breathe. But as I watch Arsen sleep next to me, knowing full well that I don't deserve him, I don't deserve anyone, I make a promise to myself. I will let Ben go and grieve for him in silence. I will do whatever is in my power to show Arsen my gratitude for having given me so much without even knowing it. If my life has taught me anything, it's that you can't hold onto anything that wants to go. Ben tried so hard to hold onto our relationship, onto our past, but it didn't matter because I still cheated on him, I still planned on leaving him. So I will love Arsen while I have him with whatever I have left in me, whatever doesn't belong to Ben, and that's that.

31

One month later.

The pain is still here.

I haven't heard from Ben, so I've been able to pretend that everything is peachy and perfect with Arsen. He doesn't ask questions and I don't bring it up. The past month has proven to be one of the happiest in a long time, but there's something basic missing, lacking…something that won't allow me to be complete. There's an underlying pain that I continue to ignore. I hope that someday it goes away and that the love I feel for him will disappear too, allowing me to love Arsen completely.

Love.

We haven't said the words yet, but I know he loves me. He must. It's written in the way he holds my hand when we sleep, in the way he combs my hair, in the way he feeds me strawberries while we drink champagne naked on his bed, and the way he makes love to me. I know it's there.

I love him.

When I'm with Arsen, I don't think about Ben. Not once, not ever. It's like Ben is an afterthought, a memory. Yet the moment Arsen steps away, thoughts of Ben swallow me whole. Melancholy fills me, and I can't shake it until I'm in Arsen's arms.

It's not the perfect situation, but we are happy and somehow we've made it work. I never went back to work, so we keep each other busy during the days with museum visits, walks in the park, and at night we make love or fuck. I know we are both avoiding real life, but when we are together we can pretend that everything is perfect.

The paparazzi know about us now. At first they were obsessed and even dragged my divorce into the whole mess, but the attention has dissipated. I don't know if Ben has read all the articles about us, but my dad won't speak to me.

The last time I saw Amy, she told me not to confuse fucking with love when I told her that I had left Ben for Arsen. She said that it was easy to confuse physical gratification with the real deal, but at the end that's all it was. Just plain old fucking.

I stopped talking to her. I don't want to believe her words. I can't.

After the usual pee in a cup, take down your weight, and check your blood pressure, I'm sitting on the bed in a paper gown opened at the front, exposing my breasts as I wait for Dr. Pajaree. Three days ago, Arsen found a small bump on the left one. After freaking out, he urged me to make a doctor appointment. I'm sure I'm fine, but here I am at his insistence.

When my phone vibrates, I stand up and grab it out of my bag. There's a text message from Arsen.

Arsen: I want you in the worst possible way. You're the drug that offers me relief…that energizes me again…that soothes me…that delivers me sweet oblivion. You're my drug of choice, Catherine. You're my addiction. My euphoria.

I blush and recall the things he did to me last night with a bottle of champagne and the places he drank it from.

After Dr. Pajaree comes in and checks my breasts for lumps, not finding anything but an enlarged lymph node, she tells me to meet her in her office once I'm dressed. I feel relieved because the small lump turned to be nothing, yet anxious because I think that she wants to ask me how I'm doing and about the magazine articles. How am I going to tell her that since she last saw us, Ben filed for divorce and that I'm currently living with a twenty four year old man?

Dressed, I make my way to her office. As soon as I'm sitting in front of her, I notice that she's avoiding looking at me directly in the eyes. Worried that she found something, I'm about to ask her what the problem is when she interrupts me.

"Cathy. You're pregnant."

In a daze, I make my way to Arsen's apartment. I can't be pregnant again. I can't. When the cab drops me off in front of Arsen's building, I swear I see Ben's black Maybach pulling away from the curb, but it's not possible. I'm imagining things because of what I just found out, so I let it go and forget about it as I pay the cabdriver.

Fumbling with the keys to Arsen's apartment door, I want to cry with happiness and apprehension. I grimace when I remember that I'm seven weeks into my pregnancy. Ben or Arsen could be the father.

When I step into the apartment, Arsen walks out the bedroom dressed in washed jeans and a light blue v-neck sweater. His blond hair is longer than usual. I'd mentioned that I love it long, so he's letting it grow.

"Damn, Dimples, what the fuck did we do this morning?" he laughs, making his eyes sparkle with a devious light. "I mean, how could the sheets get that wet?"

He pulls me in for a hug, wrapping his hands around my waist and kissing my neck. There's a desperation in his embrace that I haven't felt coming from him since the day I left Ben.

"I missed you so fucking much," he roughly whispers in my ear as he inhales my perfume. Moving his chest slightly away so we can look at each other, he brings a hand to cup my cheek. "I'm glad you're home…Now, please tell me I'm a fucking psycho and there was nothing wrong."

Oh.

How could I even begin to tell him what Dr. Pajaree found without scaring him? Will he freak out? I can't believe it myself, and I'm still in shock. Is it even possible? I want to ignore the treacherous hope gathering in my chest, I want to smother it before it kills me again, but I can't.

I can't.

I can't.

Upon leaving the office, my first instinct was to call Ben, but I decided I should write him an email instead. My chest tightens just thinking about the news and Ben. It's not like it's a big deal. Knowing my past history, this baby may never see the light of day. Would Ben even be interested?

Lost in thought, I hear Arsen talking, snapping me out of my trance. I focus my gaze on his face as questions swim in my head. I decide he needs to know. I swallow hard as I touch the base of my neck, preparing myself to deliver the best, and possibly the most painful, news in our short relationship.

"No, no. Um…uh…everything is okay. Arsen…I need to tell you something. Do you want to sit down?"

"What the hell is going on? You're scaring me," he whispers as he narrows his eyebrows.

"I'm pr—" I breathe once and finish the sentence, "I'm pregnant."

Dumbfounded, he lets go of my arm and sits down on the floor, reclining his head and back against the wall.

Well, I guess that answers my question.

"Is that even possible?" he breathes. "I mean, not to sound like an asshole but what are the chances of it even working out?"

Did he really just say that to me?

"I don't know. Dr. Pajaree said that it happens…sometimes you just get pregnant without an explanation. I'm still considered very high risk. I think she was talking about a cream to help m—"

"I can't, Cathy. I never signed on to be a father. I thought we were just having fun." His voice is drained of laughter and flirtatiousness. "I can give you that, you know. Fun. But I can't be a father. I'm sorry."

I can't say that I'm shocked by this response. I always knew that what we have would eventually end, I just didn't expect it that it would be this way—that Arsen could dismiss me so carelessly. Amy and Ben's warnings have come true after all.

"I-I…you wanted me to leave my husband. Y-you said so." I stupidly remind him.

"Yes."

"I thought you loved me. I mean, you've never said it, but I g-got the feeling you did." There. I've said it. I don't even know why I'm asking him this, it doesn't matter, we're over, but I guess I need to know. I want to know.

"Yes, maybe. I don't know Cathy." He glances around the room as if looking for an answer, the right answer, then turns to look at me once more. "I guess I do, but not enough to have a family with you. I'm not ready, and…I don't know. I don't love you like that."

Suddenly very dizzy, I step back looking for something to hold onto before I fall. When my lower back hits the back of a chair, I sit and continue to listen to Arsen break my heart with his words. Dispassionately, I notice he's calling me Cathy. He hasn't called me by that name since the day we met.

"We have fun together, Cathy. However, no promises were ever made. I thought we were just—"

"Just what? Having fun? Was this always about fucking to you? What about me?" My words make him flinch.

Good.

"I like you, you're cool. But yes…it was always about a good fucking, and you never seemed to be interested in more."

"I can't. I can't. Are you even listening to yourself? I left my husband for you! How could that be just about a good fucking? What about your jealousy? Y-you told me I was yours!" I scream at him, hysteria beginning to take over me.

"Fuck, Cathy, what do you want me to say? I don't like sharing. That's all."

"Sharing me? Are you fucking joking? Sharing me with my own husband? I cheated on him with you!"

"Well, I think it would've happened regardless. I saw a chance and took it."

My body shaking violently, I pretend that this is not happening. That this is a horrible nightmare. Yes, that's it. A nightmare. Arsen would never do this to me. Oh, God. I'm going to be sick. I close my eyes and try to fight the nausea when I hear him throw the last blow to my gut.

"I think you should go back to your husband. I love you, but not that way, Cathy. Not that way. I mean…is the baby even mine? For all I know, it could be his. After all, you were fucking both of us at the same time."

I stand up, grab my bag, and head to the door. I turn around and look at Arsen who is watching me with the saddest eyes which is odd. He's the one ending whatever we have.

I can't bring myself to feel anything. It's as if all emotions, good or bad, have been wiped from me. I'm truly paralyzed from the inside out.

"I don't know who the father is, Arsen. Not that it matters because knowing my body, I probably won't be able to carry it full term." I watch Arsen close his eyes at my words. "As for Ben, I cheated on him with you, and he filed for divorce. So yes, that won't work."

Arsen stands up and makes his way to the door. I raise a trembling hand to stop him. "Don't take a step closer to me, Arsen, or I will slap you so hard I will leave a mark. I knew this was going to happen…I knew it. It was too good to be true, but I never thought you would turn out to be such an asshole. I guess that's what I deserve…I did the same thing to Ben." Turning around, I put my hand on the handle.

"Dimples…I—" he says painfully.

"Good-bye, Arsen."

Lying in Amy's bed as she hugs me, I want to cry and scream but do neither. Staring at the sage green walls of her room, the fight is gone from me. I feel nothing.

I'm vacant.

Empty.

Hollow.

The only reminder that I'm alive is the pain around my chest. It's unbearable but welcome at the same time because it helps me drown the memories of Arsen and Ben. I close my eyes tightly and pull Amy closer to me.

My chest…

I can't breathe…

I can't.

I punish myself once more, and I recall my meeting with Ben and the way he looked at me. The disgust and hurt on his face, his painful words.

After talking to Amy about my situation, she'd agreed that I needed to get in touch with Ben and tell him the truth. He deserved to know what was going on, even though there was a very high chance that nothing would come of it. So I called him and told him to meet me at the Starbucks around the corner from her apartment.

I remember walking to the coffee shop, sick to my stomach and thinking about Arsen. I thought I saw him following me to the store. I recall turning around, thinking that I saw his blond head sticking out of the crowd, but he was nowhere to be seen.

I was sitting on one of those maroon colored couches where your body automatically sinks in because they are so worn out as I inhaled the aroma of coffee and caramel floating in the air. Soon after I sat down, Ben walked in. He had changed. I hadn't seen him in a month, and he didn't look like the same man I was married to for six years at all. He had lost so much weight that he looked gaunt, and his clothes were hanging off his body. His usually pristine handsome face was covered in a thick beard, and the only thing you could see were his lips. His maple brown eyes looked blank and bleak, and the bags under them looked almost purple they were so dark. There was so much anger oozing off him…

I knew I couldn't tell him.

And his words proved I was right. Without saying hello or asking me how I'm doing he got to the point.

"I agreed to meet you here because, frankly, I'm curious as to what you have to say. What is it?" He spits the words at me.

I told him what I'd wanted to say all along.

"I'm sorry. I'm so, so sorry. I g-guess I wanted to apologize to you once more."

Lie, lie, lie.

"Oh? Don't you think it's a little too late for that, Cathy?" he answered as I stared into his beautiful yet empty eyes.

Yes…

I knew right then and there that I still loved him so much. Not even Arsen had been able to erase it. I'd been fooling myself.

"Where is Arsen? I'm surprised you were able to step away from fucking him long enough to meet me. I mean, back when we were married I was lucky if I got to spend five minutes with you on any given day."

I flinched at his words. They hurt.

32

Love is infinite.
There is no beginning and no end.
There's no starting point and no finishing line.
Love just is.
Love is born, grows, matures, and sometimes it dies.
But the memory will remain with you
for the rest of your breathing hours.
You fall in love, you fall out of love.
But you will love again.
You always do.

It's a beautiful day. The sun is shining, making the windows of the tall buildings reflect its light. It looks like thousands of tiny mirrors adorning the Manhattan skyline.

"How are you today, Cathy?" Crystal, my therapist, asks.

"I'm very well, thank you." I smile, waiting for her next question.

I started seeing Crystal two weeks after I last saw Ben. At first, I didn't want to because I really just wanted to drown in my misery, wallow in it until I was dead. At my lowest, I actually considered suicide to make the pain disappear. It hurt so much waking up every morning and living. I wanted to be able to breathe without feeling like my chest was being knifed with every breath I took.

I wanted sweet oblivion.

To vanish.

To feel nothing.

But it all changed on my nine-week ultrasound. Because I'm considered high-risk, I had to have ultrasounds every two weeks until my second trimester, then once a month if the growth of my baby had been on target. Smiling, I touch my huge belly, but I know I won't be able to breathe a sigh of relief until I am holding her in my arms and I feel her soft little hands in mine.

As I look at Crystal, I think back to the day I decided to fight again. The exact moment when Dr. Pajaree showed me the image of my baby on the monitor. When I saw the little head and the tiniest of bodies, I broke down and cried, the numbness evaporating from my body. That little creature, my little peanut, was mine and all I had left—all that mattered. I decided to fight. It was in that moment, when everything was up in the air with my life, that I realized it was time to seek help; to open up about my fears, my mistakes, and learn not to shut the people out from my life that cared the most about me.

So, twenty-seven weeks later, I'm sitting huge, and very pregnant, on a comfy worn leather couch staring at one of the prettiest brunettes with the bluest of eyes smiling back at me. By the look of her smile, I know what's coming, and I think I'm ready to go there with her. Little by little since we started our weekly sessions, we've talked about everything from my childhood to my miscarriages, but she hasn't brought up Ben or Arsen again. I think it was in the third session when I explained to her how I had ended up alone and pregnant, but I never felt comfortable discussing them again. I suspect she wants me to introduce the subject, and I want to, but sometimes just thinking about Ben and Arsen brings back the pain, the memories. It brings back the overwhelming feeling of loving someone when all hope is lost.

So, I wait.

"How is the baby?" She smiles. She's stalling as well.

"Baby is great. She's moving so much. Sometimes I think I have a future gymnast growing inside me," I laugh lightly, resting both my hands on my belly. I love feeling her move and the guessing game of which part of her precious body is sticking out. "She particularly kicks after I've had ice cream or chocolate to eat. Oh my God. Here!" I grab Crystal's hand as I bring it to rest on the left side of my stomach.

Looking at me with smiling eyes, Crystal asks, "That's so nice. What am I feeling here?"

I smile and move her hand with mine following the trajectory of Nadia's limb.

"I think that's her butt. It could be her leg for all I know, though. I told you, she loves to move, especially when I play Taylor Swift."

Crystal lets go of my belly and sits back on her chair.

"I'm so happy for you, Cathy. Four more weeks, right?"

"Yes. Four weeks." I swallow hard as I fight to stay on the bright side of optimism, not going near to the depths of fear. "Four more weeks until I can rest easy and truly believe it, you know? Of course, my suitcase has been packed since last week, and all of her clothes are washed. Amy bought her the cutest going home outfit; and—" I smile bashfully as I straighten the hem of my dress. "Am I doing it again? Talking your ears off about baby stuff when you're supposed to be picking my brain?"

"It's okay. I'm here to listen to you talk."

"It's just…I can't stop thinking and talking about her. My whole world has become this little girl growing inside me. Nadia is my miracle. Even though sometimes I still can't believe it. Like, I wake up in the middle of the night and my hands go straight to my belly, and I just lay there, willing the baby to move so I know she's fine." I look down at my stomach and caress it as I speak to Crystal. "Dr. Pajaree says it happens sometimes. Women with my condition get pregnant and are able to carry full term without any explanation. I'd like to think it's magic." I shrug my shoulders and smile.

"I'm very happy for you, Cathy, but I think it's time we address Ben and Arsen…" She lets the words hang in the air.

"Yes…I think I can do that," I answer, fidgeting in my seat.

"Why do you think you cheated on Ben? Why do you think your marriage failed the way it did?"

"Oh, wow. You don't beat around the bush, do you?"

Laughing, Crystal shakes her head. "No. We've made a lot of progress in the past months. I think it's time we spoke more in depth about Arsen and Ben. So tell me, Cathy. Why?"

"Um…well, I know it all started going downhill after the third miscarriage. And after that, when I couldn't get pregnant, well…the strain it put on our marriage was lethal. I withdrew from him, from everything, but Ben couldn't see it. He continued to pretend that everything was okay, that we were going to be okay. It got to a point that his positivity felt like it was choking the life out of me."

"Go on," she encourages me.

"Whenever I tried telling him how afraid I was that we were never going to be parents, to tell him about my fears, he would just sweep them under the rug, saying to stop worrying about it, so I stopped trying to talk to him about it. I grew to hate his perfection, I think. Here I was, broken and lost, filled with hatred and jealousy towards other women who could get pregnant by having their husbands just touch them. It was just too much. I felt like I was not woman enough. It was the loss of my dream, the loss of ever becoming a mom that completely shattered me. I wanted to cry, scream, curse at God…I don't know. And then…"

"There was Ben."

Yes. Oh, how I wish…

"Yes. Perfect, loving Ben. Not a crack on his exterior, always the optimist. I hated that. I couldn't talk to him anymore. The more he pulled, the more I pushed away from him. But then I got pregnant for a fourth time after so long, and I thought it was our second chance at happiness."

"Do you think it was a mistake not telling him any of this?" Crystal asks.

"Um, yes. It was a mistake. I know that now. My friend Amy tried talking to me about it. She asked me if I was prepared just in case I lost that baby as well." I laugh and look up at the ceiling. "I knew I was putting all my philosophical eggs in one fragile basket, but I really didn't want to think about it. I knew my marriage was on shaky ground and that all it was going to take for it to fall apart was one soft blow to the core. And it did, although I wouldn't necessarily call it soft. When I lost th-hat baby, I think I lost my mind as well."

I touch my belly once more. "I grew to hate everything around me…even Ben. Particularly Ben. I hated when he touched me, I hated when he kissed me, and I hated when he told me that we were going to be fine. I hated it. I truly hated it."

"Why didn't you tell him all this?"

"Because by that point, I didn't care anymore. I-I think I made myself think that I didn't love him, that I hated him. I did try once…"

"Why did you hate his touch?"

"It made me think of getting pregnant. It felt like work. I resented it. I resented him. I mean, now that I've had time to think about it…I don't know. It's too late. What ifs are just life's regrets."

"Do you think all this would have been solved had you opened up to him after your third miscarriage? Do you think talking to him would have, somehow, stopped you from growing apart?"

I think hard for a moment, finding the answer deep within me. "Yes. I think…I mean, I don't think I would be divorced right now."

"But how about Arsen? You mentioned you grew to love him."

Tucking a piece of hair behind my ear, I turn to look at the window once more. It's still sunny and beautiful outside. Funny how the sun reminds me so much of Arsen.

"I'd like to think that had my marriage been in a better place, had Ben and I been in a solid marriage with open communication and not so much resentment from my part, that I would not have turned to Arsen. That I would have enjoyed his light flirting, admired his beauty from afar, but that's it. Never taking it to the next level and actually cheating on Ben. I mean, I remember how crazy I was about Ben during our honeymoon stage. I didn't even notice other men in the same room. In my world, only one man existed. Ben. I never looked at another man or wondered. Never."

"But you told me you were attracted to Arsen, very attracted to him before you actually slept with him for the first time?"

"Yes, I was. But there was this huge gap in my life and one day Arsen showed up and filled it. He made me laugh, he listened to my darkest fears, he brought color back into my life." Turning away from the window, I stare at her. "I don't think anything would've come of it had I not lost the baby, but I'll never know for sure. When I cheated on Ben with Arsen, he made me feel alive again. He made the pain go away. Whenever I was with him, I felt euphoric. He made me feel beautiful, perfect, and less broken." I pause and run my fingers through my hair. "Every time I was with him, every time we were together…I was able to forget. The people around me…my friends…my family…I didn't care about them. All I cared was about getting my next Arsen fix."

"Do you think that justifies the cheating?"

"No. Nothing can justify what I did to Ben. Nothing will ever justify the cheating. But I cheated, and it's too late to do anything about it. As cliché as it sounds, all I can do is learn from my mistakes."

"Tell me since you didn't answer before. How about loving Arsen? Do you think it was love?"

I blow air out of my mouth. I think that Crystal really wants to kill me. It's not like I can think about them without feeling the scar that has just begun to heal rip wide open again.

"Okay, this is going to be a long one. Trust me, I've given it a lot of thought."

"I'm all ears."

"They say being in love and loving someone are two different things, right? I mean, you love your best friend, but you love your husband, right? Falling in love with someone is easy. It's loving when the newness has worn off, when life gets tough, when things get in the way, when physical passion is gone, that true love remains. When love can conquer it all."

I reach for the glass of water in front of me, taking a sip because I'm suddenly very thirsty. "When you fall out of love, it doesn't mean that you stop loving someone. They just don't make your heart beat faster. You don't crave them until you don't know where they end and you begin. I d-don't know that I ever fell out of love with Ben, but I do know that I fell in love with Arsen along the way. Or maybe I confused fucking and lust for love. I don't know. I don't think I will ever know.

"But what I do know is that they both were essential to my well-being. I didn't realize how important Ben was to me until he was gone. Arsen became the air I needed to breathe, but Ben was my lungs. What good would air be if I didn't have lungs to begin with?"

"Do you still think about Arsen? Have you forgiven him?"

"I do, but thinking about him doesn't hurt as much as when I think about Ben. Arsen could easily be blamed because he pursued me, but I think it was the other way around. I think the fault lies all in me."

I have forgiven him and the way he walked out on me. I understand where he came from and, in a way, he was right. No words of love were ever said between us. No promises made. Whenever I look back to our relationship, I can only be grateful for all the things he taught me, for being my stepping stone. For that, I will always love him. Sometimes I wish I had gotten the chance to tell him how special he was to me, how much I grew to love him. Arsen taught me to move on. To live life and forget. He made me laugh when all I wanted was to stop existing. I will always love him. And also, there's the possibility that he gave me Nadia.

And now he's gone.

"Marriage is work, Cathy. You have to work at it every single day that you're together. You can't ever slack. It's hard being married. You go through great times, you go through terrible times, but it's all about what you make of those experiences. How you deal with them that sets you apart from other couples who throw in the towel. Committing fully to your partner and giving your all. Because divorce is easy, it's the easy way out."

Oh, life. Are you really that simple?

"Yes…but sometimes it's not easy. Whoever said marriage was easy must have been high on Disney cartoons."

"Good one, Cathy. So tell me before it's time for you to go, what would you have done differently?"

I think hard for a moment. "I would have been honest with Ben from the beginning instead of pushing him away."

And that's the truth.

My truth.

I just wish I'd realized it a long time ago.

33

Four weeks later.

At peace.

A sigh of relief.

I can finally breathe.

I'm speechless and in awe.

I'm amazed.

Hoping with all my soul and wishing with my whole heart has finally paid off because I'm holding in my arms my future, my happily ever after. And, somehow, I know my life will never the same.

I'm whole.

I'm complete.

As I stare at my precious baby, I can't stop myself from crying. My body is shaking fiercely from the gut-wrenching sobs escaping my mouth, and I don't care because I'm thankful, so thankful. Wiping away the tears flowing freely down my face with the back of my hand, I stare at the wrinkly miracle currently sleeping in my arms. She feels so small and fragile. I'm afraid that if I move or hold her the wrong way, I could hurt her.

She's mine.

All mine.

My Nadia.

My hope.

And even though it's just the two of us in this moment, I don't care at all. She's all I need, my reason to exist, and I will do everything in my power to make her happy. Anything and everything.

I bring her closer to my chest as an almost primal instinct takes over me. The urge to protect her and to shelter her from all the ugliness of the world becomes my number one priority, my goal in life. Gone are the thoughts of my divorce, of unworthiness, of my failed relationship with Arsen…they are all gone. There's no room for selfishness when you have a defenseless human being depending on you.

"Hi, pretty Nadia." I lift her to my face so I can smell her sweet baby scent.

So clean, so pure.

"I'm your mommy." I kiss her precious lips and fight the need to cry once more. "Can I tell you a secret?" I whisper in her ear, "I love you so, so much, my little ray of hope."

I hear my dad clearing his throat. I lift my eyes and watch him approach the hospital bed with a smile on his face. "She looks exactly like you when you were a baby."

A tissue in his hand, he leans over and cleans my face since my hands are importantly tied up at the moment. With eyes that shine because of unshed tears, he smiles tenderly at me. "She's just as gorgeous as her mother."

I feel a knot in my stomach. "Daddy, how can I love her so much when I've just met her? Is she real? Is she really mine?"

"Yes. She's all yours, my baby girl."

"I'm holding her, smelling her, kissing her and I still cannot believe it. I'm afraid this is a dream. One that will end when I wake up, leaving me all a-alone." My voice breaks.

My dad sits on the edge of the bed and wraps an arm around my shoulder. "Stop, Cathy. She's real. It's time for you to finally enjoy being a mother, baby girl. It's time to let go of all those ghosts."

Looking up at my dad, and then down at Nadia, I let the truth sink in. She is real. I'm her mother.

Her mother.

After Dad leaves for the night, I prop up against the wall with pillows behind my back. With my gown open at the front, I watch transfixed as Nadia latches on to my nipple, suctioning breast milk. It's such a simple thing, watching your child feed from your body, but it's also magical. Listening to the gentle sounds she's making soothes my soul.

I laugh as I remember walking to the maternity ward, pushing Nadia in the portable crib, and asking the nurses to teach me for the second time that day how to breastfeed her. After they warned me that I shouldn't be walking, my nurse Lili, sat me in the rocking chair and taught me the procedure all over again as I promised that this was the last time.

All I can do is watch her, study her, learn her, and memorize her. Every single curve of her tiny body, her unique smell, the way her tiny hand wraps around my finger, the weight of her warm body in my arms. The way she's imprinting herself on my skin and robbing me of my own heart.

My dad said she is mine, but I think it's the other way around.

I'm hers.

Nothing else matters but her.

When I think she's done feeding, I pull her away from my breast and begin my second attempt at burping her. The first time scared me so much that I paged the nurse to come watch me just to make sure I was doing it right. I was scared I was going to hurt her by patting her too hard.

After I manage to burp her once, I lay down with her on top of my naked chest. In the darkness of the room with only the moonlight illuminating us, and Nadia's little head resting on top of my heart, I let my barriers down for the first time in a very long time. As I caress her small back, I allow myself to think about him.

When Dr. Pajaree put Nadia in my arms soon after she was born, the first thing I did was lift my eyes, expecting to see Ben sharing this joyous moment with me. The moment we had hoped and wished for so long, to finally have a child of our own. But he wasn't there. He was gone. Instead, I met the nurse's encouraging gaze.

I took that away.

I destroyed it.

So as I lie on a cold hospital bed with a miracle sleeping on my chest, I let myself cry. I allow myself to cry because I still love him so much.

Because I was right.

It was always him.

Not Arsen.

Not anyone.

My maple-brown eyed boy.

Three years later.

Do I have a headache?

How could I have a headache in my sleep?

What the hell is going on?

I open my eyes and a pair of emerald green eyes hover above me, watching me, blonde curly hair tickling my nose, banging my head with the small jade elephant I keep next to my nightstand.

So that was the "headache".

"Momma, Momma! Wake up! Wake up!" she demands in her sweet voice.

She's about to hit me with it once more when I grab her little hand in mine, removing the deadly weapon from her fist, and begin tickling her.

"What's this, you little monkey! What are you doing in mommy's room this early in the morning?"

Laughing because I'm tickling her under her armpits, she begins to kick her small legs. "Momma! Stop! Momma!" she protests between giggles.

When we both have tears in our eyes, I stop. The sight of her dimples peeking out as she laughs can still twist my heart with so much love. Her laughter is sweet music to my ears.

"I want juice, Mommy! I'm hungry!"

"Okay, okay, you monster." I get up from the bed, grab my robe, and pick her up in my arms. It's been three years since I first held her in my arms, and not a day goes by when the need to hold her close to me is not present, not a necessity. I think back to those early days when I didn't care about anything other than Nadia. I ran my life around her schedule, and I was totally fine with it. I gladly gave it all up to be with her, not taking any of her smiles, her expressions, her kisses for granted.

Even on the days when the going gets tough, really tough, all I have to do is just think back to how much she's changed my life. How my love for her has made me a better person, one that I'm not ashamed of. And I thank her for it every single day.

After I pour some cereal and milk in a bowl and place it in front of her, I sit down and watch her eat. The curls of platinum blonde hair are sticking out in all directions, making her look like a wild child. Leaning over her, I kiss the top of her head, and go to make some coffee.

"Mommy…" she says in between mouthfuls of cheerios.

"Yes, lil' monkey?"

"I want a daddy."

I stop short and put down the jar of coffee and the mug on the table. I turn around and kneel in front of her, taking her sticky hands in mine.

"W-what do you mean, Nadia? You want to see Papa?" I hope she's asking about her grandfather, though deep down I know exactly what she means.

"Don't be silly!" she laughs. "Papa is not a daddy. My friend Lucy told me her daddy took her to the Bronx Zoo tomorrow." She grins as if I'm not getting the point. Oh, if only she knew how much I got it.

"You mean yesterday, and—"

"She told me her mommy picked her daddy before they picked her. Can we pick a daddy too, Mommy? Her daddy is nice! He gave me a lollipop, and he buys Lucy babies all the time."

"Oh."

Suddenly dizzy, I stand up and sit down on the chair. I knew this was eventually going to happen. Nadia was bound to notice that she only has a mommy and not a daddy.

I shake my head and scan the room, trying to come up with the best answer, the right answer, without making her feel bad.

"Nadia, we don't need a daddy. We have each other, and Papa and Uncle Charles."

"But I want a daddy. Lucy's daddy is nice," she protests, a pout beginning to form on her angelic face.

"Well…it's more complicated than just going to a store and picking one, baby." I touch my chest, "Our hearts choose who that person will be. And it takes time."

"Your heart will pick a daddy for me?" I want to tell her that my heart picked one a long time ago and that my heart still belongs to him, but that's a story I will tell her when she's older. Not now.

"I hope so…"

I lie. I don't want another man. I'm not ready to put myself out there. Sometimes, in the middle of the night when my body hungers for the touch of a man, it's his I want. When I'm rubbing myself, ready to climax, I picture his maple-brown eyes staring back at me as he makes love to me. And when my physical thirst has been quenched, it's his warm embrace I need.

How could I allow myself to go on a date and potentially start seeing other men when emotionally I haven't moved on? It's not fair for either party involved, and if my past mistakes have taught me something, it's that no one deserves that kind of treachery.

"Okay, Mommy!" Nadia agrees before returning to her breakfast, oblivious to how much her words have shaken me.

I stand up with trembling legs and go back to the counter, pouring myself a cup of coffee. I'm stirring some half and half in it when Nadia speaks once more.

"Mommy?"

I close my eyes, afraid of what she's going to say next. "Yes, darling?"

"Are we going to the park after?"

Breathing a sigh of relief because she's forgotten all about the daddy issue, I take a sip of coffee before answering her. "It's later, and yes. Would you like me to call Aunt Amy and Uncle Charles to see if they want to meet us there?"

"Yes! Uncle Charles buys me toys!" she says, smiling.

When she's done eating breakfast, I bathe her and put her clothes on for the day. After making sure she's busy playing with her toys in her room, I make my way to my bedroom to take a shower. While I wait for the water to heat, I call Amy.

"Hi beautiful." Amy's voice sounds groggy with sleep.

"Hi! Do you have a moment? I need to speak to you."

"Sure, babe." I can hear Charles protesting on the other side of the line as Amy shushes him to be quiet. "Okay, tell me, love."

"Um, Nadia informed me today that she wants a daddy."

"Oh my God. The poor child. What did you tell her?"

"Well, once I was able to get my brain working I told her that it wasn't that easy."

"Oh, honey, I've been telling you for the past two years that it's time for you to give someone else a chance. I mean, it's time for you to move on and start living your life."

"B-But I am living my life."

"Cathy, really? Want me to call bullshit on that? You don't have a life. Your life revolves around work and being a mom to Nadia. You won't touch the very generous amount of money Ben gave you as part of the divorce, and you won't let anyone but your Dad or me help you with her. The only time you ask for help is when you know you can't bring that little munchkin along."

"That's not true. I went out with you the other night."

"Because I had to drag you out of your self imposed prison. Tell me, what does Crystal say about this? Does she agree with the fact that you have no life? I mean, I'm sure she wouldn't like that. There has to be a healthy balance, babe."

"Well, I'll get there. But never mind about that. What am I supposed to do with the daddy issue?"

"Go on a date," she states. "Meet other men. Give other men a chance. Cathy, I know that Charles' friend Hayes, the hot stockbroker, asked you out more than once, but you've shot him down every single time. He was really taken with you, you know?"

Groaning, I close my eyes. "Don't even go there. That was the most uncomfortable thing ever. I'm thirty-three years old, and I have a daughter. I don't have the luxury to date around just for fun."

"How would you know? You won't let anyone in; you won't go on any dates…you are still pining after a man who has already moved on. I mean, Cathy, you saw the engagement announcement in the newspaper."

I feel like the air has been knocked out of my lungs. "I know," I whisper as a mixture of pain and jealousy surge over me aggressively like an avalanche.

"Ben has moved on, honey, and Arsen was in Europe the last time I heard. I think it's time you did the same. Nadia is a precious little thing, and you're a gorgeous woman. Let someone take care of you, love you. Let yourself love someone else, babe."

"But I have Nadia," I argue. Holding onto the past is a losing battle, but I don't know that I'm ready to move on, yet I must. For Nadia.

And for myself.

"It's not the same, babe, and you know it."

"Okay," I say, defeated.

"Okay what?"

"You're right. It's time for me to let go. Y-you can give Hayes a call, but I'm going to be honest with him, Amy, so don't get your hopes up."

I hear her groaning into the phone. "What are you going to tell him, you nut?"

"That I still love another man."

"What? Why would you do such a thing?" she exclaims.

"Well, maybe he'd like to be my friend. I think that's all I'm ready for anyway."

Sometimes it gets lonely, sometimes a lot. Sometimes when I see couples walking and holding hands, I remember what I had. Sometimes I wish, and wish, and wish with all my heart to have it all back again, but I know all the wishing in the world won't bring him back. So I remain quiet, never complain when it gets tough, never cry because I'm alone, and never blame anyone else but me.

Hanging up, I walk to the bathroom. It's not until I'm standing in front of the sink that I look at myself in the mirror. Reflected in it, there's a woman with vacant eyes sparkling with unshed tears.

I know that I must move on. Arsen is back to dating heiresses, and Ben is going to be married to Kerry soon. I need to let him go, let go of our memories together, of the past.

I have to move on.

Nadia deserves a family.

I wipe my tears away, hoping that I'm not making the biggest mistake by letting another man in my life because even after four years of thinking about them, it still hurts.

Especially for Ben.

I'm applying the last coat of lip-gloss on my lips when I hear a knock on my door. Instantly feeling a knot in my stomach, I take a deep breath. I can do this. I can. I put the lip-gloss away and move to open the door.

With my hand hovering over the handle, I take a deep breath as I try to calm my nerves. I don't even know why I'm so nervous. It's just a date.

When I open the door, I see a man I have met only once before and his handsomeness can still take my breath away. I don't think men should be allowed to be this handsome. It's not fair. The black haired man with the silver eyes smiles kindly at me as he takes in my appearance, seemingly pleased with what he sees. When I feel myself blush, I break the uncomfortable silence first.

"Hi, Hayes. Would you like to come in for a drink, or should we go?" I ask.

"Hello, Cathy. May I first say how beautiful you look tonight? My memory does you injustice because I don't remember you being this breathtaking." His eyes twinkle as he speaks.

"Um, thank you." Blushing, I think that maybe this was a great mistake. His comment makes me very uncomfortable. I'm so not ready for this. I'm about to go get my coat, escaping away from him, when Hayes speaks.

"I'm sorry. Too much, too soon?" He smiles ruefully, an apology written all over his face.

"Um, uh…" Sighing, I decide to be totally upfront with him. "Yes. I'm sorry, Hayes. I-I thought I was clear that this was more of a friendly thing. Um, if you'd like to leave, I'll understand. I'm so sorry."

"Yes, you were very clear, and no, I wouldn't like to leave. It's my fault, and it won't happen again. It's just…" Hayes looks at me warmly, "Never mind, Cathy. Would you like to go? We can have drinks at the restaurant bar?"

"Sure." I'm relieved that he understands my position, so I begin to relax and let myself enjoy the night with a handsome man.

Two bottles of wine later and a dinner that flew by quickly, I'm standing outside my apartment door ready to say goodnight. The air surrounding us this time is more relaxed, the tension is gone. As I stare into the face of the man that made me laugh with anecdotes from his past relationships, his work, and just life, I think that I like him. I'd like to keep in touch with him, and maybe become real friends.

"Hayes, let's try this one more time. Would you like to come in for a drink?" I say with laughter in my voice.

Hayes wavers for a second. "I would love to, Cathy. But I don't think I should."

I'm taken aback by his answer. "Why not?" I ask. Should I be hurt? I mean, it's not like I want the guy to be attracted to me, but I most certainly didn't expect that answer.

"Thing is," he scratches the back of his neck, "I like you, Cathy. I really do. And it's not like I've been pining for you after all this time, but after tonight I think I could possibly grow to like you a lot. However, you're not ready."

Hayes takes a step closer to me, making me want to take a step back. The proximity of his body isn't welcome, not yet. He takes my hand in his and raises it to his lips, planting a kiss in my palm. "When you said that you weren't ready, I didn't believe you. Not completely. But after tonight, I think you're right. You're not ready. I wish you were because I feel this connection to you, and it's such a shame. So If I go inside your apartment, I might not be able to hold myself back and do something very stupid that I will regret later on."

"Oh." I'm stunned with his honesty and the meaning of his words.

"Can I ask you something very personal?"

"Yes."

"Well, it's not really a question. It's more a piece of advice. You're obviously still very much in love with your ex-husband. Fight for him."

I feel like cold water is being poured down on me.

"Um, what? I told you what happened. W-what makes you think…No. I couldn't. He hates me."

"I don't know, Cathy. If I were him, even after everything that transpired between you two…"

"No, no. I can't. It's been four years, and he's getting married. I'm not going to spoil things for him. I can't."

Tilting his head to the side and smiling apologetically at me, Hayes remains quiet for what seems an eternity. "Okay. I will let it go. Anyway, it's been a pleasure, but it's getting late and I must go."

"Wait. W-will I see you again?"

"Whenever you want. I'm a call away."

"Even if I just need to talk to you. You know, as a friend?"

"Especially as a friend," he whispers in my ear.

After saying goodbye, I shut the door behind him and call my dad.

"Hello. That was a quick date." There's curiosity in his voice.

"Yes. It was a friendly date, Dad."

"Pft. No man ever goes on a friendly date."

"Well, trust me on that one, Dad. Do you want to hear something funny and pretty sad?"

"Yes."

"He told me he didn't want to come in for a drink because I'm obviously still hung up on my ex. It's official. I'm pathetic."

"Oh, baby girl."

"It's okay. I knew I wasn't ready, but at least that's out of the way."

"But you still need to—"

"I know, but not yet. I will when I'm ready."

My dad laughs into the phone. "Let's just hope it's not when you're sixty, okay dear?"

"Ha ha ha, very funny. How's Nadia? Was she a monster?"

"Sleeping like an angel." My dad chuckles when he mentions the word angel.

We talk some more about my date and what Nadia had for dinner, then hang up.

Lying alone in my bed as I stare at the ceiling covered in the shadows of the night, my mind rehashes tonight's events. How sweet Hayes turned out to be, how much fun it was to talk to him, and how much I like him, but how quiet my heart remained throughout the entire night. Not once did it skip a beat. Not once did butterflies attack my stomach. It was as pleasant and sweet as vanilla ice cream.

How I wish he could be my chocolate. Really. But in a way I'm relieved that nothing came of it because as crazy as it sounds, I don't want to forget Ben. I don't.

Suddenly feeling very cold, I pull the blanket up to my chin and turn to lie on my side. With sleep eluding me, I keep thinking about Hayes' advice. To fight for Ben. For a short second, I wish I could.

I wish it with all my heart because I don't think I'll ever be able to fully let go of him.

34

As I glance around the busy coffee shop, I take a deep breath, filling my lungs with the smell of coffee grinds, baked goods, and nutmeg. When my eyes land on Amy, I can already tell she's waiting for Nadia and my dad to step away so she can attack me with questions about my date with Hayes.

Oh, she's going to be disappointed.

The moment they are gone to place our orders, Amy pulls her chair closer to mine and begins her sleuthing. "Quick, tell me before Nadia gets back with your dad. How was your date with Hayes last night? Did you kiss him? Please tell me you did because gosh, that man is drop-dead gorgeous and worth a fortune. Not that you care about that stuff," Amy murmurs as she plays with a lock of red hair.

Chuckling, I pause as I let curiosity get the best of her.

"Oh my God, Cathy. You're killing me here!" she exclaims.

"It went great. And no, we didn't kiss. I hate to tell you, but apparently even Hayes agrees that I'm not rea—"

"Cathy? Catherine, is that you?" a man asks with wonder in his voice.

It's him.

With my mouth open, I lift my gaze and stare at the man with the eyes I still dream about, watching me with an incredulous expression on his achingly beautiful face. I once read somewhere that it's through eye contact that souls catch on fire.

Well, mine is burning to the ground.

Heart racing.

Exploding euphoria.

I can't breathe.

Oh, there go the dormant butterflies, awakened by one look.

"Hi," I manage to say as I try to fight through an inability to think straight. I want to get up, take him in my arms, hug him, and kiss him for all the days, minutes, and seconds that he hasn't been part of my life.

"Hi."

He stands there, staring at me as if I am a ghost he can't believe he's seeing.

"Um, How h-have you been?" I stutter like a nervous child.

"Good. Could be better. Have been better," he answers as he leans forward, closer to my chair.

I swallow hard as I try to smooth a nonexistent crease on my jeans. "Oh, t-that's great!"

He clears his throat as he's getting ready to speak when I hear Nadia calling for me. I close my eyes and take a deep breath because when I open them he'll have seen her by then. And I'm not exactly sure what his reaction will be.

Shit.

"Momma! Momma! Momma!" Nadia calls for me. I look up and see my dad watching him with hatred in his eyes and then glancing my way as if asking me what to do next. I shake my head, letting him know not to let Nadia move closer to us. When my dad gets the hint, he takes her in his hand and walks over to the other side of the coffee shop.

Out of sight, I lift my gaze to meet Ben's once more, but he's not watching me for once. His vision follows the path of Nadia's steps. Feeling not a tug but yank in my heart, I get lost in him. I absorb every new detail in his appearance. He's still just as handsome as before, but now there's a roughness in his look. He looks wiser.

Still watching him and trying to absorb his face in my memory since I don't know when I'll see him again, if ever, his question brings me back to reality.

"I-Is that your daughter?" he stammers.

"Yes." I avoid looking at him when I answer him. Instead, I study my coffee cup.

"How old is she?"

I notice that the more he speaks the huskier his voice grows.

"Three and a half." I finally raise my eyes and meet his cloudy ones.

"Oh." He seems to be doing the math in his head.

I hear someone coughing.

Amy. I forgot she was here with me. Glancing her way, Amy stares at me with bulging eyes, and nods in someone's direction.

"Ben, baby, are you ready?" A very feminine, young, and raspy sexy voice asks.

I turn to look at the much younger and drop dead gorgeous woman as she wraps her slim arm around Ben's waist. Flinching at the familiarity in her touch of Ben's body, I take her in. She looks familiar.

Oh.

That would be because she's Kerry, the intern.

The one he kissed.

The one he's going to marry.

I can feel my barely healed heart slowly crack open again, the emotional stitches rupturing once more.

I don't want to watch him with another woman, so I say a quick goodbye and leave. I don't care that I'm leaving Amy, my dad…

Oh my God.

I must go back. I need to get Nadia. I need to hold her in my arms so she can shield me from the tsunami of pain and memories threatening to sweep me away.

After tossing and turning in bed for what feels like hours, I look at the clock and realize it's already 3:00 a.m. I groan, cover my head with a pillow, and close my eyes, willing sleep to take me.

But it's not working.

As I hear the fast thumping of my heart, I can still remember the coffee

shop incident vividly.

I'm not sure whether I want to cry, or scream, or just disappear.

I want to really have a meltdown, not wake up tomorrow and wallow in sadness. But I know I can't. So as much as I would like to just not care and let gloom wrap itself around me, I know I can't.

Shit.

Ugh.

After a while, I give up the fight against insomnia. I need a glass of wine. Yes, that's exactly what I need. I get up and make my way to the kitchen. I'm grabbing the bottle of red when I hear a knock on my door.

Glancing at the clock above the fridge, I take in the time.

Who could that be?

Afraid that it's a neighbor with an emergency, I put on an old sweatshirt that I use around the house and head towards the door.

"Yes?" I ask the stranger.

"Cathy. It's me. Open the door."

"Ben?" After swallowing hard, I ask without opening the door, "What are you doing here?"

I look at the clock once more. It's 3:36 a.m.

"Cathy, please. Open the door," he pleads.

One moment I'm opening the door, and the next Ben's arms are holding me in a choking embrace.

Not knowing what to do. I don't move. I feel scared to move. Maybe I'm dreaming that he's here. If that's the case, I don't want to wake up. I want to get lost in this bittersweet dream. I want to get lost in the feel of his body against mine. Oh, how I've missed him. His touch. His smell. The way my body instantly recognizes its missing half. Inhaling his essence, I close my eyes and let myself dream a little more.

Yes.

This must be a dream.

"Cathy, Cathy, Cathy," he murmurs gruffly in my ear.

"Hmmmm?" I didn't know dreams talked back.

"Cathy, answer me. Is s-she his?" His voice breaks.

Oh, no.

This is not a dream.

Slowly I open my eyes as I drown in an ocean of maple brown. How beautiful they are. How sad they are. His hazy eyes look red and swollen.

"Answer me, Cathy. Please, I need to know. Is she his?" He asks.

"Oh, Ben. Does it matter?"

I watch as he tightens his jaw and fists his hands. "It matters to me. Is she?"

I look away from him and stare at the floor. "I don't know. I don't know if she's yours or Arsen's. I-I had been…" Shame makes my face burn and robs me of words to finish my sentence.

"Yes, I know. You were fucking us both."

Wincing at his cruelty, I carefully move out of his warm hold. I take a few steps back until we are standing in front each other. So close, yet so far. My body immediately aches for his touch…I ache for him. I wrap my arms around my stomach, clutching myself as if trying to ward off my body from further hurt.

"Ben, what do you want me to say? I've told you. I'm sorry." I rub my arms and meet his stare. "I don't know who the father is, and it doesn't matter. It won't change how much I love her." I fight through the pain I feel in the back of my throat, my stomach, my heart, everywhere. "Because she is mine. Not yours, not his. She's mine. She's all I have left of either of you, and I l-love her no matter who—"

"No matter who the father is," Ben finishes the sentence for me. "Why didn't you tell me about her? I would have helped."

"I tried telling you that day when I asked you to meet me at the coffee shop."

I watch him wince with the recollection of that day.

An hour goes by as we sit on the floor in silence.

Sometimes we stare at each other.

Sometimes we stare at nothing at all.

I play with my nails. Ben pulls his hair.

I clutch at myself. Ben rocks back and forth on his place by the door.

My hands shake. His closed fists beat the floor.

Time seems to be seeping away from us. I want to move and sit next to him and let myself enjoy his proximity and whatever time we have left together, but I don't. Instead, I watch as his hands clasp his hair. It's much longer than the last time I saw him. It reminds me of how he looked when we first met. Wild dark curls.

Looking at the clock, I realize it's almost five in the morning. He needs to go before Nadia wakes up. I don't want him to, but I don't want Nadia waking up to a stranger in the apartment.

A stranger who may be her father.

Oh, the irony.

"Ben, what do you want? How did you know where I live?" I ask, rubbing my arms.

"I've always known about this place."

"Oh."

Ben remains silent and stares at the floor for another long period of time.

"I-I think you should leave. It's almost five in the morning. Nadia will be waking up soon and—"

"You don't want me to be here. Is that it? " The confident lilt I remember in his voice is gone.

"No. Yes. I just think you should go. I don't want Nadia to wonder what you're doing here. Go back to Kerry."

I hear Ben chuckle as he reclines his head against the wall and stares at me. "Kerry and I are over."

When the meaning of what he just said sinks in my head, I feel my eyes bulging. "I beg your pardon? B-but I thought your wedding was—"

Flushing, I stop talking. I don't want him to know that I've been keeping track of his life.

"No. We were. I ended it before I came here."

"What? Why?"

"Because it's not fair to her. I saw you and I fucking knew." Ben mutters something unintelligible to himself as hope grows in my chest.

Could it be?

"I couldn't do it to her. She's my best friend. I couldn't betray the one woman who helped me to heal after you screwed me over. The one who made me realize that fucking other women was not going to make it hurt any less."

His words hurt.

So much.

I bring my legs to my chest and wrap them in my arms, wanting to shut out his words, forbidding them to make their way into my heart.

"After you left…I tried fucking Kerry, but I guess once she realized how hurt I was…I don't know. She wasn't interested. Instead, she took it upon herself to try and help me get over you, but at first I didn't listen to her…so I fucked."

"Why are you telling me this?"

"I don't know…but I've tried so hard, Cathy. I can't. Every pair of green eyes I see is yours. Every dimpled smile…every time I fucked someone and closed my eyes after…it was you I saw. It was your hands that pulled my hair. It was your kisses I felt. It was your mouth I wanted. Your taste on my lips every time I…do you know how sick I felt whenever I fucked a woman and wished it were you the entire fucking time?"

Ben starts to laugh like a crazy man. "It was you. It's still you, and it's driving me fucking insane! I can't. I need to let you go. I need to be able to breathe again without feeling as if I'm choking every time I see something that reminds me of you. I need to stop feeling such disarming pain in my chest when I remember what we had. I just want to be able to move on. But I can't. I can't."

With tears in my eyes, each word he mutters robs me a little bit more of breath, robbing me of life. "But K-Kerry? Don't you love her?"

"Can't say that I don't."

"I-I think you love her. She's very lucky. A-and I don't know what you want me to say."

"You know why I ended things with Kerry? She helped me forgive you. She helped me to see that not all women were backstabbing bitches. She told me she loved me, and I believe that I loved her back, but not in the way she wants. She was willing to give me a chance, though. And I thought we were doing great. I love her, I do, but I-I think I made myself fall in love with her. I think deep down both of us knew that it wasn't real."

He focuses on my face. "I've had the real thing, and nothing can compare to it. Fuck. After I ran into you, Kerry and I went back to our apartment and we were together. When I had Kerry's legs wrapped around me, and my dick deep inside her, I let my guard down and said your name, Cathy. I fucking came thinking about you. You. The woman who didn't want me. Who—"

"Enough. I can't. I can't hear this anymore, Ben." I feel like I can't breathe. "I can't. Please leave," I beg urgently.

"Why? Why can't you, huh? It hurts, doesn't it? It hurts so damn much. The truth hurts."

"Yes. Please, Ben, leave. It hurts so much. Are you happy now?" I can't see his face through my tears anymore.

"No. I'm not happy. I fucking regret walking in that coffee shop this morning. I've regretted it ever since I laid my fucking eyes on you again."

I clutch my legs tighter in my arms as I wipe my tears on my knee.

"Momma?" I hear Nadia's groggy voice. The sweet melody snaps me out of the living hell I'm in. Untangling myself from my arms, I get up. My voice choked in tears, I leave without looking at him and go to Nadia's room. "Please go. I need to put her back to sleep. I'm sorry, Ben. Have a good life," I speak to the air.

Inside Nadia's room, I get in bed with her and wrap her in my arms as close as possible. I'm very cold, and I hope she can warm me with her tiny body.

"Momma, why are you crying?" she asks sleepily.

"Shhh, Nadia, shhh. Mommy loves you, shhh." I can't hide my tears from her, so I lose myself in sorrow. I cry in my baby's arms. I cry until there are no more tears inside me. After some time, I hear her lightly snoring.

When I realize I have to lock the door after Ben, I stall for time. I don't want to leave her just yet. She's my safe haven.

As I hear an alien sound in the room, I glance at the door and see him watching us with tears rolling down his face.

"Cathy…" he whispers roughly, "Damn it, Cathy."

I shake my head when I see him taking a step into Nadia's room. I let go of her, get off the bed, and make my way to where he's standing. Grabbing his forearm in my hand, I make him follow me to the living room.

We stand in the middle of the room, surrounded by new memories I've created since our marriage ended. A life without him. Ben and I continue to stare at each other with tears streaming down our faces in total silence. With my heart ramming against the walls of my chest, I watch as Ben struggles to contain the trembling of his limbs.

I remember Hayes words.

Fight for him.

I take the biggest gamble of my life because at this point there's nothing else to lose and everything to gain. I wrap my arms around his large body, pushing myself closer to him until there is no space left between us. I hope my love can be enough when I utter the next words.

"Ben…I know I don't deserve you, but can we do it all again? I mean, try again?"

"I don't know, Cathy. I don't fucking know."

"If you can forgive me, if you have it in you to give me a second chance, I will give you every part of me. Every kiss…every tear…every smile. I'm yours. Always have. Always will. I promise you that I won't ever take you for granted. I promise you that not a day will go by when I won't do my best to make you as happy as you deserve. I love you. Only you. Please, Ben. Forgive me."

I pause and swallow my tears. "I know we both have changed, a-and that sometimes love is not enough to make things work. Too much has happened between us…but I have hope. I'm not asking you to marry me, or to even date me. I'm just asking you for the chance to let me back in your life. With Nadia. Let us back, let me love you. Let me earn your trust again. Let me show you how much I love you, even after all this time." I grab him by the back of his neck, pull him down, and kiss him with my whole soul, my whole heart, my everything.

And I kiss for every year, month, week, day, hour, and second without him in my life.

With the kiss coming to an end, I make him look at me and whisper fiercely against his lips, "Miracles are the consequences of daring to believe. And I dare you to believe in us again, Ben. I dare you to."

But when he doesn't respond, I have my answer even before he lets go of my waist and pushes me away.

"I'm sorry, Cathy. I can't do it. I shouldn't have come here, but I needed to know, and…fuck." He rubs his hands on his face, wiping some of his tears away. "I forgave you a long time ago, I did, but I don't think I can ever forget what you did to us. The pain is still fucking there. It's too late."

I can't move.

I can't breathe.

All I can do is stand there and listen to him telling me what I've known all along. That I destroyed us beyond repair, even if I dared myself to hope briefly.

Ben lifts a hand almost as if he wants to touch me again, but changes his mind because he puts his hands in his pockets instead.

"I should go…"

Not being able to answer him, all I can do is nod and watch him turn around and make his way through my living room to the front door, walking away from my life forever.

Just like I knew it would be.

Halfway through, he reaches down and picks up a Rapunzel stuffed doll that is lying on the floor next to some parenting and shoe magazines. "She's as beautiful as you are," he says, looking at the doll as he slowly caresses her golden hair.

"I beg your pardon?"

With a rueful smile, he turns to look at me. "She looks just how I dreamed our daughter would so many times before."

Ben is kneeling down, holding what could be our daughter's doll in his hand, and telling me that she looks exactly how he imagined she would, yet I have never felt more lost or more heartbroken than now. When I left him in the house that day, I thought I'd lost part of myself, not knowing if there was a Cathy without Ben. And as I stare into my ex-husband's eyes, I know that there's no me without him.

But I deserve this.

I deserve to be alone.

Ben is right.

It's too late for us.

"If you ever need help financially, let me know." Ben is standing outside my apartment now, looking calmer than before, but I see the sadness in his eyes.

"No. I don't deserve your help," I say more forcefully than I intended. "I-I have a job. Amy was able to get me a position at a different hotel."

"It doesn't matter. I'd like to hel—"

"No. Please, Ben, don't say anything else. J-just go. I'm so close to falling apart in front of you. I'm trying so hard to stand here and look at you and not want you," I whimper as I clutch myself tighter. "I'm trying not to throw myself at your feet and beg you to stay. Please, just go. I'm so sorry for h-how much I hurt you but please, I'm begging you…"

"I understand, Cathy. I'm sorry too."

And he's gone.

I know our love is broken past salvation and it is my fault, but watching him walk away from me once more still has the power to destroy me. As I stare at his hunched figure making his way slowly to the elevator, I realize that I'm not sure I'll be able to heal from this.

I don't think I can.

35

I don't go back to bed.

Instead, I sit on the floor on the same spot where Ben sat a couple hours ago, trying to see if I can still feel the warm imprint of his body, but I feel nothing. There isn't anything left of him in my apartment.

Nothing.

It is empty.

Just like me.

But then I remember Nadia.

Nadia.

My beautiful Nadia.

She is my will to live.

The only one who matters.

So I stand up, make my way to my bedroom, take a shower, and get ready for the day. I bury the pain deep within me once again, and prepare myself to pretend like nothing ever happened.

There is no other choice.

I have to.

I have to be strong. I'm holding hands with Nadia as we walk to her school in the pouring rain. Like every autumn before, the weather has turned chilly while the leaves begin to fall and cover the asphalt in a sea of orange, brown, and bright red. Listening to the city come alive with the sounds of cars driving over wet pavement and puddles being splashed, I watch as my daughter walks protected in her bright pink raincoat and matching boots. She's twirling her umbrella and humming, "Rain, rain, go away…"

I'm so entranced by the way her blonde curls are bouncing off her shoulders that I don't notice the man making his way towards us until I hear him saying my name. Startled, my hand goes to my chest as I peek from under my umbrella at a soaked Ben watching us with so much love.

"Ben?" I ask incredulously.

"Hi," Ben smiles bashfully as I move forward to shelter him from the rain with my umbrella.

"Um, Momma?"

Upon hearing Nadia speak; Ben looks away from me, focusing on Nadia who is openly studying him with those big green eyes of hers.

"Hi there, pretty girl," he says huskily.

"Hi. You're the man Papa didn't like. You made my momma sad," she states.

Ben grimaces. "I am, and I'm sorry for that, but I'm here to try to make it all better."

"Reaaaally? Will you buy her a cupcake? My momma says cupcakes always make a bad day better."

"If she'll let me, I'll buy her as many cupcakes as I possibly can," Ben says, smiling into my daughter's eyes.

Nadia seems to be content with his answer because she nods and says, "Momma, don't be sad anymore. He's gonna buy you cupcakes now, okay?"

I want to laugh and cry, but instead I tear my gaze away from my daughter and stare at Ben, who's watching me intensely as rain keeps falling around us.

"Cathy, I can't make promises. I don't know anything anymore…so much can happen, so much has. But what I do know is that I want you both in my life. Of that, I'm sure."

"I understand. Just give me one chance. Just one to make this right."

I watch Ben as hope is reborn within him. Fear and indecision disappear, clearing the path for our future together.

"There was never a choice for us, was there?" he says as a smile grows on his beautiful face, accentuating the thickness of his lips and the sharp edge of his jaw.

I shake my head and smile as happiness bursts inside me, bringing me to life once more.

"No."

"Come here," he says, flashing the same cocky smile I fell in love with the first time I saw him.

About to reach for him with Nadia in my hand, I let myself think of that boy with the aqua-blue fire in his eyes one last time. Silently, I thank him because he's the reason why I'm standing in front of Ben. He saved me from myself, and in a roundabout way he gave me Ben back. Without his help, and whatever it was we had, I don't think I would be here. I would probably be dead. I love him and always will because his inner fire brought me back to life. Yes, he was the fire that burned my marriage down to ashes, but in those ashes, hope was reborn.

He healed me.

Arsen.

epilogue

arsen

Missing you is a sickness I can't cure,
and it's fucking killing me.

Fuck.

It happened again.

I'm looking at a lavender ceiling instead of the familiar grey of my bedroom.

The pillow feels too fluffy to be mine, and it smells like fucking fruit.

Why the hell would I want to fuck someone who smells like fruit? It reminds me of my nana.

I feel nauseous, so I close my eyes and try to remember how I got here in the first place.

What the fuck did I do last night?

I open my eyes, and turn my head to look at who I did last night.

Figures…

Lying next to me is a naked blonde haired woman that looks exactly the same as Catherine. I guess if I can't have the real thing, I might as well screw the next best thing, right?

I'm sick.

Disgusted with myself, I get up, get dressed, and leave the blonde chick's apartment without saying goodbye. It's not like I want to see her ever again. I never do. And it works for me.

Once I step outside from the building, I look around and try to figure out where the hell I am. I glance at the street corner and read the green sign that lets me know I'm on Fifth Avenue. Well, isn't this just fucking peachy? I'm in no fucking mood to ride a cab or the subway all the way to SoHo at this moment.

With a pounding head, I decide to go in search of the closest deli. I need to take something to make my headache go away. As I start walking, I realize that I've been here before. The buildings look eerily familiar and the more I stare at them, the more a memory I've tried to erase many times before keeps popping in my head. But it's not until I'm standing across the street from the same fucking coffee shop and see her that the images of those two days come crashing down on me.

I had to let her go.

When she told me that she was pregnant, I freaked out. It was fucking shitty of me, but I didn't know what to think or how to react. I wasn't even sure the kid was mine and it scared the hell out of me. How were we supposed to raise a child together when everything was so new? For all I knew, she could still dump my ass and go back to her husband once she got bored with me. The situation was so fucking messed up, but I didn't care since Catherine was with me and not with that asshole. I just wanted to love her for as long as I had her because that was all that mattered to me. Our time together.

I saw her, I wanted her, so I took her, even if in the process I destroyed a good marriage. I saw the sadness and vulnerability in her eyes the moment I got off the jet, but it wasn't until much later that the complex of wanting to be her fucking savior was born.

All I wanted to do was fix her, save her.

Just before she told me she was pregnant, I was planning on taking her to Paris for a weekend. And maybe once we got there, go fucking romantic like in the movies and shit, and finally tell her how much I loved her.

Somehow she became my reason to be, to exist.

I loved her so damn much.

But when she came back from seeing her gynecologist and told me she was pregnant, reality came knocking on my door.

Just like Ben had.

A couple hours before Cathy came back, Ben was at my apartment telling me that the only reason she was with me was because of her last miscarriage, which sent her spinning out of control. He told me that things were getting better between them before it happened, that they loved each other, that she was never mine to begin with. And yes, I thought he was being a pussy.

Then Ben revealed something that she fucking failed to mention before. She was with me because he had left her. It had never been her. She wasn't the one to end it. But like I told him before he left my apartment, I didn't give a rat's ass as long as she was with me.

And she was.

It wasn't until after she told me she was pregnant, and I saw the way her eyes were glowing with such hope and tears, that I knew.

I couldn't do it.

I couldn't take it away from them, even if it didn't work out. Ben and Cathy deserved that baby.

I didn't.

So I did what I always do best.

I broke her heart.

I told her I didn't love her.

I told her there had been no promises.

I was lying.

When she came back to me…after Ben had left her…when she told me it was over between them…I became hers.

That night, our first together, as I held her while she slept in my arms, I thought that life couldn't get any more perfect. I finally had her and I was not going to share her anymore.

She was finally mine.

My own.

I did not expect her to come back from the Doctor's office with a dazed look.

I did not expect to see hope and anguish warring in her eyes.

I did not expect her to say, "I'm pregnant."

And when she didn't even know for sure if I was the father, it fucking pissed me off. I wanted to go to that mother fucker and beat the shit out of him because it meant that I had shared her. It meant he had touched her.

And, it fucking hurt.

That wasn't supposed to happen.

And, then I remembered the way Ben looked when he came to my place. Fucking destroyed.

I had to do it.

I kicked her out.

The moment I did, I realized what a big mistake I made. As I laid in my cold bed that night, not being able to taste her in the air I breathed, I decided I didn't care about Ben. If there was a chance that the baby could be mine, I was going to take it. I loved Catherine, my Dimples…I knew I was going to love the baby, whether it was mine or not. And in case the pregnancy came to nothing, I wanted to be there for her.

The next day, I went to look for her at Amy's apartment. I saw her walking out of the building, and instead of stopping her and begging her to forgive me right in the middle of the street, I decided to follow her. I needed to go over my speech one last time. As I was standing across the street from that coffee shop stalling for time, I saw him walk into the same shop as Catherine. I had just left her not even twenty-four hours ago, and she was already asking Ben back.

I turned around and walked away from her, from any hope of ever seeing her again. She was back where she needed to be all along, even if it killed me for a second time in my life. The only difference was that this time, I didn't think I would be able to survive because I was already dead.

It's been almost five years since that day.

Fucking hell…

It hurts.

It still hurts.

As I stand on the same corner, transfixed and feeling my fucking soul shatter all over again, I watch the familiar blonde hair and dimples on the face of a woman I haven't been able to forget. Ben is giving a young girl a piggyback ride and has an arm thrown around my girl's shoulder. They are laughing and looking like a perfect family.

I feel pain.

Mind-numbing pain.

My body is shutting down.

Catherine still has the power to take my fucking breath away after all this time.

Please turn around and look at me.

Please turn around.

Please.

Please.

I beg, pray, chant, and wish for Catherine to do so. I need to see the eyes that have haunted me for so long, the ones that stole my soul and never let it go, but she doesn't. Instead, she stares at Ben with all the love that should have been mine.

I despise him.

With her arm wrapped around his waist, I watch as he leans down and pauses for a moment before kissing her on the mouth. Closing her eyes, she stands on her tiptoes to receive his kiss. He's watching her intensely. Shit, he fucking loves her. I don't want to witness anymore of that bullshit, so I study the girl instead. She has blonde hair and looks just like her mother. So beautiful.

The little girl looks up and her gaze lands on me. She looks me straight in the eye and a sense of recognition, of having found myself again, settles in my heart.

We look at each other.

She's mine.

That little girl is mine.

I know it.

My body begins to move automatically. I need to go to her. To my girls.

As I begin to walk towards them, Catherine says something to Ben which prompts him to rest his hand on her stomach, and both of them smile at each other with so much fucking love. Straining my eyes, I notice for the first time the small bump growing inside Catherine's body.

With the fight drained out of me, I watch them for a couple more soul shattering minutes being a happy family. I know that I did the right thing that day long ago. I did the right thing by letting her go, just as I'm about to do for a second time.

And it's tearing me apart once again.

They got their happy ending. That's the only reason why I can make myself walk away, make myself say goodbye to my girls, even though it kills me that I'm not the reason behind their smiles.

And I will never be.

Fuck.

I can't.

I turn around and run, run, run, run, run, run…

Once I'm in the middle of Central Park, feeling breathless, I lean against a tree. I need to calm down. Get myself together. I look down at my hands and notice the way they are shaking so fucking bad. I fist them closed and wrap them under my armpits. It doesn't help. As a matter of fact, it feels as if an earthquake is rolling through my entire body, leaving utter devastation behind.

I close my eyes and tilt my head back, going over everything that just happened. Fuck, fuck, fuck.

It hurts so damn much.

He has both my girls.

He has the family that should have fucking been mine.

I fucking hate him.

I hate her.

I hate her for making me fall in love with her.

I hate her for leaving me.

I hate myself for lying to her.

I hate myself because I still fucking love her.

And I hate myself because when I saw that little girl…

I just knew.

She is mine, yet she's not.

Just like her mother.

I love them both.

And I don't have them.

He has them.

He has them both.

And I never will.

And it will remain that way even if I have to make sure I die in the process.

Even if it destroys what little is left of me.

He deserves them.

And I don't.

I don't.

Fuck.

Fuck

Fuck.

I am broken.

acknowledgements

J, my better half, my wonderful husband, thank you so much for putting up with me, my craziness, my obsession with my characters, the ridiculous and never-ending hours I spent writing and ignoring everyone around me. Your love and support were always my constant and without them this book would have never been completed. I love you so much and I'm so blessed to be able to call you mine.

J and M, my beautiful children, you can't read this yet but I want to thank you both so much for giving mommy the time and space needed to write this book. Play dates and playtime were forsaken but you never resented me for it, if anything you always seemed to understand when mommy said she was busy "working." Your love, laughs, kisses, and hugs were my inspiration. I love you both so, so much.

Momo, the **good** sister, you were the first person to ever encourage me to write and put the crazy voices inside my head on paper. I remember I was on my way to NH and we started texting (I wasn't driving) about S, M, and A, and the rest is history. Your help and support when I needed time to get away and finish *Arsen* were the best gift you could ever give me. I love you, sis. Always and forever.

Next I would like to thank each and every single person that helped me in creating Arsen—my very special group of BETA readers. Without your help this book would have never been completed. You guys are my own personal rock stars.

Lisa, my critique partner and the yin to my yang (LOL), I remember when I first contacted you through your blog…I wanted you to BETA read my unfinished MS and instead of politely blowing me off, you took your time in talking and explaining to me the entire process of self-publishing. You've become one of my best friends and I don't think I could go a day without talking to you. It is *that* necessary and important to me. Also, thank you so much for listening to me whine when my characters weren't talking or behaving the way I wanted them to. Without your guidance some pivotal scenes in the story wouldn't have been created. Thank you, my dear evil twin.

Amy, AKA as my second brain, and Mint, AKA as my toughest critic, you both were always there to go over the difficult chapters in my manuscript and guide me through them. Maybe you would let me type out my thoughts until they made sense or you would point out something that I couldn't see. Sometimes I got a "Nah" or "It's watery" but you were always completely honest with me. Amy, you pointed out where it should be toned down, and Mint, you pointed out where I needed to push the envelope some more. Without your input, maybe the outcome of the book would be different. Thank you so much. Oh, and thank you for the extra read-throughs…You guys didn't have to do it at all. So thank you for the bottom of my heart.

Melissa S, my Aussie twin, you were the first person to ever read anything I wrote and tell me that I had something worth reading. You encouraged me to keep going and you believed in my characters before I did. And when I was stuck with Cathy, your input and advice were the guiding light I needed to decipher her. Don't you miss our dear Cathy already?

Melissa E, my accidental BETA, remember what almost happened? I know you do…and I'm glad it never did because now I get to call you my friend. Your friendship and advice are invaluable to me. And yes, you make the best teasers ever. Also, thank you for that second read through. I must've driven you crazy…

Megan, what can I say? Do you remember when you told me you didn't **feel** *Arsen*? LOL. Well, thank you so much for being honest. Your invaluable input made me go back during rewrites and try to figure out what was missing. Also, thank you for listening to me go on and on about my characters and my story. Sometimes the conversations could be quite one-sided but you always were there for me. Also, thank you so much for your support!

Natalie, how can I describe how thankful I was when you took the time to go over my manuscript while writing your own? Seriously, your notes were so helpful and they taught me so much. You have no idea how much your help meant to me, and it always will.

Sali, HA! HA! HA! I don't know where I would be without your guidance. Your experience and advice made it easy for me not to give up when everything seemed impossible. I'm so thankful to Melissa for having introduced us…because you're not only incredible at what you do but now you are one of my dearest friends.

Beth, thank you so much for the long hours we spent on the phone talking about my plot and trying to untangle parts of the story. Your knowledge in pacing, attention to detail, and overall awesomeness are just a few of the things that make you such a wonderful person. I'm so grateful that we got to work together.

Jessica, I'm sorry your computer broke! Kidding! Seriously, I can't never thank you enough for helping me out. You know how much you helped me and I can't wait to work with you again. Can I just add that I'm so glad Lisa introduced us? You are now one of my closest and dearest friends.

Angie, I don't even know where to start? So maybe I'll just keep it short and sweet. YOU ROCK.

Kerry, Jodie, Amanda, and Lisa M, thank you so much for helpful advice and encouraging words. You guys are awesome BETAs and I'm so proud that we got to work together.

Amy Burt, Jennifer Mirabelli and Deana Wolstenholme, my very dear second, or third (who is counting, really?) round betas, thank you, THANK YOU, for going over *Arsen* and helping me tighten the plot and make sure it was a ready for the public eye. You guys saved me.

Jennifer Roberts-Hall, EDITOOOOORRRRRRR! One sentence: This book wouldn't be what it is without your talent. I never knew what being an editor's job was…I assumed the author wrote the whole thing and that someone went over it for grammatical errors. How mistaken I was. I would like to say that the author creates the story, but it is you, my dear editor, who truly puts it together. I gave you something that was too long, too wordy, and imperfect, and you turned it into a beautiful story. Thank you for being always there for me, for answering my questions, and for being my friend. I can't really put in words how much it means to me. I love ya, editor.

Jillian, thank you for being always there to answer my questions regarding the world of self-publishing. Your guidance made it seem not such a scary thing to do. Also, thank you so much for being such a great friend to me.

Angela, thank you so much for *everything*. Your beautiful work is one of a kind and you can count that I will always be a client of yours.

Regina, the cover you created for Arsen took my breath away—It's perfect. Your unbelievable talent humbles me and I can't wait to see what you come up next with my next cover.

Lili Mickey and Mint, thank you for answering my medical questions regarding Cathy's condition. The information you provided helped me make sure I did justice to her story.

I want to give a special shout out to all the bloggers and individuals that helped spread the word. No one would know about my novel if it weren't for your help. I would be nothing without your help. Thank you for believing in me and in *Arsen*.

Also, special thanks to Angie from Angie's Dreamy Reads for organizing a kick-ass cover reveal and blog tour. You were one of the first people to believe in my book. Also, thank you to Jenny and Gitte from Totally Booked, Sandra from The Book Blog, Trisha from Devoured Words, Lisa from The Rock Stars Of Romance, Dawn from Up all Night, Kathy from Love Words and Books, and Sophie from Bridger Bitches Book Blog.

Thank you to all my family and friends for putting up with me and for always being there for me. I know I'm forgetting someone and if I do know that I'm truly sorry. I love all the encouraging words, the lovely words from every single person that has stopped by my page and said hello. I love every single one of you.

This book would not be anything without the support and love from all of you. Thank *you* so, so much.

Connect with me online:

My blog * Facebook * Twitter

Turn the page for some sneak peeks at upcoming works by Lisa De Jong, Crystal Serowka, and Jennifer Domenico.

WHEN IT RAINS

by

Lisa De Jong

Coming September 27, 2013

PROLOGUE

When you live in a small town, there's not much to do on a Friday night in the fall after a football game.

When the season started that year, some of the seniors at my high school decided that we should have a bonfire after each game. It was really an excuse to drink and hook-up: two things I wasn't interested in, but I always went to hang out with my friends anyway.

That's where I was that night.

The night I retreated into darkness.

Where the night sky had no stars, the day had no sun, and all hope was drained from my body.

The night my life ended.

And Beau Bennett wasn't there. If he had been, he would have saved me just like he always did, but he was grounded that night for staying out past curfew the Friday before. In fact, it's the only weekend I remember Beau ever being grounded.

Life is a series of coincidences, and that night coincidence screwed me over.

I was there with Morgan, my best friend since third grade. She was dating the senior class president at the time, and it didn't take long before they disappeared and left me huddled near the fire with some of the other kids from my school. I felt completely comfortable being alone because I've known most of these people since I moved here when I was five. That was one of the nice things about small towns.

Or so I thought.

I was sitting with my arms wrapped around myself, trying to warm what the fire couldn't, when Drew Heston sat down next to me. My stomach did a somersault. Drew was a senior. Mr. Football as everyone called him. He was the local hero; the type of guy who would have a billboard outside of town someday. It didn't hurt that he looked amazing with his short dark hair, light green eyes and broad shoulders.

I had secretly crushed on him since the day I first walked into the doors of my high school. There was something about the way he walked the halls with his head held up high that commanded every girl's attention, including mine. I'd never talked to him, or even made eye contact with him for that matter, but there he was that night, sitting next to me in front of the fire. I couldn't believe it. Things like that didn't happen to Kate Alexander.

"Hey, Kate, how've you been?" he asked, his eyes burning into the side of my head. I couldn't bring myself to look at him. Just being near him made me lose all comprehension of the English language.

"Fine," I mumbled, biting down on my lower lip. A shiver ran through my body as I finally glanced in his direction.

"Were you at my game tonight?" he asked, bumping my shoulder with his. I could feel the heat coming off his muscular body, and it made me blush.

My thoughts drifted back to the third quarter when Drew threw the ball to his star receiver Jackson Reid, who was surrounded by defenders. My heart raced with excitement as I watched Jackson and three members of the other team jump up to catch the ball at the same time. In the end, Jackson came out victorious because Drew threw it right into his hands. It was nothing short of amazing, yet for Drew it was completely normal.

"You were great," I replied, nervously reaching up to tighten my ponytail. A breeze was gently blowing, and a few raindrops fell from the sky. I ran my hands up and down my arms in an attempt to chase the chill from my body, but it didn't help.

"Are you cold?" he asked, scooting his body even closer to mine. The way he was looking at me sent butterflies through my stomach. It wasn't like I was an outcast at school, but I wasn't one of the elite popular girls that guys like Drew usually spent their time on.

"A little. I forgot my jacket at home," I replied, feeling a few more raindrops fall on my cheek.

He stood up and reached for my hand. "Come on. I have an extra sweatshirt in the house you can borrow."

The party was being held at his house since his parents had gone out of town that weekend. I hesitated for a minute before placing my hand in his. I knew of him, but I didn't really know him. It wasn't the first time I'd been to his house, but it was the first time I'd been inside. I felt a little uneasy, but I still trusted him. I didn't have any reason not to.

Drew's house was old, but it had been well maintained with a fresh coat of paint and a wraparound porch. He opened the front door, never loosening his grip on my hand as he moved us forward. My attention was so focused on the contemporary paint colors and beautiful cherry wood floors that it barely registered we were heading upstairs.

I watched as he took a key out of his pocket to unlock one of the doors that lined the second story hallway. He must have noticed the way I was looking at him because his lips turned up on the sides. "I don't like anyone to be in my room, but me," he said, pushing the door open.

I nodded, following him inside. Had I felt a little uncomfortable stepping into Drew Heston's bedroom? Yes. Had I thought for one moment that I shouldn't be there? No. I'd known him for years. Everyone knew him and thought the world of him.

When he closed the door and locked it, I felt my heart rate pick up. I watched him glance around the room, following his eyes with mine. The walls were a deep navy blue with various football posters covering them, and it smelled as if cologne had been used to cover up the stench of his used gym clothes.

I'd only been in one boy's bedroom before, and Beau's hardly counted. He was one of my best friends. Drew remained still, staring at me with glossed over eyes. Suddenly, being there didn't feel right.

"Can you find that sweatshirt? I should probably get back outside before Morgan comes looking for me."

"Oh, yeah. Give me a sec," he said, moving to dig through a drawer in his dresser. I walked to the window at the other end of the room and looked down at the diminishing fire. The rain was falling faster against the glass making it harder to see in the distance, but it looked as if everybody had left their spot by the fire. I really needed to hurry up and find Morgan before she left without me.

The house was completely quiet sending a chill down my spine. I closed my eyes and listened to Drew's footsteps moving closer to me, my heart beating faster every time I heard the rubber soles of his shoes against the floorboards. I just wanted to get out of there. Everything about being inside his room felt wrong, and I wanted to escape it. Going up to his bedroom was a bad idea. Going to the party without Beau was a huge mistake.

His footsteps continued to move closer as I spun on my heels to head towards the door. I was greeted with dark eyes and a vacant stare. This was not the Drew I thought I knew. I wanted to run out of this house and never look back, but he was blocking my path.

"I'm going to wait outside. It's getting warm in here," I lied, motioning toward his door. My hands were sweaty, and my knees felt as if they were made for paper dolls.

He didn't say a word as he pressed his body to mine, completely closing any gap that remained between us. It was like he was in a trance, and it was scaring the hell out of me.

"It's raining outside, Kate," he said, reaching his hand up to cup my cheek. I stepped back out of his grasp, but he followed me. It wasn't long before my back was against the wall. Even if I wanted to leave, it was too late. His hands rested on the wall, caging me in with his arms. "Mmm, you smell so good," he growled, pressing his lips to my neck. His touch forced me to tilt my head in the other direction. I felt helpless.

"Drew, please, just let me go. I really need to find Morgan," I cried. My whole body was shaking from a fear unlike anything I'd ever felt before. It was paralyzing. I wanted to run out the door as fast as I could, and never look back.

But I was stuck.

He ignored me, running his lips down my jaw line. I turned my head to fight it, but he followed my movements. "What's the matter, Kate? I see the way you look at me. You want this as much as I do," he said with a husky voice that sent more panic through my already tense body. I used the little bit of fight I had left to push on his chest, but he didn't move.

"Let me go," I pleaded. His right hand came down to grip my hip hard as he roughly pressed his lips to mine. The force of his kiss sent pain to my lips, and all I could taste was the mix of my blood and the alcohol on his breath.

When his hand found the bottom of my shirt and started to work the material up my bare stomach, I tried to move my legs forward, but he was so much bigger and stronger than me. If anything, my attempts to push him away only made things worse.

He gripped my wrists tightly and pulled me over to his bed, pushing me onto my stomach. I tried to pull my arms loose, but it caused pain to shoot through my wrists. I'd never felt more terrified in my life. He continued to hold my arms behind my back and pinned my legs down with his knees.

"HELP!" I yelled as loud as I could through my panic and tears.

He clamped his hand over my mouth, yanking my head back until my neck ached. "Everyone is outside. No one's going to hear you."

That was it.

I was trapped under him, alone with no one to save me. All the fight I had was drained from my body, and the chance that anyone would pull me out of this hell was getting slimmer by the minute. Tears rolled down my face, soaking his bedspread while I fixated on the raindrops hitting the window. He forced my jeans down so that they were left slung around my left ankle. When I heard him working at his belt buckle, I felt like I couldn't breathe anymore. I'd never been exposed like that, and it wasn't at all what I wanted. I was saving myself for someone special, and Drew was taking that from me. I gasped for air, but I couldn't get any into my lungs. I tried to scream again, but no sound came out.

I felt him pressed against my backside, and it made me want to throw up. "STOP!" I screamed, trying again to free myself from his hold, but he was too strong.

He let out a hushed chuckle from behind. "Are you going to give up?"

"Please don't," I begged again. It was my last chance, and I knew it. He didn't respond, and when I heard the sound of foil paper ripping, I squeezed my eyes shut and said a silent prayer. I wanted it all to be a nightmare that I would soon wake up from. I wanted someone to come through that door and stop it from happening. I wanted to be anywhere but there.

Except no one was listening to me that night. I could hear the soft tap of the rain falling on the window, but the rest of the house was completely silent. I used to like the sound of rain, but Drew took that from me too.

He pressed into me so quickly that pain erupted through my whole body, sending a deafening scream into the darkness of the room. I squeezed my eyes shut. It felt like I was drowning, and there was no way to get to the surface. I've never felt such intense physical and emotional pain all at once. It would always be the absolute worst moment of my life.

He didn't stop. Not when I screamed. Not when I cried. He kept invading my body with each and every thrust, killing me a little more inside each time. It hurt more to fight it, so I remained still, continuing to stare at the droplets that rolled down the window. He grunted as he continued to shred my soul to pieces and I tried my best to block it out. I didn't need to have his words locked into my memory forever when I already had to live with the feel of him inside of me. I knew I'd never be the same after what he did to me.

I'm not sure how long I was in that room, but it felt like an eternity. My whole life flashed before me as I was overcome with grief. For the rest of my life, I would always regret going up there with Drew Heston.

The most important thing I lost was my entire sense of self. It took seventeen years to build my foundation, and only mere minutes to tear it down.

I hated him.

The old Kate was gone.

And she was never coming back.

And she would always hate when it rains.

IN CONTROL

by

Crystal Serowka

Coming October 2013

Bitch. Whore. Slut. Those were just a few of the names I'd been called since I began growing breasts. The boys all stared, gawking at the exposed skin above my navel. Their eyes followed the length of my bare legs, revealing their desire with a smile in my direction. No matter how hard they tried to get my attention, boys were never my thing. They were fragile. Inexperienced. Full of hope.

Girls resented my appeal, always laughing and pointing when I hopped into a different car every day after school. They never understood why I did the things I did; why I made it my mission in life to seduce men and then toss them aside like yesterday's garbage. Instead of trying to understand, they chose to spread shameless rumors. Their jealousy never got under my skin like they were hoping it would. I loved the attention. In fact, I loved it so much that I started going after their boyfriends. The girls had no idea that whatever name they called me, whatever they wrote on my locker, it wasn't ever going to bother me. I had been shattered a long time ago, and the shards of my former self were so sharp nothing else could ever harm me.

I'd been thrown away; kicked to the curb like I was the stray mongrel no one wanted. I let my guard down too many times to count and promised myself that I'd never be vulnerable again.

I was never any good at keeping promises.

His lips touched my neck, bringing me back to the moment. Wren lay next to me, his skin melting against mine. A drop of sweat fell onto my lips and I tasted the saltiness of our exertion. I'd been in this bed so many times now that I knew the softest spots on the mattress. I'd memorized the smell of Wren's pillow, the delicate fabric bursting with the scent of cedarwood and vanilla. It was October when I first visited his home, and now, with the trees dressed in bright green, I lay here in his bed, my head and heart at odds. I wanted to be with Wren, but the one time I had allowed a label to represent how I felt, I had been betrayed.

I studied his bare chest, my fingers roaming over the patches of freckles.

"Making constellations again?" he asked, resting on his elbows to watch my busy fingers.

"Just Perseus."

"You're the first person that's ever pointed that out."

"That's probably because all of your other girlfriends were dumb as rocks and didn't know a thing about constellations," I retorted.

Wren laughed quietly, not denying my words. We never discussed exes, and I was happy about that. Explaining Porter to someone who was the complete opposite of him would be an impossible task.

We lay in silence, my fingers not wanting to leave his skin. We'd been in Wren's bed since this morning, and I could have stayed wrapped in his embrace forever. Tangled in his blood red sheets, I was safe from the evil that lurked outside. In this bed, I couldn't run into anyone from my past.

"Think we should get up? We can grab some food before I head to Jay's." Wren turned on his side, his fingers leisurely roaming my skin. His effortless touch made my insides tremble, forcing me to take a few calming breaths.

I hated leaving him. I hated that I was slowly becoming one of *those* girls. The kind of girl that had nothing else to talk about but the guy they were dating. The kind that became so obsessed with her boyfriend, she scheduled her whole life around him. I wasn't that kind of girl. I couldn't possibly be turning into one.

"You already had me for breakfast and lunch, might as well fill up on me for dinner, too," I suggested, knowing it would keep him from leaving.

A devious grin formed on Wren's lips. "Suddenly I'm starving."

In a matter of seconds, he was on top of me, trapping my arms and legs with his own. Typically, I liked being in control, but once in awhile it was fun to act helpless.

"You've got me pinned, now what?" I fixed my eyes on his, concentrating on the chills that were shooting through my body.

His eyes met mine only for a moment before traveling to our linked fingers. His grasp tightened, bringing our arms higher above my head. Wren's jaw set and I knew my submissiveness had turned him on.

He leaned down near my ear and whispered, "Now I fuck you so hard you forget your name."

I exhaled, waiting for him to make his move. Wren began teasing me, his fingers exploring the curves of my body, making a point not to touch me anywhere that would put me over the edge. He caressed my upper thigh slowly, then the back of my leg. His tongue grazed my earlobe and my stomach clenched in anticipation, craving so much more than what he was giving.

"Fuck me already," I demanded.

"No."

It wasn't just his calm and collected answer that almost drove me to the edge. It was in his light kisses, his fingers brushing back curls from my face, and the way he blinked slowly as he took me in. I exhaled again, anxiously waiting to see which part of my body he'd set on fire first.

"Spread your legs," he whispered, his breath teasing my earlobe.

I quickly conceded and felt the softness of his fingers stroke the inside of my thigh. Between the motion of his hand and knowing what was coming next, I was ready for him. Two fingers slowly slid inside of me and our eyes locked together, filling me with a hunger I'd never experienced. From the very first night, Wren had instinctively known the most sensitive parts of my body. He understood it better than anyone ever had, and his touch always left me begging for more.

"Please tell me this isn't all I'm getting?" The edge in my voice made him remove his hands from my skin.

"Keep talking, Kingsley, and this *is* all you'll be getting."

It took everything in me to bite my tongue, swallowing my snappy comeback.

"Good girl." He pulled me onto his lap, and the rough hair on his jaw grated against my shoulder, leaving a pleasing sting in its wake. "Put your legs around me," he ordered. His fingers knotted through my hair, pulling my head back and exposing my neck to his lips. Wren's tongue trailed the skin of my throat, slowly moving toward my ear. "Plan's changed. Now you're going to fuck me."

"What if I don't want to?"

Without answering my question, Wren pulled my face to his, forcing his tongue inside my mouth. I sat up on my knees and guided him inside me, watching as his somber expression disappeared. He cupped my ass, pushing our bodies closer together, filling me even more. I yelled out his name like we were the only two people left in the world.

"Fuck, Kingsley…" he groaned.

Leaning back on my hands, I began to move my hips along to a silent beat in my head. Back and forth, up and down. I bit down on my bottom lip with enough force that a small trickle of blood seeped into my mouth, leaving behind the faint taste of salt and metal.

Wren pulled me back into his chest, our bodies trembling from head to toe. It was in those last few seconds when every nerve ending in my body felt like it was going to explode; it was then that I felt closest to him.

My heart was beating so fiercely, I felt the cool mattress beneath me tremble with its force. Wren's hand found mine in the rustled sheets, squeezing it twice. The comfortable silence we shared was a new experience for me. I turned on my side, studying his shadowed profile; the perfect slope of his nose, his lips half-parted with short breaths leaving his mouth. He had cheekbones that were so high, even I was envious. But his eyes were my favorite part, dark and tempting. They reminded me of the rich chocolate cake I always longed to taste, of whiskey on the rocks… His eyes expressed his feelings even before he had a chance to say them out loud.

UPCOMING NOVEL

title to be announced

by

Jennifer Domenico

CHAPTER ONE

Bloody hell! I cannot believe I overslept. I stupidly forgot to turn on my alarm clock last night. As much as I want to lament my forgetfulness, I can't now. I need to rush to get ready for my interview. How could I forget something this important? It took forever to get this appointment with the foreign language department and here I am, struggling to get dressed in time to catch the train.

I can just hear my mum's nagging voice, "never quite prepared, are you dear?" Well on that note, she might have a point. I do have a nasty habit of showing up close to late. I like to call it perfectly on time.

Rifling through my overflowing sock drawer I grab a pair of black tights. Wait. Tights in August? Better reconsider. Glancing down at my too pale legs, I desperately wish it was cold enough to cover them up. I squeeze into my plaid, knee length skirt and zip it. Cor! It's a bit tight. No time to change though.

I need to look extra smart today. Impressing the department head is my only goal. Not only do I want this job, I need it. It's time to start making my own money and stop living on the stipend my parents provide. Now all I have to do is get there.

I take one last glance in the mirror and realize I forgot earrings. Normally I wouldn't care, but this is Harvard

University for crying out loud. I run to my jewelry box and grab a pair of pearl earrings and put them in. Good enough.

In the living room, I see my flatmate sleeping on the couch. Why can't the girl make it into her own bedroom once in a while?

"Madeline, wake up." I shove the slumbering mass with my Mary Jane heeled foot.

She rolls over, waving her arms above her head. "Wha'…what the hell, Londyn?"

"You had too much to drink again, didn't ya?"

"Maybe." She grins. "Why you up so early?"

"Harvard? Ring a bell?"

Madeline sits up, her blond hair a tangled mess; the heavy eyeliner she wore the night before smeared around her eyes. The smoky eye look she was going for has morphed more into a raccoon look. Not flattering.

"You look awful," I say.

Madeline smiles. "Maybe, but I feel incredible. You should have seen him- gorgeous. A bit of wanker though."

I cross my arms and give a tired sigh. "Did you bring another one of your dirty boys in here again? I've asked you not to do that anymore. It's not safe."

"What's not safe about a quick shag between pals? I knew this one. Wouldn't kill you to have a go every now and then, would it? These Boston boys are scrumptious."

I roll my eyes. "I have to go or I'm going to be late."

"You'll do great. Hey, while you're there, can you go to Falafel Kings and get me one of those amazing sandwiches?"

"If I have time," I say. "Hey, I thought you started your no-carb diet again?"

"Ah, yeah, but I die for those sandwiches. Just a little one, no chips."

"Alright, then."

"Thanks, Londyn." She bounces off the couch and throws her arms around me. "I'm glad you wore the blue cardigan. It's got that fifty's va-va-voom factor. Like Marilyn Monroe."

"My dear girl, I'm a thousand miles away from reminding anyone of the great MM."

"You just did." She grins, and twists a lock of her hair around her finger.

I roll my eyes and grab my brown messenger bag, a recent purchase but it seems all the students here carry one. "If all goes well, I won't be back until well after lunch. Wish me luck."

"Best of British to you."

I cock my head at my silly friend. "I do love how colloquial you are after a trip back home to your parents."

"Make fun if you like, but you sound just like me with your posh Essex accent."

"I do not have an accent!" I laugh, but I know it isn't true. In the great city of Boston, everyone notices my voice. "Seriously, I have to go. Cheers."

I fly out the door and down the two flights of stairs to the street. Flinging the door of my brownstone building open, I'm blasted with the hot, sticky air of Boston in the summer. Realizing how hot it is, I pull my cardigan off and rush the three blocks to catch The T. If I hurry, I should just make the 9:45 train to the campus.

I don't trust myself to drive there as I seem to be allergic to driving; having no less than three fender benders and two speeding tickets in the five years I've been driving in the US. I couldn't take a chance with my record and Boston traffic on such an important day.

I hurry through the turnstile just in time to get on the train and find a seat. Sinking down into my spot, I lift my thick brown hair off my neck and straighten my skirt. I glance down at the gold watch on my wrist, a birthday gift from my big brother.

Staring out the window, I think about Devon. I could not be more proud of him. He graduated five years ago with his medical degree and instead of a hospital, he went straight to Harvard to work in their research center. As long as I could remember, Devon Harper was sure he could find a cure for cancer. If anyone could, I thought it very well could be him.

If I'm being honest, I have to admit if it weren't for him, my résumé might not have been the one to rise to the top of the stack at Harvard. For that, I am grateful. At the end of the day though, I am still the one that has to win over the department head.

I open my messenger bag and take out the directions I need to find the building, Boylston Hall. I'll be meeting directly with Professor Luca Di Cesare, possibly the most intimidating man on the planet to me. Devon's two hour lecture giving me tips on dealing with his combustive personality only served to make me even more nervous. It's well known the professor is overbearing, ridiculously intelligent, and extremely passionate about his work. And here I am, applying to be his assistant. Not that my dream job involves getting coffee and typing papers for a maniacal professor, but I have to start somewhere.

The train gets to my stop, just steps away from Harvard Yard. It's quiet still, the flood of students not arriving for two more weeks. When I see the building, I'm relieved. Thank goodness Boylston Hall is easy to find. I only have three minutes to spare. I stop for a moment and put my cardigan back on, collecting my thoughts before walking in. "Here goes nothing," I say to no one in particular.

I walk into the vast hall and follow the directions I wrote down. Climbing to the top of the stairs, I turn left, my heels clicking loudly on the tiled floors. Down at the end of the hall, I find his office and knock softly. Hearing no response, I twist the knob slowly.

"Hello?" I call out.

Luca Di Cesare sits in his large leather chair behind a massive mahogany desk that looks as old as Harvard itself. He's staring out the window into a courtyard, his back turned to me. "You're late," he says without turning around.

I look at my watch, flustered. It's not possible. "I thought I was on time. I apologize," I murmur.

He swings around and glares at me. "I don't tolerate lateness, Miss Harper, it's extremely rude."

A hot flush creeps up my neck and onto my cheeks, causing my skin to become clammy. This is not the first impression I wanted to make. I stand awkwardly in the doorway, unsure of what to do next.

"So," he taps his fingers on the desk, "let's not drag this out further. Sit down."

I start to walk towards the chair and trip slightly on a floor rug, spilling the papers in my hand across the floor. "Goodness, I'm sorry," I practically stutter from embarrassment. Why is this happening!?

I kneel down and collect my papers quickly, silently cursing my clumsiness. It's only worse when I'm nervous. Standing up again, I clutch my papers and stare at the imposing man before me. "I'm sorry about that," I say.

The professor continues to glare at me, withering away any remaining confidence I might have summoned. "Sit down," he says, impatiently. "Are you always so flustered, Miss Harper?"

I shake my head. "No, I'm just bit nervous is all."

I shift my eyes up to meet his and see disapproval on his face. The only thing more distracting than his expression is his features. My eyes linger for just a moment on his thick, black hair. He has one of those Roman noses I fancy, and a chiseled chin. He might be more attractive, if he wasn't so damn scary.

"You should be," he replies stiffly.

I can't help but stare for a moment into his caramel colored eyes framed in his black rimmed glasses. Although their color suggests warmth, they stare back at me; cold, empty, and humorless. He doesn't look like he could be older than thirty, but I know he's 35. I know everything about the professor's career. He specializes in teaching Italian studies and is one of the youngest professors to earn his position as a department head. He's written several books on Italian literature that I admire very much. There is much written about his impressive academic abilities but very little information about his personal life. I can't help but wonder what he's like away from work.

"Shall we get down to business, Miss Harper?" His commanding voice interrupts my senseless musings.

"Yes, of course." I settle into my seat and look attentive towards him behind the enormous desk. He seems twenty miles away.

"You have an interesting accent. Not a Boston native, I assume?" He's making small talk but his voice is startlingly dry. I notice he has a slight accent as well that is definitely not East Coast. Italian perhaps?

"I'm from England originally but I've lived in Boston for many years now."

"What brought you here?"

I wonder why he cares, but answer anyway. "I wanted the experience of living and working in America."

"You didn't answer me entirely. Why Boston?"

"My, um, my brother lives here."

"Ah, yes," he says, looking down at some papers. "The esteemed Dr. Harper. Your parents live in England still?"

"They do. London." I offer the extra information to answer him completely this time. When are we going to get to the interview questions? I spent hours thinking of answers to every possible question about my experience and abilities. He better ask me some of them.

"Is that where you get your name?" he asks.

"Yes, it is. I was, um, conceived there, on holiday." I cringe a bit as I offer this nugget of overly personal information. "We're from Essex," I add quickly. I find myself becoming just a bit impatient with his questions but I know I need to humor him. This man is the key to my future.

"Why do you want to work here? And please, don't rattle off a bunch of crap about Harvard. I've heard it. Tell me something original."

Something original? I studied Harvard's history for two days so I could impress him with everything I knew. Now, he wants original. Bloody hell.

The professor stares at me, waiting for my response. After a moment, he begins to tap his fingers on the desk again, one by one. I gaze up at him, watching as his thumb starts, then the index finger, and so on to his pinky, then back again. Suddenly, he stops.

"Are you going to answer me, Miss Harper?"

"Um, yes, of course. I really like languages. I have a double master's degree and speak five of them fluently. I can—"

"I read your résumé," he interrupts. "I said original. Everyone in this pile speaks many languages. Everyone has a graduate degree or two." He pats a stack of papers on his desk.

"What can you do for me that the other fifty applicants cannot? What makes you special, Miss Harper?"

Special? I'm not special at all. Frantic thoughts swirl through my mind. This is not going well and I need to somehow salvage what's left of this interview before he boots me out. "I want this job very much. I've worked really hard for years in order to earn my qualifications specifically to work for you, professor. No one else. I have been quite deliberate in my intention. I doubt that anyone in that stack wants this job as much as I do." I run my hand across my forehead. "I don't have much working experience but whatever you want me to do, I can learn." So much for keeping my cool.

"Why do you want to work for me, specifically?"

This probably wouldn't be a good time to tell him that I picked him because it's a well-known fact that if you can please the professor, you can do anything. That tidbit on my résumé would carry my entire career.

I decide a bit of ass kissing is in order. "Because you are brilliant and I want to learn from the best." Not entirely untrue.

Professor Di Cesare leans back in his chair, only the hint of a smile across his lips. "What are your long term goals, Miss Harper?"

This was the one question I wish he didn't ask me. Throughout my entire life, my parents and brother have been pushing me to teach. It's the very reason I'm sitting here begging for a job from Professor Overbearing. The trouble is that I know deep inside that is not my passion. I know what I want to do, but I don't know how to do it. For now, I have to come up with a believable answer for the professor.

"I may pursue teaching one day, sir," I say meekly and I'm positive, unconvincingly.

The professor leans forward across his desk and stares at me. The intensity of his gaze makes me uneasy, as if he's daring me to say something else. I avert my eyes and instead focus on his lips, silently begging them to open and utter words that will prompt me to say something intelligent.

"I don't believe you, Miss Harper," he says finally, and then leans back again in his chair.

Flustered, I realize that he can see right through me. I have no idea what to say next. I don't want to tell him about my childish journals filled with the ramblings of a wayward girl. I stare at my hands, folded nervously in my lap.

"Look at me, Miss Harper."

I look up and nervously wait for what's next.

"Maybe you aren't sure what you want to do with your life yet, but you need a path. Everyone needs direction. Perhaps I can assist you with finding one."

I nod my head, thankful he didn't ask me another question. We sit silently for a moment before I decide to break the silence. "May I ask a question of you, professor?" I ask, hesitantly.

"You may."

"What are your expectations of an assistant?"

"That's a very good question. The list is long but at a minimum I expect you to be prompt, early in fact. I want you to anticipate my needs and fill them before I've asked. I demand that I never miss anything important and I am always made aware of anything happening in the department, no matter how trivial it may seem. This is not an easy job and many have failed. Are you still up for the challenge?"

I nod my head. "Yes. You haven't scared me off just yet."

Professor Di Cesare's lips crease into a bit of a smirk. "Not yet, anyway." He stands and walks towards me, leaning his body against his desk. He's very tall, I'd guess about 6'3" perhaps, which only makes his presence that much more imposing. I'm a bit startled by his closeness to me again, and his seemingly casual stance. I would have to crane my neck to see his face so I sit motionless, scared to move.

"I think you'll do well here, Miss Harper. You can start Monday. Be here promptly at 8:15 or don't bother. Clear?"

"Very."

"Good." He walks across the office to his door. "You may go."

Oh! I jump up from my chair. "Thank you for this opportunity."

"Don't thank me yet. We'll see if you can last until winter break with me."

I gather my things and quickly leave the office. Looking back, I watch the door close and wonder if I really know what I just got myself into. Intimidating doesn't even begin to describe that man.

Back outside, I decide to call my brother to see if he is available. As busy as he is, he usually finds time for his baby sister. I dial his number.

"Ciao, little sis. Are you on campus?" Devon's buoyant voice comes through the line.

"I am. Just left Professor Di Cesare's office. You weren't joking when you said he was a difficult man, were you?"

"Did he mistreat you?" My brother's voice turns suddenly serious. I know he promised my parents he would look out for me ever since I moved to America. He worries that the professor is just too much for me to handle.

"No, not at all. I mean he certainly didn't make me a cup of tea but he did give me the job."

"You got the job? That's bloody fantastic!"

I let out a giggle. "Yes! Can you believe it? I thought I blew the whole thing but I was just honest and he hired me." I lean up against a tree. "I'm really chuffed."

"He'd be a fool not to hire you, sissy. Now we can have a lunch or two together."

"I'd like that Devon. Do you have time now? I told Madeline I would pick up a sandwich for her."

"I wish I did. I have a research paper I need to submit to the journal in a few days and I'm nowhere near finished. What do you say I take you and Madsy out for dinner tomorrow night to celebrate? We'll go to the North End and get some divine Italian."

"I would love that," I say, knowing Madeline will love it even more. She has a mad crush on Devon that everyone knows about, except him.

"Right then. Be safe getting home. I'll be round tomorrow."

"Okay, bye, Dev."

"Bye," he says and hangs up. I walk through the near empty courtyard to the restaurant location only to find that it's closed for another week. Looking down at my watch, I see that I have about thirty minutes before the next train. I meander through Harvard Square, taking in my surroundings, and feeling my excitement build. In a little less than a week, I'll be here every day. I just hope I can live up to the professor's expectations.

Checking the time again, I start to head back towards the train station. I decide to stop at a sandwich shop closer to home and pick up sandwiches for both of us. After a week of nothing but eggs, meat, and cheese, I'm sure Madeline is starved for a piece of bread at the moment.

Settling into my seat on the train, I use the ten minute ride to jot down my experience today in my journal. For each entry, I like to summarize what I've learned from that experience. One thing is obvious, the professor can smell fear. I tap my pen on my chin, deciding to borrow words from one of the American presidents, I scrawl- *Note to self: The only thing to fear is Professor Scary sensing your fear.* I giggle to myself as I put the journal away.